Black Rock: The Rising

Death Curse

Xander Weaver

Black Rock: The Rising

Death Curse

ISBN 979-8-9882784-0-5 (eBook)

ISBN 979-8-9882784-1-2 (Paperback)

www.XanderWeaver.com

The cover design was provided by Paramita Bhattacharjee from creativeparamita.com.

Release version: 1.02

Cyrus Cooper Series:

Book One: Dangerous Minds

Book Two: Rogue Faction Part 1

Book Three: Rogue Faction Part 2

Book Four: Halon Seven

Book Five: Surviving Origin Part 1

Book Six: Surviving Origin Part 2

Other Books:

Sleepwalker: The Journal of Grady Ledger

For more information, please visit:

www.XanderWeaver.com

Chapter 1

Detroit, Michigan

4 years ago

Watching Stanton pace the floor of the empty room, Gregory's anger swelled again. The walls were bare but beyond being devoid of decoration. Most surfaces of the spacious office suite were scuffed and even dented. The space was in squalid disrepair.

Stanton's voice echoed from the bare concrete floor smudged and stained from the adhesive that had once been used to keep linoleum tiles in place. There were other stains, too. One blotch much too closely resembled that of a crime scene. Gregory suppressed a shiver. He had no desire to understand the story behind the singularly strange mark.

"I know it doesn't look like much," Stanton Anakasta continued as he strode briskly across the expansive space. "But look at this view!"

Gregory took a breath and attempted to master a frustration spiraling toward the breaking point. Crossing the space slowly, he mashed balled fists deep in his trousers pockets and concentrated on the grinding sound of coarse grit

1

beneath his loafers. Stopping at the window, he sighed and looked out. They were on the corner of the forty-second floor with the cityscape spread out before them. The sun was setting to their extreme left. This was reflected in a blazing glare across the floor-to-ceiling windows which accented the greasy streaks of neglect that had collected on the glass. It had clearly been years since the office space was last occupied.

"Yes," Gregory admitted, his tone noncommittal as he eyed the desolate street far below. Even the boulevards in this part of the city were barren, empty, and forlorn. The scene did nothing to brighten his mood. The sentiment was reflected in his quiet, emotionless words. "Quite a view."

Anakasta's hopeful smile turned proud, his eyes lighting once more with enthusiasm. "I told you. Tons of space—all we could need, in fact. We can start small, and there's plenty of room to grow. And the lease is cheap—dirt cheap! There isn't a better deal in the city."

Struggling against a crushing feeling more reminiscent of claustrophobia than panic, Gregory turned from Anakasta's gaze. He'd been suckered in by the man's confidence too many times. Far too many times. It wouldn't happen again. Anakasta's most recent folly had nearly bankrupted them both—yet another joint business venture that had begun with so much promise, only to end in financial disaster. Though he'd struggled to rationalize one failure after another, Gregory had come to believe Anakasta was ultimately to blame. Though intelligent, the man was cursed. The man's once good fortune now courted increasingly dramatic failure in business.

And Anakasta wanted Gregory to partner with him once more. Gregory knew he should rid himself of the man once and for all, but the damage was already done. There was only one card left to play. That was part of what had brought them here today. After shuttering their latest enterprise only three weeks before, Anakasta claimed to have found an opportunity to make them both financially solvent. Gnashing teeth and shaking his head at the idea, Gregory reminded himself he'd come this far…there could be no turning back.

"—and that's only the shipping dock," Anakasta said.

Gregory found the man looking at him with expectant eyes. He'd tuned out his partner's ramblings. How long has the fool been rambling?

"Yes," Gregory said, hoping the imbecile wouldn't repeat himself. "The shipping dock—you were saying?"

Nodding vigorously, Anakasta waved both arms and spun in a circle, thankfully not aware that his captive audience couldn't care less about the tour. "I know," he went on, "it's forty-two floors from the street, but there are three freight elevators. I think we should go for it."

The elevators. The mention of contraptions pulled Gregory's attention fully back to the moment. His gaze fixed on his one-time friend and lingered with renewed awareness. Anakasta stood rocking from foot to foot, his hands fidgeting with nervous energy. He looked more like a child at the top of the stairs come Christmas morning—unlike the reckless speculative investor who had black-holed Gregory's last three million dollars in the previous twenty days.

Can he be this naïve?

Gregory scratched idly at the corner of his jaw, fingers raking the three-day-old stubble he'd been too despondent to shave away. Was he expected to sink good money after bad? More troubling, was Anakasta deluded enough to think Gregory would continue to throw money away? Standing here on the brink of utter ruin, Anakasta somehow thought their latest failure was but another bump on the road that was their partnership.

Three million dollars, Gregory reminded himself as he stared at Anakasta with dead eyes. The man didn't have a clue.

"You're giving this a lot of thought," Anakasta observed. "Can I assume that's a good sign?"

Gregory sighed. "This is, as they say, a make-or-break moment."

This brought an expectant, wide-eyed nod from Anakasta. "I knew you'd go for it!"

His mouth agape, Gregory was momentarily speechless. The sensation was followed a moment later by outright indignation. His blood began to boil and his cheeks flushed. Only this man could misread a situation so completely. No wonder they were broke.

Turning on a heel, Gregory stamped for the door. Anakasta stammered from behind, his words unintelligible. Then came the sound of heavy footfalls as he struggled to keep up.

"Wait! What's wrong? Where are you going?"

Eyes fixed on the floor, Gregory passed through the wide double doors of the office and entered a dilapidated hallway. He turned right and continued at a brisk pace. Loping along sideways, Anakasta fought to keep up. He struggled to draw Gregory's gaze with each clumsy step.

"I don't get it! What's wrong?" Anakasta whimpered, his very tone evidence of his blindness to their financial situation and the peril of their partnership.

Turning another corner, the elevators came into view. The sight of the battered and dented stainless steel doors, more importantly what they represented, froze Gregory in his tracks. He stopped so abruptly that Anakasta nearly toppled to the cracked tile floor in an attempt to avoid a physical collision. Gregory stared at the doors, the continuous murmur of his associate's words now merely background noise in his tunnel vision.

Over the last twelve years, Gregory Ivankovich and Stanton Anakasta had been partners. In that time they'd founded three companies and made substantial profits. Unfortunately, over the last five years, for all of their success, they'd suffered far more failure. For every million they'd made, they'd lost nearly half again as much. Gregory had finally concluded that the rhythm of the wins and losses had been hypnotic. Had he been more self-aware, he might have divested himself of the partnership before any of the three corporations went bankrupt. But they'd all failed so suddenly—so spectacularly—that there'd been no predicting each dark turn.

Anakasta was lousy luck, Gregory finally concluded. Never a superstitious man, he'd been slow in arriving at the understanding. But once he had, the facts were impossible to deny. Everything terrible that had happened to Gregory Ivankovich in the last half-decade could be traced directly back to Stanton Anakasta.

It was a sad but undeniable truth.

With this realization, Gregory had come to hate Anakasta. His life would've been different had they never partnered. The man's cheerful, optimistic, and woefully unrealistic way of looking at the world was contagious at times and Gregory had been infected more than once. Now that disease had him on the verge of financial ruin.

As far as he was concerned, Anakasta had made only one decision they would not ultimately regret. Four years ago, they'd engaged the services of a high-priced law firm. The attorneys formed a sort of corporate umbrella to shelter their partnership. There were supposed to be tax advantages, though there had to be profit for such a thing to matter. The corporate shroud was also intended to protect their personal assets. Should the company ever get into financial trouble, their personal assets would be separate and protected from those of the corporation. That hadn't mattered because Gregory had sold nearly everything of value to keep their most recent company afloat for its final 30 days.

Ultimately, the advice of the law firm had been useless…with one exception. Part of the plan included life insurance policies for both partners. Thankfully, through it all, Gregory had maintained those policies. He never let them lapse. Never a late premium. And while he'd come to blame his partner for every wrong turn in recent years, he would give Anakasta credit for something. The wide-eyed dreamer would do right by him in the end. He would fix things, even if it were the last thing he ever did.

"I don't understand," Anakasta stammered. "You said you would take a look at the offices. You promised to have an open mind."

Finally prying his eyes from the distant elevator doors, Gregory met Anakasta's gaze. "That's true. And here I am."

"So what's the problem? This is it! It's a game-changer. All we have to do is sign the lease and we're off and running."

Standing motionless, Gregory's eyes remained fixed on his one-time friend.

"Well?" Anakasta pressed. "It's now or never."

Blowing a slow pained breath of resignation, Gregory nodded. Now or never. It wasn't like he had a choice. There was no turning back. He'd already rigged the elevator, after all. Still, treading these last few yards of the hallway was more difficult than anticipated.

When Gregory spoke, there was no life in his voice. He would lose a part of himself for the action he was about to take—but he'd done the math. It was an acceptable trade. He put on the best smile he could muster and looked Anakasta directly in the eye. "Why don't you show me the loading dock?"

His visage growing bright once more, Anakasta waved a hand toward the elevator doors. He practically galloped as he led the way. Trailing a few yards behind, Gregory reached the alcove serving three elevators. The left and right elevators had their doors barred with Out-of-Order signs. Only the center set of doors remained operational.

"I don't know what's going on with the lifts," Anakasta said and pressed the call button. "I'll speak with the building manager when we sign the papers. I'm sure they won't be a problem."

A chime sounded and the metal doors parted. Gregory's mouth went *suddenly dry as he watched his one-time friend enter the car. Anakasta turned quickly, staring back from the small chamber and clearly wondering why Gregory wasn't following. Though he'd prepared for this deception, Gregory found himself abruptly unable to speak. It was as if words now might betray the anger and hatred he harbored for his partner.*

Gregory was still in the vestibule when the doors started to close. Anakasta threw out an arm and triggered the bumper on the door's leading edge. It was there to prevent them from closing. "What are you doing? What's wrong? Get in."

"You go," Gregory said. His voice sounded and tasted like gravel. He felt suddenly nauseous. "I think I left my glasses back there. I'd rather take the stairs anyway."

The confused expression creased Anakasta's face and his countenance darkened. Gregory was sure he saw suspicion cross the dreamer's eyes. He needed to say something—offer some assurance. Even as he opened his mouth to speak, Gregory still had no idea what to say.

Then he was stopped short.

The lights overhead dimmed and flickered. The fixtures mounted on the ceiling began to buzz as if infused with far too much energy. They flickered again, then flared with unnatural brightness. The bulbs inside the cab of the half-closed elevator did the same, a loud electric buzz emanating from somewhere atop the car. The halls to the north, west, and east strobed with violent flashes, painful and white, as Gregory and Stanton Anakasta shifted nervously to view their surroundings.

Bulbs at the far end of each hallway sizzled and arced with ragged bolts of electricity. Then every light went blindingly bright in the same instant. A popping sound came from every direction. One by one, the old bulbs went dark. One snap after another, the darkness advanced on the two men. A void of inky black moved smoothly and steadily down the hallways, converging from all directions.

The words left Gregory's lips before he realized he was speaking. He turned to his partner. "What's going on?"

Anakasta remained motionless in the elevator's cab, his outstretched arm restraining the automated doors. The lights overhead sizzled and sparked as they cast dancing shadows inside the stationary car. Anakasta's jaw was clamped inhumanly tight while his eyes rolled impossibly back in their sockets.

Gasping, Gregory took an involuntary step backward. Static electricity danced across his arms and legs, a sensation like a spider crawling slowly along his spine. The air had gone unnaturally dry and smelled suddenly of ozone. Lights flashed and sparked violently inside the elevator, but Anakasta stood entirely motionless, his arm still raised and preventing the doors from closing.

"Get out of there, you fool!" Gregory hissed, his plan of sending his partner to die forgotten with the strangeness of the moment.

The few remaining lights flashed bright again, and with a bang, the two men were plunged into complete darkness.

With the darkness came silence, total and complete. At first Gregory feared he might have gone deaf. He smelled the burning smolder of electrical insulation and then heard the muffled pops of wires as the conduit began to cool. His heart hammered and his eyes probed the darkness for the slightest hint of light. He wanted to call out for Anakasta, but some primitive part of his mind warned against it. He reasoned that it was an irrational fear of the darkness, but then what had just happened? Certainly something worthy of fear.

Girding himself to speak for the first time, Gregory was saved the effort when something clunked lightly in the distance. Two seconds later, the sound came again…and then once more. One by one, emergency lights clicked and powered up. They began in the distance just as the blackout had. Slowly, the dim glow worked its way up the three converging halls as one light box after another added its pale glow to the gloom.

The nearest emergency light buzzed loudly for a long second before finally engaging inside the elevator. Anakasta stood motionless where he'd been. Both hands finally lowered to his side. His hair was mussed, and Gregory could swear he saw smoke coming off the shoulders of the man's sport coat.

"My God," Gregory whispered. "What the hell was that?"

Anakasta didn't respond.

When Anakasta failed to move, Gregory stepped into the elevator, grabbed him by the arm, and pulled him into the lobby. "Hey!" His whisper was urgent and harsh. "You alright?"

Finding him mobile but unresponsive, Gregory slapped Anakasta gently on the cheek. "Hey? Are you in there?"

Chapter 2

With a slow blink, Stanton Anakasta turned darkness to light. The world was blurry, and his stomach floated somewhere shy of his throat. But he could see...something. Blinking twice more, the blur before him resolved into a portly face with thick unkempt eyebrows and wide, wild eyes.

"Hey! Are you with me?" the man before him said.

Blinking again, Anakasta gasped suddenly and huffed his lungs full of air. The taste was acrid and filled with the tang of something burning, but his body gladly accepted the accompanying oxygen.

How long did I go without breathing? Gods below, that wasn't supposed to be part of the process.

Anakasta's ears were ringing, and it felt like he was wearing a hat that was three sizes too small. Flexing his jaw, he tried to relieve the pressure in his ears.

The man before him slapped him stiffly on the back and said something unintelligible. Anakasta took another deep breath and looked at the familiar face again.

"I think this place is a bad investment," the man was saying. "It's likely to burn down at any second."

Steadying himself, Anakasta looked around. At first he didn't recognize the location and wondered if something had gone wrong. His heart began to race and his eyes bounced from one direction to the next. The man beside him spoke again, drawing his attention once more. Anakasta's mind was clearing and his breathing was improving. When he looked at the rotund man, there was a sense of familiarity this time.

"Ivankovich..." The word slipped from his lips as his mind made the connection. "Gregory Ivankovich."

Gregory arched a single eyebrow in response, then slowly nodded his head. "Yeah, that's right. You okay? You get electrocuted or something? Do you know where you are?"

Turning slowly in place, Anakasta eyed the open elevator behind him. The doors had remained open after the EM surge that had brought him here. He studied the marred finish of the stainless steel door frame and the logo stamped into the metal beside the call button. This was undoubtedly the elevator he'd seen in the police reports. He turned back to Gregory. This was the portly man he'd researched before making the journey.

Looking down at his own body for the first time, Anakasta began patting the pockets of his wrinkled suit jacket. He quickly located and retrieved what he knew to be present, a small mobile phone. Pressing a button on the side of the thin device, he was relieved to see the screen blink to life. A photo of a motorcycle filled the screen. At the top of the screen were the date and time. Raising the phone closer to his eyes, Anakasta's gaze focused entirely on the year. A smile spread slowly across his face. "I'll be damned...It worked."

Gregory's brows knitted, and his eyes pinched in response. "I think you should sit down, my friend. Something weird just happened."

"Weird?" Anakasta fixed the large man with a sudden intense, confident, and malicious gaze. All disorientation had been chased from his mind; he was now full of purpose.

"We need to talk about this partnership," Anakasta said as he slipped an arm across Gregory's shoulder. "I think it's time we went our separate ways."

Confusion fogged Gregory's visage as he let Anakasta lead him into the elevator. "What are you talking about?" the man mumbled.

Anakasta stopped in the middle of the car and faced Gregory. The lights overhead continued to flicker and buzz. It was a wonder they had survived the temporal event, Anakasta reasoned. This renewed his confidence that the *device's motors would run long enough for him to do what he'd long planned.*

Squaring himself to Gregory, eye to eye, Anakasta lashed out with a kick that shattered the big man's knee. Gregory toppled with a crash that shook the car within the shaft's walls. The man bellowed at the strike, then lay screaming on the floor.

Anakasta stepped to the doorway and looked down at Gregory. "It's time to rewrite history," he said with a disappointed shake of his head. "We both know you had this coming." He pressed the reset button on the elevator panel, then tapped the button marked Lobby.

With a single quick step, Anakasta slipped from the car. As the doors began to close, he saw recognition flash through the tears in Gregory Ivankovich's eyes.

"No!" the fat man bellowed as the doors drew shut.

Anakasta stepped back a pace and eyed the indicator above the closed doors. He heard Gregory's meaty fists pounding the floor—maybe even the walls—a second before the drive motors engaged. The number over the door changed to 41 and then to 40. Just as the digital counter resolved into the number 39, a violent snapping crash came. The digital display went dark and a horrible clatter reverberated through the elevator shaft wall. Several seconds later, a keening screech reverberated from far below, followed instantly by the sound of rending metal. The floor beneath Anakasta's feet quivered.

"They say turnabout is fair play," Anakasta said and turned in search of the stairs.

Chapter 3

Island of Nova Derrota

   88 days ago

Moving from the steep path of loose gravel and stone chips, Gavin Kray climbed to the small rock ledge and was rewarded with solid footing for the first time since starting the hike. He was more than four miles from the mountain's base, at least if he counted the circuitous path along barely visible switchbacks, ragged gullies, and sandy washes. Alternatively, he mused, aside from now being on the other side of the mountain's peak as the crow flew, he technically wasn't more than a mile from the trailhead.

Slipping the pack from his back and dropping it to the dirt, Gavin dusted callused hands on the legs of his jeans. He fished a canteen from a top compartment of the rucksack and took a slow sip of water. The expansive 270-degree panoramic view was breathtaking. The cliff dropped away only two feet from where he stood but it wasn't the three-hundred-foot plunge to the mountain slope that captured his attention. The Pacific Ocean spread out as far as the eye could see, seemingly endless to the horizon in three directions. The white tips of the breaking waves were almost invisible from this height as the water crossed the shallow coral reef and crashed against the sheer stone face that encircled most of the island. Gavin had hiked the mountain once before. It had been nearly a year back, shortly after he'd first come to this remote corner of the world.

Bagging the canteen, he retrieved a laminated map. It was crudely drawn in pencil. While not old, it had seen a lot of use recently. Gavin had studied it countless times since the old man sketched it only last week. The need for secrecy was paramount, even in a lonely place like this. So each time he was finished, the sketch was folded once more and then shoved to the very bottom of the backpack. The Kinkos laminate job was the only reason the paper remained readable.

Thank you Kinkos, Manhattan, Gavin thought with a rueful grin. From one island to another, worlds apart in every sense of the imagination. It had been just over a week since he left this place for the whirlwind trip to New York. He shook his head at the memory. They could keep the city for all he cared. The journey had been his only excursion since coming to this secluded chunk of rock to hide from the world. The place had quickly become home. And like so many things in life, this sanctuary had come at a price.

It was time to pay the tab.

The path leading here, such that it was, appeared to match what was crudely indicated on the map. So too, was the precarious ledge on which he now stood. Considering this, Gavin turned slowly in search of the next landmark. He found nothing. This small platform was a dead end. As the map suggested, it left him unable to advance further up the side of the mountain. A great vertical surface faced him; a plain of roughhewn granite was as black as any other mountain part. The color wasn't unusual. The mountain was called Black Rock, after all. A little on the nose, but damn near every kind of ore comprising the massive mountain occupying a full third of the island was actually black rock.

Circling slowly, he didn't suffer from an excess of choices. Two steps in one direction and he would be back on the sorry excuse for a goat trail that had brought him to this dead end. The only other directions led to a terminal plunge that would take him across hundreds of feet of flesh-rending granite before depositing him in the equally bone-crushing surf, which in turn waited to paste him across the ragged base of the island cliffs.

That leaves…

He turned back to the sheer rock face. This was a mountain. It was a wall *of stone. There was nothing special about it. Suppressing the urge to retrieve the map once more, Gavin kicked idly at the loose scree at his feet. The map was one step removed from childish scribble, so rudimentary that every curve and contour had long since been committed to memory. This was the spot. There was just nowhere left to go.*

"Well, shit." Gavin's quiet words were sucked away by the brisk mountain wind. "And now I'm talking to myself."

All at once, the all-encompassing wind disappeared. The lashing tare had been so persistent since beginning the mountain ascent, the second the vacuous whooshing stopped. It was as if he'd gone deaf. Vertigo struck and he wobbled on his feet. The rock outcropping suddenly felt a fraction of its previous size.

Sticking a finger in his ear, he palpated vigorously. The effort sounded like thunder and brought relief only because it proved he wasn't deaf. The silence, however, was unnatural. Snatching a fist-size stone from the ground and giving it a swift side-armed toss against the rock face, he was relieved to hear the dulcet tones of the stone-on-stone impact. Though it thumped and crunched as it should, it did not behave properly when the stone struck the vertical rock wall. Rather than bounce in obeyance of Newton's third law, the fist-sized shard of granite vaporized with a reverberating crack. Gavin jumped backward, his first impulse certainty that a rockslide had begun. The silence was interrupted by two effects. His mind had trouble reconciling to this new windless existence. First, the explosion of the stone echoed twice though there was nothing from which the sound should reverberate. Second, the sound of scraping gravel emanated from beneath one of his boots. As he rocked backward, it occurred to him how far he'd jumped in response to the exploding rock…and that only one of his boots had disturbed the gravel.

Vision swimming, Gavin's reality snapped into focus. He had backpedaled, and the effort to shift weight to his rearmost leg had gone terribly wrong. His center of gravity was already past the point of no return as his gaze flashed over a shoulder to the ragged rock face more than a hundred feet below. Commitment was his only chance for survival. Correcting his balance was already a lost cause, and firm footing was now a thing of the past. Pushing off with little traction left beneath his remaining foot, Gavin threw one shoulder over the other. He had one chance, and it would be as half-assed as it was desperate.

In a move that would have made a ballet dancer consider alternative employment, he spun for everything he was worth. It wasn't an effort that would score points for gracefulness or even style, but he rounded in time to snag the lip of the ledge with the tips of the fingers on both hands. Newton's third law was there this time, ready and waiting to sock him in the eye—this time, literally. Though his fingers found purchase on the sharp, solid lip of the ledge, his motion was not so easily halted. His feet had kicked outward as his lower body continued to spin, and his suddenly arrested fall brought both legs back toward the cliff in a pendulum swing that impacted his face with stone. A doorknob-sized lump in the wall's surface met with his chest and drove the air from his lungs. One hand slipped from the ledge, and he would have screamed if he'd had the wind to do it.

Whether through luck, skill, or bull-headed determination, Gavin maintained a grip with his remaining hand. Four fingers in a death grapple on the edge of a mountain remained the only thing separating him from certain death. The world was already silent but now it went still as well. A familiar calmness passed through him as his eyes locked on his lone hand at the edge of the ledge. Blinking slowly, he cleared the dust from his eyes and took stock as time seemed to stop. Tears ran from both eyes. A more rapid flutter of his eyelids blinked the wetness away. A similar mental effort pushed away the pain in his chest, arms, and hand. With slow deliberateness and an almost carefree detachment that starkly contrasted his situation, he turned and looked down. The mountain really was the blackest stone he'd ever seen. The near-vertical face below had been weathered by millions of years of wind and rain, resulting in razor-sharp ridges as unforgiving as any killing machine devised by man. The tide was up as well. The waves broke as they crossed the reef and crashed against the vertical stone walls that surrounded more than eighty percent of the island.

Gavin rocked slowly as his momentum dissipated. Fresh air gradually found its way back into his lungs. His eyes finally shifted upward. Four fingers. It was the first thing to deal with before something terrible happened. That detachment. It was like the calming voice of an old friend. He took a long, slow breath and was once more troubled by the unnatural silence—another breath and then a slow, deliberate heave on his good arm. A second later, he'd secured a grip on the ledge with his free hand. Bracing the tips of his boots against the cliff face, he shot a lazy glance over his shoulder for one last look at the rocks and ocean below. It wasn't the closest he'd come to death, but it was one of the more unique brushes in his short years. His attention focused on the task at hand, he pulled himself up the cliff and back onto the ledge.

No more time was wasted on introspection. Gavin dusted his hands off by striking them against the legs of his jeans. This resulted in a pair of short, bloody splits. He eyed the abrasions marring the palms and fingers of both hands and wished he'd worn gloves. The concern was quickly forgotten as he scanned the ledge for what was left of the exploding stone that had started all the trouble.

There was no trace of it. Or, if there was, what was left was indistinguishable from the crumb-size chunks littering the ledge. It was concerning. If the black rock were somehow unstable, he would have blown himself up months ago. He was hardly known for his gentle nature, and this island was riddled with the same dark ore.

Why did it explode?

His attention turned to the vertical rock face he'd struck with the stone. There, just below eye level, was a mark. It was black on black, but the pattern was impossible to mistake for a natural impression. A single thick wavy line with a circle imposed directly beneath it. Gavin leaned closer to the wall. The mark was faint but tangible. The line was horizontal but symmetrical, and the circle was perfectly round. Neither were naturally occurring, that much was clear.

Retrieving the map once more, Gavin unfolded it. There in the corner of the paper, he found the same symbol. He'd taken it for a doodle left by Fowler when the old man had drawn the map. The assumption was it was scribbled while a sick man's failing mind attempted to recall the details of the journey being committed to paper.

Apparently, this was wrong. The doodle was the key.

It had to be the right place.

So what does it mean?

Pocketing the map, Gavin leaned close to the wall and studied the strange symbol. It was about the size of a dinner plate. The black-on-black nature of its color was obviously why he hadn't noticed the mark when he'd first arrived on the ledge. One had to look at the wall from a precise angle to see the emblem, perhaps under just the right light as well. Had things gone differently, he might have missed it entirely, Gavin decided.

Leaning forward once more, Gavin placed his palm against the emblem. He felt the squish of his bloody palm against the cold stone and winced as a burning sensation lanced up the inside of his arm. The instant his hand came to rest, a massive portion of the stone face vaporized into sand. The material plummeted to the ground, landing in a pile ankle-deep around his boots. Sound returned to the mountain at precisely the same instant, the whipping wind slapping him bodily across the head and shoulders.

Offering a slow whistle, Gavin stepped carefully backward. He wasn't moving out of shock this time. Every motion was slow, deliberate, and entirely awed. A giant circular cavern had opened in the face of the mountain. He was looking into a yawning cave, accessible through a perfectly round entrance that was at least ten feet in diameter.

"I'll be dammed," he muttered.

Grabbing his pack, he retrieved a flashlight and stepped across the cave's threshold. The path sloped upward at an easy grade. He'd gone only thirty yards when he arrived in a small antechamber. Like the cave entrance, the space felt decidedly unnatural. The walls were entirely flat, comprised of smooth, mottled granite of black and gray. Though surely carved from the stone, the vertical faces displayed no signs of tool work. At least in the cursory examination by the light of the hand light, all surfaces seemed free from blemishes of any kind. Though unsure of the exact dimensions of the space, the walls and ceiling appeared identical in formation, perhaps twelve by twelve, the same as the floor. The room was a perfect cube.

Nothing so symmetrical existed in nature. Added to the way the stone portal had vaporized beneath his touch, the unnatural composition of this place began to take on a forbidding sensation.

An arched door in the far wall led to a yawning cavern. Casting the beam of his light to the ceiling, Gavin found the ceiling perhaps twenty feet overhead. It was irregularly shaped, giving the impression this part of the cavern was naturally occurring. The portal to the cave, he mused, was anything but. Nothing perfectly round existed in nature, and he couldn't explain how the door had turned to powder at his touch. Somewhat reassuringly, aside from the screwy entrance, everything was how the old man had described.

Brooks Fowler had promised the cavern would be here, even if he'd been vague about how to gain admittance. Gavin had attributed that lack of detail to the man's failing health and put that concern on the back burner. In truth, he didn't expect to find what the old man claimed to be waiting at the end of the map. Fowler had been vague and more than a little reluctant to trust anyone with the map detailing where he believed the cavern's entrance was.

"Just return the sample," he'd said. "Return the sample and forget all about the damnable place. Take nothing, or you will live to regret it."

They were the ramblings of an old man, but Gavin owed Fowler. A man who believed in the repayment of debts, Gavin promised to follow the provided instructions without deviation. Now he had one task left to perform.

Following the flashlight beam, Gavin moved swiftly for the back of the space.

He could sense the scope of the great cavern around him but focused on his singular goal. He was here to return something Fowler had taken. There would be no exploring, and he wouldn't speak of this place as long as he lived. Fowler had been emphatic on both points. Not knowing what it was about this place that scared the man so deeply, Gavin's convictions supported the promises he made.

The light beam played across something at the periphery of the path and Gavin stopped short. A sudden sense pricked the hair on the back of his neck, and his free hand tightened into a fist in response. He flashed the beam to the right expecting to see something leap from the darkness.

Nothing moved.

Gavin played the beam more slowly. The cave had been sealed. He had to be alone. His mind flashed back to how the cavern entrance had dissolved beneath his touch and the strange otherworldly silence before finding the mark indicating the entrance. Everything had happened so quickly, he had yet to reflect on the series of strange experiences. For the moment, it all added up to one thing—he didn't know what to expect from this place. He might be alone, or he might not.

Moving backward several paces, Gavin shined the light along the periphery of the path he'd walked so far. His breath caught at the sight. A stone statue knelt in the darkness. It was a life-sized replica of a man, crafted in stone and rendered in shocking detail. The figure was dressed in a frock, flowing robes and kneeling against the floor with his hands outstretched toward something at ground level. Whatever the statue was reaching for was nonexistent or perhaps missing.

Circling the statue, Gavin studied it in the harsh glow of his light. The artist's attention to detail was incredible. The stone seemed to be the same as what he'd seen on much of the island, though rather than being inky black, the ore of this piece was gray. The color was pale, almost like the black of the island rock had been rung out by the great hands of some unseen force. No, he decided. It was as if the marrow of the stone's typical richness had been sucked away. This, of course, did nothing to diminish the artistry of the work. Though he was no student of art, Gavin bet this level of craftsmanship would find pride of place in any of the world's top museums. The folds of the figure's robes rolled, flowed, and overlapped naturally. Even the crow's feet in the corner of the old man's kind eyes were crafted with lifelike precision.

The warning from Fowler returned unbidden to Gavin. Not just the words but the intensity of the old man's stare, which remained present throughout

17

their visit. "Take nothing, and don't waste a moment. Not a single second!"

Wishing he'd brought a camera or his phone, Gavin knew this too would violate his oath. He took one last look. Then, returning to the path, he pressed on. The rear wall of the cavern came into view even before his light fell upon it. A spectral green glow emanated from the base of the wall and set the space alight with a defused shimmer. A pair of small grottos had formed at the base of the wall; each contained a pool of an odd green substance. Set between the two pools was a small platform. A foot-wide trench filled with the green fluid ran from the left pool, crossed before the platform, and ended in the right pool. The platform appeared to have been hewn from the cave's stone floor. Atop it stood a crude dais or lectern. Though it looked like a place of reverence, the stand was empty.

The cave was cold, but it had gone suddenly colder. Much colder. Gavin could see his breath coalescing in a vapor cloud in the beam of his light. The green glow from the pair of pools seemed to have brightened, though he assumed this was a trick of his eyes. His vision was likely becoming more accustomed to the strange lighting of the subterranean space.

Suppressing a shiver, Gavin lowered his pack to the floor and opened the main compartment. Digging through the padded contents, he retrieved a small titanium tube. He used the top of the bag as a cradle for his flashlight and pointed it at the left of the two green pools. Then, unscrewing the end of the titanium tube, he slipped a long thin glass vial from it. The contents of the glass tube glowed green in the gloom of the cave. The color matched that of the twin pools exactly.

"Seriously, Fowler," Gavin muttered. "What did you get yourself involved in?"

Aware he was once more speaking to himself, Gavin shook his head in frustration. He knelt at the pool's edge and held the vial between the thumb and forefinger. As instructed, he carefully and deliberately released the stopper from the end of the tube. Lowering the container to only inches above the surface of the green pool, he extended the glass to arm's length. He took a steadying breath and slowly tipped the container until it was upended completely. The substance oozed from the glass with unusual slowness. Whatever it was, the consistency was thick and gelatinous.

Once the pour was complete, Gavin held the vial up to the beam of his light. Perhaps its consistency had helped because there wasn't a trace of the ooze left in the glass. There were only two more requirements before the fulfillment of Fowler's instructions was complete. He would cast the glass tube into the ocean *after retreating from the mountain. That was easy enough. That left the titanium tube used to transport the substance. Fowler said it couldn't leave the cave.*

"Commit the container to the pool," Fowler had admonished. "Don't take it with you, and don't leave it lying around that cursed place. The pool is the only way to dispose of it. But be careful. Don't let the substance touch you. One splash is all it takes."

All it takes. Hearing those words from the old man remained chilling. It wasn't just the way he'd said them—it was the look in his eyes when he offered the warning. And though Gavin had desperately wanted to know what the admonishment meant, he'd been uncharacteristically reluctant to ask.

Leaning over the green pool, Gavin noticed for the first time how the thick material appeared to be moving. It seemed to be flowing with some gentle current. The two pools were connected by a narrow channel that appeared to guard against access to the platform between them. But why? He had a clear view of the small stone dais. It was empty.

It didn't matter. He screwed the end back on the titanium tube and lowered his hand to only inches over the pool's surface. Dropping the container into the sludge, he jerked his hand back with the speed of a rattlesnake's strike. The titanium container bobbed slowly once and then again. It turned on its side as its weight settled, then deteriorated on the surface of the green ooze. In less than five seconds the container was vaporized.

Gavin didn't waste time. Grabbing his light and pack, he bolted for the mouth of the cave. He would commit the glass tube to the depths of the ocean and his debt to the old man would be paid in full.

Chapter 4

The darkness was complete and unrelenting. Keegan fought a rising sense of panic and stumbled forward. Her bare foot snagged on a granite outcropping and she went crashing to her knees. Cold stone met her splayed palm, vast surfaces of it fractured here and there with irregular splits, cracks, and crevices. Her sob echoed, each reverberation growing more distant and hinting at the size and scope of the unseen chamber beyond. Remaining close to the floor, she crawled. Without so much as a flicker of light to lend bearing, anything more might result in a turned ankle or broken leg.

Minutes passed before the tips of her fingers met a vertical surface. Probing it, she rose and understood she'd found a wall. Though her heart thundered in her ears, this was progress. Mentally flipping a coin, she began padding to the left. Her hands searched the cold, damp stone surface for anything resembling a door or a way out. Given the echo and the uneven, never-ending stone surfaces, this could only be a cavern or cave.

Logic would be her salvation. She would follow one wall to the next until she found a way out.

What choice do I have?

Minutes stretched and seemed like hours to her deprived senses. Finally, her hand brushed against something fuzzy and firm. She stifled a scream and backpedaled. Instantly regretting the foolishness, Keegan gasped and quickly returned to the wall. Irrational fears in this senseless void could get her killed.

The object she'd located was set against the wall at shoulder level. With a reaffirming dry swallow, she probed it unseen with her fingers. Stringy and dry, coarse and brittle. There was a strange fungal order. Dried moss, she decided. Working her fingers deeper into it, she found a wooden stake—some kind of shaft was placed vertically and pointed to the ceiling. It seemed to be bracketed to the wall with cold metal. Rusty iron, if the odor and her touch were accurate.

A torch?

A joyful sob slipped from her lips. She worked to slow her racing heart. It had been years since she'd attempted this parlor trick. Never in her life had she believed such a gimmick might lead to salvation. Raising her hands to the sides of the torch, or where she believed the torch to be, she focused her will. She believed in fire. "Fuego ignitios."

A billowing flame pierced the pitch-black veil surrounding her. The dried moss hanging from the sides of the ancient torch ignited with a flash and a waft of dark smoke. Keegan stepped away, eyes blinking at this new form of blindness as she laughed from a dry, parched throat.

As the flame settled and began to burn more evenly, Kegan pulled the fragile wooden stake from the ancient iron sconce. At the perimeter of the flame's dancing light, she saw another mounted torch. She set it ablaze before finding another and then another. With each added light, the oppressive black shroud was pushed back further. Every foot she gained felt like breathing room.

Looking down at herself, Keegan confirmed what she already knew. She was barefooted and barelegged. Wearing only dark panties and a white tank top, both now thick with dust and grime, her apparel made sense—at least on some level. She often wore this to bed.

This has to be a dream.

She stepped forward and felt a small sharp stone penetrate the flat of her foot. Cursing, she backpedaled. Hopping backward, she kicked away the pain. Cocking a knee and lowering the torch, she examined her foot. Blood was already seeping from the half-inch-long gash near the side of her arch. Wiping at the blood with her thumb, she was suddenly less confident in her assertion that this was a dream. When was the last time she felt pain and bled in a dream?

With light to her back and a healthy flame in her hand, Keegan was ready to search for a way out. The cavern was massive, she decided. The flickering torch offered illumination only twenty or so feet ahead and behind once she left the light of the cavern wall. Any escape, she sensed, would come from somewhere on the far side of the expansive space. She set out with renewed determination.

After moving thirty or forty yards, Keegan began to sense shapes in the distance. Though they first seemed like tricks of the eye, her pace slowed just to be safe. Who knew what dangers lurked in the darkness? She didn't yet know where she was—or how she'd gotten here, she realized with a start. The thought sent her heart to hammering.

How can I not know where I am?

Dear God—how did I get here?

She inched forward, new concern for the shapes in the distance created endless new terrors in the back of her mind. Before her imagination got the better of her, she decided she would have to deal with it. Keegan stepped forward in three quick strides. Thrusting the guttering torch before her like a gladiator branching a sword, she waved it at the darkness.

A lone stone statue greeted her. Its stark relief and life-size shape shocked her as it materialized in a flash of illumination. She nearly dropped the torch as she backpedaled in retreat.

Keegan's sob turned into a laugh as she regrouped to take a closer look at the stone figure. "You scared the crap out of me," she said to the statue as she circled it for examination.

The figure was perhaps six feet tall. It was dressed in a World War Two era German army uniform, the unmistakable Nazi swastika emblem on the right shoulder. The face of the figure had been etched with a wide-eyed expression, and the young man's mouth was captured partially agape. Every detail was rendered in exquisite detail, down to beads of sweat dappling his brow and the weeks' worth of stubble on his jaw. His uniform had seen better days. One jacket sleeve was torn at the shoulder. The trousers were torn across both knees, and the calf-high boots looked as if he'd trudged through a swamp before being immortalized in stone.

Keegan stepped backward and marveled at the figure. Who would go to so much trouble to depict a Nazi soldier? Her back collided with something. She leaped in response. Spinning, she jabbed the flame at her would-be assailant. Another stone figure flashed in a surge from the torch. It, too, was the statue of a Nazi soldier, this one wearing an officer's uniform. Crafted in the same exacting detail, the figure had been captured with one hand raised as if to protect his eyes from a bright light or glare. The figure's face was scrunched in discomfort, if not outright agony.

"Jesus," Keegan muttered.

Stepping slowly away, she raised the torch high and fanned it left and right. A dozen more shadowy forms fluttered at the edge of the flickering light. She blew out a slow breath, regathered herself, then slowly walked deeper into the cavern. Dozens upon dozens of similarly outfitted stone Nazi soldiers littered the space.

The sight of the statues was more than unnerving. It made Keegan's skin crawl. She moved quickly through the throng of World War Two figures and finally broke into an open space. The slap of her bare feet on the unadorned stone and the open space soon brought a sense of relief. She collapsed to the cold ground and pulled her knees close to her chest. Her heart still hammered, but at least the adrenaline rush was beginning to wane.

Thinking of the simple spell she'd used to bring fire to the torch, Keegan wondered if there might be a similar way to find the path out of this cavern. She was underground, that much was clear. But without knowing what part of the island or how far beneath the surface, there was no obvious path to the surface. Her hearing strained, hoping for the sound of running water—even the tickle of a gentle breeze across her damp skin might offer a hint for the path to freedom.

There was nothing.

Despair began to set in. Then the torch flashed and drew her attention. The dried moss used for fuel was nearly depleted. Her eyes went wide and she sprang to her feet. She swung the torch wildly left and right. The flame flashed and guttered before returning to life at half-power. She needed to find a wall, she decided. That's where the sconce had been, and where there had been one, there had been others. If she could find another perimeter wall, she would likely find a fresh torch.

A clicking sound echoed somewhere in the distance. A breath seizing in her throat, Keegan turned slowly. Her ears strained for the source of the sound. The clicking started once again, this time seemingly nearer. Clicking or ticking, she couldn't tell. The sound was strange in the massive place. She turned in a circle once more. It was impossible to tell from which direction the resonance was coming. She knew only two things for sure—it was coming closer, and it was now moving faster.

Keegan was confident her heart was ready to explode. She decided that running the wrong way was better than taking no action at all. With this in mind, she raised the tremulous flame and bolted away from the sound. Two things were unmistakable to her ears. The slap-slap-slap of her footfalls and the rapid-fire clickety-clack of whatever now pursued her.

A scream rose in Keegan's throat as she sensed the assailant at her heels. Choosing to turn and fight, and unwilling to be struck down entirely defenseless, she skidded to a stop and spun to face the attacker. A massive fur-covered beast flashed from the darkness and into the light. A guttural keening scream escaped Keegan's throat as the creature slowed at the last second, collided with her legs, and then nuzzled her hip with its big fuzzy head.

Brody looked up at Keegan, his big pink tongue lolling and his eyes dancing good-naturedly in the firelight.

Keegan stood shaking from head to toe and staring down at the big goofy dog. Her chest heaved, though she received no reprieve from the oxygen. She was on the verge of a panic attack. Robotically, her free hand slipped into the hair atop Brody's head. Her fingers began kneading the thick tuft of fur, and the dog grunted with satisfaction. This broke Keegan from her shock. She sank to her knees, dropping the light and wrapping both arms around the big animal.

"My God, Brody," she said in heaving gasps. "You nearly scared me to death. Don't ever do that again."

The dog nuzzled more tightly to her, and she laughed. If this were his way of apologizing, she would take it. Hugging him tightly once more, she pulled back and looked him in the eye. "Can you get me out of here?" she said. The idea wasn't as crazy as it first seemed. He'd found his way here, wherever here was. He should be able to lead her out.

The dog barked and she laughed once more. Both sounds resonated through cavernous space.

Taking up the torch once more, Keegan patted Brody on the haunch. "Alright boy," she said. "Let's go home."

As if understanding, Brody set off at a quick walk. Keegan's attention was split between prolonging the life of her torch and keeping an eye on the dog. Losing either would spell disaster.

Brody padded quickly across the expansive cavern. Along the way they passed countless other statues. Though Keegan didn't stop to examine any of them closely, she saw what appeared to be a small band of pirates gathered in a tight group. Next, they passed more than a dozen figures dressed as monks. They had shaved heads and were dressed in tattered, long, flowing robes. The monks gathered around a wide, somewhat circular structure that Keegan found challenging to identify. She stepped closer to it. With the light of the torch dancing, the surface was covered with intricately crafted detail of some kind. She reached out and ran her fingers across the vertical object, and her tactile sense told her what her vision could not.

Keegan gasped and stepped quickly backward. Raising the torch high, she cursed and backpedaled further. The limbs of a massive tree spread wide over her head, branching out and thick with rich, healthy-looking leaves. Healthy, at least if they had not been made of stone. With a trunk nearly six feet in diameter, the bough had a span of at least thirty feet. The canopy overhead was thick with foliage, and the crown of a massive carving extended well beyond the reach of her light.

Keegan backed away from the enormous work of stone and stared. The intricacies of the figures at the base of the tree paled when compared to the craftsmanship dedicated to the tree. The amount of stone required to form the massive monument to mother nature was…she actually had no concept—no concept of how much stone or time would be required for such an undertaking. Indeed the delicacy of branches, limbs, and leaves…no, she simply couldn't fathom the how or the why of any of this.

Brody huffed at something in the distance, and she realized he had wandered off. Grateful for the distraction, she followed the sound of him pawing at stone. The dog had stopped at a small obstruction on the floor. Keegan fanned the embers of her torch once more and knew that time was running out. "Which way, boy?" she said.

The dog circled the obstruction on the floor. Reluctantly, Keegan knelt before the mess to examine it more closely in the waning light. It was an old bed roll and a tattered old saddle bag. Looking closer, she realized it wasn't a saddle bag but an ancient satchel. However, unlike everything she'd found in the cave so far, these were not crafted out of stone. Releasing the rusted clasp on the bag, she flipped back the lid. The ancient leather disintegrated in her hand and crumbled to the floor.

There was no time for this, she knew. Somehow the dog's intense gaze seemed to encourage her. Reluctantly, she slipped her hand inside the rapidly deteriorating bag. Only one object appeared to be present. Wrapping gentle fingers around it, she pulled it into the light. The object was about three inches by four and wrapped in oilcloth. Leaning the torch against the ancient bag to free her hand, Keegan began to unwrap the cloth. Inside was a small handwritten book. A journal, she instantly realized. Perfectly preserved for countless years.

She flipped to the front cover and examined the book's first page. Scrawled in neat script, the only thing written was, Fenton Bitters.

The flame flickered and died, reducing the cavern once more to complete and utter darkness. Keegan shot to her feet...

...And then sat up in bed with a start. The lamp on her nightstand was faintly visible in the glow of her digital alarm clock. The windows at the end of the room were draped with sheer curtains, but she could see pale moonlight through them.

Uttering a short string of profanities, she flung herself backward in bed and pulled the comforter over herself. Frustrated with the dream and already dreading the morning, she rolled over with a dramatic flip of her arm. Her hand struck something solid and sent a shot of pain up her wrist. Pulling the object closer for a better look, a cold feeling gripped her. The small leather-bound book was visible in the diffused moonlight. Flipping open the cover, she found two words etched in a neat scrawl: Fenton Bitters.

Chapter 5

The airframe shuddered, causing Zane Greeley to curse under his breath for perhaps the hundredth time. His white-knuckled grip on what passed for an armrest in the narrow seat of the Beechcraft Model 18B threatened to tear it away entirely. At six-foot-seven, Greeley was a mountain of a man. The Twin Beech, as the aircraft was affectionately known, was last produced in the 1970s. He knew that this particular plane hadn't been among the last to roll from the production line. The wicked turbulence and the relentless drone from the pair of Pratt & Whitney R-985 nine-cylinder air-cooled engines rattled his teeth even as his anxiety ground at the enamel. He was fighting the worst airsickness of his life, and there was no end in sight. The plane's specifications passed through Greeley's mind in an unbidden loop as he fought down the gorge repeatedly rising in his throat.

A look through the starboard window did nothing to calm his nerves. The Pacific Ocean was passing far too close beneath the fuselage. Sure, if they crashed, they wouldn't have far to fall—but flying at this altitude made that crash a calculated certainty. Garboni—that sonofabitch—was to blame for this. They'd flown out of Seattle after chartering the Twin Beech. Staying under the radar meant keeping below four hundred feet. The demand had come as a surprise to Greeley and a shock to their lone pilot.

The airframe bucked once more, and rage finally won out over fear.

Throwing the seat buckle away with enough insistence to dent the stainless steel lining the walls of the passenger compartment, Greeley shoved his two-hundred-and-forty-pound frame from the seat. Though his mind was focused, his intestinal fortitude was less convinced. Despite himself, the child-like groan that slipped from his lips was audible even over the engines and the whistle of wind over the fuselage. The passenger compartment had a relatively high ceiling, but not high enough. Greeley was forced to stoop as he made for the cockpit. Having just celebrated his 28th birthday, the big man was the picture of physical fitness. He had the upper body of an action movie star, with broad, powerful shoulders, a short thick neck, and a face of angular planes demonstrating his Germanic heritage. A solid, wide forehead ended in thick brows perched atop small dark eyes hinting at an intelligence rare to men of his prodigious size and strength. Had his visage been chiseled in stone, his short blond hair and tiny ears would have made him a distant cousin to the gargantuan statues on Easter Island.

Only four seats occupied the plane's rear, the rest having been removed to make way for cargo. Pushing past the empty first row of seats, Greeley shouldered aside the threadbare curtain separating the cockpit from the cargo space. This wasn't a passenger aircraft. That particular quality, and the related specialty of the pilot had led Greeley's partner to choose Ephirm Spalding for their surreptitious flight. Spalding was a smuggler, and his Twin Beech was specially configured for the task. Float skis had replaced the craft's traditional landing gear, and auxiliary fuel tanks were stowed between the floats to extend flight range. Presently there was no cargo. Greeley and his partner, Anthony Garboni, were the only passengers.

Greeley wedged his shoulders into the narrow span of the cockpit entrance. Spalding, a cantankerous balding Gulf War vet, sat behind the yoke on the left. A headset rested crookedly across his ears, the worn out and cracked earmuffs askew on his right ear thanks to the turbulence. The cabin was dim, the weather outside gloomy as sunset approached, and the sky darker still since the sun was to their backs.

Why the hell is the sun at our backs?

They had been flying west. That meant the sunset should have been dead ahead.

"Why the hell aren't you buckled in?" This from Anthony "the Ant" Garboni. The short Italian had been born with a chip on his shoulder. He'd always been eager to make a name for himself in the Outfit, and this time he was going to get them killed. A minor league shot caller so far. Nonetheless, he

was moving up the ranks. Garboni's drive for recognition and respect put them on this fool's errand, and Greeley was regretting ever teaming up with the short shit.

"Get back there and strap in before you break that thick neck," Garboni ordered.

It was good advice. Though there wasn't a cloud in the sky, the bone-rattling turbulence had started a half hour ago. Even the pilot couldn't explain the strange occurrence. The violent shifts and jolts of the aircraft had become alarming over the last five minutes. It didn't seem like the thin metal skin of the plane could weather such an assault.

"We're too low," Greeley bellowed above the howl of the wind and the whine of the engines. He saw the pilot steal a wild glance at Garboni. There was terror in the man's eyes, and a flash of something more. Perhaps it was hope that these rational words would add support to his own advice. "You must take us higher!" Greeley pressed.

Shaking his head, Garboni grimaced. He tried to speak, but the words were cut short by another devastating jolt pushing the starboard wing low. Garboni's left hand pressed hard against the dashboard to maintain balance. The sudden shift changed Greeley's perspective. The .357 revolver Garboni clutched in the bloodless fist of his right hand came momentarily into view.

"Hey," Greeley called to the pilot. "Screw this, and screw him! Take us higher!"

Garboni raised the gun and pointed it at the pilot. "Maintain altitude," he demanded.

The pilot's eyes were wide and unblinking. He turned from his fight with the yoke and stared down the gun's barrel for what seemed like minutes. At last his eyes went forward once more. The physical battle with the plane's controls continued but they did not climb.

"What are you doing?" Greeley bellowed. "You'll get us killed."

"We stay below radar," Garboni cautioned. "I won't sacrifice the element of surprise."

"Not even to save our lives?"

The pilot slammed an open palm against the control stick and cursed in a foreign tongue. He rocked the wheel, then sat back in his seat before hammering the yoke with his hand once more. *Shooting a look to Greeley over his shoulder, the man yelled, "the wings! Go to the back and take a closer look. Tell me—are they iced?"*

Shifting his weight, Greeley freed himself from the pinched safety of the doorway. He moved aft, fighting for footing every step of the way. Twice the plane dropped entirely from beneath his feet. Had his stooped shoulders not been braced firmly against the ceiling when it happened, his neck would surely have snapped. At last, he reached the window overlooking the starboard wing. The violent turbulence made it impossible to focus on the wing with any reliability. Pressing a forearm hard against the ceiling and grinding the soles of his boots into the floor, he braced himself against the worst of the uncontrolled shaking. At least this way when the plane jolted, he was jostled in sync with it. Finally, the wing came clearly into view.

"Shit," he bellowed, though no one was near enough to hear.

Clamping his jaw in determination, Greeley shoved from the starboard wall and reached the port window in two skidding steps. Once more, he braced an arm and set his feet into a rigid stance. The port wing came into focus. Heavy drops of water spattered the outer surface of the window. Looking closer, he saw similar water slapping the wing's leading edge. The smooth curve of the wings leading edge had already collected a thick layer of ice. Though not visible, he was confident a layer of ice was also collecting along the back of the wing where the flaps hinged with the wing.

"We're icing up bad," Greeley reported as he slid through the cockpit doorway. He shifted to ensure he was pinched and stuck in a crude but effective friction restraint making a human door in the tiny entrance. At least it was enough to keep him from being knocked around the cabin. "A lot of ice along the front of each wing, and the flaps aren't too far behind."

The pilot glared at Garboni. "We must climb!" he insisted. "I'm losing maneuverability by the minute."

"How close is the island?" Garboni demanded.

The pilot bared clenched teeth. Greeley couldn't tell if this was out of frustration or whether there was something more on the old man's mind.

Garboni shoved the revolver in the pilot's face, the question silent but plainly apparent.

"Damn it!" the pilot bellowed. The plane bucked once more. He was fighting a desperate losing battle with the control yoke. "I have no idea. Under these

conditions? You think I can navigate? It's all I can do to keep us in the air. If we don't gain altitude now, nothing else will matter."

The pilot shot a quick look over his shoulder at Greeley. The fear in that brief glance suggested there was another problem.

"What is it," Greeley called over the riotous wind.

Spalding didn't waste words, and he didn't look back to answer. "We've already passed the coordinates you provided. The island isn't there!"

Greeley recalled how the plane had banked sharply shortly after turbulence had started. At the time, he'd assumed the maneuver was an effort to ensure they had the skies to themselves. Dropping his head, he shook it slowly as the realization settled in. "You've already circled back once."

It was a statement rather than a question. The old man had already made a second pass over the coordinates, apparently to no avail.

"You provided bad intelligence," Spalding snapped. A hand lashed out like a snake and tapped quickly against one of the cracked analog gauges on the instrument panel. "Now we're running low on fuel. If we don't find a place to set down, we're in real trouble."

A thunderous jolt went through the airframe, this one more violent than any before. Garboni's outstretched gun swung unsteadily and then discharged. The sound of the shot was obvious even over the wind, and endless clatter of metal on metal as the plane slowly vibrated itself to pieces. The surprise of the sound sucked the air from Greeley's lungs.

Garboni looked as surprised by the gunshot as everyone else. Clearly, his death grip on the revolver was to blame.

The windscreen cracked in front of the pilot, a small spidering fracture crawling from the pencil-sized bullet hole. The crack grew as it spread, slowly and effortlessly making its way toward the plane's starboard side. Another branch split, and then another as the tree-like etching grew. One went up while the other tangled down and to the left with shocking speed. Aided by the endless shift and shake of the airframe, the cracks spread with increasing efficiency. The windscreen began a full fledge detonation as the small peripheral spits started to pelt the cabin with pinpoints of glass.

The pilot screamed a curse in his foreign tongue once more, only to have it cut short. Half of the windscreen crumbled into his lap while the other went outward and was snatched away by the wind. When the air current caught the *vacating portion of glass, it raked the portion free from the pilot and took most of his abdominal cavity along for the ride. Half the cabin was awash in blood in the blink of an eye.*

Greeley watched the pilot's gruesome death while entirely powerless to prevent it. Worse yet, when the glass was torn from the front of the plane, it took the steering column with it. The aircraft jolted hard to port, and Greeley felt the world begin to spin. They would crash. When that happened, the doorway would offer absolutely no protection. Shoving himself free from the doorframe, he faced the cargo hold. It had gone entirely dark. With a shove, he pushed himself into the black; in his mind's eye, he saw himself buckling into the feeble restraints of that undersized passenger seat.

It was a long shot, but it was all he had left.

Chapter 6

The axe head sliced the air, cleaved the round of maple, and sank into the foot-tall stump that constituted Gavin's improvised chopping block. Rocking the handle in the grip of his glove, he pulled it free from the stump and knocked the fresh split wedge aside where it landed in the growing pile. Standing the axe upright on its head, he took the large remaining portion of the maple round in his hands and turned it into position for his next swing. Then, raising the axe once more, he repeated the process.

This was Gavin Kray's second straight day laboring to reduce more than a dozen long dead maples into firewood for the rapidly advancing winter. Two more swings and he'd finished the round. Setting the axe aside, it was time for a brief break. Tossing the pair of thick, yellow leather gloves atop the shoulder-high pile of neatly stacked wood, he retrieved a thermos. He took a deep swallow and relished the refreshing chill of the cold spring water. A snarling sound in the distance drew his attention. He turned to face it, a smile crossing his face as he snatched a battered old tennis ball from the woodpile beside his discarded gloves.

The low growl came from the far side of the dense pile of brush. There was a brief pause, and then a rapid scratching sound proceeded a jet of dry dirt spraying out into the brush. "Come here, you crazy fool," Gavin laughed. A quick, quiet whistle burst from his lips. The noise from the other side of discarded vegetation went silent.

A breath later, a black and rust-coated dog charged from around the brush pile. His ears flapped and his tongue lolled. He bolted with drive, determination, and enough speed to challenge that of a Greyhound. Paces away from knocking Gavin from his feet, the big dog pulled up short at the last second and skidded to a halt just inches from the toes of Gavin's boots. A hundred pounds of Bernese Mountain Dog looked expectantly up at him with the sun dancing against the dappled highlights of his fluffy multi-colored fur. Standing 26" at the shoulder, the dog was all sinew and muscle. He might have appeared imposing if not for the puppy-like flip of the tail and joyful glint in his eyes.

"Well?" Gavin said, gazing at the dog. "Did you get it? No...you're just happy scaring the holy hell out of it, aren't you?" He shook his head.

The dog stared up at him with anxious, unblinking eyes.

Gavin held the ball in the air and made a show of examining it. He rolled it around in the palm of his hand and pinched it between his thumb and forefinger as if trying to discern its value. "Is this what you want?"

The dog squirmed atop a fidgeting tail. His butt was still planted in the dirt, though clearly not satisfied to remain seated.

"It might be time to find you a new ball, buddy." The ball had seen better days. It was dirty, and its fabric frayed and threadbare. Cocking back an arm, he heaved the ball up the steep slope to the west, pitching it carefully between the bare branches of the dozen or so dead maples. It flew true and sailed into the green oaks and conifers beyond. The dog was off like a shot, his powerful legs pumping and big paws turning up the dry dirt for two dozen yards before he disappeared into the dry fall undergrowth blanketing the woods floor.

Grinning at the dog's unbridled enthusiasm, Gavin helped himself to another swallow of water before turning his attention to the rumble and clatter taking place at his back. Thirty yards away, almost half the distance across the hard pack outcropping that had become their work area, the small 4-stroke engine continued its ceaseless rumble. Every thirty seconds to a minute, the engine's drone was interrupted by the buzzing hiss of the machine it powered. The hiss announced the release of the hydraulic piston that pushed a ridged ram horizontally down the length of the machine's long cradle. At the end of the ram's path, with each slow, powerful stroke, a blunt wedge would meet with a massive round of wood cut from the same trees on which Gavin had been working. The mechanized log splitter might be slow, but it could split portions of wood that were too large to attack with an axe and any efficiency.

The man running the log splitter was Esker "Willy" Amstell, a stout man in his early fifties with a wiry brush of gray hair and a neatly trimmed matching beard. He was soaking wet, nearly from head to toe. He'd started the day in a flannel shirt and overalls—understandable given that the high for the day was all of fifty degrees. Hard labor had made up for the low temperature, but Esker had been too bullheaded to concede to mother nature. He had sweat through the flannel before finally giving in and discarding it in favor of his undershirt and overalls. By that time, Gavin mused, the battle of wills had already been lost. Esker had been stewing in his own sweat all afternoon.

Esker Amstell was a Scotsman by heritage, evident in his quick temper and the fragments of his hard-suppressed accent that often slipped through when he got bent out of shape. Technically speaking, Gavin reported to Esker. Together they comprised the island's maintenance crew. They fixed leaks, dug ditches, mowed grass in the summer, shoveled snow in the winter, and generally kept the island from reclaiming the estate grounds. In the autumn, they laid in a supply of firewood for burning in any of the monastery's two dozen fireplaces.

Esker was the boss, at least on paper. In practicality, his short temper and ongoing list of quirks and idiosyncrasies had influenced the island dynamic. If something was broken or someone needed help on the island, their first instinct was to reach out to Gavin. Where Esker was brooding and standoffish, Gavin was approachable if reserved. None of this had escaped Esker's attention, and Gavin couldn't help but wonder if it was part of the reason Esker kept him at arm's length.

There might have been another reason Esker had failed to warm to Gavin the way others had. Being brash, short-tempered, and perceived as generally irritable, combined with his Scottish heritage—not to mention his job on the island—the rest of the island staff had taken to calling the older man Willy. As in Grounds Keeper Willy, the Scotsman from the Simpsons cartoon series, who shared nearly every personality trait. Gavin had to take some responsibility for the moniker. He'd coined the name after making the comparison in a conversation with another member of the staff one evening shortly after joining the island's staff. The name had stuck. In a matter of days, everyone had seemingly forgotten Esker's given name. He was known now simply as Willy.

Though he didn't think Willy knew who was responsible for the nickname, it wasn't much of a stretch to put it on Gavin. They worked together. Besides, no one on the island had a sense of humor quite like Gavin—for better or worse.

Gavin watched Willy muscle a new round of maple onto the splitter before he stepped forward. Willy had the process down to a science. With the log splitter positioned properly, he could roll the rounds into position on the cleaving tray. Once there, he only had to hold the safety lever with one hand while engaging the splitter's drive piston with the other. To prevent the accidental crushing of one's hands, the system required both before the powerful splitting wedge could be put into service. Once activated, a formidable hydraulic-driven wedge-tipped piston would muscle through even the sturdiest round of timber.

Willy palmed the release button on the splitter's control panel and the piston began to withdraw down the short ramp. It left the wood efficiently cleaved, if a somewhat slow and noisy process. Gavin tapped the man on the shoulder and offered the water canteen.

Blowing an exaggerated sigh, the older man waved off the bottle and reached into his open flannel to retrieve a flask. "Thanks anyway," he said after the clatter of the machine eased to idle. Willy had long since stopped attempting to conceal his propensity for drinking. Confined to the island as they all were, secrets were challenging to keep—this one perhaps more than most since it required each quarterly supply ship to deliver a quantity of liquor that was impossible to conceal. "Knowing you, that damn dogs been drinking from your bottle. I'll stick to mine. Know where that's been, don't you know."

Willy's drinking was the other reason for his nickname. It was undoubtedly the source of his ill temper. He was fine while socially lubricated. The foulness of the man's personality tended to make appearances when he'd gone too long without his medicine. Thankfully, at least to the minds of most, this didn't happen very often. Willy was what people referred to as a functioning alcoholic. Gavin had become a believer. Willy could work harder and walk a straighter line when adequately lubricated. He was also far easier to get along with.

Willy took a second pull from the flask before secreting it away once more. Without delay, he began throwing split shards from the splitter into a chest-high pile he had already amassed. If he had to rate the man, Gavin would call him a high-functioning alcoholic. He could, and would, drink all day and never lose a step. His liver had to be half pickled by this point in the day, but he still labored like a steam engine.

Rising from his stooped position, Willy shot Gavin a look. His eyes were narrow and his nose was scrunched. He looked like he was going to be sick. "You did, didn't you," he said. "You let that filthy creature drink from your bottle."

Arching a brow, Gavin shrugged. He offered a slow nod to the affirmative and watched Willy's eyes. To his satisfaction, the sickened grimace intensified.

The color blanched from Willy's face.

"No—" Gavin admitted quickly. "I'm just messing with you. But Brody's mouth is probably cleaner than yours, even with that antiseptic you swill."

"Cleaner than my—Not an hour ago, I saw that infernal beast licking his own balls!"

Shrugging, Gavin said, "now you're just jealous. With a talent like that, I bet you'd forget all about your flask."

Willy had slipped his flask out for a quick sip and was tipping it back when Gavin spoke. The comment made him choke, a geyser shooting simultaneously from his mouth and nose. He coughed and sputtered for over a minute, doubled over and feet stomping the dirt while cursing the scorching sensation the potent drink had brought to his nose and eyes.

The scotch clearly burned. The sight of the old man stamping and cursing had Gavin laughing so hard he nearly reduced himself to tears.

When the fit subsided, Willy looked up from where he knelt in the dirt. His face was beet red, and his dirty face was streaked where falling tears had washed clean rivulets. His breathing was ragged as he fought to regain his wind. Willy looked angry. Pissed. He was a hot-blooded Scotsman through and through.

Long seconds ticked by and Gavin refused to break the silence. Veins bulged in Willy's face. Finally, the angry expression cracked and the man laughed. He slapped a knee and shook his head as a dry chuckle reverberated deep from his chest. For all of Willy's faults, he'd also been gifted with a generous sense of humor. That and he'd been drinking so he was feeling agreeable at the moment. "Kid, you're an arshole, you know that?"

Gavin grinned and looked over Willy's work area. He'd been attacking the larger cuts from the tree's base using the noisy log-splitting contraption while Gavin split the tree's thick limbs and the narrower, more maneuverable cuts from higher on the maple. They had already taken down three trees and made good progress on the fourth. They'd set a good pace considering it was just the two of them. It was getting late in the afternoon and there were additional trees still to bring down. It would be at least another two days' worth of work.

Willy eyed the pile Gavin had amassed. There was rare approval in his gaze. "I'm not as young as I used to be," Willy said after taking another sip. "There was a time when I would've been able to out-split you with one hand tied behind my back."

Gavin offered a solemn nod. Willy had a couple of decades on him, but he was pretty sure the forty extra pounds he was carrying slowed him down. "I'm sure that's true," he said with a sincerity that sounded genuine. He failed to hide the amusement that danced in his eyes with the comment.

"What?" Willy grimaced with mock indignation. "You don't believe me?"

Gavin wanted to change the subject. Willy had a good sense of humor, but he could be a talker. They could lose what little remained of the afternoon if he didn't keep him on track. It was also an excellent opportunity to voice concern on his mind since the previous day.

"How long have you worked here?" Gavin asked.

"On the island, or for the old man before Mr. Anakasta?" Willy asked. He pulled a tattered, saturated red handkerchief from his pocket and wiped his face.

"The island, I mean. I know the old man owned it long before turning it over to Mr. Anakasta. How long have you worked the island?"

A faraway look spread across Willy's visage as his mind seemed to wander. "It's got to be twenty—no, closer to twenty-five years. Why do you ask?"

Gavin motioned toward the dozen or so maple trees circling the clearing they had now used for the splitter operation. The trees were weathered and old, having long since cast off their leaves for the last time many years before. The trees had grown to a strong, full maturity before succumbing to whatever blight had claimed them. Now they were pale in color, almost as if they had been bleached white by the weather. No bark remained. Not one had even a hint of the husk that would help identify them as maples.

Rising steeply behind the plateau, the mountain began a meandering assent. And while not all the dirt and rock terrain was covered with trees, during his time on the island, Gavin had found no other groves of similarly blighted trees—maple or otherwise.

"Something happened to these dozen trees," Gavin explained. "I've been trying to figure out what could bleach them white like this and kill an entire copse so abruptly. Every tree on this steppe seems to have died from the same sickness."

Willy's face scrunched. He twisted the cap back onto the flask before turning his gaze to the trees they planned to take down in the remainder of the week. They'd taken the island's dead growth for firewood and recently signaled out this cluster for splitting and collection before the winter snows set in.

"I don't know," Willy admitted. "Can't say I've ever given it a thought."

"If there are similar trees anywhere on the island, I can't find them."

Willy offered a slow, considered nod. "Now that you mention it, I think you're right. It's odd."

The quiet rumble of the idling log spitter engine sputtered and drew their attention.

"Well, shit!" Willy cursed and snatched up the red plastic gas can. Judging by the way he lifted it, the container must've been empty. Willy had put his back into the urgent effort to raise the can. When it came up in his hands, apparently weighing nothing, he rocked back on his heels and almost spilled onto his backside.

Gavin tried not to laugh. It was better to pretend not to notice. Willy had the grace and dexterity of a hippo dancing on marbles, but he wasn't fond of being laughed at.

The engine sputtered once more and then went quiet.

"Dammit," Willy professed. "That's going to cost me more time."

Gavin picked up his axe once more. He didn't see why Willy was getting bent out of shape. The way he saw it, they had nothing but time. Being the only two men on the ground crew tasked with maintaining an island estate in the middle of nowhere had its perks. And winter was on its way. Once it hit, they would be forced to spend much of their time indoors. Until that happened, he didn't care what he was doing—as long as he could do it outside.

"I guess I'll run back for gas," Willy muttered. "I hate burning daylight like this."

If Willy couldn't find something to get worked up over, he would likely get worked up over his lack of worries. The man had a good heart, but it was just his way. Still, he seemed more bent out of shape over this small mistake than was due. They were just over a mile away from the citadel, the island's main building. Using the ATV, it wouldn't take long to run back for a fresh can of fuel.

Willy must have seen the misgiving in Gavin's eyes because he explained his frustration. "It's not the gas so much," he admitted. "If I knew I was running back before the end of the day, I would've had you load up one of the trailers to take with. I just don't like making a wasted trip. If I could take a load back, it *would at least be worthwhile."*

Gavin tipped his head to the east. "Got you covered, boss."

No one on the island treated Willy like he was in charge of their team. If only due to his age, Willy earned that right and Gavin was happy to pay the respect. It was a small courtesy, but one he hoped would eventually make headway in their relationship. Another year or two and they might actually be friends.

Spinning, Willy saw the trailer hooked to the back of the large red four-wheel-drive Honda ATV. The load bed was stacked high with bleached white split maple. Turning back, Willy's eyebrows arched. He started to speak only to have the words frozen on his lips. He tried again, this time finding them. "When?"

Offering only a shrug, Gavin slipped back into his leather gloves. "Just watch it on the curves this time, boss. You almost dumped the entire load yesterday," he admonished.

Willy's grin spread across clenched teeth. He shook his head. "Sometimes I don't know what to make of you, kid."

Chapter 7

Keegan Anakasta stood over her own slumbering form. It was a surreal experience, but this wasn't the first time it had happened. In fact, since coming to Black Rock Island at her father's request, this was happening more and more frequently. Each new experience still brought chills, but she had come to view the out-of-body events with less trepidation...if only just a little.

Her body lay semi-reclined against a pair of large pillows on the sofa along the wall of her suite. A small blanket sat draped across her legs, and a thick leather-bound book rode the rise and fall of her breasts as she slumbered. It was embarrassing how she lay there, mouth half agape and head tipped back as if passed out rather than napping.

Hopefully, no one sees me like this.

Turning from her body, Keegan surveyed the room. The king-sized four-poster bed looked small in the spacious room. With walls assembled from massive stone blocks, their roughhewn surfaces offered no scrollwork or decorative embellishment of any kind. Slate tiles covered the floors, and the exposed ceiling timber was twelve feet overhead. A pair of nightstands bracketed the bed while a wide maple desk was pushed into the rightmost corner of the room. A sleeping laptop and mouse sat beside a small pile of hardcover books. A pair of massive armoires stood along the wall opposite the couch and a gigantic eight-foot-tall bookcase ran the remaining length of the wall, its shelves stacked end to end with books of every shape and size. A pair of double doors led to an on-suite bathroom while another pair offered access to a walkout second-story balcony. The walls and floor of the balcony were constructed of the same gray stone as most of the ancient monasteries.

A great hearth assembled from stone and concrete occupied the wall not far from the foot of the sofa. Keegan walked slowly toward its dancing flames and raised her hands. No warmth could be felt. She shot a look over her shoulder and confirmed her still slumbering form. She walked closer to the hearth, paused briefly, then stepped into the flames. She passed right through. Putting a little bounce in her step, she pushed upward. Her heart began to race as it always did with this experience. Her vision went dark as she passed through the yards of stone and mortar comprising the walls and floor of the ancient structure. Though she didn't need to breathe in this form, her breath felt stuck in her throat as she waited to reach open space once more.

An unbidden gasp escaped her lips as her form drifted diagonally to emerge from both the floor and the wall of the third-floor corridor. Her vertical motion ceased, and her shoes' heels met the stone floor with a telltale click. She looked around quickly, ensuring she was alone, but she need not have bothered. The sound of her gasp and the strike of her feet on the floor were audible only to her. It was yet another mystery of the phenomenon she had yet to understand. She could hear and see more while violating the laws of gravity and without anyone aware of her trespasses. It was both invigorating and terrifying at the same time.

Keegan walked down the wide corridor dragging the tips of her fingers along the rough stone of the walls. The building was an ancient monastery built hundreds of years ago if the stories were to be believed. Her father had acquired the building along with the entire island nearly nine months ago. The previous owner was an eccentric old man named Brooks Fowler. As she understood it, Fowler had purchased the island decades before that and found the monastery in extreme disrepair. He'd sunk tens of millions of dollars into the island, intending to make it his retirement paradise. In the process, he painstakingly rebuilt the rolling old pile. It was a restoration process that took years. The result was a massive old structure with dozens of bedrooms, updated with electricity, indoor plumbing, and forced air heating. Exactly how her father had come to purchase the island remained vaguely explained at best. No matter how often she had broached the subject, he somehow managed to deftly avoid directly answering her questions.

Voices in the distance drew Keegan's attention. She found Tess Lindow and

Jennifer Fennem changing the linens in one of the staff's quarters. Tess unfurled a folded sheet and threw a corner to Jennifer on the opposite side of the stripped bed. Jennifer snagged the sheet from the air and began securing it around the corner of the pillow-top mattress without preamble. The pair's actions were practiced and routine. They'd clearly done this dozens, maybe even hundreds of times.

"It's not what he said," Tess was saying. "It's the way I catch him looking at me. He's always popping up. Maybe around a corner or at the end of a hall. I feel like he's watching me." Perhaps five foot six, Tess had long chestnut hair and a pale complexion. An array of freckles spotted the bridge of her nose and cheeks. She was in her mid-twenties and was dressed in the dark blouse and skirt that was the accepted uniform of the housekeeping staff.

"He's not watching you," Jennifer laughed. "It's his job to be lurking about. He's part of the security team. They wander around looking for trouble. They're stationed throughout the building. He's not spying on you. You just keep running into him." Jennifer had Tess's same slim build but was three inches taller. She had long blonde hair and wore wire-framed glasses that made her eyes appear just a little on the large side. They were nearly the same age and spent most of their free time together from what Keegan could tell.

Tess looked unconvinced. She tossed a pair of pillowcases to Jennifer before retrieving a pillow from the floor and slipping a case over it. "I know how it sounds," she said. "It's not so much that he's there...it's the look he gives me when I find him staring. My skin just sort of crawls. It just feels...I don't know—maybe, off somehow?"

Jennifer gave her friend a long look. "He probably has a thing for you," she admitted. "You've got the body of a twenty-year-old. Stuck out here on an island in the middle of nowhere?" She eyed Tess's skirt and smirked. "Course he wants to hit that. Tell me you haven't been paying a little more attention to the security guys than you should. Some of them aren't half bad. You're hot, and you're single. Anyone of those guys would probably give his right arm to—"

"That's not funny," Tess snapped. "Most of those guys have reptile eyes. Have you been paying attention? It's like they're cold-blooded. They scare me. Don't they scare..."

Keegan turned from the room and continued on. Girls and their gossip. Eavesdropping was the last thing on her list of priorities. Jennifer and Tess were nice enough, though Keegan hadn't gotten to know either of them. She hadn't connected with anyone on the island in the three months she'd been here.

Her original intention had been to stay for only a week—visit her dad, look in on her new stepmother, maybe get a look at this island her father had bought. Who bought an island, anyway? Her father had barely managed to keep the family solvent for most of her life. Having spent most of her school-age years in one private boarding school or another, even she knew the family had been on the verge of financial ruin more than once.

Now father has an island. What kind of mistake will this end in?

Reaching the end of the hall, Keegan stopped at the top of a great sweeping staircase. It was fifteen feet wide at the top of the third floor and widened on the way to the first level where it was thirty-five feet at the base. With stone treads and polished wooden rails, the staircase was impressive. A massive crystal chandelier hung four and a half floors above. A platform bisected the stairs halfway down with halls leading east and west on the second floor. As she could only in her strange spectral form, Keegan glided from the topmost tread and slowly descended the staircase without a single move of her foot.

Passing across the expansive lobby, Keegan passed physically through the massive pair of closed iron-banded oak doors. The late afternoon wind howled in her ears though the chill wind never touched her skin. She swept down the dozen stone stairs leading from the monastery's grand entrance and moved swiftly along the gravel path. The immaculately trimmed grass of the inner grounds was already beginning to brown with the onset of autumn. She was glad she'd arrived early enough in the season to see the island with its wildflowers and foliage in full bloom. Though the many species of trees on the island were a rich visual tapestry now as they prepared to shed their foliage at the change of seasons, it was already becoming obvious how dreary and monotone the coming months would be.

Pushing off with the tips of her toes, Keegan took flight. Drifting slowly, she flew high as she approached the crenelated wall surrounding the monastery. The fortress's many ridges, peaks, and dormers were visible from a unique vantage over her shoulder as she swept away from the structure. She drifted across the expansive gardens littering the ground, all of which had been stripped bare in anticipation of the impending change of seasons. She passed over the massive fifteen-foot-tall stone and mortar wall surrounding the monastery and its manicured grounds. Though she'd done this several times in the past, her eyes lingered on the top of the wall. It was four feet wide at the top and even wider at the base. The mortar at the peak had been mixed with what appeared to be shards of ancient weather-colored glass. Ragged metal spikes pointed skyward. None of this was visible from the ground.

Keegan mused how her father would spend millions searching the island, but he would never see things as she did. Though she didn't understand how or why she had this ability, there was no denying the exhilarating rush each expedition brought.

She soared out over the island moving quickly to the west. Crossing over the tree line, she adjusted her course northwest. The oak, elm, sycamore, and maple trees passed beneath her in a riot of color. The wind must have been up because she could see gusts rocking the branches and already sending the fantastic patchwork of color skittering to the woodland floor. Bitter's Lake came into view to the north and she adjusted course. The lake was oblong, three times longer to the east and west than it was to the north and south. It had taken its name from the island's most famous shipwreck. According to what her father had explained, the truth of Fenton Bitters's years as a castaway on Black Rock had only come to light thanks to the discoveries of the island's previous owner, Brooks Fowler. Bitter's Lake was entirely freshwater and likely the only reason the paraplegic from the 19th century survived on the island for as long as he had.

Acres of freshwater, Keegan mused. It still didn't explain how a crippled aristocrat had managed to survive in such a primitive time. There were so many questions not answered to her satisfaction. Rumor had it that Fowler was close to publishing a book when he'd abruptly left the island. The work was supposed to explain everything he'd learned about Fenton Bitters's years on the island that she wouldn't give for a peek at his manuscript. She was now in possession of Fenton Bitters's personal journal. Would it complement or contradict what Fowler planned to publish? Had Fowler been aware of the diary she found? Had he hidden it for someone to find? There were so many questions.

Those questions were why she'd stayed far beyond the two weeks initially negotiated with her father. Well, one of the reasons, she reconsidered.

The rocky bluffs began nearly a hundred yards north of the lake. Virtually the entire island was ringed by a treacherous cliff line. On foggy nights, if not for the sound of the surf pounding the foot of the bluff and the shallow reef surrounding the island, it would be easy to walk right off the ragged cliff. At its lowest point, the cliff stood twenty-seven feet above the high-tide line. At some locations along the island perimeter, the fall to the water was closer to seventy-five feet. There were at least two promontories on the mountain, she'd been told, which extended like great diving boards over the surf and offered falls of several hundred feet.

It was funny...until she'd learned to fly, Keegan had actually been terrified of heights.

The island was shaped like a lima bean laid out from east to west. Black Mountain took up a third of the island and occupied the entirety of the island's west end. And though the cliffs encircled the vast majority of the island, there was a single safe approach that didn't require boats to brave the reefs or mariners to climb the jagged rocky cliffs. A sizable shallow cove offered access via the eastern tip of the island. Though precarious, there was an approach that offered safety from the reef and the shallow rocks often located just below the surface of the water surrounding the island.

When Brooks Fowler first took possession of the land, he brought equipment in from the mainland and had the cove dredged at great expense. It was little more than a shallow lagoon at the time. Massive pylons were set into the depths of the water, and a great pier was built. This allowed cargo ships to dock. They were used to deliver the equipment and hardware Fowler eventually used to refurbish the monastery and create the modern infrastructure. Even after all his expense and labor, though the bay was vast, the inlet was narrow. Due to the constraints of the island's underlying bedrock, only a narrow channel could be carved to allow ships access to the peer. Today, only two ships currently afloat could successfully approach and dock at the island's peer. They were medium-sized cargo vessels with specialized instrumentation and highly precise maneuvering thrusters, which allowed them to make the exacting course adjustments necessary to dock without running aground. Those ships were responsible for making quarterly supply deliveries, now to the great expense of her father.

Shifting her course to the west once more, Keegan accelerated. This had already been one of her lengthiest out-of-body experiences, and there was no telling how long it would last. Black Mountain loomed in the distance, growing larger with each passing second.

Far off, the gentle rumble of an engine sounded and caught Keegan's attention. An ATV strained at the head of an overloaded aluminum trailer as it threaded its way through the forest in the direction she'd come from. A bald patch was visible in the distance, a fresh clearing in the trees that stood out against the canopy of browns, oranges, and yellows. As she drew nearer, she could see that trees had been toppled and two piles of split wood had been amassed. Gavin was stacking shards of split wood at the end of a long stack. His coveralls were tied off at the waist to reveal a tank top that was dark with perspiration. The tight, corded muscles of his arms and shoulders rippled in the waning sunlight. Not a large man, he was fit and solidly built. She knew he preferred to work with an axe and let old Willy use the mechanical contraption when they worked together.

Gliding slowly, Keegan's feet met the ground only yards from where Gavin worked. She studied him, her hands on her hips and lips in a small, tight smile. He had no idea she was here, and the experience was exhilarating.

A clatter arose from the brush behind her. Keegan spun to see Gavin's dog, Brody, returning with a tennis ball in his mouth. The dog stopped suddenly and looked directly at her. The dog's gaze caught her off guard. No one could see her; it was one of the few certainties she could count on when it came to this strange experience. She bent and looked into the dog's eyes.

He was staring back into hers.

Her jaw went slack and she took a step backward, her knees feeling suddenly weak.

Gavin gave a brief whistle and the dog darted to his side. The ball changed hands and Gavin instantly pitched it far off into the overgrowth. Brody's tail snapped back and forth in satisfaction, and then he was off like a shot leaving a short trail of dust in his wake.

Keegan was stunned by the dog's reaction. He had acknowledged her. Numbly, she trudged off in search of the dog. She had to know more. She had to understand.

Following the still-settling cloud of dust around a large pile of brush and short twisted tree limbs, she found Brody already returning with the ball. "Hey, Brody. Come on, boy," she called and slapped her thigh with the palm of her hand.

Brody's tail gave a gleeful shake, and he bolted through the overgrowth and skidded to a stop at her feet. The ball dropped from his mouth and rolled through her feet. The expectant look in the dog's eyes made Keegan smile. She was fresh out of veterinary school herself. Had she not accepted this "two-week" visit with her father, she would already be a practicing veterinarian. She loved animals, and Brody had won her heart on day one. Not being able to pet him now was breaking her heart.

But he can see me. How is this possible?

Though sitting and staring at her with excited eyes, Brody's hindquarters positively squirmed in the dirt. He was begging for a scratch behind the ears. Despite herself, Keegan bent to ruffle his fur. With Brody leaning into her touch, she had to brace herself to keep the dog from knocking her over. She laughed at his playful enthusiasm.

Then Keegan gasped. She dropped to her knees and took Brody's head between her hands. She gave him a rigorous scratching and watched wide-eyed as his tongue lolled with satisfaction. She was touching him.

I'm actually touching him!

The sound of voices pulled her attention away from the dog. It was the angry tone of a man whom she didn't recognize.

"Sit," she said to Brody. "Stay."

Circling the brush pile, three men came into view. Two strangers held guns, and one of them had his pointed directly at Gavin. The one pointing the gun was short and surly looking. He snapped words at Gavin with a bitter expression. The second man was taller and larger, broad in the shoulders and built of thick muscle. He casually held a gun at his side and looked less invested in what was happening.

Keegan watched timidly, crouched at the corner of the brush pile for more than a minute choking back even the sounds of her own breath for fear of being found. Only after an agonizingly long time did she remember no one could see her even if she stepped into the clearing. Still terrified, but wanting to understand what was happening, she finally did just that.

"Three kids," Gavin grumbled in response to whatever the short man had said. "She had three kids." His gaze shifted to the big man as if making a point. "They were going to try that head-in-a-box bullshit with them too. You have to draw the line somewhere. I'm not a good guy...but I'm not...I'm not that guy."

The short man's face went crimson. "Oh, for the love of god! Mongo, quit thinking. It's not your strong suit—just shoot him already!"

Keegan felt bile rise in the back of her throat. Gavin, however, didn't seem as concerned as he should. He didn't seem like the man looking down the wrong end of a gun barrel. If anything, he appeared amused by the little man's anger.

The quick move from Gavin's foot caught Keegan off guard. Something flew from the ground and spun toward the face of the little man. When the little man's hands went up in defense, Gavin lunged. He hammered the shorter man with a crushing blow and drove him to the ground.

Bang! Bang, Bang! Three gunshots were fired in rapid succession. Slack-jawed, Keegan gasped. Before the scream could leave her lips, a blinding flash went off and the taste of copper filled her mouth. She blinked away the residual starburst patterns seared into her retinas. The ringing in her ears was already beginning to dissipate.

She sat up on the couch with such a start that the book on her chest tumbled and clattered to the floor. Flexing her jaw and blinking quickly, she looked slowly around the room. The fire in the hearth needed to be restocked, and the room had grown colder.

"A dream?" she said aloud as if saying the words would help her find equilibrium. "Just another dream."

A sneeze caught her off guard. She idly scratched at her nose and threw her legs over the side of the couch. The blanket tangled and wrapped around her legs went unnoticed. She was staring at her fingers and the black and gray dog hair wedged under the ring on her right hand.

Chapter 8

Gavin watched Willy ride off on the 4x4, the trailer in tow. It wasn't much more than a snowmobile trailer that they'd bolted three-foot-tall panel walls to in order to haul larger loads. The sad aluminum contraption was loaded heavily with split wood stacked high near the center, its meager springs sagging and tires bulging. At least Willy was taking it easy this time. He moved slowly and consistently as he slalomed down the gentle grade, negotiated thick trees, and passed stray boulders the size of Volkswagens. He'd been too heavy on the throttle yesterday and lost at least a cord on the mile-long trip back to the compound.

Grabbing the axe once more and preparing to return to work, Gavin eyed the walkie-talkie on the wood pile. Another hour of daylight remained. Willy wouldn't get back in time to accomplish anything worthwhile. He decided to wait until he knew Willy was back at the compound, then radio and tell him not to return. It was a nice night for a walk, and Gavin was fond of time to himself. The sky to the southwest had a purple cast that suggested foul weather was on the way. It only confirmed what he'd seen on the island's radar display. The hour would be late before the weather turned inclement, so he would make the most of it.

A distinctive metallic click froze Gavin where he stood. The sound was unmistakable. Though motionless, his eyes shifted to his gloved hand on the axe handle, its head still embedded in a stump. Far too deep in the stump to withdraw quickly.

"Your buddy left just in time," a strained and pinched contralto said from somewhere behind. "For a minute, I thought I'd have to kill him too."

A slow breath slipped through Gavin's clamped teeth. This was a voice he hoped never to hear again. Eyes moving to the axe once more, his hand remained motionless with the handle loosely gripped. Anthony "the Ant" Garboni—that little prick—wouldn't come all this way alone. The little bastard wouldn't take a dump without someone to hold his hand—figuratively…maybe literally. The Ant was rumored to have some strange proclivities. Who knew, maybe paying someone to watch him use the can was one of them.

The thought brought a smile to Gavin's face. "What's up, Ant Man?" he said. His tone was light with an air of amusement as if he'd just run into an old colleague on the street and was choosing to make small talk.

"Don't start that shit again," Garboni grumbled. "And get yer hand off the skull splitter. Greeley might accidentally shoot you before we can talk."

Greeley? Garboni wasn't alone. Garboni and Greeley…the name pair was familiar. Surely their paths had crossed at some point…still, in his mind's eye, Gavin couldn't put a face with Greeley's name. Questions were competing for his attention. Was it just the two of them? Survival might depend on how many bruisers Garboni had brought. Muscle came and went from the ranks of the Outfit, but Garboni wouldn't make a trip like this without muscle on which he could count. Whoever Greeley was, it meant he'd been around a while.

Gavin's hand slipped slowly from the axe and dropped to his side. "I'm going to turn around now, Ant Man. Don't get twitchy. I'd like to have that talk before we get down to business."

"Take a step to yer left," Garboni demanded, his Brooklyn accent slipping ever so slightly into his tone. "I don't want you anywhere near that goddamn axe. In fact, make it two steps. Then turn around slowly. Keep your hands out where I can see them."

Gavin rolled his eyes at the drama. The Ant was twitchy. He was doing a fair job of keeping the quaver from his voice, but it was there. Was he really afraid? They'd gotten the drop on him fair and square. Gavin had been hiding out on the island for almost a year, as far away from civilization as a man could get in the modern world. And while he couldn't figure how they'd found him, the immediate concern was the uneasiness in Garboni's voice.

Turning to face the Ant, Gavin grinned with satisfaction. The little guy hadn't changed at all. Five foot four thanks to the platform inserts, he benefited from the slightly higher ground thanks to the grade rising to the west. He wore a dark sport coat and matching pants along with what might have been alligator skin cowboy boots. Each boot might have been made with half of an iguana given the Ant's size. His clothes were tattered and dirty with a tear in one sleeve, a muddy stain on the chest, and a large rip up one pant leg. It explained how they'd gotten the drop on him. The island had one inlet serving as a passable harbor. It was the only safe place to bring a boat to shore. There was, however, a craggy shale beach near the northernmost reach of the island. But landing a boat there was suicide. A maze of coral and jagged underwater rock formations lay just below the water's surface around the island; few points were more hazardous than the small shale beach.

The Ant's small stature was made all the more glaring because he was standing beside an absolute mountain of a man. His associate, obviously the man named Greeley since no one else was present, was at least six and a half feet tall. His head was the size of a log Gavin had nearly busted a nut lifting earlier in the morning. Unfortunately, height wasn't the only thing Greeley had going for him. His shoulders were so broad that he'd be lucky to walk through a doorway without brushing both jambs. His head was gigantic, but in fitting proportion to the rest of his body. He had an angular face, vaguely Slavic features, and piercing brown eyes that hinted at an intelligence behind a thick brow. His arms bulged with corded muscles fighting a winning battle against his black sand-stained tee shirt.

Gavin's eyes went back to the giant's sand-stained shirt. His gaze quickly returned to the Ant. The Ant's clothes were dark, so it wasn't apparent at first, but both men had recently spent time in the water. Their apparel was near dry now, but the rips and stains weren't entirely the result of the cross-country trek over rugged terrain.

"You wrecked your boat on the north shore," Gavin said. "You should have called ahead. I would've warned you about that. No one uses that beach. It's a killer."

The Ant's lips drew into a tight line, and the nickel-plated revolver in his right hand came higher by inches. "It ain't funny," he grumbled.

Gavin shot a look to Greeley and shrugged. "You're not letting this bug call the shots, are you? He's going to get you killed. I'm not kidding. You were lucky with the beach. Siding with him is proof of poor long-term planning."

"Shut. Up." The Ant growled. "You're in no position to be talking long-

term plans."

Rolling his eyes dramatically, Gavin took a fractional step to close the fifteen-foot gap between him and the two armed men. The move was natural enough because neither of his assailants appeared to notice it. "You didn't come all this way just to shoot me, did you?"

The giant looked to the Ant, whose eyes went wide in response. "You're damn right we did!"

"That's disappointing," Gavin admitted, his tone demonstrating a surprising lack of concern. "This isn't a bring him back alive type of situation?"

Greeley, the giant, offered a tiny, seemingly disappointed shake of his head. That was interesting, Gavin reasoned. The big man was armed but had yet to raise the revolver from where it hung in a loose grip at his side.

Greeley's heart didn't seem to be in this.

"This is a bring back his head in a box situation," the Ant explained. "You haven't been gone that long. I'm sure you remember those days."

All humor left Gavin's visage. He instantly took a single deliberate pace forward. He remembered those days well. One of those days had led to him hiding on an island so far off the beaten track that it didn't appear on most maps.

The Ant took a step backward in wariness, even though he held the gun. His face reddened a heartbeat later, realizing he'd just been treated like a punk. "Oh, that's right!" he laughed in retaliation. "That's why you're here. If you'd just done your job, it wouldn't be the last day of the rest of your life."

Eyeing Greeley, Gavin once more saw a lack of conviction. Not the sort of inner turmoil that would keep a man from following through on orders from on high, but there was something there…something the giant wasn't saying.

"You know what," the Ant said. "Just shoot him, Greeley. We'll walk down to the dock and steal a boat. I want off this shithole rock."

Greeley's dark .357 revolver raised at the order, but he didn't pull the trigger. He didn't even draw a solid bead in preparation to fire. It wasn't conflict in his eyes, Gavin decided. Reluctance? Perhaps remorse. In any case, Gavin had a tiny window of opportunity to leverage it against the Ant. If there was one thing he could do under pressure, it was push someone's buttons.

"You're the same chicken shit you always were, you know that?" Gavin's eyes burned into Garboni. "You come all this way and can't even shoot me yourself?"

Gavin's gaze shifted to the giant. "Is he still pulling this crap? I bet he makes you do all the dirty work—am I right? Unbelievable! Somethings never change."

A flash of recognition in Greeley's eyes told Gavin he'd struck a chord. If he didn't know better, he would swear the giant was trying not to smile. He was enjoying seeing the boss brought down a peg or two.

Garboni elbowed Greeley and gestured with the gun as if it were a crude pointing device rather than a lethal weapon. "Damn it, Zane. Shoot him! Shoot the sonofabitch!"

"You realize this is why you'll never get ahead in the organization," Gavin persisted, his gaze locked on Garboni. "Even the bosses don't take you seriously. They should've sent Greeley after me. Look at him. He would've come by himself. Do you think he needs someone to hold his hand?"

Garboni's face was shifting through more shades of red than Gavin thought possible. The little man rocked mechanically from foot to foot and swung his revolver recklessly around. He did not, however, directly point the weapon at Gavin.

"Shoot him!" Garboni bellowed.

The big man lowered his gun. "He makes a fair point, boss. I can't say I've ever seen you kill someone. Not a single man."

Gavin nodded. "That sort of thing doesn't go unnoticed. Middle management. That's all you'll ever be."

"Fuck! You!" Garboni screamed. But he looked more likely to throw his gun at Gavin than point it and pull the trigger.

"Do you think they'd send one of their best guys out here to the middle of nowhere looking for me?" Gavin pressed. "I'm nothing. I'm nobody. And they couldn't be sure I'd be here. That's why they sent you. If you get lost at sea or eaten by cannibals, no one will notice. Hell, it'll probably save one of the bosses from having to send someone like Greeley after you one day. No one retires from the life. You can't really believe there's a future in this?"

Based on the long hard stare Garboni was giving him, Gavin suspected the runt was trying to crush his skull with telepathy. Or maybe he was having a silent stroke. When he finally spoke, it became clear he'd been struggling to get his emotions under control. "Shows what you know, you prick," Garboni spat. "The bosses don't even know I got a line on you. Bringing your head back is gonna get me out of middle management. You're my golden ticket!

"And they haven't forgotten about you—not by a long shot! You're still the Outfit's number one most wanted. You're even higher than the DEA agent that screwed us for fifteen million last year. They want you bad!"

Don't even know I got a line on you?

The dumb sonofabitch came here alone… It was more information than Gavin had hoped to collect. Garboni never did know when to keep his mouth shut.

"A one-time deal." Gavin fixed his attention entirely on Greeley. "You know who I am, right?"

Greeley stared, his eyes pinched and unblinking. His head tipped in the slightest of nods.

"Then I'm making you a one-time offer. Walk away now, and no hard feelings. Keep my location a secret and we're good. My fight isn't with you. It's not with the Outfit, either. If they leave me alone, I'll leave them alone. It would be a mistake for any of us to make things personal."

Greeley stood motionless and said nothing.

Garboni sputtered. "Are you nuts? Have you forgotten? We got the guns!"

Back to Greeley, Gavin said, "last chance. I need to know now. The little shit's so worked up, I half believe he might have the balls to pull the trigger after all."

Greeley's massive chest rose slowly, then fell with the exhalation of a deep, contemplative breath. "I know who you are," he said at last. "Heard lots of stories about you. But I gotta say…two men with guns at fifteen feet? I'm tempted to find out if the rumors are true."

Gavin watched the big man's eyes. If he were about to pull the trigger, the eyes would signal the shot a fraction of a second before firing the gun. Greeley made a good point, too. Gavin wondered what sort of stories had circulated since he'd walked out on the Outfit. There was sure to be talk. Apparently, at least among the gun thugs, he wasn't vilified to the degree the bosses would like. There appeared to be a level of respect in the big man's eyes. That could be dangerous, of course. A man looking to make a name for himself could do worse than bringing back the head of the man from all those fanciful stories.

"When you left," Greeley said. "Was it really over kids?"

Gavin remained silent. He studied the big man for any hint of what was to come.

"I heard different versions of what happened that night," Greeley went on. "But only one they tried to keep quiet. It was said you left when they sent you after a mother and her two kids."

"Three kids," Gavin corrected. The words slipped out before he knew he'd spoken them. There was no turning back now. "She had three kids. They were going to try that head-in-a-box bullshit with them too. You have to draw the line somewhere. I'm not a good guy...but I'm not...I'm not that guy."

"Oh, for the love of god!" Garboni bellowed. "Mongo, quit thinking. It's not your strong suit—just shoot him already!"

Garboni's eyes were on Greeley. The moment Greeley turned to respond to Garboni, Gavin slipped the toe of his boot under the two-foot-long tree limb that was part of the scree littering the ground at his feet. He lofted the limb into the air in the general direction of Garboni's face. He was unlikely to hit him, but that wasn't the intent.

Garboni caught the movement from the corner of his eye and instinctively raised his hands in a protective stance. In doing so, he had little regard for the gun in his right hand.

Gavin hit Garboni with a crushing tackle. The hit swept the little man off his feet and the pair smashed into a pile of loosely stacked tree limbs. Before Garboni could scream from the impact, Gavin ripped the revolver from the little man's hand, jammed it up under Garboni's armpit, and fired three rounds into the side of his chest.

The loud report of the .357 was muffled by the point-blank contact with Garboni's clothing. His body absorbed a great deal of the sound as a result. Ducking a shoulder, Gavin rolled from the mobster and pointed the weapon at Greeley.

Greeley was within a foot of where he'd been standing. His gun was not raised. Instead, he held it in an upraised open palm. It was a posture that made it impossible to bring the weapon to bear.

"It's cool," Greeley said. "Everything is cool."

Gavin didn't move. Nor did he lower the gun. He studied the large man. "You picked a side?" he asked at last.

"Seems so," Greeley said simply. "You'll keep your end of the bargain?"

Gavin lowered the gun and slowly heaved himself from the leaf litter. "Absolutely. But they'll want to know what happened to the little prick."

Greeley shrugged. "Lost at sea works for me. Like he said, no one knows we're out here looking for you. Garboni kept what he knew to himself. He figured bringing you in would earn him a seat at the table."

"What about you? You're not interested in a seat at the table?"

Shaking his head without hesitation, Greeley said, "I think you had the right idea, getting out when you did. Maybe I'll get lost at sea too."

Gavin carefully lowered the hammer on the revolver and then slipped the gun into the back of his waistband. He looked into the distance to where the ground sloped away to the east. He could just make out the silhouette of the monastery ramparts against the lingering clouds as the sky grew darker.

"How did Garboni find me anyway?"

"The internet. Some guy's social media account had photos of the island. I guess you were in a few. I'm not sure. He never showed me the photos. I think he was afraid I'd get too ambitious and go after you myself."

Social media?

Gavin rolled his eyes. Jasper Epps. He'd been the only employee not retained by the new owner of the island when he took possession of the property three months earlier. For whatever reason, Stanton Anakasta had been willing to keep the entire staff, with the exception of Jasper. So off Jasper went, back to civilization…apparently to compromise a perfectly good hiding spot.

"You don't think Garboni shared the photos with anyone else?" Gavin asked.

Greeley shook his head without hesitation. "It's like you said. He was too afraid of getting beat to the punch. For what it's worth, your secrets are safe with me. I ain't gonna say nothing to nobody. I don't think anyone else is likely to come looking for you. We knew where to look, and we damn near died twice before reaching the island."

Chapter 9

The chamber had been assembled entirely of stone. Painstakingly hewn blocks fitted with precision to form a circular space. Cobwebs hung from long extinguished torches suspended from sconces evenly spaced around the room's perimeter at six different positions. Dust had collected in a thick, unblemished layer, nearly opaquing the stone floor of the chamber and attesting that the room hadn't been touched in generations. A short wall ran in a small ring at the epicenter of the space. It too, was composed of stone, the perimeter of a well that was perhaps four feet in diameter.

With no windows or even a door allowing access to the room, the chamber was entirely devoid of light. The darkness, like the silence, had gone unchanged for untold years. But then the tiniest ember of light erupted from the darkness. Little more than the spark of a single firefly, the glow emanated from deep within the well. Spectral and green, it ignited with a sputter. It pulsed slowly at first, as if trying to push back the pervading darkness. Then, after a matter of seconds, the light became solid and established.

Though only a pinpoint in size, a breach into this world had opened.

Chapter 10

They hid Garboni's body under an overturned trailer at the base of a brush pile. The location made Greeley skeptical. Stashing the corpse somewhere in the woods seemed much safer. Gavin explained that he would return after nightfall to dispose of the trash and that no one would look twice at the trailer. It was the second of three trailers, and if it didn't get pulled back to the compound, this was how they stored it each night. Gavin said he was more concerned with explaining Greeley's presence on the island. The place didn't get many visitors. None, in fact. The only foreign faces came on the quarterly resupply shipment and left as quickly as the boat could be unloaded.

"The next boat is scheduled to arrive in a couple of days," Gavin explained. "You can catch a ride out then. If Garboni had a brain in his head, he would've stowed away on the cargo carrier in the first place. It would've been the safe way to approach the island."

Greeley looked down at his tattered and torn clothes. He had the appearance of a man who had slept in a dumpster. "You're preaching to the choir."

"There's only one safe approach to the island. The lagoon on the east end can be treacherous, but a path has been cleared through the reef. It's the only way to reach the island without getting raked over razor-sharp rocks and coral just below the surface. If the coral doesn't get you, the rocks will. Garboni *really was a fool."*

Shoving his fists into his hip pockets, Greeley offered a meek shrug. A shiver ran through him. Though his tee shirt and jeans had long since dried, the temperature was dropping and he wasn't dressed for the conditions. Even if the plane hadn't gone down, they hadn't been appropriately outfitted for the island at this time of year. Garboni was more of a fool than he'd previously believed, he decided.

I was a fool to follow him here.

Gavin pointed to the east. The ground sloped away at a gentle grade. Many of the trees had lost a fair portion of their colorful canopy, and Greeley could make out the silhouette of a great structure in the distance. It was difficult to distinguish with the setting sun to his back, but a great stone wall was visible. It surrounded what appeared to be a medieval castle or monastery. "We'll head back on foot," Gavin explained. "The walk will give you a chance to warm up. More importantly, it will give us a chance to put together a story. We need to explain how you came to be here. The fewer questions, the better."

The walk back to the monastery, or the Compound as Gavin sometimes called it, was just over a mile as the crow flew. But portions of the island were hazardous. They had to navigate ridges of razor-sharp rock which pierced the surface of the island's thick loamy soil. Dense thorny brambles of brush scattered the ground and looked hardy enough to survive the worst weather conditions. They even had to circumnavigate a patch of swampy marshland. The walk would be closer to two miles by the time they reached the compound's stone perimeter.

Gavin whistled a loud, piercing pitch that echoed into the distance. The act caught Greeley off guard and instantly made him uneasy. It was a signal of some kind. He wondered if Gavin was calling to someone out in the wilderness. A stirring deep in the woods seemed to support this. Something came crashing through the brush, and Greeley felt his pulse quicken.

Greeley recoiled visibly when a black and tan dog burst into the clearing. The dog skidded to a stop at Gavin's side. The creature's tail wagged and its tongue lolled. Gavin patted him squarely on the shoulder and offered a quick scratch behind the ear. The recognition seemed to satisfy the dog. Then he continued walking as if nothing had happened. The dog moved at Gavin's side, continuing in lockstep with his master.

It didn't take long for Gavin to fabricate a plausible, if unlikely scenario, by which Greeley had come to be stranded on the island. That he had survived the shores would require no deception to explain. It was luck, pure and simple. They only needed to make it through the next couple of days, Gavin reminded. Once the supply ship arrived, Greeley would catch a ride and things could return to normal.

"You're sure no one knows I'm here?" Gavin pressed. They walked through the thick woodland, the sun little more than a twinkle behind the mountain to their backs.

"Garboni wasn't big on sharing," Greeley said with a shake of his head. Reluctantly, he admitted that the island's location wasn't even shared with him until they had left the mainland. "The little shit was so tightlipped, he was even reluctant to give the coordinates to the pilot."

"He should've been. If the pilot had known, I don't think he would have taken the job."

"You're right about that. We were in the air when he found out. Garboni had to put a gun in his ear to convince the old man not to turn back."

Gavin stopped walking and glared at Greeley. "No kidding? And he got the guy killed? I guess I shouldn't be surprised."

"The pilot was named Spalding. He died before we even hit the water. I don't think we would've survived if we hadn't been flying so low. We couldn't find the island—circled back more than once. Then the plane came down. We crashed and started floating. The next thing we know, we look up and see the damned island! There, clear as day."

Gavin stopped walking and gave Greeley a purposeful glance. "You couldn't find us from the air, but you saw us once you set down? Do you know the coordinates where you crashed?"

Greeley furrowed a brow in confusion. "No idea. We were more concerned with keeping what was left of the plane afloat. We grabbed an inflatable raft from the emergency supplies and got out right before the damn thing went under. We paddled for shore, but the underside of the raft got torn out by something in the water." Greeley thought for a moment before returning to meet Gavin's eye. "I'm not entirely sure how we made it to shore after that. Everything's a blur. We almost died twice in the course of five minutes."

They started walking again.

"What's so important about the coordinates of the crash?" Greeley said after a minute. "There's nothing of value on the plane, and the pilot was way beyond *dragging out of there. He was cut to ribbons when the windshield caved in on him."*

Gavin offered a noncommittal shrug. "Just thinking about tall tales told by an old man," he said. "It was an unlikely explanation for why this place is so difficult to find."

Walking on, Greeley waited for Gavin to continue. Seeing the far-off look in the younger man's eyes, he realized he wasn't likely to elaborate on the story. And if the concern he read in Gavin's expression was any indication, maybe he was better not hearing the rest of the tale.

A long silence stretched, but Greeley watched Gavin in his peripheral vision. He didn't seem the least bit broken up over what had just occurred. He was calm, despite having been found hiding from some very dangerous people. Though quickly circumvented, his brush with near-death should have required time to decompress. Still, none of it seemed to faze him. They were walking back to his improvised home, and Gavin had already fabricated a cover to explain the appearance of a stranger who had arrived on the island only hours ago to help kill him.

The two of them had worked together before, though Greeley was sure Gavin didn't remember him. The kid was the same back then: calm under pressure, decisive, and lethal. It was no wonder he was Fortier's number-one hitter. He was cold and calculating when on the job. But he had a conscience, at least that's what they said. That's what had brought him trouble.

"Did it really start with the order to kill the woman and her kids?" The question left Greeley's mouth before he'd even consciously decided to ask it.

Gavin walked on without altering his pace. In the silence, Greeley wondered if he'd spoken aloud after all. There was literally no response—no sign such a charged topic had been raised.

When Gavin spoke, his voice sounded far away. "I guess you could say everything started there. I never thought of it that way."

The silence stretched once more. The only sound on the winds of the surrounding sunset was the crunching of leaves underfoot and the crash of waves breaking on stone somewhere in the distance. The unexpected statement brought more than a dozen questions to Greeley's mind. He found himself suddenly reluctant, perhaps even fearful, to voice them. The order to kill that family had been the beginning of a civil war within the Outfit. Everyone had a theory to explain how things had started, though no one knew exactly what happened. It had just occurred to Greeley that he was standing with the one person still alive who actually knew the answer. He just couldn't bring himself to ask the questions.

Greeley looked up to find Gavin's eyes upon him as they walked.

"Sorry," Greeley said. "I have a million questions. Everyone thinks they know how the war began. Did you know you're the last of the principals still alive?"

A hint of a smile touched the corners of Gavin's lips. "I remember working with you on the East End," he said. "You had a good head on your shoulders. How'd you end up falling in with Garboni?"

Greeley was already shaking his head. "Been asking myself that same question for a long time now. Months. Maybe years. I still don't have an answer. I think it was a sorry lack of quality options."

Gavin seemed to consider this. He was silent for long seconds as they walked. Then, having come to some kind of decision, he spoke. "Fortier never would have given me that order. It wasn't his way. He knew I would never go along with something like that anyway. I've killed more than my share for the Outfit, but every single one of them had it coming. They were all in the game." Gavin went silent for more than a minute. "It doesn't matter how you get there, you can't justify doing that to a mother and her kids. Sure, Donny was in the game—his family wasn't. Innocent is innocent. We are who we are, and we are what we are. The line must be drawn somewhere.

"For Fortier to give that order, someone had to put some serious pressure on him. That could only be the rest of the Outfit. The order was a test. A test to see if Fortier would play ball. A test to see if I would fall in line."

"I guess you didn't fall in line," Greeley mumbled. "I'm glad I wasn't there to be part of the collateral damage."

Gavin shrugged. "You sided with me today. I'd like to think you would have done the same back then. If you'd been there then, maybe things would've turned out different." He looked squarely at Greeley. "I appreciate what you did here today."

Greeley looked away, his mouth going suddenly dry. "Maybe it was self-preservation. I knew what you did back then. Maybe I did the math and didn't like my odds."

Gavin barked a laugh. "Those must be some rumors! What are they saying about me?" He held up a hand. "Forget it. I really don't want to know. Fact is, you picked a side. Play it however you want. If I didn't believe that, you would be laying under that wagon right next to Garboni. I wouldn't be taking you back to the Compound if I didn't trust you."

Not knowing what to say, Greeley decided silence was the safest path. He had picked a side. He'd come to the island with a certain level of respect for Gavin and when push came to shove, he'd made the right call. While he didn't raise a hand against Garboni, he hadn't protected him either. The logical part of his mind suggested he should feel guilty for this. The moral portion of his mind countered and slapped down the analytical side. Garboni was a danger to himself and anyone in proximity. He'd been that way for years. This was the safe play—it was also the right move.

"Fortier's orders that day were also a warning," Gavin said. "He knew I wouldn't follow them. The simple fact that he'd given them told me he'd been compromised and was in trouble. That's why I did what I did. I needed to clear the game board and return to the penthouse to help him."

Greeley froze mid-step. This revelation hadn't been part of any postulated version of events. "That's why you wiped out the team?"

"If I didn't do the job, they were there to do me. I needed to get back to Fortier. I had a debt to repay."

Greeley heard the team had been there to kill Gavin. The story went that Gavin was supposed to kill the woman and the kids, then the team was there to put Gavin in the ground. All anyone knew was that Gavin had gotten the upper hand and survived. How and why had always been a mystery.

"A debt?" Greeley said. "To Fortier?"

Gavin's visage soured, and he shook his head. "Doesn't matter anymore. What's done is done."

Standing frozen, Greeley watched Gavin walk on. Though he knew more than ever before, he still didn't understand how the entirety of the Outfit's inner circle had been killed in a single night. Breaking into a jog, he rushed to catch up.

Ten minutes later, they entered a massive clearing where the monastery stood. A great stone and mortar wall surrounded the expansive grounds. The rambling six-story structure rose behind it, its stone block facade broken by patchworks of ancient-looking leaded windows bracketed by weathered old shutters. The roofline was festooned with jutting peaks and gables. Parapets at the corners of each outcropping marked what might have been ancient observation posts or even defensive positions. Small ornate gothic spires reached skyward from three central peaks at the roof's highest positions.

Greeley croaked audibly at the sight and stopped short just past the tree line.

"It's an old monastery," Gavin explained. "We've had trouble dating the original structure. Estimates put it between four and seven hundred years old. No one seems able to agree on it. One estimate suggested it's much, much older.

"The structure was in ruins when the island's previous occupant purchased it. He set about restoring the building, updating the inner workings, and modernizing where required as he went. He insisted on contemporary conveniences like indoor plumbing, electricity, and modern heat. Fowler appreciated history but didn't want to live in the middle ages."

"This is incredible," Greeley admitted. His eyes roved the sight. He found himself at a loss for words. The little background research Garboni had done included details about an elaborate estate on the island. He had never expected something like this.

"Brooks Fowler, the island's previous owner," Gavin went on, "spent millions restoring the citadel or monastery. At some point in the past, it may have been attacked and burned. No one can say for certain. The wall was breached in two places. Restoration specialists have painstakingly repaired it. You can't even tell where it was breached. They filled the gaps with stone and mortar that perfectly matched the existing structure. No expense was spared.

Gavin pointed to the ghostly outline of a modern two-story house to their left. All its windows were dark, the structure nearly consumed by the encroaching darkness. It sat perhaps fifty yards beyond the western edge of the perimeter wall. "Fowler had the house built before the restoration project began. That way he could live comfortably while work on the monastery was taking place. It was expected to take years, and certainly did."

The house looked small at first. Greeley quickly realized this was not the case. It was a trick of the eye. Had it not been sitting at the edge of the clearing so close to the massive wall and in proximity to the enormous citadel, it would have been more recognizable for the stately, six thousand-foot two-story that it was. It was a contrast to the ancient architecture of the monastery in every way. This home was sided in cedar, had aluminum gutters, and a steeply pitched roof of tar shingles. There was a wide wraparound porch and a balcony at the center of the second floor, which overlooked the monastery and the wall surrounding its grounds.

"Why was the house built outside the wall?" Greeley asked.

Gavin shrugged. "I've wondered that too. I suspect Fowler never meant for it to remain. Once the restoration was complete, I don't think he expected to need it. The citadel has tens of thousands of square feet. More than enough room for him and the island staff. They could all live under the same roof without running into each other."

"Island staff?" Greeley murmured and glanced at Gavin. "How many are employed here?" This was another area where Garboni's research was lacking. They should have been better prepared. They'd come here expecting to confront Gavin Kray. A solid understanding of the island topology, facilities, and staff should have been part of the essential prep work. They had flown in blind, almost literally. It was a costly mistake. Greeley knew he could have been dead at least three times over by now. First in the plane crash, next on the island reef, and lastly at Gavin's hand. There was every chance Kray would have killed him when he offed Garboni.

"Fifteen of us staff the island," Gavin said. "Three in the Anakasta family, and more than a dozen for island security."

Greeley felt a stab of pain behind his eyes. Island security? Jesus. If Garboni weren't dead already, he would have killed him.

"The Anakasta family?"

Gavin motioned Greeley forward and pointed vaguely into the distance. "The gates are around there. We're not home yet." They began walking. "Stanton Anakasta bought the island from Fowler six...maybe eight months back. He lives here with his wife and daughter. I work for him these days."

Chapter 11

"I don't understand why you're not more suspicious," Asha said. She was pacing the bedroom suite she shared with her husband, Stanton Anakasta. Wringing her hands with nervous energy, her husband's lack of concern only made the building frustration worse. "Mayhew said he showed up out of nowhere. He could be from Boston. He could be here for you."

She watched Anakasta rewrap that damnable book in oil cloth once more, place it in the wall safe, and then close everything behind the oil painting. He was taking his time responding, which only added to her irritation.

Anakasta moved to a wingback chair and turned it away from the lazy flames dancing in the great stone fireplace. Calmly, he took a seat. Amusement danced in his pale blue eyes while an understanding—patronizing—smile tugged at the corners of his lips. "Mayhew confirmed sighting aircraft wreckage in the water off the north shore," he said in a low soothing voice. "There was a plane crash. That much is obvious."

"If there was a crash," Asha countered, "why didn't it show on radar before going down? The system is state-of-the-art. We can see anything in the air within a thirty-mile radius. Besides, there was no distress call. That doesn't seem likely."

Anakasta was forty-six years of age. They had married only a year previous. A petite woman with long blond hair, Asha had deep azure blue eyes that glistened in the light and a thin, delicate frame. At twenty-five, she was twenty-one years his junior. That she was only three years older than Anakasta's daughter was a fact never far from Asha's, or likely Keegan's mind. For Anakasta's part, he seemed not to notice. He had never acknowledged it. In times like this, Asha felt she was the elder in the relationship with her husband. Anakasta was reckless when it came to certain matters.

"We're here for a reason," Anakasta cautioned. "We have an entire island to ourselves. We have a security force better trained than some armies. If we're not safe here, we're not safe anywhere."

Asha's blue eyes flashed with frustration. "That's my point. You pay these men a small fortune. You should let them protect us as they see fit."

Anakasta smiled. "You know exactly why we're here. Hiding from interested parties in Boston is only a side benefit. This is a critical time in history. This is where it all begins. We have a chance to help shape everything that follows." He breathed and released a reluctant sigh as if to say, we've been through this. "This is Black Rock Island. The world is about to change—and it all starts here."

They'd been through variations on this conversation dozens of times. Her husband's faith was as inspiring as it was infuriating. "You can't be sure of that. The simple fact that you're here changes things. There's no way to be sure events will play out the way they did where you're from."

Rising from the chair, Anakasta raised both arms at his sides. "My being here is proof enough. I wear the body of my great, great, great grandfather. What more evidence do you need?"

She rolled her eyes. This was his fallback argument every time, and it was getting old. Yes, he knew about future events. Yes, his knowledge had made them wealthy beyond either of their wildest dreams. Yes, this indicated his knowledge was correct and suggested that his presence here had not altered things in any meaningful way.

At least not when it came to his investments.

"You can't compare your luck in the stock market with what you're attempting on this island," Asha said at last. "Coming here, bringing me— bringing your daughter—that changes things. Stanton Anakasta never visited the island, let alone made it his home. You said Keegan eventually comes to the

island, but not for another seven years. You've already made significant changes to the timeline you're familiar with."

Anakasta's expression soured. He waved dismissively and began pacing. "You were never a part of Stanton's history. Stanton Anakasta died in the original timeline—a loss with no value. Everything I'm doing is for this family—you, me, Keegan, and for generations to come. Without me—without this," he waved an arm vaguely in the air, "what's about to come is all that matters. If we don't mark our place in history now, we'll be casualties of the wreckage about to be wrought."

Offering a sympathetic smile, Anakasta slipped his arms around her and pulled her tight. "I didn't just take his body. I'm correcting the course of Stanton's life and fulfilling our family destiny. It's alright. You have to trust I know what I'm doing...and that I'm doing this for all of us."

She relented and lay her head against his chest. The sound of his breathing brought her peace. The steady rhythm of his heart was calming. After a moment, she pushed back and looked up at him with tired eyes. "You've changed so much. I just worry there will be consequences. You might not sense it, but there is great power here. This island is literally humming with it."

Anakasta gazed back at her. "Of course there is. It's why we're here."

"You don't understand." Her tone turned pained, bordering on pleading. "At an academic level, you know what's here. I'm telling you—I can feel it. I can sense it growing stronger every day."

Chapter 12

Anakasta considered the unease in his wife's eyes, and it pained him. Undoubtedly, she could sense the power here. Her ability was responsible for his initially seeking her out. Their courtship and subsequent marriage were a happy byproduct of that meeting, but she was first and foremost empathic. The island would be touching her in a primal way as the Rising drew near.

"I'm sorry," he said. Taking her hands in his, he said, "I understand this experience must be unsettling."

"Unsettling? We're playing with forces beyond our understanding. You've crossed time—cheated death—changed history. There will be consequences."

Anakasta shook his head as frustration welled within. "Enough with this altered timeline foolishness. I told you, that's not how this works. I can change things, and it won't make a difference. It's not like in the movies or those silly books you read."

They'd been through this many times, and Anakasta struggled to remain patient. He reminded himself that she was only trying to protect their family. She didn't fully understand the nature of what he had done or the source of the power he'd tapped to cheat death. Irrationally, she feared that the changes he made would alter history. She was concerned about adverse effects on his life *further down the timeline. It simply didn't work that way. The book had been very clear, and his experiments had proven the prediction true. He'd jumped back in time and occupied Stanton Anakasta's body only moments before Anakasta was destined to die at the hands of his business partner, Gregory Ivankovich. The casting was possible only because he, Chandler Anakasta, knew exactly when and where his progenitor, Stanton Anakasta, died. The spell allowed him to inhabit the body of a blood relative. The timing had been fortuitous. It gave Chandler time to fully assume Stanton's identity and use his knowledge of coming events to amass a considerable fortune before the time of the Rising.*

Now the Rising was at hand. Or at least nearly. Given what was about to happen and the level of impending chaos, it was understandable that the exact timing had been lost to history. That much death and destruction on a global scale—how could anyone say for certain when things had kicked off?

At least this time around he could document the Rising for posterity. The exact how's and why's would no longer be left to the imaginations of the surviving minority. The chattel could guess all they wanted. Finally, the Anointed would know his role in the Reawakening.

"As I've explained," Chandler Anakasta went on. "When I jumped into Stanton's body, an entirely new timeline spawned. Think of it as a new line branching and running parallel to the timeline I once knew. Key events will happen just as I knew them. The changes I make have no impact on the timeline from where I come. I can shape the future of this timeline—and that's vital. This is a critical time in our history. The world is about to awake with primordial forces once more. There will be devastation and chaos. But with what I know, things will be better. We can minimize the damage and ensure a smooth, less bloody transition of power."

The color drain from Asha's face. This happened each time he spoke of what was to come. The weight of impending events seemed to impact her harder with each passing day. It had to be her sensitivity combined with her proximity to the island. There was no telling what she was going through. He saw pain in her gaze, far as well, but something more was happening behind her expression. It shifted and solidified a little more each day. If he didn't know better, she seemed to be accepting what was to come.

It was too late now, anyway. Three people were key to facing what was to come.

Keegan must be here.

He could check that off his list. Though she'd initially agreed to stay for only a week, something had changed her mind. Perhaps she sensed the power of this place as well. Her plans to return to the mainland and her new veterinary practice had been pushed back indefinitely. Though he knew destiny would draw her to the island a little over seven years from now, the cause of her journey had been lost to time. After the Rising, historic records became spotty for more than a decade. Anakasta had simply advanced that portion of the timeline to bring her here ahead of schedule.

Asha would also be key to what was coming. Her sensitivity to the island would help them survive what was about to happen. His opportunity to manipulate the Rising would require her abilities.

Then there was Gavin Kray. Of all the island misfits, he had the ultimate checkered past. In Chandler's time, much of what was known about Gavin had also been lost to history. Gavin had a past with the dominant organized crime group running operations on the east coast of the United States. They were a group of violent and bloodthirsty gangsters, the likes of which had not been seen since the days of Al Capone. How Gavin factored into what was to come, Anakasta still didn't understand. He only knew that according to vague historic reports, Gavin was on the island when the Rising occurred. He was one of the few to survive. What little was known of the actual events came from his written accounts.

"You have a bad feeling about this castaway?" Anakasta said, bringing their conversation back on track. It was better to have a new argument rather than rehashing their old debate.

"You have a security force for a reason," she said simply. "Your friends back in Boston still want words with you. It's possible, perhaps even likely, they've sent this castaway to collect you."

It was a good point. When Anakasta first arrived in this time, he'd immediately set about amassing a bankroll. It had taken less than a year to accumulate more than ten million dollars. His mistake was not doing it more surreptitiously. He'd failed to understand how many people Stanton Anakasta had wronged in his years of business. Old debtors started coming out of the woodwork. They wanted their due. Many were less than savory, the dangerous and greedy sort to whom no one should ever be indebted. Some of the more observant among them wanted to know what had led to Anakasta's sudden good fortune. They insisted on a cut of the action in trade for past associations. It was a slippery slope, and Anakasta was instantly in over his head. The island and a private security force were a mitigating approach to an escalating problem.

"Those people can't reach me here," he offered in a tone that was far calmer than he felt. A staff of twenty men protected the island at all times. "But you're right. I'm curious why the aircraft never showed up on radar. I'll speak with Dr. Cantrell before dinner."

"I'll speak with the doctor," Asha countered. "I want you to talk with our new guest. I understand Gavin is setting him up in one of the spare rooms. He'll be catching a ride on the next supply ship."

Anakasta grinned. Asha made it a point to keep him away from Dr. Cantrell. The fact continued to amuse him. Then a new idea struck. "Why don't we make things interesting? After you speak with the doctor, tell Gavin and his new friend that we'll expect them for dinner this evening."

Asha's mouth fell agape. She stammered for a long second. "Have I been talking to myself this entire time?"

Anakasta moved closer to the fire before turning to face her. "Of course not. Just to be safe, we'll have Mayhew and Kerns close at hand. But I sincerely don't believe they will be necessary. Still, I think we'll both sleep better once we've given our new guest a once over."

Chapter 13

Brody moved from the edge of the woods and into the clearing. His ears perked tall and his eyes roamed the dark landscape. Storm clouds moved in to obscure the moon and the air was charged with static electricity. The smell of freshly cut wood permeated the air, along with the sharp tang of motor oil and gasoline. Gavin and Willy had vacated the clearing only a few short hours before. Still, a twitch of Brody's nose confirmed their scents linger…Along with the foul smell of the other.

Moving slowly along the perimeter of a brush pile, the bi-colored dog took his time. Every odor told a story, any sound could hint at danger. Brody moved with steady confidence, first passing the log splitter, then the neatly stacked pile of wood. As the overturned wagon shifted into view, his pace slowed further. Crouching low, he stalked silently near. His hackles suddenly rose.

A small trailer, more of a wagon, lay turned upside down at the base of a stout tree. Its wheels were pointed skyward while the short walls of its load bed pressed into the dry soil. Brody made a slow circuit of the cart and tree before stopping at a gap at the tail end of the trailer. Pitch-black darkness embraced the prone figure beneath; it was a darkness that not even the dog's keen vision could penetrate. A subtle rustling sound at the edge of Brody's hearing put him instantly on alert. It was a nearly inaudible churning of the earth that was entirely out of place.

Blood seeped from the gunshot wounds under Garboni's arm in the featureless shadows beneath the trailer. As intended, the bullets had eviscerated the man's internal organs and reduced them to a semi-gelatinous ooze. Garboni's body lay face down in the dust.

Blood trickled from the wounds, striking the parched earth and soaking the soil. Rather than becoming saturated, the ground puckered and split upon contact with the blood. Like cracks in a pane of glass, thin fishers spidered out from the damp point in the ground. As if in reaction to this, the seepage from Garboni's wounds doubled. The brackish black arterial ooze quickly accelerated until the dead man's blood poured forth. The ground surrounding the body began to vibrate in a gentle rumble sending the fine grains of dirt and sand on the surface dancing. Blood flowed, and the earth responded. Slowly, grain by grain, the surface of the hard-packed clearing softened. Over countless long minutes, the ground parted and began pulling the whole of Garboni's body into its embrace.

A guttural growl, low and threatening, came as little more than a whisper from Brody as he stooped and glared beneath the trailer. One paw scratched anxiously at the dry soil, the dog's fangs flashing in the darkness. The hoarse growl rose louder, but then the dog seemed to think better of it. He backed slowly away from the wagon and studied it with suspicious eyes.

Turning at last, he loped purposely for the tree line. The entire time, he kept a cautious eye cast over his shoulder on the motionless trailer at the base of the tree.

Chapter 14

Moonlight spilled through the expansive lead-lined windows leaving three pale pools of light at the edge of the expansive room. The silhouetted figure remained close to the wall. Familiarity with the room meant there was no need for the lights. Thunder rumbled far in the distance and the intruder spared a moment at one of the windows to push the corner of the lace curtain aside. The moon was just disappearing behind a curtain of lightning-laced clouds moving rapidly across the fading horizon.

With the room's only remaining light suddenly blotted out, the figure froze. Keegan took a deep breath and waited for her eyes to adjust to the near-total darkness. She eyed the bed and confirmed its surface was flat and featureless. This had been one of two concerns. She'd been unable to locate Asha over the last several hours and there was a chance, however minimal, that her stepmother had turned in early for the night. The only remaining concern was a question of timing. Keegan didn't know how much time she would have to herself.

Crossing the room quickly, she placed two fingers behind the bottom right corner of the framed painting on the wall and pulled. The frame tipped easily away from the wallpaper on precision-engineered hinges to reveal the face of a sleek state-of-the-art safe. Keegan pulled a small egg-shaped plastic shell from the hip pocket of her jeans. Pinching a tiny bit of pressure at the object's center, *the top separated with a pop. She thumbed the silly putty free from the shell and into the palm of her hand. Working it between her fingers for a few quick seconds, the stiff substance gained elasticity.*

The code she tapped into the combination screen of the safe was a secret her father guarded closely. Unfortunately for him, he wasn't terribly security savvy. She'd guessed the combination on the tenth attempt when she first tried to open the safe nearly two months prior. Placing the silly putty against the biometric fingerprint sensor, she winced at the audible chime and click that signaled acceptance of the code and release of the lock. The door pivoted open and a small LED bulb engaged to reveal the contents of the safe.

The code had been easy enough to guess, Keegan's father putting far too much confidence in the biometric fingerprint scanner that was the second half of the safe's authentication control. The fingerprint scanner was good, but easy enough to bypass if the last person to use the scanner didn't wipe their print from the scanner lens. The silly putty fooled the scanner into rereading the residual smudge left on the lens. The expensive security control was effectively bypassed by a toy that cost less than a dollar.

Keegan took another deep breath to calm her building anxiety and scanned the contents of the safe. While the configuration of the safe's contents appeared to have changed only slightly since her last visit, it seemed the items present were still the same. Four thick stacks of banded currency were pushed to one side of the small space, several manila folders lay beneath a short pile of boutique jewelry boxes on the top shelf, and on the bottom shelf lay a thick leather-bound book.

Pulling the book free, Keegan laid it on the edge of the safe where she could use its light to examine the book. Inside the front cover, the first page was scrawled with faded words impossible to read in the low light. That was alright. The words were not what she had come to confirm. She flipped to the next page and tipped the book toward the light spilling from inside the safe. She could make out a fingerprint in the corner of the page, just as she'd recalled. Though the light was poor, the placement of the mark and its stark relief against the ancient yellowed paper added to her confidence. The whorls and loop weren't distinctive, but the L or V-shaped impression just off-center on the finger's pad was virtually a defining factor all by itself. She hadn't imagined it…the mark was real.

With time running out, Keegan began thumbing quickly through the book's pages. Aside from confirming the mark, she needed a page count. The cover was a close match, but books of this age and subject matter often had their covers replaced. Her father had eclectic tastes, but why he would have purchased a book like this was of mounting concern. Chances were good that he knew little or nothing of its true purpose and had purchased it entirely based on its one-of-a-kind monetary value. He'd bought countless trinkets and baubles since coming into his wealth, all simply because he was now able.

Closing the book gently, she stared at the cracked and worn leather of the cover with unseeing eyes. But what if he bought this for a reason? It was locked away in a safe rather than proudly on display like so many of his overpriced trinkets. There was a power to this book—she could feel it.

But could he?

This was one of the lost grimoires, she was sure of it. But which? How had her father come to own it, and why was he hiding it?

Chapter 15

Greeley lowered himself onto the thick oak chair beside Asha, the mortised joints of the ancient wood groaning loudly under his weight and disrupting the near silence of the room. He offered a halfhearted, self-conscious grin and pulled the chair closer to the table. A hand went to Asha's face to cover a humor-filled smile that flashed with the white of her teeth. Anakasta chuckled and smoothed a linen napkin across his khaki pants. His good-natured grin was a relief to Gavin. It suggested this would be a relaxed social exercise rather than an interrogation to further evaluate Greeley's purported plane crash.

Anakasta's lapdogs were present. Matt Mayhew stood station a respectful distance away at the corner of the room. He was on the verge of earshot but had a panoramic view of the accommodations and the room's occupants. Kerns and Hathaway were present too, though not visible. Gavin had passed Kerns on his way into the dining hall, and he'd caught a glimpse of Hathaway beyond the service door leading to the kitchen when one of the chefs made a discreet check on the room. Anakasta was using the opportunity to vet Zane Greeley, but he wasn't taking any chances.

One unoccupied place setting remained making it clear where Gavin was expected to sit. Pulling the chair beside Keegan away from the table, he took her in with a long slow gaze. Her attention was focused across the table, seeming fixed on her stepmother. Gavin suspected that was for show. Though she sat motionless, her jugular vein pulsed—actually, it throbbed. It hinted at a heart that raced despite her calm demeanor. It seemed he wasn't the only one troubled by the impromptu dining arrangements. But then, looking more closely, he wondered how much notice she'd been given regarding their presence at the table this evening. A thin gold chain adorned with an equally delicate blood-red sapphire hung just short of the outfit's plunging neckline. She was dressed in a small black number with sleeves falling just past her shoulders. The dress's satiny fabric cradled the swell of her breasts and was tailored, accentuating the flat plane of her stomach and the gentle curve of her hips. It was more of a party dress than a dinner outfit. The fall of the skirt was only slightly more conservative. Had she been standing, it likely would have fallen just short of her knee. Sitting on the chair beside him, the hem of that skirt rose halfway up her bare thigh and added to her already distracting form. Fumbling momentarily with the chair, it scraped audibly across the floor as he pulled it from the table. He dropped into his seat and silently cursed himself.

Though he couldn't be sure, he sensed Keegan's attention on him. If she'd been watching, it had been from the corner of her eye. Studying her in profile, proof of this came when her cheek darkened and her hand moved, perhaps unbidden, to smooth a wrinkle from the flow of her skirt.

He grinned. She'd been aware of the dinner invitation after all.

She said nothing. It wasn't surprising. For reasons Gavin had yet to understand, Anakasta had taken a liking to him and seemed to think he and Keegan would make an ideal match. At twenty-three years old, Gavin had grown up being the kind of guy fathers worked hard to distance from their daughters. Anakasta's enlightened view was less refreshing and more disconcerting since Gavin didn't know what to make of it. It wasn't likely to be an issue any time soon. Shortly after one of the more overt efforts to get him and Keegan to spend time together, Gavin overheard Keegan ripping her father a new one. The phrases overbearing blowhard, arranged marriage, and his personal favorite, justifiable patricide, were screamed along with a series of creative invectives. He also heard the breaking of what was likely expensive bric-a-brac.

Keegan had no tolerance for her father's interference, and Gavin couldn't blame her. His interest in them as a couple was just weird. A negative consequence of the circumstance, in situations like this, she could be downright hostile. And not just to Anakasta. Gavin could feel the icy chill of her disposition as she refused to acknowledge him.

This wasn't the first clumsy attempt Anakasta had made to further his *unusual agenda. For some reason, Gavin felt this would be a night to remember.*

Glancing around the table, Gavin was relieved that no one had noticed his clumsiness with the chair. Well, no one other than Keegan. Maybe forcing a break in the ice princess's demeanor would be an amusing distraction. He would need to find something to make what was sure to be a dull dinner even slightly interesting. And if things between Keegan and her father were going to blow up, Gavin wasn't above prepping the kindling. He shifted in his seat and tried to focus his attention on the conversation already taking place. In truth, Keegan at his side and that dress were a staggering drain on his focus.

"...lucky to have crashed so near the island," Anakasta said. "Are you a gambling man?"

Greeley smiled. "I'll admit to many unhealthy vices, but I've never considered myself overly lucky."

Anakasta studied the large man with a penetrating gaze, thoughtfulness apparent in his expression. "The waters in this area are particularly treacherous, I'm told doubly so with the coming of winter. Temperatures being what they are right now, you must have come down very close to our shores. Escaping hypothermia is no small feat."

Greeley looked ready to respond when a pair of cooks entered. One pushed a stainless-steel cart while the other carried a large silver serving tray. The man with the tray circled the table in one direction while placing drinks before each seat. The cook pushing the cart moved in the opposite direction, making a circuit while putting salads before each of the five diners present.

"Chefs Rourke and Dawe," Anakasta said by way of introductions as the men worked. He met Greeley's gaze before continuing. "Like the rest of the staff, they worked for the island's previous owner and were kind enough to stay on when my family took possession of the estate."

Dale Dawe and Michael Rourke offered Greeley friendly nods as they placed their respective accouterments before him. They remained silent, however. There would be time for that later, Gavin knew. Both men were professional chefs and took great pride in their work, even when it came to personally serving meals.

Anakasta's mannerisms surprised Gavin more than anything. For months, he'd gone out of his way to avoid interacting with the staff. Friendly enough when required, he made a point of keeping everyone at arm's length. Out of the staff, perhaps Gavin knew the man better than anyone. If Anakasta weren't so eager to pair him romantically with Keegan, Gavin was certain he would have been avoided as effectively as the rest of the staff.

Greeley looked as comfortable with the surroundings as Gavin expected. Which was to say, not at all. Anakasta looked little better. He seemed at a loss to make conversation. A difficult thing to do when you know nothing of those you're dining with and have gone out of your way to avoid many of them. Asha seemed only slightly less awkward. The uneasiness in her expression seemed constructed of trepidation. She wanted the dinner to go well but looked to be in a near panic when it came to suitable conversation.

Might as well have some fun.

Gavin grabbed one of several bottles of wine from the center of the table. Nothing loosened up folks like a couple of drinks. He poured himself a glass and then looked sidelong at Keegan. "Care for a drink?"

The silent, rigid set of her jaw was enough of an answer. That and her refusal to meet his eye. He leaned forward and snatched up her glass. Pouring it half full, he paused to offer her a glance. Arching his brows as if surprised by what she'd said, he shook his head dramatically and said, "Agreed. Time for your medicine, my dear. This will warm you right up." Pausing for effect, he said, "we just need to get the dosage...right." Pouring more, he filled the glass nearly to the brim. He heard Asha snicker across the table as he set it in place. He saw a humor-filled twinkle in Anakasta's eyes at the attempt to break the ice.

"Warm me—do I look cold to you?" Keegan retorted, speaking for the first time since Gavin entered the room.

"Ah...No. Not chilly. I was referring to your disposition. Might not guess it by looking at me, but my grandpappy was Irish." Gavin sipped from his glass. "We're firm believers in the idea that a couple of drinks can melt the chip on anyone's shoulder. Tell you what. Finish yours and I'll share mine. You'll love it." Keegan was already growing pink in the cheeks. Gavin glanced at Anakasta but continued to speak to her just the same. "But seriously, it's not like your father would skimp when buying the good stuff?" he said with a wink.

Asha chortled, and Anakasta's amused expression turned on her with one of mock seriousness. "Well, he's right," she groused. "No one will ever accuse you of cheeping out on the wine."

Everyone laughed...except Keegan.

Anakasta leaned across the table and patted his daughter's hand. "Cheer up, my dear. Be good company for our guest," he tipped his head toward Greeley.

"Oh," Greeley muttered. "Please don't put me in the middle of whatever you have here. One plane wreck is enough for today."

Gavin grinned. "She'll snap out of it. She's just not so good with strangers." His brow furrowed. "Or old people," he added. "But she loves animals. Tell her you have a cat and a dog, and you've got a friend for—"

Turning on Gavin, Keegan met his gaze with fire in her eyes. "You presumptuous son of a—"

Stanton leaned forward. "Now, now," he cautioned.

"Let's talk about strangers," Keegan virtually spat. "If Gavin didn't have—"

"Wait—wait—" Gavin interrupted.

She stopped mid-sentence and spun in her seat to face him. The pink of her cheeks had gone crimson and her emerald green eyes shimmered with electricity. As she twisted in her chair and brought her glare to full power, the hem of her skirt rose higher across her thigh to expose more of the smooth, pale skin beneath. His eyes traveled up the lines of her dress as her gaze bore into him. The black garment didn't seem to have a seam or a stitch in it. It hugged and caressed her form like a second skin. Gavin's breath caught, captivated by the form of the woman before him. The way the material strained to cup her breasts as if nearly unable to contain—

"Well?" Keegan demanded.

Looking at her for a long second, Gavin realized he'd lost track of what was happening. Then he'd recalled, wait—wait—… "Ahh," he stammered. "You said, "Gavin didn't have to," his expression breaking into a mischievous grin. "I was just surprised you remembered my name. You barely looked at me, so I was surprised you knew who I was. Sorry. Please, continue?"

Once more, everyone at the table burst out laughing. All except Keegan. But even there, Gavin saw the trace of a smile tugging at the corner of her downturned lips. She lowered her head. It wasn't quick enough to hide the amusement in her eyes, at least not from him.

Anakasta slapped the table, still laughing hardily. His daughter had a long history of pushing people away. Clearly, seeing someone call her out on it was to the man's liking.

Keegan turned back to the table. She took a breath and spoke through half-clinched teeth. Her gaze remained lowered toward her plate. "Of course I know who you are. You're the immature boy with the beautiful dog." Her voice dropped to little more than a whisper, and she spoke from the corner of her mouth. "Brody's love for you is your single redeeming quality." The words were touched with the slightest of smiles.

Asha laughed at this last barb. "Keegan studied veterinary medicine," she explained for Greeley's benefit. "She loves animals—that dog in particular."

Nodding, Greeley leaned back and looked across the table. "That's right— the black and tan dog. That's Brody?"

Gavin nodded but didn't offer anything more. He watched as Keegan drained the last of her wine in three aggressive swallows before setting the glass back on the table. Snatching up the wine bottle, Gavin poured what remained into her glass while she offered him a pointed, if amused, look.

"Are you trying to get my daughter drunk?" Anakasta said, amusement obvious in his voice.

"I'll drink to that," Keegan said, this time sipping from the glass. A chorus of laughter broke out around the table.

Turning his attention to Gavin, Anakasta said, "I've meant to ask. What made you decide to bring your dog to an island like this? With the wildlife being what it is, this isn't the safest place for a dog to roam free."

The island was home to a pack of wolves that had been something of a problem in recent months. There were signs of their presence all over in the form of footprints, droppings, and the ravaged carcasses of other small creatures. While they had always been present on the island, traces of their presence were recently found closer to the monastery. It was starting to raise concerns. Wild creatures typically gave inhabited areas a wide berth, at least until civilization encroached on their domain. Though nothing had changed in the island's ecosystem, the wolves seemed to be stalking the perimeter of the citadel at night.

"Actually, Brody isn't my dog," Gavin admitted. "I didn't bring him here."

Anakasta's brows arched and he looked to his wife for clarification. She seemed equally confused. "I don't understand," Asha said, her eyes narrowing. "That dog follows you around with rare loyalty."

Considering this for a second, Gavin nodded. It was true. "As far as I can tell, he's been on the island longer than any of us. Truth be told, he adopted me.

Before I met the fleabag, I never cared much for dogs." He scratched the two-day-old stubble on his chin as he considered his statement and pondered the dog. "He grows on you, I'll give him that."

All of this was true, Willy Amstell and Jasper Epps had come to the island along with Brooks Fowler, the billionaire who had first sought to use the island as a private residence and retreat from the world. Willy and Jasper were the original grounds staff and the first to report seeing a stray dog wandering the woods. Sightings went back to their early days on the island. And through the years, despite the harsh winters and predatorial wildlife, the dog had survived on his own. It wouldn't come near Willy or Jasper. The rest of the staff had tried approaching him at one time or another, but he never allowed them to get close. Even Brooks Fowler had attempted to approach the animal without success. Then one day, Gavin was working alone out near the northwest end of the island. He'd been on the island less than a week at that point. The dog had approached him, of all things. They'd been inseparable ever since.

Judging by their expressions, Anakasta and Asha didn't know whether to believe the story. Even Greeley seemed dubious. It was understandable. Brody was a domestic breed that had somehow come to be lost on an island a thousand miles from nowhere. If he'd gone feral for several years, the odds of him turning around and becoming domesticated again were unlikely. Beyond unlikely.

"Is such a thing possible?" Anakasta said, directing the question to Keegan, their resident expert.

Shaking her head, Keegan said, "Academically speaking, no. If Brody was abandoned on the island or shipwrecked here for years, his distrust of people is understandable. But from all I've read, a dog left in an environment for such a time won't one day walk from the woods and choose a master. It just doesn't happen."

Turning his gaze to Gavin, Anakasta looked upon him from beneath arched eyebrows. He clearly expected elaboration from Gavin, though none was forthcoming.

"That said," Keegan continued, "I've spoken with the staff about this curiosity. They all share the same story. Willy, as Gavin said, was here from the beginning. However unlikely and unconventional, the dog seems to have bonded with him."

Gavin shrugged. "What? I'm lovable. Neither man nor beast can resist me. Just you wait," he eyed Keegan salaciously. "You'll fall under my spell. It's only a matter of time."

The conversation grew more mundane as empty plates were cleared and additional courses came and went. The wine flowed freely, though after making his point by draining the remains of the first bottle into her glass, Gavin let her pour for herself the rest of the evening. He'd broken the moment's tension, allowing everyone to loosen up to some extent. In all seriousness, he had no desire to poke fun at Keegan's expense. Chiseling away a thin layer of ice was enough for him. That and seeing how Anakasta reacted to the chisel work. He still couldn't figure out why Stanton wanted to see him paired with his daughter. A father supporting the would-be suitor of his stunningly beautiful daughter went against the nature of every established father/daughter, father/suitor dynamic established since the dawn of time.

At least now Anakasta seemed accepting of Greeley. Friendly even. Perhaps the interest was genuine, though Gavin suspected Anakasta was playing an angle. His carefree banter carried on through the first and second course, just long enough for even Gavin to think Greeley might be in the clear.

The chefs entered with steaks, placing the thick cuts of meat on plates before each of those present. Rourke and Dawe were no sooner clear of the room, and Anakasta was on the second bite of his steak when his gaze shifted to Greeley once more. This time Gavin saw something new in the man's countenance.

Suspicion.

"There is one thing I still don't understand," Anakasta said, his gaze penetrating. His attention was centered on Greeley, the focus palpable. Asha froze with her fork and knife, halfway cut through a sirloin strip. Keegan hadn't eaten much. She'd been pushing a chunk of meat around her plate on her fork, suddenly frozen with Anakasta's words.

For Greeley's part, he sat straighter in the chair. His eyes moved from Anakasta to Asha and Keegan before finally stopping briefly on Gavin. The room seemed to grow suddenly cold. Attempting to ease the tension, Gavin poured himself some more wine.

Chapter 16

Tom Hathaway watched the dinner conversation from the crack between the swinging service doors separating the dining room from the short corridor leading to the kitchen. He couldn't see Mayhew, but he knew his boss was a discrete distance from the table on the opposite side of the room. Mayhew wouldn't be able to eavesdrop on the conversation, so he'd tasked Hathaway with learning what he could about the island's suspicious shipwrecked survivor. They should have planted a bug, Hathaway quickly decided. Between the murmurs of voices coming from the dining hall and the banging of pots and pans in the kitchen only twenty-five yards away, he only caught fragments of what was said.

A new voice caught Hathaway's attention, and he turned to the kitchen. Abandoning his post, he quickly traveled the hall and stopped at the entry to the massive industrial-grade kitchen. It was lined with stainless steel counters and outfitted with multiple gas stoves, a pair of oversized subzero refrigerators, and there was a door to a walk-in freezer that took up the entire next room. The new voice belonged to Tess Lindow. She had just entered the kitchen and was having a hushed but animated conversation with Dale Dawe, the head chef. Her arms moved with exaggerated effusiveness and her eyes danced with excitement. Energy flickered in her blue eyes, and a broad smile stretched her lips. She laughed and lay a hand on Dawe's shoulder as he cackled in response.

"Such a flirt," Hathaway grumbled to himself. But then she could afford to be. It was that tight little ass and those pouty lips. He wondered what kind of turn-down service she and her friend really offered Anakasta. While Tess and Jennifer were each gorgeous in their own right, there was something exceptional about Tess. Hathaway found himself going out of his way to look in on her while making his rounds. The extra attention hadn't gone unnoticed, he knew. Still, she hadn't done anything to encourage him—nothing to reciprocate the attention either.

He wondered who on the island she was banging. Anakasta for sure, but that had to be part of her job. The boss had a lot of miles on him; he wasn't as young as he used to be. With a body like that, Tess had to have someone servicing her needs. It couldn't be one of the security team—anyone on the squad tapping that was guaranteed to talk about it. Besides, Hathaway would gut anyone who laid a hand on her. That had been made crystal clear in recent months.

She was off limits.

That left one of the cooks…or that prick Gavin. Or Willy, though Hathaway was pretty sure the old Scotsman had no lead left in his pencil. Surely not with the way he drank.

Tess exchanged another few words with Dawe. The cook handed over a small package wrapped in white butcher paper. She smiled broadly and gave him a wink, clearly satisfied with whatever it was. A nod, a quick wave, and she turned on a heel. With a flurry of that ruffled little skirt of hers, Hathaway watched her march away. The seductive sway of her tight bottom made his groin ache. And the bounce she had in her step…she'd be hellfire between the sheets. Those pouty lips…there was a whole list of things he could imagine that would take the pout right out of them.

"Jesus," he muttered. "It's just not fair."

He didn't know who she was banging, but he would get a piece of that ass one day. One day really damn soon.

Throwing an icy glance in the direction of Dale Dawe, Hathaway turned quickly back down the short hallway to resume his post.

Chapter 17

Zane Greeley took another bite of the thick juicy steak and eyed Stanton Anakasta from across the table. He'd done a little research on the man before boarding the plane to the island. That little shit, Garboni, claimed he had everything under control, but Greeley was never willing to take him at his word. Knowledge was power, and every scrap of information he could gather on the island and its owner would aid in the operation to retrieve Gavin Kray. There were references to some holy order that had built an Abbey near the turn of the century, and the island had been the home to some wealthy aristocrat sometime in the 19th century. Beyond that, little was known about the island itself. It seemed history had a habit of forgetting the island even existed.

Stanton Anakasta wasn't much better. In his youth, he'd been a player, chasing the almighty dollar with one grandiose get-rich-quick investment scheme or strategy after another. Years had gone by where nothing seemed to break in Anakasta's favor. He amassed a sizable debt to shady investors on both the east and west coast of the United States. And just when it looked like he was about to go broke for the last time and lose it all, somehow Anakasta managed to strike it big. He'd made his fortune in the stock market, of all places. Leveraging the last of his assets in one final gamble, Anakasta had sunk one hundred and twenty thousand dollars into a single no-nothing stock that skyrocketed overnight. Cashing out with a cool half million, he invested the proceeds into a pair of similarly obscure stocks. A week later, Anakasta had paid off all his debts and was sitting on over four million in liquid currency.

It seemed that a lifetime of bad luck had been paid out in full during the first part of Stanton Anakasta's life. For the last five years he'd apparently lived a disproportionately charmed life. Something had clearly changed.

"You were north of us when your plane went down, were you not?" Anakasta said. The words roused Greeley from his musings.

The statement caught Greeley by surprise because he sensed a trap. The problem was, the deception wasn't immediately obvious, and Greeley had never considered himself particularly good under pressure. "Ah... I'm sorry?" he said through a mouth full of steak.

Anakasta grinned, though Greeley noticed a distinct lack of amusement in the man's penetrating gaze. He was being studied now, there was no question. "Your plane went down off our north shore, isn't that right?" Anakasta pressed. "According to the briefing relayed by my head of security, this is what you reported when you were interviewed."

Interviewed. A polite word for the interrogation that had taken place. Though he hadn't been physically harmed in the interview, the threat of harm seemed close at hand the entire time. Moments after passing through the compound's front gate, the security team had descended on him. He'd been whisked away to an interrogation room and questioned for well over an hour. Anakasta's men were good. Certainly more professional and thorough than the police of the greater New York area based on Greeley's experience. These guys were well trained—likely ex-military. They stank of it.

"A Beechcraft, I believe," Anakasta continued.

Nodding, Greeley said, "That's right. Your people said it was somewhere off the north shore. I wasn't the pilot, so I can't be sure. We went down fast. I'm not entirely sure where we are, to be honest. I know there aren't many islands out this way. I was damn lucky to wash up here."

Anakasta sat, his gaze fixed on Greeley. "Lucky? Is that how you feel? Tell me... are you a gambling man, Zane?"

"Poker," Greeley said. "And blackjack. But mostly poker. Why?"

"Well, as you said, it takes incredible luck to wash up on the shore of the only island for thousands of square miles. What did you say your intended destination was again?"

"The drill site on Mud Cat Atoll. We were carrying replacement parts for their drilling equipment."

Letting the silence hang, Anakasta watched Greeley with a sharp eye. Without a word, he raised his fork and knife and cut another bite from his steak. He took his time placing it in his mouth. Everyone watched the man slowly chew the rare meat. Greeley was interested in how the act held the attention of everyone at the table. Even Gavin seemed unsure how to react or what might come next.

"For an island so far out in the middle of nowhere," Anakasta said. "We lack for few modern conveniences. We receive regular shipments to restock our food stores, and it takes us perhaps a little longer than most to receive replacement parts when something breaks down. But when it comes to technology, we're as cutting edge as any first world nation."

Cutting more of his steak, Anakasta slipped it into his mouth and began to chew. This time he spoke around the food. "Take internet access, for example," he said. "We have a gigabit microwave satellite uplink. For an island no one bothers to put on navigation maps, we can access the web at speeds faster than most homes in America.

"Then there's our radar system," Anakasta said and swallowed. He glared at Greeley, the implied accusation and challenge evident in his sharp stare. "Exactly the same sort of technology protecting the perimeters of the American White House. From personal experience, I can tell you that it will pick up a single-passenger aircraft from more than thirty miles away. Truly up-to-the-minute technology, I assure you. No backwater, second-rate gear for us out here." His gaze swept the table before returning to Greeley. "Not when the safety of my family is involved."

Offering a slow nod, Greeley understood where Anakasta was going with this. In his judgment, letting the man speak his mind would be best. Greeley sensed that interrupting to cut to the chase would only imply guilt or cast further suspicion on his surprise appearance. Anakasta ran this island as he saw fit. The smart play was to let the man call him out and hope he could smooth things over enough to catch a ride out on the next supply ship when it departed.

"I understand," Greeley admitted but offered no elaboration.

"Perhaps you can explain why your Beechcraft never appeared on our radar," Anakasta said as he finally reached the point of his speech. "Or why your pilot never sounded a distress call? If you crashed and washed up on our shores, surely you went down within thirty miles of the island. If you'd been more than a mile or two away, you would not have known the island was here and would have frozen to death in these seasonal waters. That you're alive and well suggests your arrival here was no accident."

Laying his fork and knife down on the plate, Greeley sat back and squared his shoulders. His eyes focused on the plate for several long seconds as he took a calming breath. He'd known this moment was coming. Gavin had warned of the island's radar system. And though Anakasta was paranoid, he was no fool. The story of the crash wouldn't hold up to scrutiny.

"I apologize for the deception," Greeley said in a quiet tone. "I heard there was a supply ship scheduled to arrive soon. I was hoping to catch a ride out before I had to explain the mess I'm in. It was a mistake. I should have come clean from the start."

"Why are you here?" Asha asked, speaking up for the first time since a palpable tension filled the air.

"Entirely by accident," Greeley explained. "As you've guessed," he said, meeting Anakasta's gaze. "We were flying below radar on our way to Mud Cat Atoll. Under the radar, because we weren't delivering a load of authorized inventory. We were trying to avoid Ardonic Corp's security protocols on the way in."

"Contraband?" Anakasta said. The arch of one brow suggested he'd never considered the scenario. "You were smuggling contraband to the workers on Mud Cat?"

Greeley nodded. "Tobacco and booze are restricted unless you buy them from the company store. Maybe not such a big deal in theory, but workers are forced to pay exorbitant rates. The operation's quartermaster claims the prices are justified given the astronomical expense of transporting recreational goods to the remote location. But really? The company's just taking advantage of its workers in every way it can."

Sitting silently and staring at Greeley, Anakasta tapped an index finger idly on the table. Long seconds ticked by. "So you thought you'd cut the company out of the equation and deliver goods to the island at a cut rate? Is that it?"

Greeley shook his head instantly in reply. "Not a cut-rate," he explained. "A substantial savings. We weren't just shaving a buck off a fifty-dollar bottle of cheap bourbon. We've been offering better liquor at fair prices. A far cry cheaper than even the cheapest swill from the company store. The catch being we had to sneak it onto Mud Cat Atoll. And if the security goons at Ardonic Corp caught us, they'd confiscate it for themselves—maybe even kill us for making an end run around them. These offshore operations can get away with anything."

The callous edge in Anakasta's eyes had softened. He offered a slight nod, but contemplation was still evident in his gaze. After a sip of wine, he returned to work on his steak. As he placed his knife to the meat, a thunderous boom erupted in the distance. Everyone shifted in their seats, most nearly coming to their feet. The chandelier overhead shook and clattered while the wall sconces rattled against stone walls. A second explosion followed, the sound somewhere far in the distance but still frightening and intense. To Greeley's untrained ear, it sounded like cannon fire.

Anakasta quickly raised placating hands. "Nothing to fear," he said in a surprisingly subdued voice. "It's alright." A chuckle escaped his lips as bewildered expressions crossed the faces of everyone at the table.

Everyone except Gavin, Greeley noticed. Of the lot, Gavin was the least surprised by the distant explosions. Less ready to launch from his chair in panic, his response was unusually calm and measured. Conversely, Keegan looked as on edge as Greeley felt.

"It's okay," Gavin said. "It's a thunderstorm."

Greeley's gaze shifted to the great hewn lumber of the rafters two stories overhead. He looked quickly at the thick stone walls of interlocking blocks, each about a yard square. Every brick likely weighed more than an SUV. Another crash erupted, this one seemingly more distant. It gave him an opportunity to examine the tones. They seemed to reverberate through the building's stone structure.

"He's right," Anakasta chuckled. "This old building is beautiful, but the materials aren't the least bit modern. I'm afraid they make for drafty conditions in the winter, and the first few thunderstorms take some getting used to."

Greeley swallowed hard. "That," he grumbled, "is a thunderstorm?"

"Just the start of one, I'm afraid," Anakasta confirmed.

"And you get used to it? I might need clean shorts." Greeley's complexion had gone pale but was beginning to regain its original color.

Keegan shook her head. "I'm still not convinced. I've been here through one storm so far. I don't think I'll ever get used to that!"

93

Gavin laughed and poured himself another glass of wine. Unbidden, he poured one for Keegan as well. This earned him a wry, but not entirely unaccepting look in response, Greeley observed.

"About this smuggling run," Anakasta said as he focused the conversation once more on Greeley. "Booze and tobacco, you say?"

Greeley nodded.

"And illicit drugs?" he pressed.

"No," Greeley said instantly. There wasn't a breath's width of hesitation in his response. Along with it, there was steel in his eyes. "No drugs. Never drugs."

"Never?"

Greeley shook his head. "Had a nephew who OD'd a few years back. I'm no saint, but I know where to draw the line. It doesn't matter what kind of money is involved."

"A smuggler with a code?" Anakasta said. Amusement danced in his tone. "That's refreshing. Perhaps we're cut from the same cloth. Nothing wrong with making a buck, legal or not, so long as no one is harmed in the making."

There was genuine humor in Anakasta's expression and Greeley realized he'd passed the assessment. But seeing the expressions both Gavin and Keegan cast on Anakasta, he suspected something more had been gained from the conversation. Then, as quickly as the accusatory flicker had touched both of their visages, it was gone.

"My partner was afraid some of the islands surrounding Mud Cat had radar installations to stop smugglers," Greeley said and finally merged his fictitious crash with the reality of what had happened. He made it a point to come in below four hundred feet well before the atoll, just in case. But flying that low caused ice on our wings. It was going to be the last run until spring. I guess we got greedy."

"What made you fly so close to Black Rock?" Keegan asked, pointing out the most obvious flaw in the greater lie.

"Our pilot," Greeley replied in a dour tone showing respect for the dead but implying frustration for the man who had crashed them. "He was a substitute. He was worried about flying so low for that long and wanted to stay within range of the few islands dotting the route. If something went wrong, he figured

we could make for land."

"A terrible idea," Anakasta grunted. "Not enough islands to make burning the extra fuel worth the trouble. And water temperatures this time of year…it was just dumb luck that you didn't freeze to death before making landfall. You should buy a lottery ticket when you return home," he chuckled. "If your luck holds, you may just win the grand prize."

"In the meantime, you'll be our guest," Asha said. Judging by the look she gave him when she commented, Greeley suspected she was trying to cut Stanton's reading of the riot act short. The explanation for his arrival here seemed to have satisfied her as well. Her expression had warmed substantially since the start of the meal.

"Quite right," Anakasta said with a nod. "The supply ship is a few days out." He waved his knife slowly in the air in a circular motion. "As you can hear, there's a weather system moving in at the moment. We're due to get a break in about 24 hours, then its big brother is due to hit. The captain might push his arrival back accordingly, depending on how long the second system takes to move through. But never fear. You'll be our guest until we can arrange to get you back to the mainland."

Releasing a contemplative breath, Greeley eased back in his seat. So much had already happened; he only wanted to get off the island. At least now he had a frame of reference for the timing. He didn't realize just how wound up he'd become until hearing those words. The death of Garboni didn't weigh on him in any tangible way; being rid of the little bastard would be advantageous in the long run. If Anakasta proved to be true to his word, the next few days might even be relaxing.

All the same, Greeley felt a gathering sense of unease. There was a nagging sense of dread deep in his gut. Though he didn't understand its source, he took it seriously.

Something was wrong here.

Realizing he'd allowed the conversation to lapse into momentary silence, Greeley added, "I appreciate your hospitality. I'm just not looking forward to dealing with the insurance adjusters when I get home."

"Or the accident investigators," Anakasta added. An amused smile tugged at the corner of his lips.

Chapter 18

"You've been quiet," Asha said, directing her attention to Keegan. "This is the most excitement we've seen in some time. What do you think of it all?"

Keegan had sat quietly through the bulk of the conversation. She'd watched it much like a spectator at a tennis match, her gaze shifting from speaker to speaker and offering nothing. Though there was interest in her eyes, she apparently had nothing to contribute. This was out of the ordinary for someone usually very insightful and opinionated. As was the expression on her face. Though she'd clearly been uncomfortable with the dining arrangements from the start, something subtle had changed over the course of Greeley's story.

The animosity wasn't entirely unwarranted, and Asha reminded herself she could be misreading Keegan's body language. Stanton had made a point to place her beside Gavin in yet another less-than-subtle attempt to break the ice between them. It was entirely possible the animosity coming off the poor girl right now was in response to her father's unwillingness to mind his own business.

If only you understood what is at stake.

Still, something seemed off. Though they sat shoulder to shoulder, Keegan seemed physically unwilling to turn her head even slightly in Gavin's direction.

Even more strangely, though Keegan acted cold regarding the rare interaction with Gavin, Asha sensed a lack of sincerity in her bitter demeanor. The quality of her standoffish nature toward Gavin seemed somehow…hollow.

Perhaps with time…

"I think it's a miracle anyone survived the crash," Keegan said. "Maybe we should be out on the beaches searching for survivors."

Greeley's downtrodden gaze found his plate and the conversation went quiet. Keegan looked around the table, at a loss for understanding. All eyes seemed to roam the room, obviously uncomfortable and unsure of what to say.

"The pilot went down with the plane," Gavin said quietly. He eyed Keegan sympathetically, perhaps seeing the confusion and concern clouding her expression in response to the sudden silence of the room. "The only other passenger aboard was tangled in his seatbelt when the plane went under."

Keegan looked to Greeley, but her expression had an uncharacteristic lack of sympathy. "Your partner and the pilot went down with the plane?" she said. It sounded as if she wanted clarification on the point. "I'm sorry, but you don't seem all that broken up over it."

Her tone was filled with accusation. Asha saw suspicion in Keegan's expression. Having been a part of the family for only a short period of time, Asha had worked hard to win Keegan over. The effort remained a work in progress. Very close in age themselves, they should have had much in common. But being her stepmother now, Asha was in an untenable position. It left her striving to understand Keegan's moods and read her expressions. They were the keys to walking the delicate path to find harmony in the family. Keegan didn't seem satisfied with part, or perhaps all, of Greeley's story.

Greeley looked suddenly very pale. "Anthony and I weren't close," he explained. "That doesn't mean losing him is easy." His gaze dropped and his visage seemed to cloud with a murky pain that obviously embarrassed him. "The worst part was seeing the pilot. The windscreen caved in and collapsed in his lap. The shattering glass gutted him right there. I've never seen anything like it."

Color filled Greeley's cheeks. Holy crap—Asha's stomach churned, and her heart sank as moisture filled the corners of Greeley's eyes. Her eyes began to tear in response.

Greeley shook his head slowly as if making some silent decision. He raised his head and met Keegan's stare. "Anthony died, but the pilot was eviscerated right there in front of me. He didn't want to make the flight, but we talked him into it." He heaved a deep breath. "Crazy thing is, you know what makes me feel the worst? For the life of me, I couldn't tell you the captain's name."

Gavin looked at Greeley, his jaw agape. There was something unreadable in his expression.

Keegan's look was less prosaic. Anger flashed in her gaze. Apparently not satisfied, she wasn't going to back down. Gavin must have noticed because, thankfully, he intervened.

"Easy there, kitten," Gavin said, placing a hand on Keegan's where it sat atop the table. "The man's clearly in a lot of pain. Don't make him bare his soul to a bunch of strangers."

Keegan's eyes went wide at Gavin's touch. She yanked her hand away as if scalded. There was color in her cheeks when she met his eyes fully for the first time since they had taken adjacent seats. She looked about to speak, perhaps scream. Instead, she swallowed the words. Her eyes turned to her father. Asha saw that Stanton was as confused as anyone at the table.

Slamming back against her chair, Keegan shot to her feet. Spinning with a flourish of her skirt, she slapped the swinging kitchen door with the flat of her hand and was gone. The door squeaked quietly as it flapped back and forth in the room's silence.

No one knew what to say.

"I should go check on her," Asha said and placed her napkin on the table.

"No," Anakasta said. "Stay. Leave her be. She just needs to cool off. She's overreacting. Sooner or later, she'll realize it."

Greeley looked to Gavin, perhaps more stunned than anyone with the unusual display.

"You're wondering what that was all about," Gavin stated matter-of-factly as he looked back at Greeley. The big man just shrugged.

Anakasta spoke instead. "The mother of all misunderstandings, I'm afraid. Keegan got it in her head that I wanted to pair her off with Gavin here, and she's appalled at the thought."

"To be fair—" Asha began.

"Now stop that," Anakasta grumbled. His tone reflected a distinct lack of

patience for the subject and hinted that there had already been much discussion on the topic. "I know damn well what I said, and I know even better what I meant. It was a misunderstanding, and I'm tired of her acting foolish just to drive the point home."

Another thunderclap struck and sent a percussive wave through the dining room. It was enough to derail the conversation and send all eyes skyward. It sounded like a small eruption and sent a chill down the length of Asha's spine.

"The storm is upon us," Anakasta said.

Chapter 19

Jimmy Kerns rolled his eyes and watched as the normally mild-mannered and quiet Amar Harihassim cackled and swept up the last of the chips. Harihassim was known simply as Hari to the rest of the team. At a towering five foot eight and weighing all of one hundred and fifty pounds, the quiet little sonofabitch was one hell of a poker player. Born in Egypt to an Egyptian mother and American father, he'd been raised in the United States. Kerns had initially not wanted to like the quiet little man with his strange indistinct accent and olive complexion, but he'd managed to grow on him. It was hard not to like him. He'd become like the brother Kerns had never had.

"You lose again, my friend," Hari chuckled as he swept the chips into a heap before him. "That is what, three nights in a row?"

Canto sat with his elbows pressed hard into the table and his fists balled tightly. "Four nights," he corrected through clenched teeth. "And I still think you're cheating."

Kerns already knew where this was going. As much as Hari was good-natured and easygoing, Canto was a hothead and constantly spoiling for a fight. He was the stereotypical hot-blooded Italian. He had a mane of thick jet-black hair, eyebrows that were just as bushy, and nearly as much hair sticking from the collar of his shirt as he had atop his head. It would have been easy to disregard the man's bluster but being a couple of inches over six foot and weighing in somewhere just over two-fifty, the guy had arms like telephone poles and a neck thicker than anything Kerns had ever seen.

"Let it go," Kerns said and shot Canto a tired look. "He's either far luckier than either of us or much smarter. Either way, he wins. I plan on cleaning you both out next time."

Canto looked about to say something but paused. He took a breath, then drained the last of his Scotch. He shot a threatening stare in Hari's direction before moving his gaze slowly back on Kerns. The rant was about to escalate. Instead, Kerns slid the half-empty bottle of Scotch in Canto's direction. It would either defuse the tension or add fuel to the fire. With Canto, under the circumstances, the attempt could go either way.

Long seconds passed. Finally, Canto snatched up the bottle and poured himself two fingers. He paused to glare at Kerns once more. The stare finally broke into a grin—the big man relented by pouring two fingers for Kerns. Turning to Hari, he poured only a splash of the rich liquor. "You're a lightweight, and we're all still on duty," he grumbled.

Kerns sighed and relished the bullet they had all just dodged. Canto was decent enough, but drinking with him was like playing Russian Roulette with four rounds in the cylinder. He turned to the security console along the wall and the man monitoring it. "Hathaway, you want a nip?"

Tom Hathaway sat with his back to the group, his gaze pointed at an array of flat panel displays tiling the wall. By long-standing agreement, the group had decided the one to draw the short straw would monitor the camera feeds for the shift. To keep his attention as sharp as possible on the boring detail, whoever drew the short straw wouldn't be allowed to drink. In fact, none of them were supposed to be drinking. Kerns believed it was an unspoken benefit of the night shift. They had to stay sharp and maintain morale, so concessions had to be made. Cards and a couple of drinks were a small price to pay for vigilance, particularly on an island in the middle of nowhere protecting people of no importance in a place where nothing ever happened.

Sitting around bored inside all night beat walking a perimeter in the cold and rain, at the very least. The hours were crap, and spending time with Canto was like a nightly proctology exam, but at least the money was good.

"Hathaway? You with me?" Kerns said, this time his voice raised.

Hathaway cocked his head but didn't turn away from the displays. "I'm good," he said simply.

Canto chuckled. "He's perving over the cleaning girls again."

Kerns eyed the wall of video feeds. Six screens hung side by side, tiled four rows high on the wall. They displayed live footage from all over the complex and the dock in the lagoon, the tool shed, and various other outbuildings. Since twenty-four screens were insufficient to display footage from the seventy-eight cameras on the island, each cycled automatically from one camera to the next in six-second increments. All but two of the displays, Kerns noted. The two screens most in line with Hathaway's gaze had been taken out of the rotation. On them, he saw a high-definition feed of two women moving laundry between two sets of industrial-sized washers and dryers. One of the cameras had a close, in-room feed of the two women as they worked, while the other showed a distant shot from a room down the hall. Even in this second shot, the women were only barely visible.

Christ, he really is watching her again.

This was the third night in a row that Hathaway had skipped drawing straws and volunteered to monitor the feeds. At first Kerns took it as a sign the guy was just sick of dealing with Canto. Who wouldn't be? But twice was a coincidence and three times was a pattern. The way the guy was eye-fucking those two girls had gone from amusing to concerning.

Hari finished stacking the last of the chips into neat, even piles and eyed Kerns across the table. "You won't have a chance to win this back for a while," he said. "Mayhew is moving me to the day rotation. Drone four is back online, and they need an operator."

Canto smashed a beefy fist on the table and grinned. "Hell yes. Here I thought I would need to break a couple of your fingers to change your luck. I guess this will do just as well."

The little man's eyebrows shot up, clearly unsure how to interpret the comments from the much larger man. Though he smiled, Kerns knew Hari was worried this wasn't a joke. For his part, Kerns was even more concerned Canto was serious.

"We've had those drones running for weeks," Kerns said. He spoke to change the subject, but this topic had been on his mind for sometime. "I know we're running a topological survey, but I've seen the hardware. This stuff is far more precise than necessary. And way more expensive."

Hari nodded. "A survey doesn't explain the sensor arrays on these drones *either. They are equipped with ground-penetrating radar and detectors to identify specific compounds and ores. Of course, this is in addition to the advanced capabilities already common to this type of craft. Technologies such as lidar, sonar, laser imaging, and in this case, the largest hydrogen fuel cells I have ever seen on drones.*

Kerns had heard most of this before. No one seemed to fully understand what Anakasta was looking for on the island, though most of the security team agreed he was searching for something specific. This was no effort to conduct a topological survey of the island.

The advanced abilities of the drone fleet made Kerns consider another of the security team's problems. "If we have that kind of flight time and detection ability, why don't we use a drone or two to search for that downed plane?"

The new arrival on the island had been big news for the entire security team. A stranger arriving out of the blue caused a minor uproar, particularly since the arrival had caught the team flat-footed. And though their benefactor, Stanton Anakasta, hadn't made a big deal out of it, their team leader, Matt Mayhew, had practically gone supernova. That Gavin Kray discovered the stranger before the security team was a colossal black eye for the entire security force.

Hari offered a sheepish grin and seemed reluctant to meet Kerns' eye.

"What is it?" Kerns prompted.

"As I understand it, two drones were used for just such a reconnaissance. They found considerable pulverized debris at the base of the rock face on the northeastern perimeter and the remains of an oil slick just beyond the reef due north of that position."

Kerns felt his cheeks warm. Why was he always the last to know these things? This only helped to remind him there was no chance of vertical movement in the chain of command. His placement on night duty with the likes of Canto was only further proof of it. He didn't have any kind of special training like Hari, and Mayhew barely knew his name.

With a sigh, he glanced over to Hathaway, who remained motionless before the wall of displays.

"Tom," he said. "Want me to spell you for a bit? You can stretch your legs and get some fresh air."

Hathaway didn't reply.

Chapter 20

Tom Hathaway had tuned out the drone of the voices in the room behind him. The endless yammering of his so-called team was pushing his tolerance into the red zone, well past the boiling point, but then she had saved him. The appearance of Tess Lindow in the hallway on the third floor had been his singular focus when coming on shift for the evening, and she had appeared just in time to save his sanity. Moving from one of the staff bedrooms with a large laundry basket pressed to her breast, Hathaway watched as Tess followed Jennifer Fennem down the long stone hallway. They stopped before a wooden panel in the wall. Jennifer flipped the small door open and both women dumped the contents of their baskets into what Hathaway knew to be a wide laundry chute running vertically through the center of the building, down to the first basement level where the laundry facilities were located.

Hathaway scratched idly at the inflamed patch of gray-green skin just below his elbow. He adjusted the sleeve of his uniform and watched as the two women collected bedding from each room on the floor. He lost sight of them as they entered each bedroom since, disappointingly, no cameras were allowed in the staff bedrooms. Thankfully, the two women worked efficiently, and Hathaway's patience was rewarded when he reacquired Tess five to seven minutes after she entered each room. Like clockwork, Tess and Jennifer made their way to the end of the hall each time and deposited their loads down the laundry chute.

Staring through unblinking eyes, Hathaway used the high-definition cameras to track Tess as she moved up and down the vast stone halls. He enjoyed the way her uniform clung to the gentle curves of her slender form. His mouth went dry as he contemplated the sway of her hips as she walked the corridor length.

Jennifer had just entered the next room on their itinerary, and Tess was clearly about to follow when she stopped suddenly and looked down the hall. Hathaway tapped the keyboard on the desk before him and zoomed out on the camera's view in time to see Keegan Anakasta advancing down the hall. Hathaway felt his breath catch. Tess was his favorite, but Keegan was a distant second place on his list, and seeing the two together made his pulse quicken.

He watched as the pair stepped within a pace of each other and began to speak in what Hathaway interpreted to be hushed tones even through the silent feed of the surveillance system. He watched the smiles between the two girls and zoomed the camera to better study the gleam of their eyes and what he believed to be the seductive pout of their lips. His mind raced, wondering what conspiratorial gossip was moving between the two young women.

Hathaway loosened the collar of his uniform and harshly scratched at the inflamed and aggravated flesh just below the collar of his shirt. The rash had grown substantially worse in the last day, but his intention to stop and have Doc Cantrell take a look at it after his shift was entirely forgotten as he began to fantasize about what he would do if given the opportunity to get both Tess and Keegan alone in one of the dark nooks of the massive building. He'd toyed with the idea of cornering Tess more times than he could count, but now the idea felt like fuel oil burning in his veins.

Chapter 21

Pulling the zipper of her North Face insulated jacket higher against the permeating chill, Keegan blew out a breath. The vapor cloud coalesced and shimmered in the beam of her flashlight. Her hand was already growing icy against the aluminum grip of the long, frigid Maglite. Gloves would've been a good idea, she decided in retrospect before trudging on.

The ceiling was only five feet high. At five foot eight herself, it forced her to stoop. The passage was three feet wide with walls that repeatedly changed in construction as she followed the path's nearly a hundred and seventy-yard length. While portions of the tunnel had been hewn from solid stone, some were constructed with marble bricks, limestone, and other less obvious material. Different sections were not reinforced at all. A few stretches were composed entirely of bare earth. These were further supported by trusses and beams, some of which looked to be a century or more in age. Oddly, the occasional support had been replaced very recently.

Careful to mind her head, the ground underfoot kept Keegan's pace slow and methodical. While efforts had plainly been made to keep the walkway clear of obstacles, small chunks of stone and natural debris scattered the path. With the beam of a single flashlight to find her way in otherwise utter darkness, and given that no one knew she was here, turning an ankle would prove harrowing if not eventually fatal. To that end, she'd worn boots to protect her feet and ankles. Intended to be a hip and stylish take on combat boots, their smaller size and shape made them distinctly feminine even though they were laced nearly to her knee. The boots and the coat were a concession to the conditions she'd expected to face in the tunnel and a stark contrast to the nearly knee-length black skirt extending past the insulated coat falling just past her hips. Black cashmere stockings snaked from the top of her boots to end just above the knee. The bare flesh exposed between the top of her stockings and the hem of her skirt felt painfully exposed with the bitter cold clawing at gooseflesh. Icy tendrils seemed to coil in the folds of her skirt as they contacted her legs with each step. It was foolish attire, she decided. Warm jeans, wool socks, and a stocking cap would've been a better choice for this excursion.

She trudged on, her head ducked and eyes cast high to follow the flashlight's beam. There was a soothing reassurance that came with the heft of the Maglite. Her grip tightened reflexively with that understanding. It had the weight and heft necessary to strike a killing blow and was a weapon unto itself. Not that she was afraid of the dark. Admittedly, the distance of her journey and knowing she was underground made every step unsettling, as was seeing the air vaporize before her with every breath. It was a persistent reminder that the oxygen around her was finite—yet another incentive to mind her footing and complete the journey as quickly and quietly as possible.

At last, the telltale curve of the cavern wall became evident. The path had been arrow-straight until this point; some minor course correction had evidently been required when the tunnel was forged. Her way swept to the right and followed the gentle bend. Rounding it, the passage ended in an eight-foot-tall cube-shaped room. The walls were cast entirely from poured concrete. As was the floor, for the first time not composed of earthen materials.

Standing fully upright for the first time in more than ten minutes, Keegan rocked her head from side to side and marched silently in place as she worked blood back into her extremities. It was an effort to raise her falling body temperature. Traversing the tunnel felt like time in an industrial freezer. Here, even with every exposed inch of her skin partially numb, the cold was less extreme.

Her eyes went to the ceiling.

Taking a steeling breath, Keegan doused her light. The three-foot square outline of light on the ceiling became more distinct. Even at a distance, she recognized its source to be razor thin. Reaching out, she felt for the ladder on the wall. With eyes focused on the light from above, she began to climb.

Chapter 22

Tess Lindow practically bounced down the last few steps on her way to the second floor of the monastery. It had been a long day, and she was looking forward to unwinding. She'd just fed Brody the scraps of steak volunteered by Chef Dawe, and the big dog had been beside himself with excitement over the treat. Everyone on the island loved that dog, and he was constantly spoiled as a result. The thought of the big Bernese's lopsided grin, lolling tongue, and frantic tail brought an unbidden smile to her face.

"You're in a good mood tonight," a gravelly voice intoned from a distance. It carried the trace of a Texas drawl, and Tess felt her heart jump to her throat with a start. She turned to see Tom Hathaway advancing down the broad stone corridor only a few yards away.

"Tom," she said and forced a convincing but insincere smile. "You scared me. What are you doing here at this time of night?" She had just descended to the second floor of the west wing. This was the entrance to the staff quarters. He had no business here, given that the security teams were boarded on the first floor of the north wing.

Hathaway looked her up and down with a slow, deliberate stare. His gaze was predatory and unsettling as if he were undressing her with his eyes. "Just out for a walk," he muttered. "That alright with you?"

"Of course," she grinned. Their quiet surroundings seemed suddenly oppressive. She felt the hair on the back of her neck prickle. "Just not used to visitors in this corner of the building."

Saying nothing, Hathaway studied her with a penetrating gaze. He moved in closer. At this time of the evening, she was alone in this corner of the compound, and they both knew it. Tess eyed the staircase and thought of making an excuse to double back. She could head for the third floor. As if sensing this, Hathaway moved and blocked the path of retreat.

"I forgot," she said in a trembling voice. "I have an appointment with Doctor Cantrell. I better get going before I'm any later." It was a weak excuse, but explaining that she'd be missed seemed the intelligent play. There was something reptilian and dangerous in Hathaway's glassy eyes, something she'd never seen before. It sent her heart racing.

Hathaway moved closer but didn't respond. Tess stepped quickly backward. Her back met the rough cold surface of the stone wall and she shuddered. Closing the last two feet, Hathaway looked down at her small, five-and-a-half-foot form. Wordlessly, his eyes roamed her face. A hand slowly rose to pull a stray length of chestnut hair from the corner of her eye. The tips of his fingers brushed her face and slipped the lock gently behind her ear. The sense of his skin on hers made her stomach turn and her face flush.

Perhaps taking her reaction for something it was not, Hathaway smiled. It was more of a sneer, Tess decided. There was nothing charming or disarming about it. The expression lacked any sense of warmth. The lustful quality filling his eyes had grown more intense.

"I—I really need to be going," she stammered.

"No need to play hard to get," Hathaway said in a cold, dry voice. His gaze had shifted and he looked down the open collar of her blouse. His fingers leaped suddenly to the top button and teased at it.

"Stop," she said and slapped his hand away.

He grinned, wide and toothy. "Alright," he drawled. "Hard to get then." A vice-like hand clamped around her throat. Her head snapped back and bounced against the cold wall. He squeezed, and her eyes rolled. His free hand returned to the button. Rather than release it, he tore the material away with a single effortless motion. Pale flesh and the delicate lace cups of her pushup bra met his eye.

Tess tried to scream but couldn't expel the air. She tried to make a fist, but her brain was already oxygen-deprived. Vision swimming, her hand slapped uselessly against the cold stone at her back. Knees buckling, she failed even to collapse to the floor; her attacker had her pinned to the wall with a single meaty hand and throttled her long delicate neck.

The world began to grow dark.

"Hey asshole," a distant baritone voice warbled as Tess's eyes rolled for what she knew would be the last time.

Chapter 23

The room was dimly lit, murky shadows encroaching from every corner and falling in on Gavin from every direction. The only illumination came from the weak fire in the wide stone hearth and a single lamp's dim bulb in a distant corner. Sitting on the edge of the bed, Gavin held an extinguished pair of small flashlights in one hand. His gaze was fixed on the flicker of firelight, and the contents of his hands had been long since forgotten. He shook his head and banished the distraction with quiet remorse. They were memories of a life he couldn't forget, but he at least hoped to outrun them. Such contemplation had become commonplace in his private time. Solitude and introspection had brought him to the island in the first place.

If only he'd known what he was walking into when he'd first arrived. The island was supposed to be a refuge—a place for him to escape the past and the rest of the world. It didn't take long to learn how small his place in the world was. With the arrival of Anthony Garboni and Zane Greeley, it seemed his past was inescapable. If he couldn't find peace at this far corner of the world, could he ever? Then again, for all its complications, all the surprises he could've lived the rest of his life without, Gavin had to admit there was one undeniable benefit. There was one bright point with the potential to make all of it worthwhile.

Shaking his head once more, this time with frustration, Gavin rose from the bedside. He stuffed the flashlights into the half-empty rucksack on the chest at the foot of the California king. That one bright point was why he hadn't caught the first supply ship out of here nearly three months ago when things started to get complicated. Since that day, events had continued to snowball out of control.

Gavin scrunching his brow and grinding his teeth, crossed the room to the en-suite bathroom. The simple feeling of his bare feet in the thick pile of plush carpeting normally relaxed him. But not tonight.

He considered his trip to Manhattan, what had happened in the cavern at the top of the mountain, and now the appearance of Garboni. It felt like his life was a series of standing dominoes, and he couldn't shake the feeling that the three had toppled rapidly.

What's really going on here...

If he was right, more dominoes were soon to follow. This island was strange. An off the charts kind of strange, both figuratively and literally. And while he might know more about this place than anyone else on the island, he didn't have it figured out—not by a long shot. Without using a light, he pulled open a cabinet door beside the bathroom sink and grabbed a bath towel from the stack. He didn't need to see what he was doing. These accommodations had been his home since shortly after arriving on the island. This house was one of several outbuildings. It had been built by Brooks Fowler decades ago, one of the first amenities added to the island when he first made it his home. When the billionaire took possession of the island and began to renovate the then-dilapidated monastery, his first order of business was to build this modest house. It was his home until restoration was complete, and the citadel was ready for habitation.

That modest house was about five thousand square feet, the bulk of which was consumed by the open-plan first floor. A loft dedicated entirely to the master bedroom suite, a spacious bathroom, and a small office consumed half of the second level. The bedroom and office abutted a simple wood beam railing that overlooked half of the ground floor. Gavin knew the building by rote and liked the darkness. He seldom used lights unnecessarily, particularly enjoying the darkness on rainy nights like tonight.

A nearby flash of lightning lit the large picture windows on the face of the house. The entire southern exposure was thrown into a momentary, retina-searing flash of white. The brilliant lightning strike was followed an instant later by another causing an almost strobe-like effect. Gavin had his back to the windows when the lightning struck but began to turn in response to the display. Every lurking shadow disappeared instantly with the stuttering pulse of light—

every shadow except for one.

As Gavin finished turning to take in the brilliant display, he became aware of a figure at the center of the room. The form was silhouetted against the blinding flash. Perhaps thirty feet separated them. The shape was near the balcony, presumably with its back to the railing. Thunder boomed, rattling every window in the house. It was a concussive wave that physically impacted Gavin's chest. A heartbeat passed, and he wondered why he'd ever taken it as gospel that Garboni and Greeley were the only two hitters to make landfall. The figure before him was too small to be Zane Greeley—too small by a long shot.

His breath seized in his throat as Gavin's hands balled into fists. The strobing flash of white light disappeared. In contrast, the room was reduced to utter darkness. The brilliance of the flash had resulted in temporary night blindness. Still, a vision captured in the last split second of light was frozen, burned momentarily into his cornea. The figure held something overhead—and the figure was lunging.

Chapter 24

"No one knows exactly how old the place is," Willy Amstell was saying. "The last owner restored the citadel based on the best guesses of experts he flew in for the task. The underground levels survived some kind of catastrophic fire, so they had the base architecture to work with. As I was told, they made educated guesses about the design and layout for large portions of the upper floors."

Zane Greeley nodded and followed Willy's outstretched hand. At that direction, they moved into another long stone corridor. Like many of the halls they had already traversed, the walls were largely unadorned. Like the floors, the walls were comprised of massive stone blocks roughly three feet wide and as many tall. The place looked ancient and medieval. If not for the electric wall sconces every twenty to thirty feet, he would have believed he'd been transported back to the middle ages.

"I'm guessing some upgrades were part of the remodel?" Greeley said and eyed one of the light fixtures.

"Oh, right you are," Willy chuckled. He pulled a battered and dented flask from his breast pocket and sipped. He tipped the open end slightly in Greeley's direction. "Sure I can't offer you a nip?"

Willy had given Greeley a guided tour of the citadel and explained what he knew about the place's ancient and mysterious history. Greeley was fascinated by the size and scope of the building. He wondered what it must have been like to undertake such a construction project back in the day. He shook his head. "No, thank you, Willy."

The older man chuckled and shrugged. "Running water and electricity were installed when Mister Fowler reengineered the place. It's still drafty as shite, but he installed a hot water inductive heating system throughout the above-ground floors. There's forced air in some areas. It all depended on what could be fitted given the construction.

"You know, there are dozens of fireplaces throughout the old pile? But for the life of me, I can't imagine what it must have been like to live here four hundred years ago."

Greeley stopped in his tracks. "Four hundred years? Is the place really that old?"

Taking another sip, Willy nodded. "Aye. Some say it's much older. Truth be told, no one knows for sure. I'm told artifacts have been found proving she's four hundred years if she's a day. Rather troubling that no one knows for sure."

A scuffing sound followed by something hollow impacting on stone drew Greeley's attention. His eyes flashed to Willy. The old man had heard it as well. "Is that normal?" Greeley said.

Willy shook his head. "Haven't a clue."

A muffled voice came from the distance, and Greeley felt his suspicion grow. He turned a corner and found a long, dimly lit corridor. A staircase rose to the left, climbing to the second floor. Another murmur of a voice, slightly closer this time, and he knew he was on the right path. He bounded up the stone treads taking them two at a time.

At the top, he rounded a corner and stopped suddenly. Greeley blinked at the unexpected sight. A man in a dark suit had a young woman pinned against the wall. Her mouth was agape, her eyes rolling, and her hand slapped ineffectively against the wall at her back. Greeley had seen the man before. He was part of Stanton Anakasta's security detail. One of his three primaries, if he wasn't mistaken. The guard raised a hand and tore open the woman's blouse with a single violent motion.

"Hey asshole," Greeley yelled and charged. He was already throwing a haymaker of a left hook.

The guard turned just in time to catch the blow squarely in the eye. He released the woman, who instantly sagged to the floor like a discarded rag doll. Greeley raised a battered leather-soled shoe and kicked the dazed man away from the young woman. He was turning to check on her when he saw movement from the corner of his eye. The guard was pawing at a gun. It was slung in a shoulder rig underneath his coat.

Greeley wouldn't allow the prick to get his bearings, let alone pull a piece. He pivoted and closed the gap. The gun slipped from the shoulder holster, only for Greeley to slap it away with a meaty paw. "No sir," he grunted. "You'll have to play fair." He grabbed Hathaway by the lapels and yanked him to his feet. A devastating right fist to the man's breadbasket and the bastard was back on his knees.

"Miss Lindow," Willy was saying in the distance. "Are you alright?"

Greeley turned to find Willy kneeling over Tess who was rubbing her throat and gasping for air. She looked at him and the stooping security guard, also retching for air. Her eyes were wide and uncomprehending. Her blouse had been torn away, though she hadn't realized it yet. Greeley slipped the borrowed dinner jacket from his shoulders and tossed it to Willy. "Cover her up," he said before turning his attention back on the woman's attacker.

Greeley spun just in time. Hathaway looked up with wild eyes. Something flashed in his hands a fraction of a second before he lunged. Countless street fights told Greeley's lizard brain what was happening, even if his rational mind was slower at the math. He backpedaled in time to avoid an eviscerating stroke from the four-inch folding knife. The blade swished as it cut through the air an inch short of Greeley's belly. Tess screamed in the background.

Hathaway clambered to his feet and advanced on Greeley. The knife blade swung lazily from side to side; Hathaway's gaze remained reptilian and focused squarely on Greeley's face. The man had skill with the knife, Greeley could see. Formal training. Likely some second-tier special forces asshole. Not surprising. Private security contractors tended to hail from similar backgrounds. There was a glassy quality to the man's eyes, Greeley observed. Perhaps from a blow to the head, or he was hopped up on something.

Greeley took a feigning step toward his opponent. Rather than retreat, Hathaway charged. The move was entirely unexpected. Raising a hand, Greeley caught the downward arc of the stabbing motion as Hathaway rushed him. Their limbs became tangled, and Greeley went over backward. He crashed down on the unyielding stone floor and felt the wind driven from his lungs. Hathaway bore his weight upon him and pressed the advantage. They grappled hand over hand for control of the knife. Hathaway took the opportunity to pivot his weight. He drove a knee into Greeley's ribs repeatedly in a kicking motion. Swinging only his knee, the man had little windup; still, the blows were effective as they caught Greeley below the ribs and threatened his kidneys.

Greeley shifted and mashed a knee upward to strike Hathaway's groin with a devastating crunch. Though a tremor went through the man's body, the reaction was nowhere near what it should have been. Greeley ground his teeth and clamped his grip tighter on his opponent's wrists. The sonofabitch was on something, now there was no question. If Hathaway freed the knife, Greeley knew he'd be lucky to only take a poke or two before getting out from under him.

Raising a knee once more, this time shoving with every ounce of his strength, Greeley flung his opponent headfirst in a cartwheeling spin down the hall. Greeley's grasp on the knife and wrist of Hathaway disintegrated as the man went spinning yards out of reach.

Tess screamed and Willy cursed, but it must have been in surprise. Greeley saw them huddled at the base of the wall a dozen feet away. They were safe, but only if the guard remained engaged. If he lost this fight, they would surely pay the price.

Rolling, Greeley found his feet at the same time as Hathaway. Both men crouched low, ready to lunge or repel a lunging attack. A feral, wide-eyed savageness belayed the laconic expression Greeley was accustomed to seeing on the face of the islands' security guards. Hathaway's lips were pulled back to bare pristine dental work that was entirely out of place when paired with the wild spittle drooling from the corners of his lips. His eyes were bloodshot and unblinking. Behind the eyes, he seemed more animal than man.

Hathaway lunged, leading with the knife and putting all his speed behind the attack. Greeley reacted on impulse, his motivation to end this strange attack before something happened, and the savaged man somehow gained the upper hand. Focusing his attention on the incoming blade, he seized the wrist and elbow of Hathaway's knife hand as the man closed within arm's reach. Pushing the knife away at the wrist and drawing the elbow tight to his ribs, he stepped out with his left leg and threw his hip into his attacker's oncoming motion. Hathaway was off balance and committed to forward momentum. His legs were ripped from beneath him when they contacted Greeley's leg. Upon impact with Greeley's hip, Hathaway lost what was left of his control. Greeley used Hathaway's knife hand to spin him in the air and drive him to the ground. Hitting the floor as one, Greeley deliberately drove his two hundred and fifty pounds down. Between the twisting and the impact, the bones of Hathaway's *arm shattered. Multiple ribs snapped audibly as Greeley's unforgiving weight impacted Hathaway's more fragile form.*

A wheeze escaped Hathaway's lungs as Greeley climbed from his inert form. Dusting his hands on his pant legs, Greeley looked at the stone dust covering his clothes. He saw Tess and Willy staring at him from their huddled position at the base of the wall. Greeley's jacket was draped like a tarp over Tess's narrow shoulders.

Rasping like an enraged wounded animal, Hathaway slapped at the floor with his good arm. His feet kicked and his backside raised as he began a clumsy, broken ascent from the floor. Greeley closed a big fist and leaned forward. A mighty crack reverberated down the corridor as he struck the man with a devastating blow to the side of the head. The hollow thudding echo followed instantly as Hathaway's head impacted the floor.

Greeley offered his hand to Tess, who looked at him with tear-filled eyes. "Are you alright?"

She said nothing but allowed him to pull her to her feet. Willy stood on shaky legs, using the wall for support. His eyes pinched as he stooped to examine the unmoving form of the sprawling guard.

"He alive?" Willy said.

Greeley nodded. "He'll need a doctor. Lots of broken bones. He's on something—wasn't going to stop. I didn't have a choice."

Tess appeared to gain her bearings at last. She pulled the dinner jacket tight across her shoulders with a visible shudder. Stepping forward, she heaved back a foot and planted a solid kick to the side of Hathaway's chest. Greeley heard yet another rib snap in response. "Serves him right," she grumbled. "He's been creeping on me for months. I just never thought it would come to this."

She wound up for another kick but seemed to think better of it. Both Willy and Greeley looked at her from beneath arched brows. Hathaway was face down on the cold floor, breathing through bubbles in his bloody drool.

"This might be a problem," Willy said after a long silence. Tess and Greeley just looked at him. "I don't know how Anakasta will take this. One thing I can tell you, this shitehead's boss will defend him." Willy's Scottish baroque was raspy and cold. "Mayhew already doesn't like our friend here," he eyed Tess and motioned to Greeley.

"He was going to rape me," Tess said simply. Her eyes were drying and she

had already regained her composure. It was rare wherewithal, and Greeley was impressed. "Even Mayhew can't overlook that."

"Mayhew?" Greeley said.

"Mayhew is head of security. You think this one's a bastard?" Willy remarked. "Wait till you see Mayhew in action. He'll find a way to blame all of this on Tess. No," he quickly decided. "He's more likely to blame it on you," he said to Greeley. "He already has an axe to grind. Can tell it just by the way he looks at you. He'll say you started the fight. Who knows…might even get Anakasta to believe it. Stranger things happen."

Greeley was skeptical until he saw the indecision in Tess's gaze.

"It's possible," she admitted. "Either way, it's trouble none of us need. We can't risk being sent back to the mainland."

Willy didn't argue. Worse, he nodded in agreement.

Looking back and forth between the two, Greeley couldn't understand what he was hearing. "That man tried to rape you." He was apoplectic. "That can't stand!"

Tess's eyes searched his. There was something she wanted to say, perhaps something she wished to explain, but there was indecision in her gaze. "You don't understand. Neither one of us can afford to be fired. All of us here…we must remain on the island."

"You're worried about your job? That's crazy! Are you—"

"She's right," Willy interrupted with a sad shake of his head. "Besides, looking at this poor sodden mess, he's heading back to the mainland for sure. He won't be a problem for anyone here. I'd say you solved that problem right proper."

Greeley felt his blood boiling. He didn't know what to say.

"The question is," Tess was saying. "How do we explain…" her hand moved back and forth over Hathaway's prone form. "This."

Greeley couldn't believe what he was hearing. He'd worked with some messed up people—worked for some even more messed up people—but even they lived by a code. Something like this was wrong, even for every one of them. He was about to explain as much but was distracted by the curious expression on Tess's face. She was studying the hallway. She seemed to be sizing up the location and position of Hathaway's body.

"He's more or less at the bottom of the stairs," Tess remarked.

Willy looked confused.

"So?" Greeley grunted.

"Move him over a little," she said to Greeley. "Given his condition, no one will doubt he fell down the stairs. The rest of us just walk away."

Greeley felt his blood boil anew. "You would walk away from this? After what he tried to do to you?"

She nodded without hesitation. "He can't stay on the island in this condition. Even the Doc can't work miracles on this. They'll have to send him out with the supply ship. Being removed from the island will be punishment enough. He'll be replaced and never allowed back."

Greeley shook his head. Being expelled from the island hardly seemed like a fitting punishment.

What is it with these people?

Then again, Greeley decided, what was it to him? He needed to keep a low profile, perhaps more than anyone. If Tess wanted to let this go, it was certainly in his best interest.

"Fine," he grunted. He grabbed Hathaway by the back of the collar and belt. Lifting him like a grain sack, he shifted him two feet to the left. Tess studied the positioning and motioned for some fine-tuning. Only then did Greeley place the man gently on the floor once more.

"If anyone starts asking questions, or if Hathaway starts telling stories," Tess said, "I'll tell Doc Cantrell what happened. She's got no patience for this sort of thing. She'll make sure he's sedated until the ship arrives. I'd bet money on it."

Greeley rubbed at the headache forming behind his eyes. What was with these people? Could everyone on the island be this messed up?

Chapter 25

Teeth clamped firmly, the figure charged. The few short yards separating them disappeared instantly as the heft of the rigid black shaft of the flashlight swung back in preparation for a bone-crushing strike. The glow of the lightning strike was unexpected, though it had made the target unmistakable in the otherwise poorly lit bedroom. The lightning flash had cost the element of surprise. The strike must have been within yards of the house because the percussive blast had been immediate and struck like a violent shove to the back.

A blast of light would have blinded the target—how could it not?

Shifting her weight, Keegan closed the last few steps and began to bring the Maglite forward in a cleaving downward swing. Having her back to the light display, she'd been spared the associated blindness. Still, she'd lost Gavin when the room blinked into darkness. In the span of a heartbeat, there was nowhere for him to go. He was where he'd last been because there was no time to flee.

Her grip tightened on the flashlight's bulk as she swung forward and down, propelled by weight and inertia. Time seemed to slow; her heart hammered; the foot-long Maglite split the air with a whoosh.

She understood instantly that she'd failed to connect. Her downward swing continued too far. Her forward charge carried her onward and dangerously off balance. The fraction of a second it took for her to recognize the crushing grip on the wrist of her outstretched arm was an eternity to her confused mind. She stumbled, off balance and clumsy with dizzy momentum, even as the vice-like grip tightened with overwhelming ferocity.

Then she was airborne.

The world spun, her eyes seeing nothing of use in the darkness. Her internal gyroscope registered chaos as her wrist and arm were tugged and wrenched. She sensed her head falling and her feet going high. Then came a spinning sensation. The contents of her stomach bucked with the whirling change of orientation that seemed to last long seconds.

The late-night excursion lost all of the appeal it held only minutes before.

Impacting flat on her back with a bounce, Keegan pinched her eyes against the pain that was sure to follow. But when heartbeats followed and no crushing pain passed across her hips or ran up her spine, she freed the lung full of air trapped in her breast. Her eyes opened to find dim flickers of light at the periphery of the darkness. Both arms were pulled high over her head and clamped together at the wrists. Her legs were pinned. She twisted against the restraint and was surprised to sense a soft pillowy surface beneath her back.

Blinking against dry eyes and darkness, she quickly became aware of the crackly pop accompanying the meager glow at the room's perimeter. A blast of thunder rolled in from the middle distance once more. Her heart raced and a defeated sigh escaped her lips. She suddenly understood what had happened. Her eyes finally adjusted to the waning light, and the face of Gavin Kray materialized above her. He was seated across her legs and leaning over her to pin now numb, outstretched arms to the mattress above her head.

His amused smile materialized in the flickering firelight.

Chapter 26

Sitting atop her, Gavin was careful to keep Keegan restrained. Her slender wrists were clenched in his fist and pinned against the mattress where she'd landed. He'd dodged the swing of the Maglite easily enough, though he'd almost reacted aggressively after the altercation with Garboni earlier in the day. Gavin and Keegan had played these games for over a month, but now a real threat had come to the island. Gavin was about to break his attacker's arm when he recognized a more child-like weight moving against him. Fortunately, he pulled his punch before doing any harm.

He was about to speak and explain what had happened earlier in the day. They needed to stop the ongoing game where she tried to get the drop on him. Then he was struck by the electric excitement dancing in Keegan's green eyes. Her body twisted and strained beneath him. A gasp escaped her throat and her breasts heaved against the sheer fabric of her blouse.

She wore a long-sleeved sweater. The fine threads of its weave strained against her lithe form. It had a daring hem intended to accentuate her bare midriff, and it had been hoisted devilishly higher when he'd pinned her hands above her head. His eyes roamed her body, taking in every detail. The way the firelight danced across pale flesh, the gentle ripple of shadows across her smooth midriff, and the tightly corded flex of each delicate muscle as she strained against him pushed all thoughts of discussion from his mind. She wore a short

123

black skirt that had billowed wide when she'd been airborne and thrown head over heels across the room. Cashmere stockings started at shoeless feet and ended just above her knees.

She bucked and twisted beneath him once more, but it was clear she wasn't trying to escape. Her eyes were wide and hungry. It was a gaze desperate to draw him closer in a way impossible while physically restrained. Another lance of lightning filled the room, followed by a rolling cacophony of thunder that seemed to reel from one end of the island to the other.

Gavin's eyes roamed her body again, and he saw her lips move. He could hear little over the thunder of his own heartbeat. The fingers of his free hand danced gently over the exposed flesh at the base of her ribs. Electricity passed between their bodies. Her skin felt feverish beneath the pads of his fingers.

This was crazy, he reminded himself. There was a corpse laying out there in the woods. He needed to dispose of it before the drones launched and Stanton Anakasta was given a reason to start asking impossible questions. Gavin had been with Keegan for only a short time...she was well aware of his past. She knew he'd come to the island to lay low and hide from people who would kill him, or worse. He had a short window of opportunity to dispose of Garboni.

There was no time for...this.

Gavin's analytical mind had already weighed in. There was only one foolproof way to dispose of Garboni, and he would need Keegan's help to pull it off. Every minute counted. Worse yet, he would have to share what he knew of the strange cave at the top of the mountain to do it. That meant breaking a portion of his promise to Fowler. For the moment, at least, there was no perfect solution.

The drones were the immediate problem, Gavin knew. They were one of Stanton Anakasta's many secrets. Without fail, they launched nightly after everyone on the island had turned in. The autonomous octocopters conducted an ongoing search of the island. What they were searching for, Gavin had yet to determine. The odds were in his favor for the moment. There were thousands of square acres to search and only four drones in Anakasta's arsenal.

Gavin had never been a gambling man. That meant the chances of the drones stumbling on Garboni were still too high. It was vital to dispose of the corpse before the automated sentries went operational for the night.

"Are you kidding me?" Keegan said at last, her voice a hoarse whisper. Piercing eyes flashed with fiery determination. "What the hell are you waiting

for?"

His gaze moved across Keegan's form once more. She bit anxiously at the corner of a pouting lip, her eyes pleading in a way that made him want to taste her. Her body twisted and wiggled; he realized he was already hard—Jesus, how could he not be? His grip on her wrists slipped and one of her hands suddenly broke free. It lashed out, grabbed him by the shirt collar and pulled him to her. Their lips met, her tongue thrust across his in a dance that sent fire across his spine. She arched her back, pressing the fullness of her breasts firmly against him with a conviction that ensured there was no turning back.

Their lips mashed and their tongues clashed. All the while, a small voice was fighting to be heard in the back of Gavin's mind. The body... they had to dispose of the body. He'd been forced to leave Garboni out there in the woods. If he didn't get rid of the corpse quickly, the Outfit wouldn't be the only one putting a price on his head.

"Alright," Gavin said, pulling himself back from Keegan's embrace. He was out of breath and still unsure of what to say. She had a way of erasing all concerns from his mind. Right now that could get him killed. It could get them both killed. "Let's slow this down. We have to talk."

A pert smile stretched her lips, and he saw an amused flicker dance in her eyes. A single slender finger rose. She wet her lips with a slow, sensual, snake-like lick. Then she placed her finger against them in a silencing gesture. At the same time, the thumb and forefinger of her other hand pinched at the tiny teardrop zipper of her sweater and began to pull. The sweater had a high neck, clinging to her breasts and throat in a nearly skintight fit. The zipper was delicate and indistinguishable in the fabric's weave until she freed the clasp from where it was secured beneath her chin. In one smooth, agonizingly slow motion, the zipper passed down the length of her long slender neck, over her clavicle, and between her breasts. As the zipper parted, porcelain white skin showed in the dancing flicker of the firelight.

Reaching the end of its run at the base of her sternum, the fabric fell away with only a tiny ticking pop as the strain on the mechanism was relieved.

"If you want me to beg," she said in the ghost of a whisper, "it's not a problem." A devious smile parted pouting lips. "But you'll be on your knees before we're through. I promise you that."

His fingers caressed the smooth cashmere fabric of her stocking just above her right knee. Just beyond it he felt the warm, impossibly smooth texture of her bare flesh. His fingers moved slowly up the outside of her leg, pulling up what little remained of her black skirt as he reached her backside. His thumb moved up the outside of her hip, and he took her backside in his palm. This confirmed his suspicion—there were no panties. With her petite frame, half of her bottom fit perfectly into the palm of his hand. It was one of the many wonders of her body that never failed to make him physically ache. He gave her a firm squeeze and felt his erection quiver in response. A throaty gasp choked from deep within Keegan at the same time.

A moment later, her free hand moved decisively again. This time it shoved harshly at his chest and pushed him back. He rocked backward onto his knees. Her hands snapped into action, unbuckling his belt with whiplash-inducing speed and agility. She took down his zipper with a snap healthy enough to pull start a lawnmower or chainsaw. And then he felt both hands encircle him. She squeezed, and he could hear the thunder of his own heartbeat in his ears. Her eyes were locked on his—a look that made it clear that no more delay would be tolerated. It was now or never. He pushed his jeans lower on his hips, and she pulled him to her.

Chapter 27

Lower Manhattan

New York State

Three months ago

Gavin followed the liveried butler through the richly appointed apartment and a doorway in the far wall. The dour-faced man then motioned for him to continue by himself. Brooks Fowler rose slowly from behind the wide mahogany desk. It was all Gavin could do not to recoil at the sight of the man. Hunched and limping, his hairline had been reduced to a little more than a pair of bushy gray sideburns. Dry, parchment-like flesh blemished with liver spots covered his face and hands. His eyes were hooded, and one corner of his mouth drooped slightly as he offered what had once been a kind and warm smile.

"Old beyond my years," Fowler said with a hoarse chuckle. He finished rounding the desk and offered a quivering hand. His grip was weak, and Gavin could feel every skeletal bone.

His mind searching for an explanation, Gavin opened his mouth to speak. No words came. Fowler was in his mid-fifties. It was a fact unreconcilable with *the man standing before him—a man who had to be pushing one hundred. He was a man who appeared to have one foot already in the grave. Gavin knew Fowler was sick; it was his reason for abruptly leaving the island. But this? What sort of illness did this to a man?*

"Fifty-two," Fowler said with a nod and what might have been a self-deprecating grin. "You were trying to recall my age? I'm fifty-two." He raised two frail, insect-like arms halfway in the air as if to prove the point. The effort caused him to wince, and he quickly lowered his hands. Gavin noticed the cane clutched in a white-knuckled grip for the first time.

Fowler had vacated the island weeks earlier via emergency medivac helicopter. He'd been flown to a ship fifteen miles off their shore, then according to Doc Cantrell, he'd been taken to a facility not far from the Oregon coast. Since the island's sickbay was state of the art and equipped to deal with anything short of organ transplant, whatever had forced Fowler's evacuation must have been serious. Until now, if anyone knew the man's true condition, they hadn't been talking.

"Judging by your reaction," Fowler began, "I take it Doctor Cantrell has been true to her word? She has remained silent as far as my condition is concerned?"

Not knowing what to say, Gavin walked slowly to the massive floor-to-ceiling windows covering the entire north wall of the room. He had a unique view of the historic Kronenburg Museum. It faced him from across four lanes of traffic. At twelve stories tall, he looked down on it from Fowler's home on the fifteenth floor. A crisscross of thick aluminum pipes formed a framework across at least eleven stories of the structure. The building's black and white marble finish looked freshly laid, though Gavin knew the museum to be one of Manhattan's oldest privately funded institutions.

"They cleaned it up well," Fowler said. He stopped several paces behind Gavin. "Six years of effort and twenty-seven million dollars spent, to date."

Gavin's stunned expression caused Fowler to chuckle. It had a wheezing quality. "Superior stonework stands the test of time, but nothing lasts forever. Patching was required; large portions needed to be resurfaced," he paused, and his tone became more conspiratorial. "And while it's not for public knowledge, they had to replace three large sections of the facade." He shook his head in disappointment. "Far too much pride in the Kronenburg lineage. They somehow believe that knowledge of this would blemish the family reputation."

Gavin laughed. "Family reputation? Wasn't it one of the Kronenburg girls

128

with that sex tape scandal last year? Something about a suitcase full of coke and a couple of guys dressed as Muppets?"

Fowler shook his head and somehow managed to pale even more. "I abhor tabloid gossip." He waved a hand, then paused as if thinking better of what he was about to say. "And I recall being told it was cocaine and three chaps dressed as characters from something called…anime?"

Gavin laughed. Color touched Fowler's cheeks for the first time and Gavin finally saw a flicker of amusement in the old man's eyes.

Gavin nodded, not knowing what to say next and wanting to know why he'd been summoned across the planet to this place. He eyed a pair of sofas arranged in parallel around a glass coffee table. "Why don't we sit?"

Fowler turned a milky eye in the direction of the furniture and offered the slightest of nods. He set out in short, shuffling steps. Gavin didn't know whether to help or stay out of the way. The shock of seeing his friend in such a state made the decision for him as Fowler reached the furthest sofa before Gavin could reach a conclusion. Fowler turned and lowered himself into the seat at the end of the couch with an audible wheeze.

Gavin slipped into the seat across from the old man and said, "I'm sorry, Brooks. I knew you were doing poorly, but this is…well, it's unexpected."

It took Fowler more than a minute to regain his breath. In that time, he studied Gavin. "You're not the only one at a loss for words," he said finally. "My doctors are equally flummoxed. Never seen anything like it. They think it's some unique form of progeria."

Gavin winced. The diagnosis was troubling on multiple levels. "I read something on that once. It's supposed to be a genetic condition unique to children, as I recall. Rapid onset aging." He left out that it was a fatal genetic condition. That writing was on the wall.

Fowler arched what was left of his thinning eyebrows. "You never cease to impress me, my boy. Entirely correct. And you hit upon the crux of the problem. The damned doctors haven't a clue what they're talking about because they're dealing with something unknown to medicine."

"Then you know what this is?" There was hope in Gavin's tone. If Fowler knew what was happening, perhaps there was a way to mitigate the disastrous effects.

Fowler responded with a crisp nod. "Did it to myself, I'm afraid."

Gavin said nothing.

"Entirely unintentional, I assure you," Fowler went on. "But there's no denying the results. Just look at me."

Dozens of questions flooded Gavin's mind. His eyes roamed the frail form before him, and the list grew. He opened his mouth to speak, but Fowler cut him off.

"It's the island," Fowler said. "By now, you must know it's an extraordinary place."

The way Fowler said extraordinary concerned Gavin. It was as if a bell had rung in his mind, racing his pulse. The island had been his refuge, a sanctuary where the world couldn't reach him. But hearing this described now in such a way, with that tone, was like awakening some new sense to the place. His eyes narrowed and his tone became concerned. "Special?"

"You've noticed it, haven't you? Perhaps not overtly...it impacts your senses in very subtle ways. Some seem more in tune, perhaps more receptive to it."

Gavin slowly shook his head. "I don't know what you mean." But that wasn't entirely true. Now that the words had been spoken, he felt he knew something. He just wasn't sure what.

"I paid thirty-two million dollars for that chunk of earth and rock," Fowler explained. "That's nothing compared to what it cost to renovate the monastery and bring infrastructure to that remote corner of the world. Everything needed to be shipped in, literally shipped. That includes the manpower necessary to perform the work. The project cost me just over seventy-eight million by the time I moved my home to the island."

Fowler leaned forward and placed both palms atop his cane. His good eye seemed to narrow on Gavin. "That's a lot of money, even to me. I wasn't throwing it all away, don't you know? What do you suppose made that remote, godforsaken rock such a worthy investment?"

Seventy-eight million dollars.

The number might as well have hung in the air before Gavin's eyes. It was a figure so vast he couldn't place it in perspective. How could that kind of investment generate a worthwhile return? Placing it in the context of what he already knew of the island, it didn't make sense. No mining was taking place, and the chunk of land had no historical significance to his knowledge.

Gavin shook his head. "I have no idea."

"That portion of land is one of the oldest on the surface of the planet," Fowler explained. "Most islands of its size, located in relatively similar regions of the world, are volcanic in nature. They form as the result of volcanic activity beneath the sea. Our Black Rock is unique because it is part of a land mass that's tens of millions—possibly hundreds of millions—of years old.

"While the rest of the planet suffered worldwide upheaval: earthquakes, tsunamis, the global tectonic plates shifting, polar reversals, and continental drift, Black Rock remained unblemished. As far as I've ascertained, every other portion of the earth's crust has buckled, shifted, risen, and fallen beneath other layers of earth or ocean. All except for our little island in the middle of nowhere."

His mind reeled at the concept of millions of years of planetary change; Gavin wondered if the old man's mind was now failing along with his body. It seemed the more logical answer. The science required to prove or disprove the claim was undoubtedly beyond Gavin, but he supposed a man of Fowler's means could pay to gather the necessary proof. Still, to what end?

"I'm not the cat with the sharpest claws," Gavin admitted. "But how does that make the island valuable?" The island might prove valuable for scientific research if the claim proved accurate. But then why spend tens of millions rebuilding an ancient burned-out citadel, and why turn it into a home?

"Black Rock has unique properties," Fowler said after a long pause. He leaned back in his seat and took a slow, contemplative breath. "You've heard the myth about the fountain of youth?"

Gavin barked a laugh. The absurdity of the comment caught him off guard, and the exclamation escaped him before he'd had a chance to process the thought. At least now the conversation was starting to make sense. Fowler's mind was at least as poor as his physical condition. If he chased fairy tales, he would destroy his vast fortune before this strange disease finally did him in.

"I apologize," Gavin offered quickly. "I didn't—"

Waving a weak dismissive hand, Fowler said, "not at all. You'd be a fool to take my words at face value. Surely, I sound like a nut. And in my current condition? You must be thinking my mind is worse off than my body." His smile was sad but genuine. "You're a wise young man, Gavin. Wise in the ways of the world with experience in things most of us could never begin to imagine. You've come a long way since Salem, and you survived the streets of

Atlantic City. It's also why you're here today."

Gavin shot forward in his seat, his eyes narrowed, and his fists balled where they sat on his knees. Fowler wasn't supposed to know about Atlantic City, and no man alive knew about Salem. His gaze flashed to the closed office door, expecting it to burst open at any second. He ground his teeth and took a breath. Atlantic City wasn't the real threat here. If Fowler knew about Salem, his problems were much more significant.

"No one is coming for you," Fowler said quietly. The disappointment was evident in his tone. "You're safe here with me, my boy. I've known about both since you first appeared on the island. I knew you were coming. You have nothing to fear."

Though he slowly opened his palms to lay them flat on his knees, Gavin did not sit back or relax. He eyed the old man with palpable suspicion. "What do you know about Salem?"

"Time is short," Fowler said. "As you can see looking at me, my time is shorter than most. My deterioration can be stopped, but only with your help. I have—and will continue to—keep your secrets. In exchange, I will share mine and ask that you do the same."

Gavin eased himself back on the sofa. His senses were now tingling and at full alert. Every muscle in his body felt coiled and ready to respond to a threat he couldn't identify. His rational mind sensed danger all around. Another part of his mind found truth in the old man's words and wanted to hear more.

"The island has a new owner," Fowler explained. "A man named Stanton Anakasta has purchased the property from me. He will be taking possession in approximately two weeks."

Gavin's heart fell. His sanctuary was no more. The admission that Fowler knew of his past had made this likely, but the island under new ownership made the need to relocate a certainty. He realized for the first time he'd been too lax in his precautions as no fallback plan was in place.

Fowler raised a restraining hand. "Mister Anakasta has agreed to keep the entirety of the island's staff on under his employ, except for Mister Epps. It seems Jasper was convicted in his late teens, and Mister Anakasta's security detail is unwilling to overlook the transgression."

Relief mixed with concern as Gavin processed the new information. Jasper Epps was a decent guy. A few years older than Gavin, he didn't have a violent bone in his body. He liked to smoke weed. It was likely related to the arrest in his past. But if this Anakasta guy was protected by private security thorough enough to find Epps's conviction, why would they keep any of the staff on? A professional security team would be far more likely to start fresh with an entirely new workforce. "Why would Anakasta keep any of us?"

"Before we get to that, I want to warn you. I'm not entirely sure what to make of the man. I don't mean to speak poorly of anyone, but I make it a point to look out for my people above all else. With that in mind, I had Stanton Anakasta researched. It seems he was virtually penniless until a few years back. Then out of nowhere, his wealth skyrocketed. There was no obvious catalyst for his financial good fortune, and such turns make me weary. That said, I made the deal because I could get him to keep all of you on.

"To your question, keeping the staff appeals to him for three reasons. First, I have vouched for all of you, saying you're highly skilled and well-suited for work in the environment. Second, I may have exaggerated how difficult it is to locate staff willing to work in such a remote and solitary location. And third, I was entirely honest when I explained how trying it is to get a skilled staff to stay at said remote location for protracted periods."

Gavin grinned. "All of that to save our jobs?"

Fowler took on a grave expression. "All that to protect my friends and potentially save them from my fate." His tone was dry and serious. "Did you ever wonder what keeps talented people like Dale, Bill, Tess, or Jennifer at a place like Black Rock? All of the others? They have a unique motivation to stay."

In his idle time, Gavin had considered the motivations of everyone on the island. Admittedly, he'd spent time musing over some more than others. But in the end he'd assumed that, like him, each had been searching for a quiet, simple, uncomplicated existence. He simply shrugged in response.

"Tess Lindow was diagnosed with stage three leukemia shortly before coming to the island," Fowler explained. "Bill Anders had a rare form of inoperable brain cancer. Doctor Cantrell was suffering from a lesion...well, the complexities of the doctor's condition are beyond my ability to explain. Sufficed to say, she was paraplegic and bound to a wheelchair. There was no known course of treatment."

Gavin raised a hand. "Just a second. What are you talking about? I've known these people for the better part of a year, and I've never seen them suffer from so much as a cold. Not one of them is being treated for a serious medical condition. And Doc Cantrell sure isn't stuck in a wheelchair."

A grin spread across Fowler's face. It managed to subvert his deformities. In it, Gavin finally saw a flicker of the man he'd known only a few short weeks before. "Precisely!" Fowler laughed. "Within days of reaching the island, each case showed rapid improvement. No matter how incurable or permanent, every case miraculously and spontaneously began to improve."

Gavin asked the only question that mattered, given the claim. "How?"

Fowler shrugged. "Unknown. But it's something unique to the island. I've tried to figure that out since I first set foot on the ancient rock." His expression soured. "And it's that search that led to my current condition."

"Returning to the island can't cure you?" Gavin couldn't believe he was asking the question. That he was willing to contemplate the wild claim was a form of insanity all its own.

"I'm paying this price because I took something from the island."

Gavin felt his mouth go dry. More questions flooded his mind.

"There's a small box on my desk," Fowler said. "Fetch it for me?"

His mind still spinning, Gavin quickly crossed the room. A small, 4x6-inch box was one of the few objects on the surface of Fowler's sprawling desktop. The wood was old and dark, burnished with a patina that looked generations in the making. Two delicate hinges were visible along the lid's back edge, and a fragile brass latch secured the front. Returning to the couch, Gavin handed it to Fowler.

Fowler lay the box atop his knobby knees and motioned for Gavin to sit on the coffee table. "The box is an antique, entirely unrelated to what's inside," he explained. Releasing the clasp and flipping back the lid, Fowler revealed the box's crushed velvet interior. A cutout had been made. Into it was placed a long, thin silver tube.

"The container is titanium," Fowler said. "This must be returned to the island. And this is vital—the tube cannot be opened until you return to where the sample was gathered."

Gavin studied the titanium cylinder, though he did not reach out to touch it. "What's in it? Is it dangerous?"

"Inside is a glass vial that contains the sample itself. The sample is a substance of which I know precious little. I fell ill shortly after removing it from the mountain. I left the island in hopes of improving my condition.

Unfortunately, it seems that was a mistake. I haven't had an opportunity to study the material. At this point, I fear my only chance at salvation is returning it to Black Rock."

"Wait, you said, the mountain. What does that mean?"

"I spent years searching the island for the key to its remarkable healing properties. I finally found something wondrous and terrifying, near the top of the mountain. I'm still not sure how I gained access to the cave. You'll have a challenge figuring that part out for yourself. I wish I could offer some advice, but I'm afraid I recall little of the day I collected...this."

Eyeing the vile with growing suspicion, Gavin considered what he'd just heard. "You collected this substance at the top of the mountain and want me to take it back. You think that will heal you?"

This time Fowler shrugged. "Heal me? Who can say. Honestly? I hope my rapidly deteriorating condition ceases. After that? I have no idea. But something must be done. At this rate, I'll be lucky to see the month's end."

Considering the man before him, Gavin found truth in the statement. The Fowler before him wasn't even a shadow of the man who'd been airlifted from the island weeks earlier.

"Ok," Gavin said. "How do I do it?" A fiery determination was already stirring in his belly. If there were a chance to help the old man, he would do what he could.

Fowler smiled, relief glistening in dewy eyes. "First, don't open the titanium outer container until you've found your way into the cavern. Once you do, and once inside, open this. You'll find a glass vial containing an iridescent green gel. Don't let the gel come in contact with anything. Nothing at all," he cautioned. "The glass containing the substance is the only thing I've found that it can't consume."

"Consume?"

Nodding, Fowler said, "precisely what it does or how it does it, I never discovered. It either burns other materials like acid or consumes them like a parasite. I have no idea what the substance is or what it's comprised of. Letting it touch your skin would most certainly be fatal.

"Once you're done, drop the titanium tube in the green pool and dispose of the glass vial in the sea. The green substance doesn't leave a residue, so once it's out of the vial, it will be safe to dispose of the glass. Dropping it in the sea just seems a prudent safety precaution."

"Wait, what do you mean pool? You're saying there's more of the toxic green stuff?"

Fowler nodded. "Can't say that it's toxic, but yeah. There's more. A fair amount of it. That's why I didn't think it would hurt to take a sample." He raised a feeble hand of cracking, weathered flesh. "Biggest mistake of my life."

Closing the box, Fowler latched the clasp and handed it to Gavin. Sitting back on the sofa once more, the man looked exhausted. "Just a couple more things." His voice was equally dry and weak. He pulled a folded white paper from the breast pocket of his cardigan. "This map explains how to find the cavern near the top of Black Rock. Once you've returned the material, destroy the map. Never go back to the cavern. It's not worth the risk of becoming like me." He looked slowly around the room. "There's a book over there on the credenza. You'll need that as well. The island has a wealth of strange history. Much of it has been lost...some has already resurfaced. I fear more will soon come to light. Just remember Salem and keep an open mind. The world is a far stranger place than most of us have ever had reason to believe."

Gavin collected the book from the counter. It was a thick, battered old volume bound in leather and wound closed by a leather thong. A strange symbol was carved into the thick hide of the cover, along with the title, The Personal Journal of Fenton Bitters.

Fowler broke into a rattling cough that seemed ready to shatter the man's frail frame. Gavin sat beside him and waited for the fit to subside. Finally, Fowler spoke. "One last thing before my jet takes you back." Gavin knew Fowler's jet was waiting to return him to the west coast of the United States. From there he would board a ship specially chartered to take him back to Black Rock island. Looking at the remains of the once vital man before him, he only hoped he would arrive in time. "You need to understand why the island has remained largely untouched for millennia. It holds another secret—one which makes it nearly impossible to find unless one knows where and just how to look for it."

Chapter 28

Greeley pushed through the double doors of the infirmary. The defused white glow of the sterile medical facility was calming. It distracted from the way it was situated in tight quarters. Nonetheless, it was immediately apparent that it lacked little when it came to the latest technical hardware. A pair of hospital beds sat in stalls at the back of the room, each surrounded by more high-tech gear than he'd seen outside a science fiction movie. A massive flat panel display hung on the wall beside each bed, and some expensive-looking contraption hung on an articulated arm over each pillow.

Only one of the beds was occupied now, and it was the patient he'd come to see. Tess Lindow lay in a semi-reclined position on the left of the two patient bays, the lights around her turned low. A blood pressure cuff was secured around one arm, and a bag of saline hung from a stand at the head of the bed. Her eyes drooped, suggesting she'd been sedated.

"You must be Mister Greeley?" a quiet voice said from a room to the left. "I'm Sydney Cantrell." The woman offered a hand as she entered the room. "Most folks just call me Doc."

She was in her early thirties, if Greeley had to guess. Her long blonde hair was pulled back in a ponytail; it was so blonde, it was more accurate to call it white. Her skin was equally pale, in contrast to ruby red lips. She wore no *makeup that he could see. Cantrell flashed a bright, friendly smile set off by the most dazzling pair of blue eyes Greeley had ever seen. The thick black frames of her glasses did little to hamper her attractiveness. If anything, they only made her appear more scholarly. At nearly six feet in height, her medical scrubs did little to hide what was obviously a fantastic figure.*

Greeley made a mental note to ask who'd done the hiring for this place. It was more like casting for a Hollywood film. He grinned and shook the offered hand. "Nice to meet you, Doc. I wanted to check on Tess. She's had a rough night."

Doctor Cantrell raised and consulted an e-tablet. Tapping several times on the screen, she gave a confirming nod. "Vitals are good, and the inflammation in her trachea is down. From what I understand, she'd be in much worse shape if not for you."

Greeley's lack of comprehension must have been visible on his face.

Cantrell smiled. "Tess told me what happened, and Willy was in to tell me the story we can't share with Mayhew. Speaking of which, I understand we have you to thank for this?"

She motioned to a closed curtain on the far side of the room. Greeley followed as she pulled back a slit in the fabric and stepped through. Tom Hathaway was laid out flat on his back with a brace around his neck and a temporary inflatable cast around both arms and one leg. A jumble of intravenous drips was suspended from both corners at the head of the bed, the bags feeding a series of tubes disappearing beneath the inflated rigs on each arm. Both eyes were black with deep tissue bruising, and his nose was splinted.

"Numerous broken bones and one dilly of a hematoma," Cantrell offered with surprising levity. "Sounds like he got off easy from what I've been told."

Seeing the lack of concern in the doctor's expression, the weight on Greeley's shoulders lifted. The doc must have noticed as much because she gave him a light punch on the shoulder as if to say, attaboy! She tipped her head toward the main room and led him back through the curtain.

"Tess and Willy explained their concerns," Cantrell said. "I'll keep Hathaway sedated until the supply ship arrives. By the time he wakes up, he'll be halfway back to the mainland. Hell, given the concussion he's nursing, I might not have to fudge the numbers. A medically induced coma might be just what the doctor ordered." She met his eye. "You don't believe in half measures, do you?"

Greeley shrugged. "It was him or me."

"So they said. I've never cared for these security folks. More trouble than their worth, if you ask me. Never had these troubles working for Mister Fowler."

Cantrell's e-tablet chimed and she raised it once more. Her brow furrowed in response. Rapid tapping ensued. It became instantly evident to Greeley that something was wrong. Cantrell began muttering under her breath and tapping more aggressively on the screen.

"Something I can help with?" Greeley offered.

She was chewing at the corner of her lip. It was an attractive trait. Still, Greeley found his mind drifting back to Tess. He wanted to check on her. He needed to know how she was doing after the attack.

Cantrell looked up and blanched. It was as if she'd forgotten he was there. "Sorry," she muttered. "Just got blood work back on our friend in there," she nodded to Hathaway's bed. "Some of these numbers are off the chart. Hormone levels that just don't make sense."

"Is the machine busted?"

The doctor stopped tapping and slowly looked up at Greeley. She seemed to be considering the concept. She shook her head. "No, I ran a full battery of diagnostic tests to rule that out." She was saying the words, but she didn't appear convinced. "But maybe you can help. Do you mind giving blood?"

Stomach-churning at the thought, Greeley took an instinctive step backward in response. He hated needles with a passion. There weren't many things he feared, but the idea of drawing blood made his insides feel like bubbling liquid.

"Afraid of needles?" the doctor said matter-of-factly.

Greeley's forehead wrinkled. "I wouldn't say afraid."

Backpedaling to the open bed beside Tess, the doctor said, "here's the thing. I've been getting some really weird values in the blood work from an alarming number of people. At first, the numbers were just a little off, but in time they started to skew more and more. Weirder still, it's not everyone on the island. Some folks are entirely normal. I've been trying to sort this out. I need to know what I'm dealing with before it gets serious. It could be environmental, biological, or…" her voice trailed off. "Let's just say I don't know what I don't know. That's where you can help. You just arrived. You're the neutral base I *need for my comparison."*

Greeley's stomach churned audibly, and his expression darkened.

The doc waved a calming hand. "It's just a little blood. A big strong guy like you can't be that sensitive to needles, can you?" While she spoke, she pulled vial after vial out of the cabinet on the wall.

His stomach gurgled again.

The doctor shoved a wheeled stool in his direction with her foot. "Have a seat. This will take two minutes." She followed his eyes to the small pile of containers stacked on the bed. "Sorry," she said with a wince. "I'm also testing hormone levels so I'll need a little more than you're probably used to giving."

Chapter 29

Blinking sleep from her eyes, Doctor Sydney Cantrell sat upright with a start. Her heart was racing. Thunder crashed in the distance. The infirmary had no windows, so she had little insight into the storm raging outside. She turned and eased her legs over the side of the long-reclined chair normally used for dental examinations. The buzz and chirp of medical equipment could be heard in the primary medical bays next door. She sighed and tucked a lock of stark blonde hair behind an ear.

A moment later, the sights and sounds of the dimly lit room were entirely forgotten. A clouded expression passed across usually cheerful and expressive eyes. It was as if a cloak of detachment had settled over her only seconds after waking. She stepped past the shoes she'd discarded in preparation for a brief catnap and crossed the cold tile floor past the bureau. The thick black-framed glasses, necessary for seeing anything more than a few feet away, were entirely forgotten. She retrieved a thick candle from a nearby cabinet and fished a small box of matches from the back of a nearby drawer. Her actions were slow and mechanical as she struck a match and set each of the candle's three wicks alight. A moment later, the antiseptic walls of the infirmary danced with shadows cast by the flickering flames.

With the light in hand, Cantrell passed silently through the primary medical bay and into the hallway beyond. Her pace was slow and purposeful, traversing one corridor after another as she moved into the citadel's depths. Other lights merged with her at the ends of hallways or the intersections of corridors. Other silent, similarly robotic figures fell into formation behind her without uttering a word. The deeper she went into the structure, the colder the stone floor beneath her delicate bare feet became. She didn't speed her pace or even seem to notice.

Five minutes later, she crossed the intersection of a pair of wide hallways in the bowels of the basement. Thirty yards later, the path doglegged to the right. A vast storeroom with a low ceiling was awash in cobwebs. There were piles of provisions draped in ancient-looking sheets thick with accumulated dust. A narrow path zigzagged between the haphazardly arranged piles of castoff furniture, tools, and ancient equipment. A tall, wide antique mirror was among the collection of forgotten, eclectic artifacts. It was framed in an exotic, ancient natural wood and suspended from a base made of the same material. The sheet that had once protected the beautiful old antique lay crumpled and covered in dust at its base. Cantrell took no heed of anachronism. The flames of her candle danced as she navigated the treacherous pathway with practiced ease. The short procession of silent, blank faces followed at an unhurried pace.

The back wall of the room was draped with an ancient tapestry. The design of its stitching was impossible to distinguish in the meager light, but it hung from a massive iron rod bolted to the face of the stone block wall. Setting the candle atop a tall wooden barrel, Cantrell pulled back a corner of the hanging tapestry. The rough stone block wall was marked with a glyph. The sigil, a little larger than a dinner plate, was etched deeply into the dark stone of the wall just below eye level. It was a thick wavy line suspended atop a fist-sized circle. The line and the circle were a fathomless pitch-black set in shocking relief against the gray hews of natural stone.

Turning to the figure behind her, Cantrell raised the palm of her free hand. The shadowy form standing there slowly drew a sharp crude implement across her flesh. Turning again, Cantrell placed the same outstretched palm against the shape etched in the wall's surface. Blood from her palm squished audibly as she applied pressure. A long second passed, then a portion of the wall vaporized silently beneath her touch. Black sand particles washed across her bare feet as a ten-foot diameter opening in the form of a perfect circle appeared in the wall. Offering no reaction, Cantrell collected the candle once more and stepped across the threshold. The thick tapestry behind her bucked and thunked quietly as the procession moved to follow through the portal.

Traversing a short corridor, Cantrell entered a wide circular chamber. A pair of burning torches hung in wall sconces at the three and six o'clock positions on the perfectly curved brick wall. A vaulted ceiling of intricate stonework rose thirty feet overhead. The procession at Cantrell's back spread out, nearly a dozen people crowding the room. All wore the same blank expression, stood silent and near motionless, and were in various similar states of undress. Most looked as if they'd risen directly from bed. Cantrell seemed to be one of three still on the clock as she and two representatives from Anakasta's security detail were the only ones fully dressed.

Cantrell paid the group no attention as she moved to the center of the room where a circular dais stood perhaps three feet above the stone floor. The platform was no more than four feet in diameter and was assembled from a dark, ancient-looking timber. The planks were unevenly spaced, and several were entirely missing along the edge close to the gathering. Had anyone looked, the darkness of the well below would have been a yawning abyss.

As one, the group knelt before the platform and the well beneath it. A figure ascended a short set of stairs at the back of the platform. The lithe nude form of a petite woman walked uncaring across the rickety old planks. She stopped at the center of the platform and seemed to consider the group. Her features were indistinct, cloaked in the dancing shadows produced by the torches at either end of the chamber. Long light-colored hair cascaded down her back, shoulders, and breasts. Thick locks hung haphazardly across her face, further cloaking her appearance.

All heads in the room bowed in unison. Unbidden, a low tone emanated from the group as if they were one. The tone grew in volume until it reverberated through the confines of the circular space. Echoing for long seconds, the group shifted suddenly as one into a low, whisper-like crescendo. Though their words were unintelligible, every assembly member was perfectly synchronized in tone and modulation.

Cantrell's downturned gaze never shifted. If it had, she might have noticed a spectral green flash emanating from the depths of the well.

Chapter 30

After surveying the group for several long minutes, the naked figure stepped from the front edge of the platform. Her bare feet silently impacted the stone floor. She turned with a flourish that sent her long silky hair billowing. The move lacked the numb, mechanical precision the rest of the group displayed. Pale, flawless skin was briefly visible in the torchlight before being consumed by shadow once more. Seizing the narrow plank at the front of the small platform, she tossed it aside. A second board quickly followed, uncovering the cavernous space beneath. It was an ancient well, its smooth stone walls visible only to a depth of a few feet before being consumed by darkness.

She stared into the abyss, the sound of the group chanting while her eyes searched the darkness. Her vigilance paid off. A flickering green glow, little more than the light of a single candle flashed to light deep from the darkness. She raised her hands to the ceiling, threw back her head, and howled like a feral animal.

All faces rose to the figure as she stood on the last solid plank suspended over the mouth of the well. She turned to the congregation. In one hand she held a dagger, its sharp pointed blade of silver flashing in the guttering light. A new, guttural, and equally unintelligible chant slipped from her lips. As one, the group took up the mantra. The long verse was completed and then repeated. On the third chorus, the figure jumped from the stone wall's lip. She turned to the pit and lay her elbow across the edge of the well. Her empty hand extended over the abyss as if in offering. Without hesitation, she raked the dagger's tip down the length of her arm, rending flesh and slashing vein and artery alike. Blood blossomed from her body and poured silently into the depths and the tiny green glow.

For several long seconds, nothing happened. The group at the figure's back continued to chant the same unintelligible murmur, and blood flowed freely from the leader's arterial breach. Then the pinprick of light from the depths blossomed. Through thick locks of hair, the figure watched the specks pivot and dance as they ascended the vertical stone shaft. Clearing the mouth of the well, the phenomenon came more clearly into view. It looked like motes of dust caught in the breeze and forced through radiant green moonlight, only these moved in erratic directions as if they had a life of their own. They shimmered as if lit from within. The tiny specs glowed like fireflies, though each was no larger than a grain of sand. At first there was only a handful of drifting flickers, but as more blood was sacrificed to the well, more tiny embers began to ascend.

The figure stood stoic and silent until the flow began to slow. A physical shuddering gripped her legs. Seconds later, her knees buckled. Slapping a fist on the side of the well, the dagger still in hand, she braced herself to remain standing. As if in a show of reluctance, she slowly raised her damaged limb. Pointing it to the apex of the arched stone ceiling, she placed the dagger on the side of the well and limped away on weak legs. Cantrell was already on her feet and moving to fill the figure's position. She lowered her left arm over the pit and took up the blade in her right.

The nude figure watched while, one after another, those present sacrificed what they could. The Rising was close at hand. Their work would be instrumental. The blood on her damaged arm was already drying; it had become tacky and thick. Slapping the palm of her good hand at the crook of her elbow, she applied pressure and wiped the dark substance down the length of her arm.

The skin of her damaged limb had entirely healed. A tight smile played at the corners of her lips, and a new chant sprang forth in a whisper.

Chapter 31

A brief flicker of light caught Greeley's attention. It pulled him from the edge of sleep. The low buzz, hiss, and occasional chirp from nearby medical equipment immediately reminded him where he lay. Raising his head, the low after-hours light of the infirmary came into view. Tess lay supine atop a bed in the observation bay to his right. She was still hooked to an IV drip and appeared to be sleeping comfortably. The louvered accordion-like wall separating the two stalls had been retracted, allowing them to share the space.

Another flicker of light danced across the ceiling and he instantly understood what had awoken him. He rocked silently onto an elbow and looked out over the foot of the bed. Doctor Cantrell had just slipped from a doorway at the room's periphery. Oddly, she held a thick candle even though the room's after-hours lights were enough to move freely. There was something off about her movement too. Each step was slow and methodical, yet somehow unnatural. She looked like a puppet being guided by the hand of a puppeteer still learning his craft. As she turned for the exit, he noticed the socks on her feet. She had no shoes. Or glasses, he realized with growing curiosity. Recalling the thick-framed glasses supporting the equally thick lenses when he first met the woman a few short hours before, it seemed unlikely she had the visual acuity to go long without corrective eyewear.

Interest piqued, he slipped soundlessly from the bed and moved to follow.

Pushing through the double doors at the entrance to the infirmary, he moved with exaggerated slowness. These doors tended to thump when they wobbled back and forth on self-closing hinges. And while he didn't know what the doctor was doing, her odd behavior suggested stealth was his best path to discovering the answer.

Cantrell moved at a plodding, ever-constant pace, first down a short corridor and then down a winding stone staircase. At its base, she turned left at the junction of three wide hallways. They were somewhere near the center of the citadel, so the only light came from the guttering flicker of the three flames in Cantrell's hand. Greeley followed just beyond the periphery of the bubble of light to avoid exposure.

His caution proved advantageous when, three turns and one level later, two more dark figures joined Cantrell. One was male, the other female; Greeley didn't recognize either. He had yet to meet most of the island staff. Further concealing the identity of the newcomers, the first held a small flashlight while the other a short taper candle. Both kept the light sources low at their sides leaving their faces cloaked in eerie shadow.

Neither of the newcomers spoke. None of the three acknowledged the others in any way. The two fell into step behind Cantrell with robotic precision. After two additional turns, the procession picked up another member in precisely the same way. By the time the group reached what Greeley guessed must be the basement or even a subbasement of the facility, the line was nearly a dozen strong. Concern for being discovered forced him to hang back so far that keeping the group's cloud of light visible in the distance was increasingly difficult.

Turning one more corner, Greeley found himself surrounded entirely in darkness. His throat seized, stopping even his breathing as he listened for an indication he'd been discovered. Something told him being found now, way down here, would have dire consequences. And just as there was no light, he could hear nothing. This brought a claustrophobic sensation that sent his heart racing. He'd descended four, five, maybe six staircases—there was no way of knowing now. By his estimation, he was deep in the center of the citadel and somewhere in its basements. His hand tapped nervously at his hip pocket searching for his mobile phone. It could be used as a light source, but he knew it was not to be. The phone had been destroyed in the plane crash and subsequent submergence in the sea. It had been summarily discarded as a result.

Swallowing hard, Greeley took a deep breath. Attempting to calm his mind and forestall a growing panic, he tried to apply logic. Turning one hundred *and eighty degrees, he stepped slowly forward. Keeping to a steady pace, a half minute later, the fingers of his outstretched hand met the cold surface of the stone wall. Turning right and treading slowly, he dragged the fingers across the rough stone surface.*

Feeling an opening in the wall at his left, Greeley turned and stepped through the doorway. Though a vague turn-by-turn map was forming in his head, he already knew it would take time, and a lot of luck, to find his way back to the surface. He cursed himself for not bringing a light—and for his curiosity.

Chapter 32

Jolting upright with a gasp, Keegan's eyes instantly took in the dark room. Low flames danced in the hearth and thunder continued to rumble in the distance. Gavin lay asleep on the bed at her side. The comforter was pulled halfway across his torso. She watched his chest rise and fall in a slow, reassuring rhythm. The sight brought a contented smile. The rolling rumble of thunder seemed to be coming from every direction. Clearly, the storm was a long way from subsiding. A far-off blast of lightning brought the room into relief for a fraction of a second and the air eased from her breast just as the grin was washed from her expression. Whatever had drawn her attention must have been lightning.

Eager to return to a well-deserved slumber, she adjusted the sheet across her naked form. A pulse of light from the far end of the room drew her attention with a quick turn of her head. The pulse of light had been brief, but the flash was dull and slow-moving—decidedly not lightning-like. The large free-standing mirror on the far wall shimmered with a barely perceptible glow. Her eyes narrowed. Was the apparition a trick of the light, or was her mind having fun at her expense?

The mirror's wide silver surface rippled, and she nearly jumped from the bed. Her eyes wide, she tapped Gavin on the arm. "Wake up," she hissed between clenched teeth.

Gavin didn't move. The steady rise and fall of his chest weren't interrupted.

Keegan's eyes darted back to the mirror. At the same time, she shook Gavin violently with an outstretched hand.

Still nothing.

Cursing under her breath, she slid to the edge of the bed. With a tug, she freed a sheet from the tangle of bedding and pressed it firmly to her breast. She moved slowly toward the mirror, the strange experience with the antique mirror in her bedroom flashing to the forefront of her mind for the first time since the incident occurred.

How could I forget an experience like that?

Is it happening again?

She considered that this might be part of some ultra-realistic dream...then she wondered if her mind was capable of such considerations while in the middle of said dream. The answers, of course, were beyond her. She mentally chastised herself for even worrying at a time like this. Amusingly, this last thought, the mental reprimand did the most to convince her this was not a dream. She decided she could only berate herself so severely in a conscious state. This juxtaposition brought a smile to her terrified expression.

She drew to within three feet of the mirror in time to see its surface ripple once more. Her reflection seemed to be looking back at her from a pool of quicksilver. Then as quickly as the ripple had formed, it was gone.

She stepped closer still.

Being this close, there was no question—a distinctive mild glow emanated from the mirror's surface. But if this mirror was related to the one in her room, it wasn't a sibling. The glass was entirely flawless, and not the slightest of aged patina had accumulated on the mirror's silver coating. The silver layer beneath the glass on antique mirrors provided a reflective surface. Many antique mirror designs used mercury and tin to produce a reflective surface. Scarce antiques used real silver in that reflective coating. If this mirror was related to the one in her room, it was a distant cousin rather than a sibling. It looked more modern in both design and construction.

This raised the question, related or not, might it have the same properties as the mirror in her room? The surface rippled once more as if in answer to the unvoiced question. Her reflection dissolved and was replaced with darkness. The vision was at once unsettling and foreboding. Keegan's eyes dilated as she searched for form in the void. The light wasn't at first visible. What registered first was a sense of movement in the abyss. Long seconds passed. What she perceived as movement soon became apparent as the flickering perimeter of light moved closer to the opening on the other side of the portal.

A hand going to her mouth, Keegan struggled to suppress even the sound of her breathing. If I can see through, can someone see me? She was suddenly conscious of the sheet draped across her front and bare, exposed backside.

The guttering flicker of candlelight neared the far side of the portal. Keegan could see large objects draped in wide dusty white sheets. The sound of multiple figures moving in the darkness startled Keegan and made her take a defensive step in retreat. When she did, the image in the mirror faded and lost clarity. Her view of the other side lost focus. The sheet-draped objects became cloudy and indistinct.

Not wanting to give up on the experience so soon, Keegan stepped quickly back to the mirror. Focus and clarity instantly returned. A figure came into view on the other side of the glass. Doctor Sydney Cantrell set aside a bulky candle and pulled a tapestry from the wall. She turned to a figure out of frame. Keegan saw another hand rise into view. It drew a blade slowly across the palm of Cantrell's hand. The woman didn't so much as wince as blood splattered the floor. Turning back to the wall, Cantrell pressed her hand against the stone. The rock disintegrated beneath her touch as if it were nothing more than a wall of sand.

Keegan fought the urge to retreat. She must not be visible to those on the other side of the portal. If she were, she would already have been discovered. Struggling to hold her ground against the rising sense of panic, Keegan watched as one after another, shadowy forms filed through a doorway secreted behind the tapestry.

Numerous figures had passed her vantage point. Other than Doc Cantrell, she hadn't seen enough to identify any of them. She suddenly wished she'd tallied their numbers. Now, more than anything, she wondered what they were doing. Leaning forward, Keegan's fingers touched the surface of the mirror. There was a slight resistance, then her hand passed entirely through the material. Her eyes grew wide and she tipped further forward. Her arm extended into the void. Heart hammering in her chest, she wondered what kind of foolish mistake she was making.

When submersion reached past her elbow, an overpowering sense of vertigo gripped Keegan. The room tipped and the world spun. The dim illumination of the bedroom disappeared, and she felt a cold jolt as her bare backside impacted with the ridged stone floor. Stifling a sound somewhere between a scream and a sob, Keegan pounded at the ground around her. There was no plush, soft carpeting. Her hands slapped on solid stone tile. Inky black surrounded her.

Gasping and waving her hands in the abyss, Keegan struggled for understanding. Her eyes fluttered, and she finally began to adapt to the conditions. It wasn't entirely dark, she realized. A dull glow emanated from somewhere at her back. Jolting to a knee and spinning, she became aware of two things simultaneously. The first was that she was naked. She'd lost the sheet when she fell through the portal. Second, the light was coming from another mirror in this strange place. Looking into it, she saw Gavin's bedroom reflected. It was like looking through a window. The room flickered in the low flames dancing in the fireplace.

Crawling forward, she intended to touch the mirror and get the hell out of here...wherever here was. But her hand stuck upon something slippery and wet on the floor. Her forward motion ceased. With great trepidation, she raised greasy, slick fingers into the light emanating from the surface of the mirror. Though the substance looked black in the dim illumination, she knew exactly what it was.

Blood. Cantrell's blood.

Eyes shooting upward, Keegan noticed the thickly woven tapestry on the wall for the first time. The sight of the figures moving behind it flashed through her mind. As did the strange sight of the wall disintegrating under Cantrell's touch. Keegan's lips moved with a silent oath as concern for her friend. It was a worry that outweighed the terror of her predicament.

Climbing to her feet and scanning the surroundings, Keegan used the end of a dusty tarp to wipe the blood from her hand. The fine grit came off like dark soot on the pads of her fingers. Selecting one of the smallest dust-mottled sheets, she slowly pulled it from its protective position over a short pile of ancient ladderback chairs. She wrapped the grimy material around her shoulders and tried not to choke on the billow of particulates sent spiraling in the air. She stepped to the tapestry. Pulling back the corner, Keegan was relieved to see the dim flicker of torchlight in the hallway beyond.

Taking great care, she pulled back the curtain only far enough to squeeze through and moved into the narrow empty corridor. The moment the tapestry flapped shut behind her, Keegan could hear the low murmur of chanting nearby. She bunched up the sheet and knelt close to the floor. Then, knees on freezing ancient stone, she crawled toward the source of the sound.

Chapter 33

Gavin pulled back the comforter to expose Keegan's naked back. Lazy splashes of light from the fireplace played swirling shadows across the surface of her flawless skin. He nudged her gently and said, "I need you to wake up."

Stirring, Keegan raised her head and looked at him through blurry eyes. Confusion was obvious in her expression. "What time is it?"

"Not all that late, all things considered. But there's work to do, and I need your help to do it."

She looked troubled. Rolling onto her side, she looked ready to say something. Opening her mouth, she started to speak but stopped short.

"What's wrong?" Gavin prodded.

Pausing, the confused set of her brow appeared to darken. "I don't know," she admitted. "There's something on the tip of my tongue. It just disappeared in a flash. Seemed important." She shook her head slowly, then shrugged. "Must have been nothing."

He nodded as if this explained everything. They hadn't had a chance to speak in private yet. This was his first time alone with her since dinner. There'd been no time to talk at dinner, and well, things had been too hot and heavy when *she'd attempted to get the drop on him showing up unannounced as she had.*

She wouldn't like what he had to say. He struggled for a way to broach the subject. It was the first time during their relatively short relationship that he wondered how she might react to news of his past. He wondered if it might drive a wedge between them. She knew something of his history, but only a little. Knew he'd come to the island to hide out. If only in the broad strokes, she knew what his past entailed. Tonight would offer first-hand exposure to his history and the baggage he'd hoped to avoid.

"They came for me today," he finally blurted out. "I killed one of them. His body is stashed out in the woods."

Gathering an arm full of bedding, Keegan pulled it to her breast and sat up. She arched an eyebrow but said nothing.

"I told you there was a chance…that they might come for me one day," he said by way of clarification.

Her searching gaze softened as if deciding this wasn't part of their ongoing game. "Jesus," she whispered. Her fingers rubbed the sleep from the corner of one eye. "Sorry. Yeah, I know."

Gavin's skin suddenly went cold. What? "You know?"

Keegan nodded. Traces of a blush touched her cheeks. It seemed to take effort for her to maintain eye contact. "I was watching."

He said nothing, his eyes pinched, confused.

"I saw it," she clarified. "I was eavesdropping. I didn't catch it all, so I don't understand exactly what happened. I saw two men holding guns on you, then I saw you jump the little guy and take him out."

Gavin leaned back on the bed and contemplated this information. Although familiar with her unusual ability, he didn't fully understand it. She didn't either, for that matter. Some called it mind-walking while others referred to it as remote viewing. But she'd only been able to do it over very short distances.

"Where were you, physically, I mean?" he said finally.

Her answer came in a hushed tone. "My room."

His jaw dropped. "That's a new record," he offered with enthusiasm. "Way to go!"

"Don't deflect," she admonished. "Explain. What the hell happened? And

what's going on with your friend? Greeley, is it?" Her tone had softened too, the English influences sneaking into her accent even where she'd worked to eliminate them from her dialect. The majority of her adolescent life was spent in UK boarding schools. Later she'd studied veterinary medicine in France. She was every bit as American as he, still her accent had been a turn-on since day one.

"I'm not sure I'd call Zane a friend," Gavin said with a shake of his head. "He came in with Garboni. Garboni's the little prick I killed," he clarified. "If things went to plan, they were taking me out of here dead or alive."

"The man you brought to dinner tonight came here to kill you?" Her voice was filled with wonder, but her tone bordered on irate—or maybe indignant? He was having trouble reading her roller coaster of emotions. "Is that customary where you come from?"

Gavin offered a shrug. "I gave him a chance to pick a side, and he leveled up. We're good now. Greeley knew Garboni was an anchor, chained and wrapped around his neck. Garboni had a way of bringing bad things to good people. Greeley just picked the right side before he could be added to the list of collateral damage."

"Meaning you would've killed Greeley too?"

Gavin shrugged.

"Could you have done that? I saw your situation. It didn't look likely."

Grinning, Gavin said, "Greeley thought I could. That's all that mattered."

She became quiet. He could see the wheels of contemplation working behind her eyes.

"I know this isn't what you signed on for," Gavin offered. "And I'm sorry. But I need your help. I can't get rid of the body by myself." He motioned toward the massive windows overlooking the home's front yard. "Not in these conditions, and not in time. I can't risk your old man finding the corpse with his damn drones. And I can't just dump the body in the ocean. If it somehow ends up on shore, there would be no explaining the bullet holes in him."

Leaping from the bed, Keegan took the sheet with her. Gavin was left naked and cold. "You know very well that man is not my father," she sputtered and paced. Gavin watched as the tangle of blankets was dragged back and forth across the floor.

Reluctantly, he slid to the edge of the bed and retrieved his jeans. Pulling them on, he said, "I still don't know who or what he is. Right now, I'm more worried about Garboni. I need to get rid of the body. Again, only possible with your help."

She stopped pacing. Her expression was unreadable in the dim light. The fire had died down to nothing; the tiny lamp in the corner of the room offered little illumination but strangely generated endless shadows in the expansive space.

"Look," he said. "I understand you're upset. I need you to believe that I didn't have a choice. If you knew the kind of people—"

Keegan murmured something, and Gavin stopped short. "I'm sorry," he said. "What was that?"

"I'm not upset about that," she said. "You told me about the Outfit. It wasn't likely, but you said it was a possibility. I hoped you were exaggerating, but...well, it's not really like you to embellish. I guess I'm not all that surprised when it comes down to it." She thought for a moment, standing motionless in the darkness. "More than anything, I don't understand Greeley," she said at last.

"You mean, why he changed sides?"

She nodded.

Gavin considered his response. It should have bothered him more too. Somehow the circumstances made things different. Perhaps it was because he and Zane had walked similar paths. Both had done things of which they weren't proud. Explaining to an outsider wasn't easy. Once you were in the life, getting out—even changing the rules—wasn't a recipe for survival. No one got out. Ever. Then again, few had done what Gavin had. It was why he was now hunted.

Gavin went to the hearth and dropped three new logs into embers crumbling in their death throws. Stoking the ashes with a poker, he coaxed a lazy flame to life. It licked at the periphery of the first log for long seconds before finally flashing as the dry bark ignited. Seconds later, a wave of warmth washed over his bare torso.

"I wasn't just giving Zane a chance to live," Gavin said. "I gave him a chance to leave the organization. A chance to walk away and start over. It was an opportunity few ever see. He was smart enough to recognize it for what it was."

She approached the side of the bed and sat facing the fire. "You're saying you trust him?"

Gavin didn't answer. Time will tell.

Keegan changed tactics. She draped an arm around him and wrapped the sheet over his shoulder. The act exposed her nude silhouette to him, and he groaned with appreciation—as much for the view as the offer of warmth. She flashed a pert smile in response. He slipped an arm around her bare back and the other beneath the bend of her knees. Effortlessly, he lifted her onto his lap. The warmth of her flesh against his chest warmed his blood and skin in unison. She tightened a cocoon of sheets around them.

Teasingly, the tips of her fingers traced the contours of his erection, pressed hard against the inside of his jeans. Her breath was labored, warm, and damp in his ear. When she spoke, her voice was little more than a husky whisper. "We don't have time for this, do we?"

His only reply was a heartfelt, exasperated sigh.

She squeezed him quickly before sitting back to offer a playful smile. "Ok," she said. "Never thought I would ask this, but how do you propose we get rid of your stiff?"

Despite himself, Gavin laughed. Their present circumstances aside, this wasn't how he wanted the evening to progress. He'd promised to keep the cave a secret. Now he had no choice but to take Keegan to the top of the mountain. It was the only safe place to dispose of the body. The place terrified him in a primal way. Nothing particularly disturbing had happened on his last visit, but there'd been a chilling sense of foreboding that permeated the interior of Black Rock. Exposing Keegan to that was the last thing he wanted.

"I know how to do it," he said finally. "I just can't get the corpse there alone. There's a cave near the top of the mountain."

She shot him a look. "A cave? For real? Why haven't you mentioned it? That's kind of cool."

Chapter 34

"No, not cool," Gavin mumbled. "You'll understand when you see it. I'm pretty sure it's what your father—what Stanton's been turning the island upside down searching for."

Dispelling his claim of urgency, Keegan saw a glint in Gavin's eyes. His hand rose high and cradled the nape of her neck. He kissed her gently. The slow caress of his fingers, lips, and tongue became more passionate, and she felt her skin flush with renewed anticipation. Their lips parted and his eyes searched hers. His free hand brushed a lock of hair from the corner of her eye. With a delicate touch, he tucked it behind her ear. She looked at him with hungry eyes, her gaze washing over his face and neck.

They were good at this, she reminded herself. She'd intended to spend only a week on the island. Just long enough to visit her father, and God help her, get to know her new stepmother. Meeting Gavin had devastated those plans. Leaving was now the furthest thing from her mind. They could do this for—

Keegan's eyes went wide. The flat of her hand met Gavin's bare chest and she pushed away. "What's that?" she stammered. "What the hell?"

The sheets fell away, but Keegan didn't care. She turned them, shifting so they were sidelong to the firelight. She cradled Gavin's forearm delicately in *the palms of both hands. Her eyes flashed from the tattoo on the inside of Gavin's forearm to the confused expression on his face.*

"What?" he said simply.

"What?" she barked. "Where did that come from?"

Confusion clouded his expression. He said nothing.

"It's new," Keegan said, running a finger across the emblem. But it's not, she silently noted. Her fingers silently crossed the dark ink and confirmed there was no swelling or irritation of the flesh. "Where did this come from?"

Gavin looked at her through pinched eyes. He gently extracted his arm from her grasp and sat back. "Are you alright? You're not making sense."

Keegan started to speak but stopped short. Suddenly aware of the chill air and her naked form, she gathered a fist full of the blankets from either side and pulled them over her shoulders. She fought back a deep-seated shiver that had nothing to do with the temperature.

"That mark," Keegan's tone was almost accusatory. "Where did it come from? How did you get it?"

Gavin followed suit and pulled the loose covers over his stomach. He cast her with a dour expression. "I've told you this story," he said in a voice dripping with concern. His gaze dipped to his forearm. "Three or four years ago, back in Chicago." He met her eye once more. "What the hell—what's wrong with you?"

"That sigil," Keegan muttered. "It wasn't there an hour ago."

His brows knitted. "Sigil? Wait—what do you mean an hour ago?"

"An hour ago—" her tone grew more aggressive. "As of sixty minutes ago, you didn't have a single tattoo. I would know—certainly if there had been one on your bloody wrist!"

Gavin remained silent. His expression, however, spoke volumes; his visage was a mask of deep-seated concern. He lay his hands in his lap and studied her.

Keegan's mind raced. The tattoo wasn't new, but it had appeared out of nowhere. It defied all logic...no, that wasn't true. It defied conventional logic. There were less conventional explanations. She had to consider where they were.

"Let me see it again," she said.

Slowly, and with obvious reluctance, Gavin presented his forearm. "Maybe we should go see the Doc," he said. "Something's wrong."

She shook her head. "Doctor Cantrell can't help with this." Even to Keegan's ear, her English accent suddenly became more pronounced. This happened, she knew, under times of great excitement or stress. "I'm not sick. But something has happened."

The tattoo was precise in its detail. Only slightly larger than a silver dollar, it was monochrome but stark in contrast against his flesh. A pair of wavy lines paralleled each other, set apart by a perfect circle bisected at the center. Half of the circle was absolutely black, while the other half was a pale shade of gray. The outside of the ring was thick and black. Another ring circled the first, shaded gray like the half-and-half-colored solid circle at the center of the image.

The circle and the wavy line reminded her of something. It was a memory dancing at the edge of her perception, just slightly beyond reach. She could sense understanding waiting beyond the bounds of her perception. It was like a taste on the tip of her tongue, something she knew well yet could not identify.

"Tattoos don't just materialize out of thin air," Gavin said with a halfhearted smile. "Besides, I remember getting this—well, more or less. I've told you the story. The trip to Chicago, the drinking, the bar? You remember?"

She searched his eyes. The story was entirely unfamiliar. We've never talked about this. She knew it with absolute certainty. A question formed in her mind when the taste on the tip of her tongue suddenly brought forth a memory. Her eyes darted back to his arm. She lay the palm of her hand across half of the image. With only half of the tattoo visible, Keegan knew why the sigil looked so familiar.

She stared at the single wavy line and the black half of the circle. An unbidden whisper escaped her lips, "Nae'ja-dinn."

Chapter 35

The concern in Keegan's stare was troubling. She clearly had no idea what he was talking about. How could he perfectly recall their conversation while she knew nothing of it?

"Code 10-31?" Gavin said hesitantly. "The bar? That doesn't sound familiar to you at all?"

Keegan shook her head.

She was convincing.

Considering how he'd explained the night from years earlier the first time around, Gavin suddenly felt like he'd been given a second chance to tell the story correctly. He'd made a mess of it the first time, spending a bit too much time on the mysterious girl who had talked him into getting the damnable tattoo in the first place. Actually, talked hadn't really been the case, and that was where he'd messed up the story. He sounded like a fool and had the mark to prove it. How she maintained any respect for him after that story, he still didn't know.

He eyed her suspiciously. "You don't know what I'm talking about?"

Unmitigated concern blanketed her face and convinced him this was no game. No simple attempt to wipe the board clean and let him retell the tale in a way that was less embarrassing. But...

How can she not know? Is it a symptom of the medical condition impacting others on the island? Is it the first sign of it hurting Keegan?

The thought nearly made him shudder visibly. He fought the knot spooling in the pit of his belly and the consideration that he might be the one remembering things wrong. There was a third possibility, after all. Too many unexplained things were happening on the island. This could be one of them— entirely unrelated to the strange illness, the cave, and the threats from his past.

For now, he would roll with it and see where the memory loss—or whatever this was—took them.

"Code 10-31 was a bar on the South Side in Chicago," Gavin explained. "I was in town on—" he stumbled visibly for a moment; this part of the story was still difficult to admit aloud. "I was working an out-of-town job for the Outfit."

"Busting kneecaps," she clarified. There was no surprise in her tone, nor was there criticism.

He shifted uncomfortably, his head finally moving side to side in a, more or less, type statement. "I was protection. The brass thought I was scary, so I made good protection on a milk run every once in a while." Gavin didn't find himself very intimidating when he looked in the mirror. He was aware of his reputation within the crime family and the surrounding underworld where the family operated. This reputation made him the ideal so-called muscle for out-of-town assignments.

A milk run.

That easy protection detail had turned out to be anything but simple. A firefight the night before had left all but three on their protection detail dead. One of the survivors took a bullet to the belly and spent three days in the hospital before suffering an aneurysm and dying while his release papers were being processed. Another man had been luckier and walked away with a through-and-through shot to his shoulder. Gavin had personally taken a blow to the head that was diagnosed days later as a severe concussion. Still, less than twenty-four hours after the shootout, he, the other remaining survivor, and a few others from the crew had somehow managed to find themselves drinking at a bar called the Code 10-31.

"I avoided working outside of the family's sphere of influence whenever possible," Gavin went on. "That trip was out of my hands. They sent me to Chi-

town, and I ended up at the 10-31 with a couple of the guys to kill a few hours on our second or third night in town. I was recuperating with a guy I was traveling with," he thought for a long second. "And I think we met up with a couple of guys from a local Outfit while we were there."

Odd that most of his memories from that trip were foggy at best, he thought. Probably not that shocking given the severity of his concussion. Still, the more he considered it, there seemed a clear delineation between solid and foggy memories. He could recall everything prior to arriving at O'Hare International Airport. There he had relative clarity. It was as if every memory after landing was impacted in some way.

"What kind of name is that for a bar?"

The question pulled Gavin back to the moment, and he grinned. "10-31 is the Police code for a crime in progress. I know what you're thinking, a bar named after a cop's call-out code is likely a police bar. Let me tell you, this place was anything but. It was wall-to-wall lowlifes. Looking back, it actually was a great name for the place. At any given time, at least a dozen crimes had to be in progress. Drug deals, gun deals, prostitution, you name it."

Keegan looked troubled. "There's no way you got drunk and ended up with that inked on your arm. It's a nice story, and if we were talking about a skull or something, I might buy it. But this is way too esoteric."

Gavin adjusted his position on the bed. He was suddenly aware of his nudity and the room's chill despite the blanket he now clutched more tightly. He'd messed up this part of the story the first time around. And while he didn't understand how he was getting a do-over, he would make the most of it. Taking a slow breath to buy just a little more time, Gavin finally forged ahead. "The night was a blur—it still is, actually. I woke up the next morning with the tat and didn't remember stopping at a shop, let alone sitting for the work. It's been years, but I'm still not entirely sure what happened."

The blank spot in his memory troubled Gavin far more than he could verbalize. There were people who would literally skin him alive if given the opportunity, and they would only do that after getting far more creative with prolonged forms of torture. It was a byproduct of the life he'd led working for the Outfit. It wasn't enough to say that he never got blackout drunk. He never got drunk at all. Such an act was beyond reckless. It was likely to get him killed in the most gruesome ways imaginable. He'd been working on unfriendly soil that night. There was no way he would have compromised himself in such a way.

"There was a girl involved," Keegan said knowingly. Her expression suggested this was a guess, but not a stretch of her imagination.

Gavin could remember the silhouette of an attractive woman from that night. He could even remember the silky luster of her hair and the way it caught the dim light as it framed her face…but frustratingly, no matter how hard he tried, he couldn't recall her features. In his memory, her face had no detail. There were no distinguishing characteristics.

A shrug was Gavin's only response for a few long seconds. Finally, he said, "I don't know her name, and I can't remember her face to save my life. It's embarrassing."

A smirk played across Keegan's lips. "I take it you didn't spend much time looking at her face." Her tone was playful, but the accusation was plain enough.

The empty feeling Gavin sensed when he thought of the young woman's face was replaced when he thought of her eyes. He looked squarely into Keegan's emerald gaze and was instantly transported back to that night. He could hear the clatter and rumble of the surrounding bar and smell the stale beer mixed with the sour bodies surrounding him. Music, much too loud, pounded from distant speakers. A small table was at one side, and a woman sat atop his left knee. She had a trim, athletic frame, and his arm rested easily around her waist. She was young, though likely a few years older than him, and it was appealing. Her lips were moving though he couldn't hear the words. Her hand moved to pull a curtain of black hair aside and meet his gaze with a penetrating set of green eyes that danced with light and amusement.

Gavin shivered and snapped physically back to the present. Sucking in a lung full of air, he felt suddenly oxygen deprived. Keegan threw the blankets aside and instantly pressed herself close to him. He felt the warmth of her naked form against his own. "Are you alright?" she said in a near shout and gave him a shake. Gavin instantly sensed this wasn't the first time she had asked this question.

He realized he was laying on his back, though he didn't recall laying down. He offered a slow nod, then looked into her eyes. The same green eyes he now remembered from his missing night at the 10-31 years earlier. A shiver ran through him, traveling from his head all the way to his toes. He pulled the comforter tightly around them and then shifted to look her in the eyes. "You know the bar I'm talking about," he said. "You've been there."

Keegan looked confused. "I've never been to Chicago. And, no offense, I wouldn't be caught dead in a place like that."

Gavin didn't understand, but he saw the sincerity in her expression. In fairness, there was a lot that didn't make sense. The woman from that night had been a blind spot for him. He'd struggled for years to recall any feature that would help him understand who she was. Countless hours were spent in a futile effort to recover even a single clarifying feature that might help him understand how the events of that night had come to pass. He needed to understand the woman, the strange connection was still felt with someone he'd only known for a few hours, and how their short time together had marked him mentally and physically for the rest of his life. For years he'd fought to recall the name and face of a woman he'd felt some strange, deep connection with after a brief, chance meeting. And now he believed he was looking at that same woman. Yet, somehow, she knew nothing of his experience.

"I'll Google the bar," Keegan said. "The name isn't familiar. But I'm positive I've never been to Chicago. Not once in my life. A couple of layover flights at O'Hare, that's the closest I've ever come. In fact, that's the only time I've ever set foot in Illinois."

Gavin shook his head. "Looking the place up won't help now. It burned a night or two after I was there. Might have even been the next day, for all I know. Someone said the place was eventually rebuilt, but they called it something different when it reopened. I guess the owner wanted to class the place up a little with the reboot."

"It burned?"

"To the ground."

Keegan shot him a sharp look. "Right after all of that happened to you? That doesn't seem odd?"

A shrug from Gavin was the response. "The place was an overpacked series of code violations when I was there, and it was crammed with every form of ne'er-do-well you can imagine. I'm not the least bit surprised. Though, now that you mention it, I recall reading they had a hell of a time figuring out how the fire started. I think there was pushback from the insurance company—something about not wanting to pay out on the claim or something. There was a lot of talk in the Outfit because they wanted to understand it too. I don't think I ever heard what actually happened."

Chapter 36

Gavin engaged the choke, turned the key, and tapped the ignition of the massive four-wheel drive ATV. The starter triggered with a low buzz and the throaty four-cylinder engine sparked to life without hesitation. He adjusted the angle of the Stetson on his head to ensure the guttering rainfall would drain clear of his shoulders. Tightening the collar of his waist-length leather coat, he reduced the choke and slipped the leather work gloves back onto his hands. A twitch of the tip of his left boot and the transmission dropped into first gear. He gently feathered the throttle with the thumb of his right hand and the ATV eased forward. The 450cc engine growled as all four tires bit into the slippery earth.

Even sitting directly over the machine's engine, Gavin had to strain to hear the burble of the exhaust over the sound of the driving rain. Though bone-chilling, the weather had advantages. No one would be outside in these conditions, and it was equally unlikely that Anakasta could launch his drones under the deluge. And though the lightning had died down for the moment, the storm's intensity seemed to promise further escalation.

Gavin rounded the west side of the Out House, as the two-story house outside the monastery walls was affectionately known. The citadel and its massive encompassing wall were to the east. Though he'd been the smaller building's sole resident for nearly as long as he'd been on the island, Gavin never took his privacy for granted. There were eyes everywhere, he believed. It *was only a question of when they were watching and what they believed they were seeing. Upon returning from the woods earlier in the evening, he had secreted the ATV in the woods beyond the edge of the clearing where the Out House and the citadel stood. His trip to dispose of Garboni's body was a foregone conclusion and the four-wheel drive would be required.*

Only fifteen minutes earlier, talk of Gavin's tattoo had died an abrupt death. Keegan said a word, or a name, that was unfamiliar to him. Nae'ja-dinn. When he asked what it meant, she refused to elaborate. She even went so far as to chastise him for speaking the word aloud. This, of course, only made him want to know more. But she would have nothing of it. Discussion ceased, though he could see an entirely new level of concern in her eyes. The significance of the word, somehow related to the symbol on his wrist, troubled her deeply.

Keegan's sudden apprehension for the tattoo was perhaps the most troubling of all. The emblem had been there for years. He'd had it when he met her and couldn't understand why she thought it appeared out of thin air. He remembered the trip to Chicago that had precipitated the rash decision, even if he couldn't precisely recall the specific events leading up to the branding as he now thought of it. A girl had been involved, of course. He'd never cared much for body art and would not have done something like this if not appropriately motivated. A woman and too much booze. The details of the night remained foggy to this day, but he knew one thing with certainty. The tattoo appeared out of nowhere.

Braking at the base of the stairs leading to the two-tiered deck behind the house, Gavin shifted to neutral. Every window in the house was dark. Lightning danced in clouds far to the east. Wind buffeted him with chilling rainfall and his eyes searched the surrounding darkness. Keegan approached from his blind side and laid a hand on his arm. He recoiled in response, eliciting a satisfied, devilish smile.

She leaned close to be heard over the whistle of the wind. "You're a little jumpy."

He nodded. "I was getting worried. What took so long?"

She was dressed in similar foul-weather gear. A wide-brimmed western-style work hat was pulled low across her brow, and the collar of a waterproof duster hung past her knees. She had on the same boots she'd been wearing when she'd visited him only a few short hours before. "I was watching the windows," she tipped her head toward the Out House.

Gavin was confused at first. Then he realized she was referring to the citadel.

His house currently obscured their view of the surrounding wall and the multiple stories of the massive structure beyond. This was why she hadn't come down from the deck. She'd been around the corner of the house and watching the compound.

"There were lights," she went on. "Low flickers moving around behind the windows. It looked like someone was using candles or flashlights."

Gavin nodded. It was odd but not unheard of. Perhaps a breaker had blown in part of the compound. "So we're not the only ones teaming up to stay warm tonight? Now you're a peeping Tom?"

She rolled her eyes and socked him in the ribs. The punch was largely ineffective, mostly resulting in a splash of water that hit her in the face. It made him laugh. She slipped a hand from a glove and wiped a wet hand across an equally wet face. "Not quite," she retorted. "I wanted to be sure no one was watching."

It wasn't frustration he saw on her waterlogged face. It was a concern. "Someone's watching?"

She shook her head. "Not that I can tell. It was the candlelight. I was only watching for a couple of minutes, but I saw candlelight moving through the second and third floors of the north wing. I could swear I saw the same somewhere in the west wing at the same time."

Gavin frowned. "That's a lot of people up and around for this time of night."

"And using candles?"

Gavin patted the seat behind him on the ATV. Keegan gathered up the length of her long coat and pulled it to the side before stepping on the foot peg and throwing a leg over the seat behind him. Keeping the headlight off as before, Gavin tapped the accelerator and eased the bulky ATV slowly ahead. The knobby tires bit and ground at the muddy surface that had hours before been the sod of the yard. As they passed the corner of the Out House, his eyes went past the perimeter wall and searched the dark upper windows of the monastery. Though he saw no unusual lights suggesting the use of candles, he did notice a glow coming from the inner perimeter of the grounds within the surrounding wall. The exterior lights were on, as they were every night. And if those lights were functional, the facility still had power.

Chapter 37

The way Gavin explained it, they were looking at a mile-long ride to the site where Garboni's body was stashed. It would be a slow, plodding trip following a course closer to two miles by the time they made it. Keegan kept her hat tipped low and her body pressed tightly against Gavin's back to minimize her exposure to the wind and rain. Their course was circuitous, using Gavin's prodigious knowledge of the island's topology to keep them on rock and heavy forest growth whenever possible. As Gavin explained, the tracks from the ATV would stand out if Anakasta managed to put the drones in the air. The entire trip was a gamble. If they could keep their journey out of the telltale mud bogs most likely to give them away or get them stuck, it would save the need for an elaborate explanation later.

That was all well and good in Keegan's mind. The damn rain was the foremost concern in her mind. She would've been happy to take the ride if she hadn't been soaked to the bone five minutes after leaving the cozy confines of Gavin's bed. All that had happened in the last eight hours troubled her. Strangers on the island. One dead and the other changing sides the way he had. She couldn't claim to understand the sort of world these men had come from, but it was a change of fortunes she couldn't imagine. Keegan always believed she had a good sense for people, and Greeley seemed on the level, as unlikely as it seemed. She certainly had a better feeling about him than she did about her father. That man was an entirely different set of worries.

Dear old dad... Without question, there was something off about him. He seemed genuine in some respects, but off in far more ways. Over the last couple of months, a certainty had formed in her mind. Stanton was not her father. She'd had his DNA tested by Doc Cantrell; a current sample compared to one taken from a gift he'd given her as a little girl. Though the science said it was the same man, she was confident it wasn't. They were strangers. What he knew of their time together and of her personally seemed gleaned from secondhand accounts rather than personal experiences. It felt more like he'd read a biography rather than participating in her life, limited as his participation had been.

Keegan had never been close to her father. She'd been trundled off to boarding school early in her formative years. Her mother had died during childbirth and her father had never really settled into family responsibilities. He'd outsourced those duties to others, and Keegan had grown up abroad. The rational part of her mind reasoned that, as an adult, she didn't know her father personally. Still, the Practitioner in her sensed that something greater fueled the sense of unease. She had an instinctual drive to remain guarded in his presence.

Gavin turned the ATV around a tight corner and adjusted their course by nearly one hundred and eighty degrees. Keegan's eyes were closed, the side of her face pressed against his back to absorb what little warmth escaped through his coat. The sweeping turn across rough ground caused her to stir. Eyes flashing open, she raised her face and peered over his shoulder. A staggering splash of rainwater was her reward. Coughing suddenly, she blew water from her lips and blinked her vision clear.

"Falling asleep back there?" Gavin chuckled.

"If only," she grumbled.

The ATV came to a stop. Keegan saw piles of split wood stacked around the clearing. A great steel contraption sat to one end of the open space; a pair of red plastic gas cans upended beside it. The log splitter, she decided. Turning on the seat, she saw the overturned trailer in the opposite direction.

Gavin pointed the ATV toward the trailer and engaged the headlight for the first time since their journey began. He maneuvered the machine into position. At last, she climbed off the ATV. Her legs ached from poor circulation.

Gavin slipped from the seat of the 4x4 with practiced ease. "Wait here. You don't need to see this."

He began to move, but she stopped him with a restraining grip on his arm. "It's okay," she said. "We're in this together. I'm not afraid."

His visage in the light of the ATV's single headlamp shocked her. Driving rain streaked his face; pain was obvious in his eyes even shadowed as they were beneath the brim of his hat. It was a type of anguish she'd never seen in another person, let alone someone she cared so deeply for. She read his gaze and sensed the words not spoken—You shouldn't have to see what I have done.

Her gloved hand found his and gave it a squeeze. "We do this together," she said.

Chapter 38

The two-wheeled trailer was overturned at the base of a small tree. With the massive stone outcropping to the immediate right of the location, it seemed the wind and rain had collaborated to leave the body's hiding place as one of the few relatively dry locations on the island. Seeing Keegan shiver violently, Gavin waved her over to the lee of the twenty-foot-tall rock face a few yards from the scene. It was massive and jagged, though relatively flat on the surface facing them, the tree, and the trailer. It looked like it had been coughed from the depths of the island by some great cataclysm. More concerning, for the life of him, Gavin couldn't recall seeing the massive shard of stone there earlier. Though he'd spent days working in that clearing, the trees had been his focus. The rocks and boulders in the area hadn't even been blips on his radar.

With Keegan out of the weather for the moment, Gavin slowly circled the trailer. Nothing had changed since he'd stashed Garboni's body. Not that there'd been a reason to expect different. Only Willy had ever been out this far, and Willy wouldn't be back until well after sunrise tomorrow, assuming the rain let up by then.

Bending low at the knees, Gavin wedged his shoulder under the hitch lock at the end of the trailer. Rising slowly, he brought the front end of the small aluminum cart into the air. Keegan stepped forward, ready to lend a hand. "No," he said with a grunt. "Stay back. It's not heavy, but it'll go over hard after the tipping point."

He registered Keegan's confused expression from the corner of his eye. Moving forward, he walked the trailer backward, pushing it up onto its tailgate until the hitch assembly pointed directly at the sky. Then with the smallest of shoves, he edged it past the tipping point. The trailer fell over with a crash, its hitch assembly splattering in the mud, and the load box coming to rest on beefy wheels.

Though she was already standing at a safe distance, Keegan jumped at the sound of the rattling crash. Gavin waggled his brows and proceeded to dust soaked gloves off on sodden pant legs. He stopped short when he saw the color drain from Keegan's face. His gaze followed hers to the patch of ground sheltered by the trailer.

Garboni's corpse lay face down, half-submerged in dry soil. The earth around the perimeter of the body had been turned up in a way Gavin had never seen before. Kneeling beside the body, he looked more closely at the phenomenon. Churning seemed like the most appropriate way to describe it, he decided. It was as if the soil beneath the body had bubbled and slowly rolled away to pull the body into an earthy embrace. Soil particles stacked two or more inches high made a perfect perimeter around the body. The material was comprised of exceedingly fine-grained particulates visible even in the light from the 4x4.

Keegan squatted beside Gavin and leaned over the body. "You did this to him?" Her tone was incredulous. "It looks like he was skydiving without a parachute."

Gavin shook his head. It was precisely what the body looked like. If he didn't know better, he would've thought the body impacted here...after falling from a great height. It looked like he'd cratered into the landscape. "I've been around more than my share of dead people. I've never seen anything like this."

"But you shot him?"

It was true. He'd done it...and she'd witnessed it.

Gavin grabbed Garboni by the shoulder and sleeve of his jacket. With a tug, he rolled the body onto its side. He planned to show Keegan the gunshot wounds. Not that he cared to share his handiwork, but damned if he could figure out how three bullet wounds could possibly result in the body augering into the soil in such a way.

With a heave, Gavin rolled the body. Keegan gasped and attempted to backpedal. Her squatting position conspired against her, and she went sprawling to her backside. The maneuver sent her out of the shadow of cover provided by the vertical rockface, and she landed in the mud. Shoving the corpse away, Gavin pulled Keegan to her feet. Her boots slipped and skidded precariously. Her face was pale and her eyes were wide. In the struggle, they both nearly took a spill.

Keegan sagged into Gavin's arms, a sob escaping her shuttering form. The reaction wrecked him in a way that taking a human life never had. He'd done this to her. Bringing her had been a mistake. Killing Garboni hadn't been a choice, but bringing her here was. He should have sheltered her from this experience—from learning who and what he actually was.

"I'm sorry." It wasn't enough, but it was all Gavin could think to say.

Keegan choked back another sob while hanging in his arms. She slipped her face from where it was pressed to his chest. Her mouth moved close to his ear. The rasp of her husky voice sounded hollow against the clatter of surrounding rain. "You couldn't possibly have done that to him," she said.

Gavin turned to look at the body for the first time since he'd turned it over. The once fleshy and jowly face of Garboni was now bloodless and emaciated. His skin was parchment thin and stretched tight across the bones of his skull. The tightness of the tissue must have caused the jaw to extend because the mouth was agape, the tongue shriveled, tiny, and nearly unrecognizable. The eyes were entirely gone, the orbital sockets sunken and hollow.

Chapter 39

The trip up the mountain turned out to be easier than Gavin expected. Most of their path crossed expanses of rock and beds of gravel. The higher they moved in elevation, the less the risk of accidentally leaving tracks in the mud. There was little need to find a circuitous route, and time was saved. The small trailer was attached to the hitch on the rear of the ATV and the couple made it three-quarters of the way up the southeast face of the mountain before the climb became too steep for the four-wheel drive.

Gavin eased the ATV to a stop, applied the parking brake, and killed the engine. They'd stopped on an extreme upward slope, so he left the transmission in first gear for good measure. The rain had eased from a driving downpour to a steady, consistent soak. Thunderheads loomed in the distance and foretold of another violent assault soon to come.

Keegan climbed from the ATV. She kept a gloved hand on the machine's rear cargo rack until she'd negotiated the treacherous footing. The mountain's slippery gravel had replaced the island's omnipresent mud. This portion of the trail was littered with loose rock scree and shale of every consistency. Gavin recalled the hazardous footing from his last trip. The foul weather conditions and the need to tote Garboni would make things considerably more treacherous.

"How far is it?" Keegan asked as Gavin climbed from the ATV.

"A couple of hundred yards." He kicked at the loose slate-like stone lining the path for emphasis. *"The trail is narrow and steep. And it's entirely covered in this crap."* It was why he needed her help, but he left that part unsaid. Dragging the body up this last stretch by himself would have been next to impossible.

Gavin looked at Garboni's emaciated form crumpled in a heap against the trailer's tailgate. Gravity and the increasing vertical climb had pulled the corpse to the back of the load bed. He looked like a bag of bones shrink-wrapped in ancient leather, then stuffed into an oversized filthy suit. Amusingly, Garboni's boots sat beside the body. One had somehow wriggled itself upright along the load bed wall and was nearly filled to the top with accumulated rainwater.

Slipping one hand around the knotted tie still loosely looping the neck of the body, Gavin grabbed at the belt and hefted the corpse. He lifted Garboni from the trailer with little effort. The fat bastard was short, but he'd been pushing two-twenty when he was alive. Gavin shook his head. He might be eighty pounds now, and a portion of that was thanks to the saturated state of his clothing.

"Maybe you should stay here," Gavin said. He lowered Garboni to the ground and dusted his gloves against each other. Everything about the strange state of the body made his skin crawl.

Keegan shot him a pained look. *"You brought me to help. Let me help."*

"That was when I thought I'd be dragging a two-hundred-pound fat ass up the mountain in the rain. For whatever reason, he's half the man he once was. There's no reason to risk taking you up there. The path is shit." And the cave…he didn't say it, but he didn't want her anywhere near the cave. Just being near it brought a hollow feeling to his guts.

Her only response was to glare back.

Gavin didn't move. He could explain how he'd nearly fallen from the cliff on his last visit, though he wasn't sure the new information would support his argument. It was just as likely to work against him.

"We're wasting time," Keegan grumbled, pointing a thumb over her shoulder. *"The weather is about to step up its efforts. Shut up and grab his arms."*

Gavin grinned. He looked at the body for a second and then back at Keegan. *"You got the legs?"*

She nodded.

Removing his gloves, Gavin proceeded to take off his belt. He ran the leading edge under Garboni's back and looped it up under his arms. Fastening the belt for its largest size, he bent and lifted the body briefly as a test. Garboni's arms dangled at the sides but his taught, jerky-like flesh kept them from moving far or too freely.

Keegan scowled while she watched Gavin slip his hands back into his leather gloves. "Did I just watch you build a handy-dandy corpse carrier?"

He pointed at Garboni's feet. "Loop your belt once around his ankles, then do the same. Your back with thank you." She would fare better on the trail as well, being able to put more of her attention on the path and her footing.

"Did this a lot, back in the day?"

Gavin felt his cheeks color. He hoped she couldn't see it in the dark and the rain. He'd come up with the trick there on the spot, though he wasn't sure the declaration would instill additional confidence.

Keegan did as suggested, removing her belt and looping it around the feet of the dead man. "I'm burning this belt," she said. "Actually, I'm burning all these clothes."

Two minutes later, they were trudging up the slippery gravel slope.

Chapter 40

The last forty yards up the mountain proved to be the most challenging part of the climb. They were forced to clamber hand over hand while traversing a precarious stretch of near-vertical rock scattered with loose stone. Toting Garboni's body proved a harrowing experience and a testament to their teamwork. Gavin was thankful the rain had slowed to a heavy drizzle. Both his and Keegan's vision was less compromised, and there was less chance of the ground washing out from beneath their feet. After thirty-five minutes, they reached the tiny stone plateau Gavin recalled in vivid detail.

He dropped Garboni's body with a hollow squish and rolled his shoulders. His back and legs ached from the exertion. Gently stomping his feet, he warded off the cold and worked circulation back to the numerous deprived parts of his body. He was relieved to see Keegan following suit. She looked exhausted. The water-drenched Stetson had long since fallen from her head. It hung from a strap draped over her shoulders and down her back. She flicked water from inside the sodden thing and looked ready to throw it from the cliff less than three feet away. She inched near the ledge and peered over.

Gavin grabbed her arm. "Careful. That first step is a neck breaker."

Her eyes were wide. Nothing was visible in the black abyss beyond. For that matter, the only sound was the ever-twisting whistle of the wind. "How far is it?" she asked.

"Several hundred feet. After that, you pretty much bounce and splatter on stone until you hit the water."

She stepped quickly away from the ledge. Her heels impacted Garboni's body, and her arms began to pinwheel. Gavin grabbed her arm once more. He offered a silent but hopefully reassuring smile.

"You're joking about the fall, right?" she grumbled in a dry, humorless voice.

He thought back to his close call, hanging from the ledge and the view he'd had from that perspective. Taking a calming breath, he slipped his hands from his gloves and shoved them slowly into his back pocket. "Wish I was."

Her gaze moved quickly around the small landing. A lightning flash in the distance washed over the bleak, confined, boulder-strewn surroundings. "Did we make a wrong turn?"

The path they'd followed ended abruptly at the east. A sheer drop greeted them at the south edge of the platform. The west edge was exactly the same. A great slab of vertical stone formed a wall at the back of the shelf to the north. There was just enough room for the two of them and the supine corpse at their feet.

Gavin examined the sheer rock wall he remembered from his last visit and recalled the way it had literally vaporized beneath his fingertips. It was solid and immovable once more.

There was no sign of the cave entrance.

He wrapped his fist against the stone. It was entirely unyielding. "I don't get it. The entrance was right here."

Keegan placed a hand against the wall. Sighing, she sagged physically against it and slid to take a seat on her backside. Everything about her appearance screamed exhaustion, and Gavin wondered for perhaps the tenth time how she'd made it this far given the weather and the load the two shared. Being this close to the corpse didn't even seem to faze her now.

Gavin watched how she pressed herself to the stone wall and suspected Keegan took some comfort in it because it was literally the furthest she could move from the cliff's edge. He couldn't blame her.

The lack of a cave defied reason, and Gavin couldn't reconcile the experience *he'd had with what he now saw.*

Was it all a dream?

He pulled a small flashlight from his coat pocket and played the bean across the wall's surface. Keegan laughed at his thorough examination. "There isn't enough room to lay down," she said. "I hardly think you've overlooked the cave entrance." Though she'd maintained a sense of humor, her English lilt had slipped out with the words.

All at once, the whistle of the ever-present wind went silent. The change was disorienting. In her exhausted state, leaning against the wall, she shifted quickly in response and slapped outstretched arms against the wall to her back.

Gavin knelt instantly and placed a steadying hand against her shoulder. "It's happening," he said in a sharp whisper. "Move slowly away from the wall."

He didn't know why the warning had sprung to mind, but he didn't question it. The events of his last visit remained a confusing blur, and his memories of the cave entrance were hazy and indistinct. Something was happening and it was similar, if not an exact repeat of his last visit.

Taking Keegan by the hand, the couple rose and stepped past Garboni's body. The crunch of gravel and grime sounded like sandpaper as it ground beneath their feet. In the dead silence of the night, even the slightest sounds seemed magnified. Keegan turned toward the ledge, but Gavin stopped her. "No," he said. "Keep an eye on the rock face. Something is about to happen."

Her eyes were wide. "What happened to the wind?" she whispered. She sounded on the verge of panic. "It's not just me—do you feel that? There's something in the air."

Gavin kept her hand clasped tightly in his. Something in the air? He felt the cold metal of his flashlight in one hand and the feverish warmth of hers in the other. He sensed nothing in the air, though that prior sense of foreboding had returned in force.

Something at the center of the rock face began to shimmer and caught Gavin's eye. The color shift was subtle, but the beam of his light quickly found the spot. It was just below eye level at the center of the wall. Keegan took a step forward as an engraving materialized from the unadorned stone. She gasped and sagged physically. His restraining arms were the only thing to keep her from collapsing atop Garboni's body.

Gavin recognized the symbol on the wall before them. He wrapped his arms around Keegan and held her close. His eyes probed the symbol. It seemed to fade in and out of visibility, distinct one second and barely distinguishable the next. A single thick wavy line with a circle imposed directly beneath it. The line was as black as obsidian and carved deep into the wall's surface. The circle, centered about two inches below the line, was every bit as dark and carved just as deep.

"This is it," Gavin said.

"No!" Keegan croaked. She grabbed him by the coat and looked him in the eyes. Lightning flashed in the distance, but no thunder followed. "We can't. Not here—not with that…that thing. We have to go back."

Gavin grimaced. "The cave is here. You don't believe me?"

She offered a violent shake of her head and glared with wild eyes. "It's the symbol. If there's a cave, we can't go inside."

"It's alright," he said with a reassuring smile. "It's a little creepy, but I've been there before. We'll be in and out before you know it."

She shook her head once more, this time more violently. Water flitted from the loose strands of hair. "You don't understand—It's the same symbol from your tattoo."

Gavin's brow furrowed. He pushed a saturated sleeve back on his waterlogged coat and shined the beam of his light on the inside of his arm. The tattoo was more complex, but she was right. The core of his ink was based on the same sigil. Additional lines were added, but based on the same core iconography.

How the hell did I miss that?

"What does it mean?" It was the only question he could think to ask.

Keegan's brow furrowed, and Gavin watched as her gaze moved slowly between the mark on the wall and the similar ink on his arm. "I…I don't know," she stammered. "There's a link, but…"

"It's okay, watch." Gavin stepped over Garboni once more and pressed the palm of his hand against the center of the sigil. It seemed more like the memory of a dream, but he now recalled this was what he'd done the last time.

Nothing happened.

Keegan shook her head. She looked ready to argue but stopped short. A faraway look crossed her expression as if suddenly recalling a long-forgotten memory. "Blood," she said quietly. "It was the blood." Her words were little more than a whisper.

Blood. Gavin recalled the slash on his palm and the gooey squish it had made on impact with the stone on his last visit. Is that the key?

Pulling the fixed-blade knife from the horizontal sheaf on the back of his belt, he quickly drew the blade across the palm of his left hand. The moment his palm made contact with the sigil, a massive portion of the stone face vaporized into sand. The material plummeted to the ground to land in a pile of ankle-deep grit. Sound returned to the mountaintop at precisely the same instant. Keegan's hand went to her mouth and tears filled her eyes. Her gaze shot left and right as if trying to make sense of the experience.

"Do you know what you just did?" she hissed.

"Quick, grab his feet," Gavin said.

Chapter 41

The inside of the cavern was oppressive, but not just in temperature. There was an anxiety-inducing quality to the space that had nothing to do with the darkness nor the countless tons of rock suspended overhead. Keegan pulled off her hat and looked to Gavin for confirmation. "You've been here before?"

He nodded.

"Was it this hot then?"

"Not even close." He was slipping out of his coat and had already discarded his hat. His gloves were pushed quickly into the back pocket of his jeans. "Brooks Fowler told me there was no volcanic activity on the island."

"There isn't," she confirmed. "I've done my homework. The nearest volcanic activity in the region is at Mud Cat Atoll." They both knew that was far to the north. "And Mud Cat has been dormant for at least thirty thousand years."

She turned back to the yawning mouth of the cave. Lightning danced in the distant sky and rain pounded the platform only a few feet away. "And the freaky ass door? Do you have any idea what that was?"

"A Casting," Gavin offered in a low tone. "Something archaic."

The look on Keegan's face displayed her surprise. "A Casting," she said slowly. "And you know what that is?"

"I'm familiar with the subject matter," he offered cryptically.

At a loss for words, she simply stared. When he failed to elaborate, she spun a finger in the air in a, get on with it gesture.

Gavin sighed audibly and took a long moment to respond. He seemed to be coming to a decision that weighed heavily on him. "My mother was a witch. She was burned alive. Her death curse changed the course of my life, so yes... I'm familiar with Castings."

The light in Keegan's hand dipped and illuminated the floor. She would have laughed at the outrageous claim if they weren't standing where there were after having done what they'd just done. It also explained why Gavin had been so accepting of her creepy proclivity for out-of-body experiences. Considering the expressions she'd just seen cross his face, he must have decided she'd gone through much the same process before deciding to share her ability with him months earlier. Looking back now, he'd accepted her claims without scorn or incredulity. It was as if this sort of thing somehow came naturally to him. At the very least, he had prior experience with the paranormal.

Gavin raised his light and grinned. "I know you're familiar with the practice." He paused for what seemed like forever before continuing. "It's just been a long time since I ran into anything like..." his voice trailed off. He motioned in the direction from which they'd come. "Like this. Well, this island. But that portal pulled the same disintegrating act last time. Disturbing," he said with a nod, then added, "Actually, I'm a little more concerned about how the wall reconstituted itself following my last visit."

Images of a similar disintegrating wall deep within the basements of the citadel flashed through Keegan's mind's eye. The experience had a dreamlike quality. The memory flooded back to her in a wash of emotions. The primal fear of witnessing the strange ceremony in the next room, the silhouette of the featureless naked figure leading the group—the experience was lost to her until this moment. It was as if the memory had been taken or suppressed until this moment.

"I've seen a door like that once before," she admitted.

Gavin's face was a mask of confusion. It grew instantly into concern. "Something to do with your coven?"

She shook her head. She looked at the desiccated corpse at their feet. "Let's *call it the next problem to deal with. It might make this seem downright run-of-the-mill. Show me the rest of this cave? I'm starting to wonder if the two might be related." She shook her head. "But you're not getting off the hook that easy. When we're done here, you're telling me all about what happened to your mother." She looked around the shadowed confines of the cavern. "First, let's do whatever we came here to do. There's something…wrong…with this place."*

The comments did nothing to alleviate Gavin's concern. He looked ready to ask a question but seemed to think better. "If you like what you've seen so far, you'll love this." He tipped his head in the direction of the cave's dark confines.

Great.

Gripping the belt slung beneath Garboni's shoulders once more, Gavin prepared to move on. Keegan lifted the body at the feet and grunted her readiness to move. They reached a large chamber after following the only path available to them. They found themselves in a massive stone gallery with walls testing the limits of the flashlight beam. The stone ceiling rose to a natural dome high overhead. Though the ground was rough with gravel, a path of smooth stone led from the chamber entrance and seemed to snake a deliberate path through the gallery.

A dark form loomed in the distance. Gavin's light fell upon it as they moved with the dead man stretched between them. The sight caught Keegan off guard. She stifled a scream and dropped her burden.

"Yeah," Gavin said. "I had pretty much the same reaction." He played the beam of his light across the kneeling form of the intricately carved life-sized statue.

Stepping around Garboni, Keegan moved close to the stone figure. "It's amazing," she muttered, her tone reverential. "The level of detail is…well, it's astounding." A cold feeling turned deep in her gut as her eyes probed the stone surface of the figure. She sensed another lost memory struggling to break through.

I've seen figures like this before. Many, many more…

Gavin said, "I'm no aficionado, but the craftsmanship isn't what concerns me."

Keegan shielded her eyes from the light's glare and offered Gavin a concerned glance, wondering what she'd missed. While this figure was vaguely familiar, she couldn't fully recall the experience tugging from the corner of her mind. It felt as though her subconscious was slapping at her conscious mind in an attempt to deliver a message.

That message felt like a warning. Something vital.

"The purpose of art is to tell a story or invoke emotion," Gavin said. "Given this level of detail, it might even be to immortalize someone. But if that's the case, what's this monk doing?"

The statue depicted an old monk in flowing robes. He had a balding hairline, a neatly trimmed beard, and thick callouses on his fingers. Kneeling, his hands were outstretched as if reaching for something close to the floor's surface. Whatever he was reaching for was not present.

"You're right," Keegan said. Her voice was little more than a whisper. She felt reluctant to disturb the silence of this cavern. Even the storm outside wasn't audible here. The complete lack of stimulus felt increasingly oppressive. "This is a lot of effort with no clear intent."

"And it's only the beginning."

Gavin turned his light further into the darkness. Another statue loomed beyond. This figure was every bit as intricately detailed, depicting a man in a World War One-era military uniform. His hat was folded beneath his equipment belt, alongside which hung a battered Calvary man's saber. An empty holster drooped from one hip. Interestingly, the figure appeared to be captured mid-stride. He'd been depicted running; his head turned sharply to peer over his shoulder as he moved.

A violent chill shot through Keegan. She felt it from head to toe. Déjà vu. Swallowing hard, she tried to focus on the immediate predicament. Her hand slipped into Gavin's. She could not mask a shiver so fierce it was more of a tremor.

"Are you alright?"

Keegan blinked slowly and nodded. "That's a Russian infantryman insignia." She was pointing to the battered and worn hat pinched between the figure's torso and belt.

Gavin spun and directed the light some thirty yards away. Another figure, this time some native tribesmen, came into view. The man was perhaps five and a half feet tall and dressed in an animal skin loincloth. A quiver of arrows was slung across his back, the delicate feathers of the arrow fletchings, each distinctly visible in richly crafted detail. This figure was depicted in mid-stride as well. He had a crude wooden bow in one hand, and his face was a pinched rictus of either determination or terror.

"My God." Keegan's voice boomed loud and echoed across the stone walls. It suggested the cavern was more extensive than she'd first guessed. "How many are there?"

"I didn't stop to browse," Gavin admitted.

Tempering the growing unease in the pit of her belly, Keegan took several slow, meditative breaths. Gavin was watching her with concerned eyes. Reaching out to touch the tribesman, she stopped short. It was as if she felt it was somehow wrong to violate the artwork in such a way. "They appear to be the work of the same craftsman," she said.

"You think?" Gavin looked skeptical.

"Who can say for sure," she admitted. "But this level of artistry doesn't come easy. It's all so…intricate…and exacting. It's hard to believe more than one person would be up to this level of work."

Gavin cleared his throat and said, "I hate to admit it, but this place is creeping me out. Can we do what we came here for? We need to get back before someone notices we're missing."

She met his gaze and was struck by the concern in his expression. He might be creeped out, but that wasn't the reason for the comment. Her growing discomfort was palpable, and he hadn't missed it. Gavin was just too kind to call her out on it.

"Let's stash the body and go," she agreed.

Raising his burden once more, Gavin pointed his light toward what should be the rear wall of the cavern. "We're not hiding him. We're here to dispose of him."

Keegan didn't understand the distinction.

He led the way to the pair of sunken grottos bracketing a small raised stone platform. Keegan's eyes were instantly drawn to the twin pools because they glowed with an iridescent, spectral green goo. Thick and gelatinous, the substance seemed to churn and circulate in almost imperceptible eddies and currents.

Keegan stared, mesmerized and speechless.

"I know," Gavin said. "Strangest crap I've ever seen. And from what I

know, it will consume just about anything."

Her mouth working in silent slow motion, Keegan was struck by a dozen questions. The alien green glow from the pools left her nearly unable to speak. "How," she finally croaked in a dry, gravely tone.

"Kind of a long story. The pools were originally discovered by a shipwreck survivor named Fenton Bitters. Brooks Fowler found Bitters' journal about a year after he moved to the island. That led him to the cave. Somewhere along the way, Fowler learned about this green goop."

"And the goop is…"

"Hell if I know. Fowler nearly died trying to test it. He couldn't even take a sample for the longest time. Everything he used to try and extract a sample ended up instantly consumed by the corrosive crud. Turns out it eats just about anything, manmade or synthetic."

Keegan stepped backward reflexively. "Maybe we should be concerned about the fumes."

Gavin shook his head. "No fumes. Fowler was finally able to take a sample. Hand-blown glass is about the only thing that doesn't get absorbed by the sludge. The trick, apparently, was to have glass with high carbon content. He did finally get a sample."

"What did he find?"

A shrug from Gavin. "I don't think he ever tested it. He got sick before he got that far. We're talking really sick. He thinks this stuff did it. It's why he was willing to sell the island. He just wanted to be done with everything associated with that pursuit."

This was news to Keegan. She'd never heard how her father came into possession of the land or heard more than a few comments about the elusive previous owner. Her mind swam with new questions.

Gavin wasn't nearly as distracted. Hefting Garboni by the collar and belt, he swung the sagging remains over the side of the leftmost pool. Then, very gently, he lowered the remains to the surface of the green fluid. The surface of the thick gelatinous material seemed to resist at first, as if a membrane had formed. A moment later, there came a sucking sound and the body was physically pulled from Gavin's grip. He jumped back so quickly, his feet seemed to dance to catch up to his pinwheeling arms.

Keegan grabbed Gavin and pulled him further from the radiant green glow. "What the hell was that?" She snapped.

"Don't know," he said with a slow shake of his head. Gavin's eyes remain fixed on the pool. The body was already slipping entirely beneath the surface of the green ooze. "It felt like something beneath the surface grabbed on and pulled him out of my hands."

Keegan shook off a fresh wave of chills. "We're done?"

Gavin nodded vigorously. "Let's get the hell out of here."

Chapter 42

The chill, damp air of the chamber stirred with a circular current that seemingly had no source. Decades-old cobwebs were swept from the wall sconces and the tight joints where the circular stone wall met the stone ceiling. Had anyone been present to witness the event, they would have felt the room's temperature rise more than fifteen degrees in less than as many seconds.

At the same time, the pinpoint of green light struggling for breath from the bottom of the well flared. A spectral green flame the size of a large candle guttered, flickered, then found footing in the inky black abyss.

Chapter 43

Stanton Anakasta burst into the control room and threaded his way between a series of long tables stacked high with complex electronic components. A massive flat-panel display hung on the wall at the room's far end. Across from it sat a pair of technicians at a long counter. They sat behind wide monitors of their own, one displaying areal telemetry dotted and etched with waxing and waning measurements. While the second screen showed the same visuals as the first, the imagery was awash in dramatic colors; most were shades of blues-tinged with the occasional splash of orange or yellow.

"You found something?" Anakasta barked without preamble.

Asha stood beside the pair of men at the table. She manipulated the display of her hand-held tablet and moved the colorful blue and orange images to the large screen on the back wall. "Drone two discovered the anomaly twenty-seven minutes ago. There was a lightning strike in the vicinity, and we lost contact with the octocopter. Drone three just arrived on-station." She nodded to the screen. "This is the infrared feed."

Anakasta groused and studied the indistinct, moving aerial image. He could see a dense canopy and thick tree trunks, but thermal imaging wasn't ideal on the cold island night. Certainly not, given the harsh weather conditions. Everything was awash in frigid driving rain.

"Switch to ultraviolet," he muttered. "I can't see a bloody thing."

One of the men at the twin consoles entered a series of commands with swift strikes at the keyboard. The big screen flashed and went to night vision mode. Anakasta instantly saw what he'd missed. A small aircraft lay pitched nose first, almost standing perpendicular to the rocky soil, one wing torn from the fuselage and the tail section entirely missing.

"Is this the plane our new friend Greeley came in on? I thought he crashed at sea?" Anakasta's comment was directed at his wife.

Asha shook her head without hesitation. "Can't be. Based on his account, that was a small twin-engine craft with sea floats. The drones have found wreckage off the coast to support that. This is a much smaller, single-seat fixed-wing aircraft according to measurements. No chance it's the same plane."

The nose of the aircraft had impacted sharply with the surface; there was no question concerning the result of the crash. The nose cone was twisted and mashed, evidence of a violent impact. Anakasta noted the coordinates at the corner of the display. "Is that zone correct?" he barked. "I thought we cleared that grid days ago."

"Two days ago," Asha confirmed. "We've already reviewed footage of these exact coordinates to confirm. The aircraft wasn't there on our last pass."

Anakasta's face was growing dark with anger. "You're saying we have more uninvited guests."

Asha's response was unusually noncommittal in tone. "Perhaps. But I'm not so sure." She tapped one of the technicians on the shoulder. "Mark, review that zoom location for me one more time."

The display on the large screen flashed several times in rapid succession. With each flicker, the frame jumped to zoom closer on the aircraft just aft of the crushed nose cone. The cockpit's canopy had fractured at its apex, while the side closest to the camera had largely disintegrated entirely. The dark image froze, streaked with rainfall, frozen in time. The details were difficult to distinguish, everything resolving to one shade or another of gray on black.

"What am I looking at?" Anakasta grumbled.

Asha tapped the screen directing attention to the collapsed portion of the canopy. "This appears to be tree growth." If she was right, a portion of the tree had already grown up through the bottom of the cockpit and sprouted through the hole in the glass.

"Impossible," Anakasta said quietly.

Chapter 44

The doors to the infirmary flew open and Gavin stormed in. His stride showed determination, and Doctor Cantrell saw a fire blazing in his eye. He had a reputation for being one who didn't anger quickly, and she had never seen him like this. Interestingly, Keegan Anakasta was close at his heels. Though the couple's relationship was a poorly concealed secret when it came to the island staff, it was unusual for the two to appear in the public areas of the complex.

"Where is she?" Gavin fumed. "Where's Tess?"

Cantrell raised a restraining hand. She didn't intend to bar the couple from access to the infirmary; she simply wanted to keep the situation from escalating. Though Gavin was the youngest of the men on the island, he was also fiercely protective of his friends. He projected an air of confidence that had a way of uniting the staff in a way no one before him had managed. Technically he had no authority, but from what she had seen, that didn't appear to matter. He breathed with the confidence of a natural-born leader. "Slow down," she warned. "Tess was released about an hour ago. She's doing well, both mentally and physically. Far better than her attacker, I might add."

Gavin looked confused at the comment. "Hathaway," he said as if to clarify the point.

"You don't know what happened?"

Keegan stepped from behind Gavin and shook her head. "We just heard Tess was attacked last night. Dale said she was brought here."

Her gaze shifted from Keegan to Gavin; a smile touched Cantrell's lips. "Then you haven't heard the story?"

The couple shook their heads in unison.

"It seemed we have the newcomer to thank for coming to Tess's rescue," she explained. "Zane appears to be as capable as he is large." She motioned to a drawn privacy curtain at the perimeter of the room.

Gavin pulled the curtain away in a single brisk motion. Tom Hathaway lay semi-reclined in a wide hospital bed. Thick casts wrapped each arm and one of his legs. His head was wrapped in layers of thick white gauze. He looked like a comatose mummy. Only his eyes were visible through the bandaging; both were circled in thick purple-black bruising.

"Greeley did this?" Gavin said. Satisfaction quickly softened his expression. Judging by his tone, he wasn't entirely surprised. "When can I talk with this prick?"

Cantrell stepped forward. She tugged the curtain closed and glared at Gavin through her thick glasses. "That's not going to happen."

Gavin looked ready to argue. Keegan put a restraining hand on his arm and guided him toward the middle of the room. "It looks like justice has been served, if only temporarily," she offered.

"I can't let you speak with him, even if I want," Cantrell added. "For what it's worth, I intended to keep Mister Hathaway under sedation until he could be escorted off the island. It turns out that won't be necessary. He's currently in a coma. He won't be talking to anyone."

Though Gavin looked concerned, Cantrell didn't read worry for Hathaway in his expression. "And Tess is okay," he said quietly. "What happens to Greeley?"

"We have Willy to thank for that. At least as far as Mayhew is concerned, Hathaway did that," Cantrell motioned to the drawn curtain, "falling down the stairs. It's clear Mayhew isn't buying the explanation but since no one is contradicting it," she tipped her head once more to the closed curtain, "what can he do?"

The tension eased visibly from Gavin. His hands slipped into the pockets of his jeans. The ferocity slowly drained from his eyes.

"I need to draw blood from you and Miss Anakasta while you're here," Cantrell said after a long pause.

"Blood?" Keegan said. "Why?"

The look Gavin offered seemed to ask the same question.

"Just a routine examination," Cantrell explained. "I've taken samples from the rest of the staff. Obviously, since you're not staff, your participation is not required, Keegan. But if you're willing to contribute, it's appreciated."

Keegan was puzzled by the request. "You do this often?"

Gavin didn't respond. Cantrell didn't like lying, so she went for a splitting of the truth. "Not often, but with some regularity." She felt Gavin's penetrating gaze but was relieved when he didn't call her on the deception.

Preparing a table for the blood draw was a matter of only minutes. Keegan was the first to contribute. A set of six vials were taken. Though she was surprised by the amount, Keegan didn't protest. When it was Gavin's turn, things were different.

"Give me a minute with the Doc," he said.

Keegan nodded and slowly crossed to the far end of the infirmary. She began reading the numerous medical posters on display. Cantrell knew what was coming and attempted to redirect the course of the conversation preemptively. "It's not like you to be seen in public together."

It took a lot to make Gavin uncomfortable, but this seemed to do the trick. "You know about that?"

Cantrell tied the tourniquet tight around Gavin's arm. She pushed her black-framed glasses back on her head and grinned. "Twenty-two years old, an accent, and eyes like that?" She glanced in Keegan's direction. "This sort of girl doesn't stay single for long. She's also too bright and driven to stay in a place like this for long unless there's a good reason." She let an uncomfortable silence grow between them. "Besides," she said with an arch of her brow. "Who do you think prescribes her birth control pill? I'm literally the only game in town."

Though the color of his face darkened a shade, there was a twinkle in his eyes.

"The biggest tell is the way she looks at you," Cantrell whispered. "That's

hard to hide."

Gavin groaned. "We'll have to try harder."

Clicking a new vacutube into the tap still embedded in Gavin's arm, Cantrell knew she had avoided the subject at hand for as long as he would tolerate. "What do you want to know?"

"What's the real story behind the blood samples, and why so much?" he asked.

"Visits to my end of the floor are up more than three hundred percent in the last three weeks." By that, she meant the infirmary. She snapped a new tube in place and began drawing a fourth vile. "Mostly minor things, headaches, nausea, fatigue, and the like—but all in volumes much higher than normal. The last two days have shown dramatic hormonal shifts in at least two of the staff." She looked at the closed curtain across the room. "Our new guest is the most aberrant example yet. His readings were off the charts in extremely unusual ways."

"And you suspect a contagion of some kind?"

"Yes—Well, no." She stammered and fumbled in an attempt to switch out the next sample tube. Gavin put a calming hand on hers and drew her eyes to his.

"It's alright." His tone was as calm as it was disarming. "No one expects you to have all the answers. Just tell me what you do know."

Cantrell offered a frustrated smile. "The fact is, I don't know much. Not everyone on the island seems to be affected. Those who are don't seem to have anything in common. Some of the results are a little concerning. Some exhibit metrics which might suggest their condition is ramping up to something worse. But they could just as easily be winding down from whatever this is…the test results could show they're on the mend. I don't have enough data to work with."

Gavin nodded. "So you need more data. And you're on top of that." He tipped his gaze to the tap in his arm. "When will you know more?"

"I'm collecting new blood draws from the entire staff today. Until now, I've been working with draws taken haphazardly when appropriate. I have an eighty percent sample rate. Today I'm getting data from everyone. I'll know more tonight."

She lay the last vacutube on the counter and pressed a cotton swab across the needle in Gavin's arm. *Extracting the collection assembly, she deftly used a bandaid to secure the cotton.* "See, Doc? You've got this. Let's see what more data tells us and go from there." *He eyed the curtain on the far side of the room for a long second before continuing.* "To be clear, are you saying these odd test results might be related to the attack on Tess last night?"

Sitting back in her chair, Cantrell looked frustrated once more. "I think Tom Hathaway was already a ticking time bomb. His psych profile didn't include the building blocks for a very nice guy. Experience tells me what happened last night was only a matter of time. That said, his numbers were worse than anyone so far. Considering those results and the impact likely to result? Who can say? It's possible."

Gavin considered this. "One more question," *he said. Leaning forward and offering a smile, he carefully pulled the glasses from Doctor Cantrell's face.*

"Hey," *she stammered.* "What the hell?"

Turning the thick black frames in his hands, Gavin raised the lenses to the light on the ceiling. He scowled before looking back to Cantrell. He examined the thick glass lenses and then placed them over his eyes. "Care to explain this, Doc?"

Cantrell had gone pale. Her hands began to shake. She folded them in her lap but knew Gavin had seen just the same. "Explain what?" *While the words came, her heart wasn't in them.*

Gavin passed the glasses back. "These things are nearly as thick as Coke bottles, yet they have no corrective value whatsoever. Why wear them?"

She found herself unable to answer. No reasonable explanation could be offered. If she wore them for cosmetic reasons, the lenses should be thin and light. She couldn't attribute this to personal vanity. Nor could she explain the truth. It was far too unusual to be believed.

"I think you used to wear glasses exactly like these," *Gavin said at last.* "But something changed and you didn't want to change with it. Sound about right?"

Her palms growing damp, Cantrell studied Gavin.

Can he know?

"You haven't been here long enough," *she offered finally.* "You wouldn't understand."

Gavin studied her for long silent seconds. "I met with Brooks Fowler recently. He made some fairly outrageous claims about this place and the people working here. Do you care to comment?"

She remained silent, though her heart was galloping beneath her breast.

"Fowler said there was a reason he worked so hard to ensure the staff could remain on the island. He implied he didn't know what would happen to many of you if you left. He didn't know if your conditions would reassert themselves."

Cantrell found it impossible to meet his eye.

"You're entitled to your secrets," Gavin said. His voice was neutral and patient. "But I raise the question to you for a couple of reasons. First, if something on this island has such miraculous healing properties, in your professional opinion, could that same something be causing these unusual test results? Second, if you know what's bringing about the healing, I suggest you start there when you look for causation. And third—"

"I don't know how this place helps us," she blurted. "Only that it does. I haven't found anything here that can explain it, but I can confidently say that something miraculous happens on this island."

Gavin studied her. At last, he nodded. "Alright. But clarify this for me? Fowler claimed you were wheelchair-bound when you came to the island. Is that true?"

She met his gaze with moist eyes and nodded. Her voice was husky and pained. "I'd been confined to a chair for eleven years."

"And being here changed that?"

She nodded.

"Just being here? You didn't have to do anything? Didn't eat or drink anything unusual? Maybe visit a particular part of the island?"

Looking squarely into his eyes, she shook her head. "I've asked myself the same questions—asked them of everyone under my care, for that matter. I consume the same food and drink as everyone else. And as far as travel? I'd only seen photos of the island until about a month after I was out of the chair. I came here to work and never actually left the confines of this building until well after I regained the use of my legs."

Gavin seemed to consider this. "Last question then." He pointed to her glasses, now folded at the center of the table. "Why wear bulky fake glasses that serve no purpose?"

She laughed, embarrassed and relieved by the question at the same time. Offering a shy shrug, she said, "a miracle cure restored my ability to walk. My background—my life—is based in medicine, in science. As overjoyed as I am with this shocking turn of good fortune, part of me is terrified by it." She fumbled with the glasses, folding and unfolding the frames. "I've worn lenses like these my entire adult life. I suppose they're a bit like a security blanket. Just something familiar to hold onto when the world isn't making total sense."

Nodding as if satisfied, Gavin smiled. "The explanation makes sense to me." He squeezed her hand and pushed away from the table. "I'll leave the science to you."

Cantrell began to slip the glasses over her face but stopped short. Pulling them away, she gave them a long glance. Slowly folding them, she watched as Gavin exchanged quiet words with Keegan. He offered a wave and a smile, then the two were gone.

Setting the glasses aside, Cantrell considered the conversation they'd just had. It felt like a weight had been lifted, a burden somehow removed from her shoulders. Gavin was the only one among the island staff not aware of the unique properties of the place. Sharing had felt cathartic. He'd raised a good point as well. Might the island's supernatural properties be influencing their physical states in a negative way? Perhaps too afraid to challenge her good fortune, the idea had never crossed her mind.

Chapter 45

Gavin slid his tray along the counter. He scooped a generous helping of scrambled egg, grabbed two slices of toast, then snagged three strips of the crispiest bacon from the pile. He nodded good morning to Chef Dawe, pawed a bottle of orange juice, and headed for the tables. Having the cafeteria to himself was a relief. Gavin took a table at the center of the room. He was still processing what Doc Cantrell had explained as he attempted to reconcile it with the information Brooks Fowler supplied on the whirlwind trip to Manhattan. There was something special about the island, that much was clear. The experience in the cave at the top of the mountain, combined with the terrible turn Fowler's health had taken suggested the benefits of the island might not be without equally terrifying costs.

The island had beautiful qualities, many uniquely appreciated by Gavin, specifically due to geographic isolation. But there was a darkness to the place as well. He'd been aware of a sense of malignancy since the first time he set foot on shore. The source of the hollow feeling simmering in his gut was difficult to quantify. Though he'd come from a line of powerful Crafters, he possessed no power himself. The high expectations of his clan were instilled in his bones back in the early years of his childhood. The elders had subjected him to every assessment, evaluation, and appraisal known, no matter how painful or arcane.

Drinking down half of the orange juice, Gavin considered Keegan. She had *the gift. She was both knowledgeable and powerful—more powerful than even she was aware. Her power as a Seer was just the tip of the iceberg. In time, she would grow into a wider range of abilities, it was a certainty. The island seemed to magnify what was unquestionably a natural talent. The place was a supercharger for those with a gift, and her abilities were outpacing her facility to control them.*

All of this ultimately caused Gavin to circle back to the root of his concern. He had yet to gain confidence in his understanding of Stanton Anakasta. The man had paid a literal fortune for the island. And while he was making complex attempts to hide his efforts, the man was using his so-called security team to search every square inch of the land.

But for what?

The journal of Fenton Bitters seemed a likely target. Bitters was the island's most famous and controversial tenant. Shipwrecked in the 19th century, the man was crippled by Polio and left with nearly no use of his legs. Information detailing the man's early life was readily available online. The only son of aristocratic parents, history credited him for developing telescope technology that was generations ahead of its time. His devices used complex gear-driven mechanisms to combine multiple lenses resulting in precision optics able to see over an incredible distance. A Bitters Scope, as the devices were known, was expensive and in high demand. It was said Bitters was making a Pacific voyage to personally deliver one of his most intricate new instruments when the ship he'd chartered was lost at sea.

The story of Fenton Bitters devolved into one of history's lost hero tales with that fateful journey. Some believed Bitters died in the shipwreck. Others claimed the accident was all an elaborate ruse, and that Bitters lived out his remaining years as a hermit in some quiet corner of the world. Perhaps most interestingly, some reports claimed Bitters was stranded on an unknown island far off the western coast of the United States, and that he was ultimately rescued by a cargo vessel that was itself blown off course by one of the massive storms frequent to the region. These reports were vehemently challenged by skeptics primarily based on two factors. First, it was claimed that Bitters was rescued 26 years after his ship was reported lost at sea. And second, it was said that upon his rescue, Fenton Bitters had regained full use of his legs and no longer suffered the debilitating adverse effects of Polio.

Gavin wouldn't put much stock in any of the information…if not for the journal Brooks Fowler handed to him at the end of his Manhattan visit. Fowler had researched every aspect of Bitters' life and believed with absolute certainty the man had spent more than a quarter century on the island. The journal, Fowler claimed, detailed much of what happened in that time. There were gaps in what was documented in the man's own hand, Fowler was equally certain. And while he had never gained insight into the experiences too sensitive for a man like Bitters to commit to paper, the way the book had been authored made it clear some experiences had been redacted.

Stanton Anakasta was likely searching for traces left from Bitters' time on the island. That and something Fowler referred to only as the Shard. Apparently, the small plinth and podium Gavin had found empty in the cavern at the top of the mountain were supposed to contain an object of some intrinsic value. Uncharacteristically, Fowler had been unwilling to describe the object. Gavin had failed to discern a description of the Idol, and Fowler refused to explain the artifact's significance.

These people were all nuts, Gavin had long since concluded. Recent events only reinforced the assessment. If he had a brain in his head, he would catch the next ship out and never look back. It was a survival instinct he would never obey, but it didn't change the wrongness of this place. There was a quality to the island he needed to fully understand. But more importantly, there was Keegan. As long as she was here, so was he.

The sound of Willy's Scottish brogue filled the room before the man came into sight. When the old man passed through the double doors in the corner, he was gesticulating in grand gestures and puffing out his cheeks. Greeley was at the man's side, seemingly hanging on every word. Willy slapped his hands together, the clap echoing off the walls of the vast, empty room. Gavin noted how Chef Dawe fumbled to keep control of a large pan he was moving behind the buffet. Willy's antics startled the man, and Dawe grabbed at the pan with his spare hand to keep from spilling the contents. Whatever it was, it must have been hot because his ungloved hand recoiled. Dawe muttered a silent curse and shot Willy a withering glance that went unnoticed as the man filled a plate while still telling the remainder of his story to Greeley.

"So I says to the lad," Willy went on with a shake of his head and shoved half a dozen limp strips of bacon onto a plate already stacked to overflowing with scrambled eggs, toast, and some kind of Danish. "You only claim to have one testicle. The point is, she'll have to prove you wrong!"

Greeley let out a barking laugh and shook his head. Gavin suspected the big man was humoring the old guy and was surprised to see genuine mirth in Greeley's expression as his laughter died to a chuckle. Odd since Gavin had endured every witticism old Willy had to offer in recent months and found the man only truly funny when he was three sheets to the wind. Given it was barely sunrise, even Willy couldn't be drunk so early.

"Good morning," Greeley said and thumped his tray down on the table across from Gavin.

Gavin nodded, still examining the camaraderie between the old man and the big man. "Did the bar open early?" Gavin said. "I haven't seen Willy in such good spirits without the help of his spirits, and I can't remember the last time he made it to chow before the sun crossed the horizon."

Willy folded a strip of bacon in half and immediately jammed the entire piece in his mouth. He glanced at Greeley and arched an eyebrow. "What did I tell you? He's nothing but piss and vinegar in the morning. You try working with that."

Greeley smiled. "Willy said there's a problem with one of the antennas on the roof of the north wing. There's supposed to be a brief break in the storm this morning. I'm going to help him pull down the aerial and rewire it. Willy said it's used for the internet uplink?"

Gavin sat back in his seat. He suspected the old man's motivation had more to do with a sudden inability to access internet pornography, and was very tempted to make the point. Deciding to take the high road, he eyed Greeley. "You have electrical experience?"

Greeley nodded. "I worked as a contractor for a few years. Nothing too complicated there. Mostly heavy lifting from the sound of it. Willy said you use some industrial panels all along the north wing. My biggest contribution will be the lifting."

Willy leaned over his plate and stabbed at his eggs. He grumbled his words without making eye contact. "I'll take advantage of yer help while I can. This Nancy-boy ain't good for lifting nothing."

Gavin grinned, glanced at Greeley, and rolled his eyes. "If you're working with this old cuss today, it will give me a chance to get some real work done." He thought about something Doc Cantrell had said and decided it was a good time to bring it up. "The storm has delayed the supply ship. The ship's captain isn't willing to navigate our reefs given the unusual currents caused by the weather."

Gavin saw the fork stop moving halfway to Willy's mouth. The old man's watery gaze seemed fixed on the table, though it was unlikely he saw the room before him. Wrinkles of concern tugged at the corners of his unmoving eyes.

Greeley didn't look pleased with this news, though he was handling it better than Willy.

"Not to worry, boss," Gavin said somberly. "I checked out the inventory log. We're stocked with enough essentials to last at least five weeks without rationing. That includes enough refreshments to keep the party going even if we have to hold out another month." Gavin thought of briefing the old man on the status of their medical supplies, equally well stocked for the coming delay, but he saw tension leave his eyes. A second later the fork was refilled, and a fresh mouthful of eggs was shoved through the crack in his grizzled old beard. A sustained daily intake of booze was all Willy needed to survive. He only ate breakfast to keep up appearances.

Willy was the textbook example of the functioning part in the phrase, functional alcoholic. He glanced briefly at Gavin and offered the slightest nod of his head. Sincere relief flashed across his eyes. "Better take that to go," he said to Greeley. "That break in the weather won't last for long."

Greeley looked confused about what had just happened. His gaze shifted quickly between Gavin and Willy. He opened his mouth to speak, but Gavin cut him off.

"We'll still get you out on the next supply ship," Gavin said. "It might take an extra couple of days, is all. Some gnarly reefs circle ninety-eight percent of the island. Supplies come in on a specially designed ship. One that can navigate the break in the reef and run a tight enough line. They can't do that in rough waters. There's nothing to worry about as long as they come in along the right course and when it's smooth sailing."

Greeley didn't look fully pacified, and Gavin knew what he was thinking. The sooner the big man could get off the island, the more certain they could be that no one would be coming this way looking for Gavin. They were reasonably sure that Garboni hadn't shared word of his luck finding Gavin's hideout. Still, once Greeley returned to the mainland, he would be in a position to ensure Gavin's trail was covered.

Willy and Greeley were just out of earshot when Keegan passed through the cafeteria doors. She retrieved a cup of yogurt from the open-faced refrigerator at the end of the buffet counter and poured coffee from a carafe on a nearby table. She met his eye for a long second, a smile touching the corner of her lips. Then she sat at a table near the front of the room. Propping an e-tablet on its stand, she dabbed at her yogurt with a spoon while she tapped and occasionally swiped at the device's screen.

The complexities of their relationship required this, unfortunately. They couldn't be seen socializing in the public areas of the compound. While they shared concern over Stanton Anakasta's interest in them as a couple, Keegan bristled at the idea of anyone attempting to pair her with any man against her will. Gavin's concerns ran deeper. Until now, he'd been reluctant to elaborate on his point of view. The sense evolving inside him, Gavin knew with certainty that he would soon need to put all his cards on the table. It was time to level with Keegan and explain who he was and from where he'd come.

Bill Anders was at the buffet counter adding additional scrambled eggs to the pan under the heat lamp when Harper Hegan came in. "Good morning, Harper," Anders said. "Just putting out fresh eggs. If you're interested, I'll have flapjacks up in a couple of minutes."

Harper didn't respond. She didn't even seem to notice Anders's presence as her eyes scanned the room. Gavin feared what was to come. At somewhere in the neighborhood of thirty, Harper Hegan was a force with which to be reckoned. Five-eight in height, she had a trim, athletic figure that most men would describe as being all-leg. Long blonde hair framed a tan complexion of flawless skin accentuating high cheekbones and full, often pouty lips. She was an unabashed flirt when it came to interactions with nearly every man on the island. The girl was gorgeous but entirely too slutty, in Gavin's opinion. He'd had to fend off her advances since first arriving on the island.

At first, troubled at the thought of having to fend off new advances so early in the day, Gavin eyed the woman and felt his blood go cold. Her ordinarily flawless hair was tangled and unkempt, as were her clothes. She wore her traditional working attire comprised of jeans and a button-down blouse about two sizes too small for her bust line. Today the outfit looked days old and slept in. Understandable if this were a walk of shame, assuming the woman had any dignity left. According to the grapevine, she'd been occupying herself with the attention of Michael Rourke these recent weeks. The junior member of the three-man kitchen staff likely had no idea what he was in for.

The icy glare in Harper's expression raised warning bells for Gavin. Her eyes swept the room and landed on Keegan. Keegan had her back to the woman, a point that suddenly concerned Gavin greatly. That and the angry bloodshot glaze of Harper's eyes. The dark half-circles under her eyes he'd first taken for excessive makeup were, in fact, more concerning. And lips, usually parted in a salacious self-satisfied grin, were slightly parted in what looked like a subtle, silent growl.

Harper took two stalking steps in Keegan's direction, and Gavin knew he *needed to act. There was a predatory quality to the woman's expression that was already reflected in the speed of her advance. Warning Keegan would do little to defuse the situation. He needed to pull the attention entirely away from her. Harper looked ready to tear the woman apart.*

"Hey, Harper," Gavin called. "Just the woman I wanted to see. You must be reading my mind."

Harper's stalking advance froze and her gaze shifted to him. Keegan quickly turned, Gavin seeing confusion and then concern in her posture. She'd read Harper's intent just as he had.

Nostrils flaring in a primitive, predatory manner, Harper turned on Gavin. Kicking aside a chair, she bolted forward. Harper was the island's quartermaster, responsible for the up-to-the-minute inventory of key supplies and arranging the restocking of everything required to keep everyone and everything operating at peak efficiency. Gavin's mind spun for a subject he could use to deescalate the palpable tension quickly filling the room. Even Dale and Bill had stopped working in the kitchen to watch what was happening.

"I need to put in a new order," Gavin said with what he hoped was a disarming smile. "If you have a minute, maybe you can sit down and discuss it?"

Harper skidded to a stop and eyed him from across the table's width. Her nostrils flared once more, her eyes darkening. A clamped set of teeth became further exposed. "Are you alright?" Gavin asked in a gentle tone. "I can get the Doc for you. Maybe you should sit down?"

Keegan had slipped from her seat and was moving slowly into Harper's blind spot. Gavin knew this to be a mistake but couldn't express the concern without risking the escalation of this strange primal reaction. He needn't have bothered. Harper snapped her head quickly in Keegan's direction. Something akin to a hiss escaped her throat as she angled toward Keegan. Keegan froze, her eyes going wide. Backpedaling, Keegan attempted to put space between herself and the feral creature staring daggers.

"You think you're clever," Harper growled, speaking for the first time. Her words were directed at Keegan. "Playing your games and thinking no one knows?" The last word was drawn out nearly into a sentence of its own. "I can smell you on him!" These last words came out harsh and accusatory.

Harper's gaze shifted back to Gavin. He opened his mouth to speak, intending to draw her attention away from Keegan before things went entirely wrong. Again, it was a wasted effort. Harper lunged in his direction, diving headlong across the table with fingers splayed and nails bared. Caught entirely off guard, Gavin twisted and spun in his seat. He dodged a lashing hand as likely to take out his eye as it was his throat. Still, Harper caught him by the open collar of his flannel and the two crashed to the floor.

Throwing forearms up before his face and neck, Gavin felt the bite of long fingernails as Harper swiped wildly with dizzying speed. In the blurring motion of her swinging hand, an impossible sight further confounded Gavin's attempt to rationalize his situation. The nails of Harper's hand had elongated into jagged and razor-sharp talons. Left-right combinations rained down, splitting the flesh on the backs of his arms. A primal, feral scream was added to the assault, making him sure he was no longer dealing with a person. In this condition, the poor young woman had been reduced to something savage and animalistic.

"The Shard," she snarled in a voice that was no longer human. "Give it to me! She will swallow your soul—"

Gavin grabbed the woman's left wrist but missed her right as it wound back in preparation for another flesh-rending swipe. When her free arm lunged, he snatched it by the wrist as well. Without pause, Harper dove forward with jaws spread wide. She was aiming for his throat.

Her teeth had also changed suddenly, incisors elongating with rough razor-like edges and ragged points. Gavin twisted his neck beyond the range of her biting attack but knew she would get him on the second attempt if he didn't take action. Leveraging his advantage in size and strength, he pushed her backward and forced her wrists against her ribs. Even still, her head snapped forward with snake-like speed. Her neck twisted at an unnatural angle as her teeth hammered shut repeatedly.

The effort was futile. Her bite could land nowhere near him. With her momentarily subdued, his mind raced.

How in the hell do I restrain her?

A blur flashed overhead, followed by a thud. Shattered glass tinkled to the floor around Gavin's head as the now inert form of Harper Hegan tumbled from his grip. Keegan stood silhouetted in the overhead light, her tablet computer's bent and twisted remains clutched in a white-knuckled grip.

Turning quickly with a bloodied and balled fist, Gavin prepared for another attack. He needn't have bothered. His attacker lay unconscious, a mop of gnarled hair shadowing her face and her body twisted in a heap. The claw-like nails on her hand began to retract slowly. Gavin sensed Keegan drawn closer by the sight.

"What the hell is that?" Keegan mumbled. "She said something, but I couldn't make it out."

The Shard?

For some reason the phrase resonated with Gavin, but he couldn't pin it with context. And something about his soul? He shrugged. "Gibberish," he grumbled and leaned over to gently spread the fingers of Harper's half-closed hand. A grotesque figure was burned into the fleshy palm of her right hand. The shape was crude, its perimeter set deep into puckered and welted tissue.

Keegan dropped to a knee and bent forward for a better look. But even as they watched, the shape shrank, the skin raised up, and the sigil slowly disappeared. As unnatural as the fangs and the talons had been, somehow the disappearance of the emblem was more disconcerting. This was not a natural immune response by the body.

Gavin pushed Harper's mop of hair aside and tipped her unconscious head to the light. He pulled back the corner of her lip in time to see the last of the jagged incisor retract and disappear into her gum line.

Keegan shook her head. "I've never seen anything like that before," she offered in a quiet, contrite tone.

"I have," Gavin said.

Chapter 46

A deep baritone rumble emanated from the bottom of the well. In the span of a few short seconds its resonant base grew, as did its ferocity. The torches suspended from stones circling the periphery of the chamber billowed to life with flames as one and bathed the room in light for the first time in more than a century. The room's ancient mason work, stone walls, floor, and ceiling fit generations ago by master artisans long perished, quavered at fitted joints and sent particulate dust clouds billowing through the confines of the small space.

A gout of cloying green light lanced vertically from the base of the well. Oily and undulating, the tower of ephemeral plasma came within feet of reaching the mouth of the pit before stopping its vertical surge, hanging suspended in mid-air for long seconds, and then finally plummeting back into the bowels of the abyss.

The torches extinguished as one, but the electric green-black glow from the bottom of the well continued to blaze with intensity.

Chapter 47

36 miles southeast of Salem Massachusetts

October 1692

The black chalk ground across the coarse fibers of the parchment. Though he worked with a speed one might attribute to impatience, anyone with more than a moment to study his work would find it an effort of a skilled hand. Illustrating a skill level well beyond anything expected of his eight modest years, there was no question the boy had talent. Offering a quick glance at his subject matter, he tucked the chalk into the palm of his hand and stroked the chalky page with the tip of his finger. With care and precision, he turned the wide, dark line into an inky and foreboding shadow that matched his subject with perfection.

A vast space yawned before the boy, the center of a small barn cleared except for a crude table or workbench of long-hewn planks across sturdy, battered old sawhorses. The hard-packed dirt floor was clear of the dust and debris common to similar old structures, in this case, to help prevent the fire from spreading. A series of small logs lay stacked in a small cone shape beneath a massive iron vat. The logs crackled and popped in the near-silent space bringing little heat to anything but the bottom of the basin.

A gust of wind rattled the panels of the old building, and a plank somewhere on the roof high above tapped gently in resistance. The space beyond the hayloft was lost in shadow, light from the six small lanterns hung from thick posts arranged in a rough circle at the center of the space. Glancing at the figures surrounding the workbench, the boy made another calculated observation and quickly captured it on paper with a series of deft strokes.

One of the women rounded the end of the table and retrieved a pair of stout candles from a slouched canvas bag on the floor. She placed them on the table beside a thick leather-bound book. "Those are just rumors," the woman was saying. "Scandal and hardship make for the best tongue wagging."

A man and a woman stood shoulder to shoulder opposite her, the man's eyes meeting the words with a disapproving glare. He looked ready to object to the statement but seemed to think better of it. With a shake of his head, he went back to lacing a loop of bailing twine through a series of rings.

The two women and the man were all dressed in similar attire, threadbare clothes of off-white and gray that had clearly seen many seasons of manual labor. The women wore long skirts of coarse fiber, frayed and patched the garments hung to just above their ankles. Their sleeves were equally worn, both women having patches at the elbows and the sleeves cuffed tight at their wrists. The man wore trousers and a tunic of a similar course and tattered material, though where the women were reticent to show even a modicum of flesh, the man had his sleeves rolled to the elbows and his shirt collar open at the topmost button.

"Come now, Karina," the second woman offered, her tone scolding. "You know as well we—the darkness spreads by the day. It will be coming for us sooner rather than later. Is it so hard to believe in killings at our very own back door? Four dead. Butchered like cattle!"

The spooked look in Karina's eyes spoke volumes. Offering a shake of her head so forceful it nearly toppled the hair from the tight bun on the back of her head, her voice cracked. "They can't be so close. We need more time. Each passing day brings converts—the Dark One grows more powerful by the minute."

The man stopped what he was doing and turned slowly to his wife. "We all know what's at stake, Dendra," he offered in a calm, quiet voice. "There's still time," he said to Karina.

While Nestor and Dendra were in their late twenties, Karina was well into her thirties. They all knew she'd seen more darkness in her years, having lost her husband and twin daughters to disease more than a decade before. "I have to believe we have enough time," Dendra said and shot a glance at the boy sitting at the base of a haystack at the perimeter of the lamplight. "By the Gods above and below, we'll fight for our boy and every innocent soul those vile creatures wish to claim."

Karina smashed her small fist down and rattled everything on the makeshift table. "For that, we need all the help we can get!"

"Karina," Nestor warned.

Dendra shot the older woman a withering glare. "We've been through this. I'll not go through it with you again. This is our responsibility. This is our fight."

"We have protected the people of this town for years," Karina countered. "It's time for them to repay the kindness. They must stand beside us. At the very least, we need to know they don't stand against us."

"Our protection has brought prosperity to the town," Dendra admitted. "We ensure a plentiful harvest, safe seas, and a bountiful catch. In turn, the village allows us peace and sanctuary. But the people here have no power. We can ask nothing of them."

Her eyes flashing with anger, Karina slapped an open palm firmly in the center of the thick leather-bound book. "We have the power to use them. One way or the next, they can be made to help us."

Nestor shook his head slowly but said nothing.

"That is not our way," Dendra snapped. "What you suggest is blasphemy."

"It is not," Karina countered. "It's been done before. We can—"

"That is the reason our kind was hunted nearly to extinction." The tone in Dendra's voice made it clear the matter was not open for debate.

Karina refused to yield the point. She glared across the table, the nails on her extended hand slowly elongating and growing razor-sharp as they stretched across the surface of the ancient book. Dendra's lips drew into a tight line. Her eyes pinched slightly, a second before blue-green electricity danced across her irises. Though her face didn't shift, somehow there was a ferocity in her expression that had not been there before. Springing backward, Karina slapped a hand to her breast and gasped; the nails of her hand had retracted and were once again normal.

Dendra's next words were measured and calm. "We will not make matters *worse by undoing what goodwill we have accumulated."*

She might have understood he was less confident in the assessment if she'd seen her husband's gaze. He'd been to town earlier in the day. If reports were to be believed, the killings were already being answered. Two had been slain by something as yet unidentified. The bodies had been found in the woodland, mauled and eviscerated in a way not even common to the wildest of the beast. There was something sinister to the scene if reports were to be believed. Strange symbols etched in the surrounding dirt using both blood and human entrails.

The four who had been killed were a different matter. Townsfolk influenced by paranoid gossip and rumors up north had panicked. A mob seeking justice and furious for revenge struck out at those they believed responsible for the travesty. Three innocents were hanged, and one was drowned; all tried and convicted of witchcraft. None of them were practitioners, Nestor knew. Any Caster with even the slightest hint of talent would have been known to the three in this room. No one with natural ability was within a hundred miles of the farm. It was the reason they had laid down stakes in this part of the country.

Seeing the flash of light in his wife's eyes, Nestor knew better than to relay what he'd heard earlier in the day. Karina was already on the verge of panic and Dendra might reconsider her willingness to abide by the coven if she knew just how close the forces of the Dark One had drawn. To Nestor's best estimation, they had a day, perhaps two at the most. It should be enough to complete the ritual. He needed to keep them focused and on task.

"I think we can all agree there is little time," Nestor said. "If we work through the night, all will be ready by sundown tomorrow."

Karina still looked unconvinced. "You're sure the enchantment will hold against Blood Casters?"

Nestor understood her concern. Pound for pound, Earth Casters couldn't wield the unbridled power of those proficient in Blood Casting. While the Earth was vast, plentiful, and nurturing, at its core, the force wasn't capable of the ruthless and violent power that came from unfettered access to a raw life force. "They have to find us before they can—"

A blue stone at the end of the table interrupted Nestor when it flashed to life, a radiant azure glow drawing every eye in the room. The light pulsed for the span of a dozen heartbeats before setting the darkness alight with a swirling pale blue glow. Even the young boy promptly tossed aside his tablet and joined the group, his eyes wide and mouth agape.

Nestor stammered and pointed to the cauldron simmering atop steady flames only a few paces away.

"They are here," Dendra said, completing his thought as she darted to the bubbling vat of murky water. Nestor, Karina, and the boy were quickly at her heels.

Dendra leaned over the wide lip of the massive bowl. With a wave of her hand, the surface of the bubbling substance went placid and still. The fluid's shadowed and inky surface began to glow with an inner light, as if someone had set a match to a lantern deep in the bowels of the cauldron. As the light reached the surface, an image materialized. It was a bird's eye view of the clearing in which the barn stood. The structure's bowed roofline was clearly visible, as was the fifty-foot ring of dirt and short grass surrounding the barn. A thick canopy of trees began beyond the ring, the leaf litter dappled with the browns and reds of autumn. Movement could be seen through the boughs of the wispier trees as shadowy figures darted from one trunk to the next.

At least two dozen dark figures converged on the barn from all directions.

Wood shattered and sprayed the group with dry splinters as the inside of the barn exploded. A woman screamed. Nestor attempted to shield his wife and son from what must have been black powder charges magnified by some kind of blood-cast hex.

Then everything went black.

Chapter 48

The boy woke to a ringing in his ears and a stabbing pain that reached from the base of his skull to the back of his eyes. He heard voices, but they sounded distorted, fading from his side, then off into the distance before coming back again—all in the span of a heartbeat. Blinking his eyes did little to push away the darkness. It only brought a fresh stab of pain and a roiling burn in the pit of his belly as the world began to spin.

"The boy is awake," a voice called only a second before young Gavin felt a boot impact his ribs. "On your feet, boy!"

The bell-like tone began to sound more like a rush of water drowning out rapid hammer strikes. Gavin realized he heard the thunder of his heartbeat in his ears. Sensing the cold, damp earth beneath his cheek, he pushed out with a hand and tried to sit up. His hands were bound with iron manacles. The sight of his hands swam into focus in time to see chain links scrape against each other and thin flakes of rust tumble into the still night air. Distractedly, he noted his fingers were still black with smudges from the drawing chalk.

The clamor of voices filled Gavin's ears and he looked slowly around. A turn of his head sent a shot of pain down his neck, well past his shoulders; his vision dimmed once more. He swallowed hard to force back a throat full of rising bile. Taking a deep breath, he forced his eyes open once more. At least two dozen people surrounded him. Most carried farm implements, rakes, shovels, pitchforks, heavy hammers, and at least two carried long, unwieldy grain cycles. He counted at least four with guns; two with rifles, at least one musket, and one with a flintlock pistol.

"Blast it; get the boy on his feet," a voice demanded.

A hand seized Gavin by the back of his collar, and he was yanked from the ground. His mind swam to understand what was happening and who these people were. A hand cracked across his face. He heard the snap of skin and saw stars before sensing the pain. The shock of the impact didn't so much hurt as help to drive the cobwebs from his mind.

"Answer me, boy!" a man howled.

Gavin's gaze snapped up and to the side, where it met the eyes of his tormenter squarely. Blood boiled in his veins. It filled him with a strength of will he'd never experienced. He shot a gaze of narrowly focused fury directly into the eyes of the red-faced man glaring down at him. The look rocked the man back on his heels, instantly producing a puppy-like squeak. He seemed to think better of the hand raised for a follow-up strike.

As shocked as Gavin's attacker was by Gavin's expression of defiance, Gavin was far more taken aback. Mister Smithson? The sight of the town's pastor was wholly unexpected. Still, Gavin didn't let his mask of defiance falter.

Gavin shoved at the man holding the back of his shirt. Unfortunately, this assailant wasn't as easily deterred. The man kicked Gavin's legs out from under him and sent him crashing into the hard-pack dirt. Gavin never saw the face of the man holding him. When he fought against the grip at his back, he received a blow to the back of the head for his effort. Undeterred, Gavin turned once more to the Pastor. The man glared down, his face a kaleidoscope of concern, worry, angst, and fury. Seeming confused by his own emotional instability, the man turned and disappeared into the crowd. The unruly mob came into focus for the first time. Three dozen people by Gavin's estimation. And to his shock, more than half were townspeople armed and enraged. It was a lynching if he'd ever seen one.

Turning again, Gavin followed the gaze of the angry mass.

No!

His heart sank. He recognized the clearing in which the mob stood, and the attack on the barn flooded back into his mind. The exploding mass of wood, the blinding flash of light, and the hammer blow of sound that had struck from all *directions. He knew with certainty the goal of this vigilante group.*

Three tall wooden posts had been driven into the earth at the center of the clearing. Arranged in a triangle pattern, the penultimate post had been placed closest to the crowd while the two remaining were placed twenty feet behind the first and perhaps forty feet from each other. Bushels of tree branches and brush had been piled like kindling at the bases of the two rear posts. That was precisely what they were, he knew with certainty—burning stakes.

Bound to the left rear post was Karina. Her back was to the wide beam, her hands bound behind her back. Judging by the awkward way she futilely fought for freedom, her feet were also bound. Her eyes were wild, and she seemed ready to chew through the thick rag stuffed in her mouth. It was looped around the back of her head to form a crude but effective gag.

Nestor was bound similarly to the right rear stake. Kindling was stacked so high that it obscured his knees. Without question, Gavin knew what was about to happen. Stories about this sort of execution had been circulating for months, making their way from the north. These were said to be trials, but no one was fooled. They were executions.

Gavin broke from the front of the crowd and ran for his father. He made it only a handful of steps before he was struck bodily from behind. Crashing face-first into the hard earth, Gavin reached out in an attempt to right himself. The attempt was stymied by the three thick links of chain connecting the manacles around his wrists. A fist struck the back of his ribs as he attempted to roll free of his tackler. He rolled in time to take a dizzying fist to the face and a boot once more to his ribs. The air was driven from his lungs by the impact. He saw multiple dark figures converge over him, their features lost in the shadows of the dancing torchlight. Fist blows rained down on him.

When Gavin opened his eyes again, he was back where he'd started and placed in the front line of angry onlookers. He glanced around more slowly this time, attempting to gauge how long he'd been unconscious. The crowd hadn't settled—they still wanted blood. Karina and Nestor were still bound to stakes, but both had given up fighting against their restraints. The front-most stake had changed in the time he'd been out. Tree branches were now densely stacked around the base of this one as well. By Gavin's estimate, they were piled nearly three feet high.

This group didn't mess around. They knew their work. They had done this before. He looked over the crowd once more. Of the three-dozen present, perhaps two-thirds were locals. Gavin was awestruck. While his family had never been close to the people of the town, they had a kinship. They might have had the courtesy to keep each other at arms distance, but there had never been animosity before—never hostility.

There had to be a reason for this.

Gavin's gaze fell on a dark-clad figure standing alone at the edge of the crowd. He wore a long dark coat and a wide-brimmed black hat which cast his face in shadow. He held a small thick book bound in ancient-looking leather. It was a grimoire, Gavin knew instantly.

The figure's hat tipped and turned. Though he couldn't see the face in the shadow beneath it, Gavin could sense the figure's eyes upon him. An icy chill ran up and down his arms, despite the burning he felt in his blood.

Chapter 49

Biting at the coarse rag tied as a gag around her head, Dendra twisted against the thick post at her back. Her ankles were bound together with what looked like bailing twine and her hands were manacled behind her. The rusted iron links between the cuffs bound deeply into the wood with every savage twist of her hips and shoulders. Thanks to her bare feet in contact with the earth, she was able to draw a measure of strength. Her people drew power from nature; unfortunately, what energy she could gather was dissipated nearly as quickly by the iron in contact with her wrists. It was one of the few things Earth and Blood Casters had in common. Almost all beings of supernatural power had a weakness for iron.

A change in the aura of the crowd pulled Dendra's attention in that direction once more. Gavin was stirring from his slumped position on the ground. He'd been unconscious when she'd been led from the dark confines of the barn where the mob had sequestered her alone. The sight of her beaten and battered son forced away the fear she felt for herself and her coven. Even seeing Nestor and Karina bound to stakes, and knowing the fate awaiting them, somehow paled compared to the fear she felt for her boy. The moment she'd seen the gaunt man in the wide-brimmed hat holding the grimoire made it clear that while the fate of her people would be painful, it would be swift when compared to what the savage and his people had in mind for Gavin. The man with the book was one

220

of the Nimm, a sect of Blood Casters her coven had evaded for nearly two generations.

The Nimm eyed Gavin as the boy slowly pulled himself to a sitting position. A dim glow emanated from the figure's eyes, the only thing visible in the inky black shadow beneath the hat. Nearly a dozen of the crowd members held torches, yet somehow the light never reached the face of the Nimm. With the slightest wave of his hand, the dark figure motioned two of the torchbearers forward. They were men Dendra had known for years, and they approached with swift intent, their guttering torches held high.

Seeing this, Gavin once more attempted to gain his feet, only to find they had been bound with the same bailing twine used to restrain Dendra. He toppled to the ground, and a pair of men grappled to restrain him again. As he fell, Dendra saw the glassy look in her boy's eyes. His face was bloody and already beginning to swell, but it was the dull look in eyes usually so observant that added fuel to her already boiling rage. He'd already taken too many blows to the head. She knew her boy would take a much worse beating before he accepted what was about to happen to the rest of his family.

The pair of torchbearers passed Dendra without so much as a glance. She shot a look over her shoulder in time to see one of the men touch a flame to the dry pile of thick brush surrounding her husband. The rag in her mouth muffled the sound of her hoarse scream and a sob. Her rage intensified tenfold. In one last desperate act, she called to the earth and any power the forces of nature could provide. In her mind's eye, she could see a flame being set to the feet of Karina as well.

This would be the end of them all. She had to do something.

Dendra's eyes went to the dark figure at the front of the gathering once more. The Nimm stepped forward and his face met the light. "You could not outrun us forever," he said in a dry, raspy tone. "Your fate was sealed back in the time of the ancients. You're the last of your kind." He eyed Gavin briefly. "The boy lacks your ability, but that won't matter. He is of your bloodline and will make an appropriate sacrifice."

The threat made Dendra's blood sing with rage. She knew the sacrificial rites to which the Nimm was referring. Her eyes scanned the crowd and found Pastor Smithson. Every Sunday he preached of fire, brimstone, and eternal damnation. Though he was a fearmonger by nature, Dendra knew with certainty there was a hell beyond even his most fevered nightmares. And the Nimm would see that her boy experienced it.

Biting into the gag with savage ferocity, Dendra threw back her head and bellowed an incoherent curse at the heavens. There was only one way to face an evil this pervasive, and for a chance to save her son, she was willing to damn herself to the abyss. Though she couldn't speak the words, visions of her intent formed vividly in her mind.

The Nimm laughed at the sight of Dendra's distress. "Call to your Gods," he bellowed. "Not even they can save you now."

Screams emanated from behind Dendra's back. The flames reached Nestor and Karina simultaneously. A swirl of cold air kicked up and stirred the stillness of the night. The temperature dropped by more than a dozen degrees. Every eye in the gathered horde moved skyward as thunderheads rolled in from the east. Seconds later, even the full moon was blotted out by wicked roiling storm clouds.

Chapter 50

Bellows of pain grew ever more intense. Gavin twisted his face from where one of his captors held it pressed to the dirt. Thunder boomed. It had to be close because Gavin felt the concussive blast impact his back and the earth below him shake. The pair of men on his back slipped away with a start and he rolled from their grip. He spun up and onto his knees in time to hear Karina's screams fall suddenly silent. The flames surrounding her had to be six feet tall. Through the guttering light, he could see the woman's form sagging forward, her hair gone and her clothing ablaze.

Gavin screamed at the sight. Tears streamed down his face. His father was faring no better. If anything, the flames around him were taller. Nestor went quiet, the fight against his restraints quickly slowing, and then ceasing entirely. The battle was lost. His flesh was already an unrecognizable ruin.

Lightning turned night into day as at least five lightning bolts lanced from the sky at once. They converged on a single tree at the edge of the clearing with a detonating force unlike anything Gavin had ever experienced. The tree was splintered into shrapnel, and the dirt at its base turned instantly into a three-foot-deep crater. The explosive blast sent most of the mob stumbling to the ground. Nearly all present were clutching their ears or their eyes; many had blood trickling from both.

His ears rang once more. Gavin looked up in time to see his mother shake her head violently. The gag preventing her speech went tumbling away. The sight wasn't lost on the Nimm. Gavin saw fear coalesce on the man's dark visage. Somehow the dark figure was one of only three who managed to remain standing through the lightning strike.

The Nimm pointed to the nearest of the standing men and then at Dendra. "Fire!" he bellowed. "Now!"

Until those words, the man had looked as shellshocked as the rest of the group. Whether it was the words of the Nimm or the figure's focused gaze upon him, Gavin saw the man snap from his stupor. Without so much as a stumble, he snatched one of the still-burning discarded torches and darted for Dendra's stake. The Nimm motioned to a second man from the periphery of the crowd. A second later, he was on his feet and sprinting to the stake with a torch of his own.

Gavin shook the manacles uselessly and eyed the rusted iron chains. They'd used iron on his parents, which meant the dark figure was of their world. Maybe they didn't know he had no power, though if they suspected that, Gavin guessed he would be tied to a stake and set ablaze right now as well.

So why isn't he trying to kill me?

One problem at a time, he decided. A half-dozen loops of baling twine were looped around his ankles. He could deal with that more easily than the manacles. He scanned his surroundings in hopes of finding something sharp. People were still struggling to their feet, most still looking to the skies and trying to make sense of the lightning strike—many likely fearing the next blast. An impact to his ribs told Gavin his captors were once more placing their attention on him. Two men were on him and attempting to force him to the ground.

Thunder cracked once more, and the air was suddenly thick with driving rain. Gavin looked up, hoping his mother had called the storm to smother the flames. It would be too late for his father and Karina, but if she could soak the wood surrounding her before they could set it—

"No!" he bellowed at the new blaze before him. The dark figure's people had made quick work of the flames. An inferno already surrounded his mother. The blaze was converging on her by the second; tongues of red and yellow already danced at least four feet in the air and were singeing her tattered clothes.

Dendra did not scream. No fear touched her visage. A look of focused rage was directed at the man in the hat, and it was a fury Gavin had never before experienced. "You'll not take my boy, Nimm," she called across the sound of the whistling wind and driving rain. "So many years, and you make the mistake of a first-level conscript?" her tone was as scolding as it was menacing.

Gavin didn't know what his mother meant, why she wasn't using her power to escape the flames, or why the dark figure looked panicked by these few simple words. The wind gusted and ripped the hat from atop the head of the ancient dark figure. When the firelight struck him full in the face, an incredible transformation occurred. The eyes drew wide into an inhuman almond shape, and their glow became yellow. His lips drew tight to the gums as a row of razor-sharp teeth replaced those previously human. Gavin blinked in dismay as the figure's incisors continued to extend to jagged, wicked points. The hands of the man-creature began to change as well. His fingers elongated, the nails extending into ragged animal-like talons.

"Mother!" Gavin called. He'd heard stories of these creatures but never seen one in the flesh.

Dendra looked at Gavin and smiled. Though there was love in her eyes, it did nothing to tamper the rage in her expression. Her gaze went instantly back to the dark figure, the man she'd called Nimm.

The Nimm stepped quickly and snatched a discarded musket from the ground. His boots slipped in the mud as he struggled to shoulder the long gun. Gavin instantly understood the creature meant to shoot his mother. Whatever her Casting, it terrified him to the core.

Having pulled himself to his knees once more, Gavin pushed away from the man grappling his right arm. He lunged for the knife on the far hip of the man holding his left side. In doing so, his boots slipped in the mud. He twisted as his feet went out from under him and used the additional momentum to grab for the distant blade. Tearing it from the sheath and landing on his hip in a splatter of mud, Gavin slashed the bindings at his ankles in a single swipe. The pair of men he'd just slipped went down in a tangle of flailing limbs, unable to keep their footing in two inches of mud growing deeper by the minute thanks to the ongoing downpour.

Gavin looked up just as the Nimm secured his own footing and steadied the barrel of the long gun. In the distance, Gavin could hear a rapid flow of words steaming from his mother's lips. It was a language he didn't recognize. Gavin darted in the direction of the Nimm. With certainty, he knew his mother was working a Casting of some kind. The strange language meant this was something unique. Something powerful. This understanding was reinforced by the look of anger and fear he saw on the grotesque face of the Nimm.

The Nimm thumbed back the hammer on the rifle and Gavin saw the figure's talon-like finger wrap around the trigger. With fifteen feet still between them, Gavin knew he couldn't close the gap in time to prevent the shot. Before processing the idea, the blade sailed from Gavin's hand. It crossed the distance with preternatural speed and sank into the neck of the Nimm with a splattering crack. The Nimm stumbled forward half a step, dipping the rifle and discharging it into the mud with a boom. The gun slipped from his hands as he sank slowly to the ground.

Gavin didn't waste a second. Off and running, he darted for his mother before the Nimm had fully reached the ground.

The sight of his mother nearly stopped Gavin's heart. Flames danced almost eight feet in the air as if fueled by some unnatural force. Dendra remained upright with her back to the post; her hair burned away along with her clothing and most of her flesh. Much of her face remained, her lips still somehow moving with words Gavin recognized as somehow familiar now. A smile touched her mouth when he met her eyes. Still, her lips kept moving with the silent chant. He suspected whatever she was doing had allowed her to persevere as long as she had.

Gavin realized he'd frozen at the sight of his mother. Looking at the flames, there was nothing he could do. If this torrential downpour did not affect the pyre, there was nothing he could do to stop it.

"You are a fool, boy," a wet voice gargled from a dozen paces behind Gavin. He turned to see the Nimm ambling closer with a black powder pistol in his upraised claw. "The blade must be made of silver. Did your mother teach you nothing of the Nimm?"

The figure was half-covered in mud, a black inky substance oozing from his neck with every self-congratulating word. The creature shook his head, and Gavin prepared for the gunshot that would end his life. But then Nimm shifted aim by several degrees. Gavin instantly understood the gun's single shot was intended for his mother.

The Nimm shook his head and called to Dendra. "All of this rain and wind means nothing. The death curse of an Earth Caster has no power over me. The Dark One grows too strong. You have already lost."

Dendra's silent chant stopped and her tattered lips drew into a satisfied smile. She spoke when Gavin wouldn't have thought such a thing possible. "I needed the mud," she said. "But if you look carefully, you of all people should recognize this as no Earth Casting."

The Nimm stepped forward two more paces. He and Gavin saw the massive sigil scraped into the mud just beyond the perimeter of Dendra's flaming pyre. The series of interconnected shapes formed an oblong tableau perhaps six feet wide and three feet tall. It was etched deep into the mud as if carved there by the invisible finger of a giant.

The dim unnatural glow of the Nimm's eyes went suddenly electric, and he stumbled. "You— you would invoke— how?"

As Gavin watched, he understood the sigil was incomplete. The last corner of the muddy sigil took shape, crafted by some unseen force.

"No!" the Nimm growled. He raised the pistol once more and took aim.

Gavin was already in motion. Turning, he threw himself between his mother and the gun. This happened just as she freed her hands from behind her back and thrust them into the sky. Completing whatever incantation she'd worked in tandem with the sigil in the mud, Dendra bellowed the last words of her Casting with complete conviction of body and soul. Though Gavin missed most of the proceeding words, he clearly heard the final phrase as she bellowed, "hear me, Nae'ja-dinn!"

A massive blast of air hit Gavin from the front a fraction of a second before the led musket ball struck him in the back. He crashed forward and slid to a stop in a pile of crisp, dry leaf litter. He rolled over in time to see a gaping three-foot-wide hole torn in the night. The woodland floor was warm, dry, and covered in vegetation where he lay. Beyond the rip in the night, he could hear the wild whistle of the wind and see the ceaseless downpour of rain.

Time seemed to have slowed on the other side of the portal. He saw the standing figure of the Nimm and the cloud around the breach of his upraised pistol as it expanded in slow motion. An expression of horror was gradually spreading across the creature's dark features. Then Gavin noticed a wave of light moving across the night. It seemed to be shifting away from the portal and toward the Nimm.

No, that wasn't right, he quickly decided. It was only his perspective that made it appear that way. His mother was the energy's point of origin. The wave moved swiftly, seeming to gain speed as it went. Sweeping across the Nimm, the figure was instantly vaporized. Then moving more quickly, the energy expanded to cross the remainder of the rain-soaked clearing. In a flash, the confused and ineffective mob was turned to dust exactly the same way.

A second later the energy wave was gone.

Clutching his left shoulder and feeling the trickle of blood running down his back, Gavin sat up in the darkness. The portal before him slowly contracted, and his view of the clearing beyond the barn where his family had died faded away. That energy was his mother's death curse, he suddenly understood. And while he'd heard talk of such things, no one had ever described it as anything so powerful.

Whatever she'd done to supercharge it was…terrifying.

Gavin climbed to his feet and realized three things instantly. Wherever he was, it was nowhere close to home. The vegetation was different, and what had been a full moon only moments ago was now only a quarter. Second, he was in bad shape between the gunshot and the beating he'd taken. The wilderness around his was swimming in and out of focus one minute and spinning the next. And third, he was standing in the wilderness, bare-ass naked. Whatever brought him here, apparently his clothes had not come along for the ride.

Chapter 51

Stanton Anakasta followed his head of security, Matt Mayhew, through the thick vegetation. With each step, his designer boots squished at least two inches deep in the mud. The damp, bone-penetrating cold was making the walk even more unpleasant, if such a thing was possible.

"How much further?" Asha Anakasta said from behind Anakasta and Mayhew. "And why couldn't we drive? This weather is awful, and I'll be lucky if I don't break an ankle by the time we get back."

Anakasta pushed a thick bramble of buckthorn aside and bit back a curse when one of the thorns pierced his heavy leather glove. He slashed the vine with a machete, then paused to glare at his wife. "If you can't walk through this, what makes you think we can drive through it?" He'd attempted to leave her back at the monastery, but she'd insisted on seeing the aircraft for herself.

Offering her own withering glare in response, Asha swung her machete at another tangle of briar. The blade came within six inches of Anakasta's leg and caused him to recoil. She smirked in response, her message delivered. She pushed past him, the blade swinging viciously left and right as she charged forward. He watched her go, now forging a trail all by herself. She was dressed in khaki cargo pants, heavy knee-high boots, and a thick insulated jacket over which she wore a vest festooned with pockets and compartments filled with God only knew what. Her long hair was pulled into a tight ponytail, and a floppy bush hat was pulled low over her head. He looked down at his expensive hiking boots and the bright blue of his denim pants. He was covered in mud and muck well past the knee. His boots had done little to protect him, let alone keep him warm.

Say what you would about his wife, she did pack for every possible contingency. Perhaps it was time to stop chastising her for gluttonous travel standards. Shivering, he pulled at the inch-long thorn in his glove and decided to learn from her example.

"Just another two hundred yards," Mayhew offered in a calm, professional tone.

Glancing over his shoulder, Anakasta confirmed the presence of three more men from the security detail. They were all outfitted in black foul-weather gear. Each carried a heavy-looking automatic rifle. Thunder cracked in the distance and Anakasta was reminded that the break in the weather wasn't supposed to last much longer. "Have the recording equipment ready when we reach the crash site," he ordered. "I want to gather data as quickly as possible." He left out that he didn't want to be out here when the skies opened up once more. It wasn't yet 11am. The sun had failed to penetrate a sky filled with dark, roiling clouds and the surrounding forest was getting darker rather than brighter. There was no question that the latest weather report was accurate. A new wave of the storm system was only a short distance off.

Asha quickly ran out of steam, and Mayhew took over blazing the trail. Perspiring and clutching at her side, she fell silently in step behind Anakasta. The crashing rumble of the surf smashing against the nearby bluff reminded Anakasta how close the crash site was to the north edge of the island. If a plane had indeed crashed out here, it had only made landfall by a narrow margin. According to the drone footage, had it been another seventy-five feet northeast, it might have struck the cliff face or even been claimed by the sea.

Anakasta's gaze swept to the right. If the craft had come down several hundred yards to the east, it might have landed in the island's only freshwater lake. Though the water had been explored by divers using sonar, Lidar, and numerous advanced imaging techniques, they had only looked at the floor of the seven-acre body of water once. The drone had only found the crashed aircraft because it was moving past this location onto the next unexamined grid as it continued to search the island. His plan to explore every meter of the landmass never considered looking for anything that might have changed position between drone sweeps. Finding this downed aircraft had been a stroke of luck, *pure and simple. Had the plane come down in the lake and fully submerged, it would have gone unnoticed indefinitely.*

The lake.

Just thinking about it sent a literal chill down Anakasta's spine. It was yet another of the island's mysteries. The only source of fresh water, it somehow maintained a resting temperature of twelve degrees Fahrenheit year-round. And with no salinity at all, it somehow managed never to freeze. The water had been tested and confirmed to be untainted and pure, the result of snow runoff from the mountain as well as a collection of eons worth of rainwater. There was simply no scientific explanation for the body's ability to maintain sub-freezing temperature without ever accumulating even a centimeter of ice.

"Here we are," Mayhew called.

Anakasta stepped from the wild growth into a small clearing at the base of a strange-looking tree. Its boughs stretched high and wide overhead, the canopy still half full of red and brown leaves. The quality of daylight seemed more akin to dusk, perhaps even closer to nightfall. Anakasta squinted up into the tree in search of what had brought them here.

"It's over here," Asha said. She already had her backpack off and had retrieved a powerful LED flashlight. Pointing the beam vertically from her position halfway around the tree's massive trunk, she whistled quietly in awe.

Anakasta and his men moved to her side and added their lights to hers. There, perched vertically in the bower of the tree was the short, narrow fuselage of a single-seat aircraft. The plane's nose cone had flattened, clearly absorbing substantial impact as it came to rest in the tree crook, the aircraft suspended and perpendicular to the surface some twenty-five feet off the ground. One wing was completely missing. The other was twisted and mangled among the branches. Shining his light along what he could see of the still partially attached wing, what Anakasta saw concerned him. Branches had grown through holes and tares in the wing. This was only semi-recent growth, perhaps a season or two old. Worse yet, the silver metal skin was mottled and blotched with mold and accumulated tree sap.

"Record everything," Anakasta ordered. He looked to Mayhew. "Put your best climber in the tree. I want video and photos from around and inside the airframe."

Mayhew began issuing orders to his men.

Asha directed her light to the shattered glass above the cockpit. "You see it, don't you?" she said. "That vine coming out the crushed metal at the tip?"

Anakasta pinched his much older eyes in response. The flattened nose of the plane had several wide tares where the conical form met with the rest of the body. "Yeah. What of it?"

Asha moved her light vertically up the length of the fuselage to where the ragged metal hinted at the missing tail section. "Two vines are entering there," she said. "It looks like one of them has grown through the aircraft and found its way out through the nose cone. It doesn't make sense."

Anakasta met his wife's gaze. "Growth like that would take years." His estimate of a season or two of growth was already being reestimated as he evaluated the scene anew.

She extinguished her light and lowered the volume of her voice. "That's what I mean. We have footage of these exact coordinates captured days ago." She pointed overhead. "This wasn't here last week."

Anakasta scowled. He knew she was right. Even if the plane had been missed in visual scans of the area, each drone carried a state-of-the-art sensor array tuned to report even trace amounts of metal. It could detect ferrous material buried even several feet below the surface.

"How long do you think?" Anakasta said.

Asha glanced at the black-clad man climbing along thick limbs and branches high overhead and raised her voice to be heard. "We need samples of the vines entering the tail section and multiple samples from the growth protruding from the nose cone. Also, see if you can find a serial number. I assume you know where to look?"

"Yes, ma'am," a dry professional voice responded.

Unseen by the group, wet foliage moved beyond the perimeter the security team had formed. Brody pushed silently through the green growth and withered brown vegetation, his eyes missing nothing. His fur was soaked and matted, dark and concealing him in the endless shadows. Four large paws moved noiselessly through the leaf litter. The large hound had the stealth of a predatory jungle cat. It took only minutes to complete a circuit of the perimeter. Then, with no one the wiser, he disappeared into the darkness.

Chapter 52

Her back to the wall of the narrow medical bay, Keegan watched as Doctor Sydney Cantrell slipped the hypodermic needle into the port on the line connecting the bag of saline to the catheter on Harper Hegan's arm. Harper bucked wildly against her restraints, eyes wide and teeth snapping in a manner both animalistic and feral. Cantrell depressed the plunger on the syringe. Harper's reaction was almost instant. She sagged, her efforts quickly becoming weak and then lethargic.

Harper's attack on Gavin had been shocking. If Keegan hadn't witnessed it for herself, she wouldn't have believed the young woman capable of such violence. The fangs and talon-like nails had yet to retract. It was as if she'd mutated into something demonic. Upon regaining consciousness, she'd become even more aggressive. Thankfully Gavin had been decisive, restraining Harper with the electric cord from a kitchen grill. Harper was unconscious for a matter of minutes, and had she not been bound upon waking, it was unlikely anyone could have stopped her without hurting her or being seriously injured themselves.

Doctor Cantrell was leaning over the bed and shining a penlight in Harper's eyes. The elongated, exaggerated almond-like shape of her eyes was alien and disturbing. "This is incredible," the doctor said. "I've given her enough sedative to blitz a large farm animal. She's lucky to be breathing—she sure as hell

233

shouldn't be moving."

Keegan stepped to the foot of the bed for a better view. Harper's head turned slowly from side to side, her jaw opening and closing in slow motion. Razor-sharp teeth extended from tight lips, and a low guttural growl whispered from somewhere deep in her chest. Arms and legs tugged ineffectively at the restraints. The drugs seemed to have slowed her to quarter speed, every movement now seemed to take place in slow motion. Harper's eyes were rolled back so that only the bloodshot whites were visible. The display sent goosebumps across the flesh of Keegan's arms.

A long powdery smear along the calf of Harper's left leg caught Keegan's eye. Before she knew it, she had reached out to touch the chalky substance. It seemed to be made of powder so fine it was only slightly gritty between her fingers. The tactile sense was somehow familiar, but she couldn't place it. It was like being reminded of a memory just beyond the bounds of recollection.

Cantrell put a hand on Keegan's wrist and gave it a gentle shake. Keegan realized the woman had been speaking to her. "She just attacked you?" Cantrell apparently repeated. "Are you alright? Can I get you something?"

"I'm fine," Keegan said and shook the chill from her skin. Blinking rapidly and feeling the sense of déjà vu fade, she pointed beyond the curtain toward the perimeter of the room. "Do you mind?"

Slipping past, Cantrell pulled the curtain aside and led Keegan from the medical bay. As she stepped from the claustrophobic confines of the space, Keegan observed Harper was in the same bed Tess Lindow had used only hours earlier.

Cantrell eyed Brody who heeled close at Keegan's knee. Perhaps not the most sanitary of circumstances, this being a medical facility, but the dog was a fixture on the island. He'd become accepted as one of the staff. The dog trotted forward to accept a treat pulled quickly and discreetly from Cantrell's lab coat pocket.

"You've had a busy twenty-four hours," a tired voice called from the corner of the room. Gavin pulled himself from one of several chairs at the base of the wall. He pointed to the curtained medical bay from where Keegan and the doctor had just emerged. "Tess was in there just a couple of hours ago."

Keegan smiled, both at the sight of Gavin and amused they'd been thinking the same thing. She raised a hand, about to reach out and touch Gavin but then thinking better of it. She shot a quick glance at the doctor. Her heart sank, and she awkwardly rerouted her hand to the hip pocket of her jeans.

If Gavin or Cantrell noticed, neither showed it. Cantrell looked exhausted and Gavin's attention was fixed on the doctor. "Things are escalating," Gavin said.

Keegan didn't know what that meant, but apparently the doc did. Cantrell's tired expression grew somehow darker and more contemplative. Lips pursing in a sour pose, she stood silent for several long seconds. At last, she nodded. "More blood work has come back. Dopamine levels are scrambled, and almost everyone tested has Pancytopenia."

"Pancytopenia?" Gavin grumbled, clearly not understanding.

"It's a blood condition where the red and white cell counts are negatively impacted along with platelet tallies," Cantrell explained. "But even that's not an accurate diagnosis. It's just the closest I can find."

Keegan felt suddenly dizzy. Gavin must have noticed because she suddenly felt his steadying arm around her. He did it without meeting her eye, likely to reduce the attention the action was likely to draw. She felt his hand squeeze her hip twice. It was an, are you alright, sort of motion. Leaning into his shoulder and taking a deep breath, she felt the spinning room slow and her legs grow more solid beneath her. She placed a hand atop his and gave it a solid squeeze in return.

"Does that point to a cause?" Gavin said, referring to the characteristics of the unusual blood levels. "Maybe a condition?"

The doctor was slow to answer. "Not really. It's an indication of aplastic anemia... or bone marrow failure. It could indicate numerous serious conditions. None of which would explain it happening to people in numbers."

A memory of dancing torchlight flashed in Keegan's mind, and suddenly she was huddled naked in the corner of a dark room. Shadowy figures moved slowly nearby. They chanted softly, a murmur of words that somehow felt like another language. Two figures were upright while the others knelt on cold stone and earth. One figure was slim and nude. Folds of pale light and inky shadow enveloped her. Though the nude female figure seemed familiar, her face somehow remained just beyond the light. The second upright figure was much larger, distinctly male, and at least partially clothed. The light seemed to conceal his identity with an equal degree of malicious skill. This figure pushed away from the side of a short stone wall and moved drunkenly. He stumbled back to the group kneeling on the floor. No sooner had he knelt than one of the prostrate figures rose and moved to the wall. It was a well, Keegan saw with sudden clarity. She watched as the new silhouette raised a dagger and drew it slowly and calmly across his inner arm.

Keegan felt her knees grow weak once more as she blinked the darkness away. Gavin's arm around her tightened in response, but he said nothing. Though she'd missed portions of his conversation with Cantrell, she sensed he'd continued despite her...whatever this was. He was attempting to conceal whatever she was now experiencing.

"So, we don't know more than we did." Frustration was evident in Gavin's tone.

"We know it's getting worse," Cantrell countered. "Not everyone is affected either. Your levels are entirely normal," she nodded at Keegan, "as are Keegan's and Mister Greeley's. Zane might make sense as he's new to the environment— but the rest of you? It just doesn't track."

"Maybe it's a question of timing," Gavin countered. "Greeley's been here a day, I've been here about a year, and Keegan only a couple of months. Maybe it's a short time compared to the rest of those impacted."

The doctor was already shaking her head. "I've considered that. It doesn't hold up. Willy has been here as long as anyone, and he's not symptomatic. And neither is Tess. There's just no associative correlation—no consistency."

The image of the group huddled in the darkness of the small chamber flashed once more in Keegan's mind. This time she saw part of the vision more clearly. A dark figure was drawing a glinting blade across pale flesh. Black fluid gushed from the resulting wound. She watched as the blood fell over the side of the short stone wall. She watched as the figure made a blood sacrifice to something in the bottom of the well.

When Keegan spoke, she barely recognized the dry frailty of her voice. "Anemia...What if they're several pints low on blood?"

Cantrell smiled but shook her head with determination. "Anemia describes a low red cell count specifically. What we have here is—"

"No," Keegan snapped. "Fine, forget the term." She was lightheaded, and while the clinical term was on the tip of her tongue, she couldn't find it. "What about the blood? What if they were all down a couple of pints? Would that put them in a similar condition?"

Again, Cantrell shook her head. "I don't see how that's possible. And there's no way simply being low on blood," she gestured to the drawn curtain behind her and the bed beyond it, "could do that to an otherwise healthy young woman."

Gavin studied Keegan for a long second before turning his gaze to the doctor. "Setting the crazed behavior aside," he said, "would massive blood loss explain the Pancytana..."

"Pancytopenia," Cantrell corrected with a tired grin. She seemed to consider the question once more, given the revised criteria. "I'll admit, it explains the blood-related manifestations. That still wouldn't explain the hormonal offsets I've recorded. That would have to be entirely unrelated."

Gavin nodded. "One thing at a time. Assuming it's not all directly related, maybe this will start to make more sense. It also means we're making progress."

Cantrell looked unconvinced. "The patient has no wound suggestive of an injury or condition that would result in massive blood loss. And how do you explain at least eight symptomatic cases? You think eight people injured themselves so severely that they tanked their levels to the point of becoming zombies?"

"Some are worse than others?" Gavin clarified.

Cantrell nodded.

"Then I'll need a list of everyone you tested and those with zombie blood," he said with a smirk.

Cantrell raised a hand and took a step back. "To be clear, I wasn't claiming they are zom—"

Gavin laughed. "Of course not. Though Willy has been about two drinks away from turning into one for as long as I've known him. In his case, I wouldn't rule anything out." He gave the doc a conspiratorial wink.

On a superficial level, Keegan was relieved. Doctor Cantrell seemed not to have noticed, or at least found anything unusual about her intimate proximity to Gavin. The same could not be said about Tess and Jennifer, who now stood at the end of the room. The girls were shoulder to shoulder and pointed an almost twin-like conspiratorial gaze at her. Jennifer whispered something to Tess and bumped her with her hip before moving away. Both women chuckled, their eyes never leaving Keegan.

Crap.

Keegan watched as Jennifer grabbed a magazine from one of the chairs along the wall. She looked briefly at the cover before tossing it on the end table with a *pile of other well-thumbed issues. Jennifer dropped into a seat with a tired sigh, sinking low into a slouch with a bored expression. Tess crossed to the opposite wall. She slipped a blood pressure cuff over her wrist and shimmied it up her arm.*

Approaching Tess, Keegan said, "need help with that?"

Chapter 53

Tess was attempting to cinch the blood pressure cuff one-handed. The Velcro kept snagging and hindering her efforts. She was quickly becoming frustrated. Meeting Keegan with a curious glance, she replied with caution in her tone. "Sure, if you don't mind."

Keegan unfastened the snagged cuff and adjusted its position. She aligned the inflation tube with the crook of Tess's arm and held it in place while she secured the strap. Her fingers on Tess's wrist, Keegan eyed the wall and began squeezing the bulb to inflate the cuff. She felt Tess's gaze on her the entire time.

"I didn't realize you doctored people, too," Tess said as Keegan released the last of the air from the instrument.

Keegan eyed her but said nothing.

Tess could feel her face turning pink in response to the brief penetrating stare. "You're a veterinarian, am I wrong?"

The sharp edge in Keegan's gaze dissolved into a warm smile. "I am." Pulling the cuff away, she wound the tube and hung the device from a hook on the wall. "You were going to do this all on your own?"

Tess didn't understand.

"You came over here and got started like you knew what you were doing," Keegan explained. *It was an oddly phrased question and they both knew it. Color rose in her cheeks, and Tess knew why the conversation had become so clumsy. "It's kind of late. Is everything alright?"*

Tess shrugged. "The doc has me stopping in several times a day. After what happened, I think she's just overprotective."

"The attack," Keegan said quietly. "That was horrible. How are you? I should've asked—it's just—how do you— He really hurt you, didn't he?"

Grinning, Tess said, "Not to worry. What do you say after something like that, right? Anyway, Zane was there, and everything was alright."

Both girls' eyes snapped up to meet and went wide simultaneously. They shared a deer caught in the headlights look for several long seconds as the tension grew. Tess suddenly realized Keegan shouldn't have known anything about the attack since it had been reported that her attacker, Tom Hathaway, had supposedly fallen down the stairs. Obviously, Keegan had let her understanding of the incident slip as well.

Still wide-eyed, both girls finally broke into laughter. The seriousness of the circumstance had finally become too much. "There are no secrets in a place like this," Tess said when her laughter tapered off.

Keegan looked suddenly uncomfortable again. Tess watched the young woman's gaze shift uncomfortably to Gavin. Keegan shifted quickly and shot her eyes to the floor, likely realizing she'd further given herself away. Tess giggled in response and slapped her knee.

Tess waited. Keegan caught her gaze once more. This time a stricken expression clouded Keegan's confused eyes.

Laughing again, Tess slapped Keegan's arm. "Oh, cheer up. That's old news. You might be fooling your old man, but you're not fooling any of us!"

If it was possible, Keegan only looked more concerned. "You mean you— I mean to say, you—" She tried another set of combinations, all of which left her equally tongue-tied.

Tess laughed so hard she was forced to wipe tears from her eyes. She nodded. "Sure, I know." She pointed to Jennifer across the room. "She knows." The girl sat with her hands folded and watching them. An amused expression was painted on her face even though she was beyond the range of overhearing the conversation. Tess had no doubt her friend was entirely up to speed on most of what was being said.

"We all know," Tess clarified.

Keegan looked shocked. What had briefly been a mortified expression quickly dissolved into a blank, droopy-eyed gaze; presumably as she attempted to understand how they might have been found out. "How?" she finally whispered.

Tess was grinning widely. "First of all, you two work way too hard to stay away from each other. Only guilty people do that." Leaning close, she offered clarification in a quiet, conspiratorial voice. "Plus, me and Jen do the laundry around here. Given what you and Gavin have been up to? You can't hide that sort of thing from the people who do the laundry." She shot Keegan an exaggerated wink at the close of the statement.

Keegan's complexion paled. Her cheeks went pink before transitioning to a shade of crimson.

Oh, God.

Chapter 54

Moving at nearly a sprint, Keegan dragged Gavin back to her room in the upper reaches of the citadel. Hitting the last stretch of stone hallway, Gavin was relieved not to pass any of the island staff or security team members. Keegan shoved the key in the lock beneath the doorknob and powered through the door. He ducked into the room quickly at her heels.

"What's so important?" Gavin protested. "A running chase through the building isn't subtle, you know?"

Keegan shook her head, impatience clear in the focus of her dark eyes. "Not important. That cat's out of the bag," she mumbled. "We have bigger things to worry about, trust me."

Gavin watched as she darted around the room turning lamps on, one after the next. The spacious suite was chilly, and the air was stale. It was an attestation to how much time she'd spent with him in the exterior house. They needed a fire. Kneeling and adjusting the flue, he added a pair of fresh logs to the fireplace. He began shoving crumpled newspaper and crumbled tree bark beneath the bottom logs. Gavin was reaching for the box of matches when the paper and bark burst into flames with an audible whoosh.

Rocking back on his heels, Gavin set the matches aside and turned to Keegan.

He eyed her from beneath arched brows. "You're getting better at that," was all he could say.

She shook her head and didn't look happy. "No—It's getting easier."

Rising, Gavin dusted his hands over the fire before turning to her. "Isn't that the same thing?"

Shaking her head once more, Keegan looked upset, maybe even angry. "You get better at something because you practice and hone the skill. Repetition and focus are the keys to Casting, just like playing sports, learning a musical instrument, or anything else."

Gavin nodded. "Sure…"

"But this is getting easier—not because I'm practicing or improving. Something fundamental is changing, and it's directly impacting Casting."

Gavin remained silent, his gaze one of growing concern. He slipped his hands into the pockets of his jeans and nodded slowly. His brow creased and he began to pace slowly. Flashes of a dark, terrifying night in the forest filled his mind. Memories from so far in his past, they felt more like a dream. Three fires, a torrential storm, and the Casting of a death curse that had thrown him forward in time. It was a night that had changed his life forever. Whatever was happening now—

"Gavin!" Keegan shouted.

Pausing mid-stride, Gavin shot a look at Keegan. "Sorry?" he said quietly.

"You're not even hearing me. What's wrong? You just went into your own little world for a few minutes. Did you hear a word I said?"

"Sure," he said in a quiet, distant voice. "You said you think something fundamental has changed."

She crossed her arms and glared with unvarnished irritation. "Gavin, that was five minutes ago. You're saying you didn't hear anything I said after that?"

Looking down, Gavin saw he was pacing again. He dropped heavily on the foot of the bed and leaned his elbows on his knees. "I'm sorry. No…you just got me thinking. Start over?"

Crossing the room, Keegan knelt on the carpet before him. He looked up to find her angry expression replaced by one of concern. "What is it?" she said. "This means something to you. What are you thinking?"

There was a power to this place, of that they were both aware. Keegan was a gifted Crafter even before coming here. Something about the island seemed to intensify her ability. It was being magnified or supercharged.

"You grow more skilled and powerful the longer you stay here," Gavin said. "What if this place is benefiting from you the same way you're benefiting from it?"

Keegan was clearly confused.

"Crafting is reciprocal," he explained. "It's the reason Casters originally formed covens. The power of one is shared with the group. Similarly, the more powerful the group becomes, the more powerful each member of the coven also becomes."

Chapter 55

Keegan stared into Gavin's eyes and processed his words. He had no powers, of that she was certain. They had talked about it many times. He'd claimed as much, and just as obviously, she could sense no supernatural ability in him. Crafters could discern the aptitude in those around them. He had none. But he spoke with a confidence and understanding that came from experience. She could sense that in him as well.

Why have I never sensed it before?

Though she had explained what little she understood of her out-of-body ability and her study of Crafting, he had never volunteered any personal knowledge on the subject. It was natural, even logical, to assume that he had no familiarity with the topic since few did. Those in the know had esoteric knowledge at best. The few fringe groups claiming to practice Crafting, in her experience, were posers, cranks, or outright charlatans.

"What do you know about Crafting?" she said. The words were cautious, even guarded. For the first time in months, she felt like she might not know him as well as she believed. Covens have been outlawed for generations. The claim he'd made earlier now rang back in her mind. *My mother was a witch,* he'd said. *She was burned alive.* It was a claim that didn't seem plausible. Not in the modern world. The last coven was destroyed generations ago. Those few talented enough in Crafting would never be reckless enough to gather, let alone join in a coven. What little literature remained had been outlawed, possession of it punishable by death. Most had been destroyed. She'd never met another Crafter, though she believed there were others out there—true Crafters, not the witless twits gathering to play witch and dress as goths.

There was a pain in Gavin's eyes, she could see it and sense it as if it were her own. He knew what he was talking about.

But how?

"You're a Crafter?" she asked, the words not even a whisper.

He shook his head slowly. "No. You've got talent. If I were, you'd know. I believe you're more gifted than even you realize."

Placing a hand on his cheek, her tone became imploring, her words desperate for understanding. "Then how—how do you know these things?" Questions now stacked in her mind. So many questions. He'd been entirely accepting of her strange abilities. Powers that had scared—terrified her—were easily accepted by him. It was like he knew her even before they had met.

"I watched my mother and father die," Gavin said. The few short words seem to take all of his efforts. They were forced into the world using a quiet, mournful voice that seemed to require a tremendous effort of will. He met her eye again, an attempt to support the import of his conviction. "Burned at the stake."

A frozen fist seized Keegan's heart. Icy tendrils spidered through her breast as her breath choked. Her eyes searched his, first for clarification, then for understanding. His claim made absolutely no sense. Speaking of covens and executions by burning. Such things hadn't happened for hundreds of years. Not since—

Her eyes went wide. "My God!" she croaked and shot to her feet.

Gavin sat back, startled by her outburst. His face was ashen, eyes dark with foreboding.

Keegan stalked from one end of the room to the other in quick, rhythmic strides. She muttered to herself continuously, then stopped abruptly. She looked at Gavin, seemingly confused and awed all at once. Muttering once more, she resumed pacing at a frenetic pace.

"Oh, for fuck's sake," Gavin bellowed at last. The outburst snapped Keegan from her high-speed internal mental monologue. "Would you sit down before *you wear a hole in the floor? I've got more to tell if you give me a couple of minutes to work up to it."*

Keegan darted across the room. She dropped to her knees before him once more and looked at him with wild, rarely blinking eyes. "Gavin Kray," she said with an affirming nod. "I didn't place it—well, why would I? Kray, short for Kravenell—one of six families destroyed—murdered—in Salem. That was September and October of 1692."

Gavin sat back, his expression unreadable. "You know of the Kravenell clan?" he finally muttered.

Keegan nodded quickly. "The Kravenell coven was attacked by a mob. Your mother was Dendra Kravenell? She's said to be the most powerful Crafter of the greatest generation—the last generation. She used her death curse to—"

Her eyes taking on a mischievous glint, Keegan slapped Gavin on the side of the knee and released an uproarious laugh. Choking on her amusement, she said, "you know you look pretty good for a guy well over three hundred years old!"

Chapter 56

Gavin countered with a near slack-jawed expression. "You know the Kravenell—you know our story?"

She nodded vigorously. "It's no exaggeration to say it's legendary in some circles." Her disposition soured suddenly. "Though I'll admit the idea of a death curse being quite that effective? I can't say I ever bought into that. Figured it was a conflation added to the telling over time."

Gavin shook his head. "I don't know where you got your information, but it sounds pretty accurate. It was months before I worked out the how and why of what happened to me. There was a mob trying to kill me and mine one minute, and seconds later I was sitting bare ass naked in the middle of western Wyoming with a hole in my shoulder from a missing musket ball?"

It was Keegan's turn to look confused. "Naked? Musket ball? Seems some bits were left out of the telling."

"I still don't understand it entirely. Whatever Casting my mother used to blast me forward in time didn't account for anything not of my body. I lost every stitch of clothes in the crossing. Luckily the lead ball I'd just been shot with was taken along with my clothes. That might've saved my life. Better than any surgery. Plus, it was two days before I found help, and there was no way I could've gotten that bullet out of my own back."

"You were shot?" Keegan's tone was incredulous.

Gavin grinned. The idea of a time-traveling naked youngster wasn't a problem for her, yet the fact that he'd been shot in the back represented the most relevant concern.

He shrugged. "The last act of a desperate Nimm," he explained.

"A Nimm shot you?"

He arched an eyebrow. "That was missing from the telling as well?"

Keegan offered a slow nod. "Story goes, you were set upon by a mob led by some crazed small-town preacher. Dendra Kravenell's death curse wiped them out. Her boy, Gavin, was spared when a slit in space swallowed him whole."

"A portal," Gavin corrected and wondered who had recounted the tale of his mother's curse, one that had claimed the lives of everyone present. "I read of the so-called Salem Witch trials," he went on. "History's watered-down rationalization of the killings preceding that night, as best I can tell. Still, I never came across a telling of my story. As far as I knew, the events of that night were lost to history."

"As I understand it, there was a coven about a hundred miles to the south. After all that happened, how could they not investigate? They counted a Seer among their numbers. Story goes, they put the events of that night together before going into hiding themselves." Keegan shifted uncomfortably. "I've read of the Nimm before. I thought they were figures of overactive imaginations. You're saying they were there that night?"

"One of them was. Vicious bastard too. Seriously had it in for my family. He must have put the townspeople up to what happened. While we were never close with the people nearby, there had always been a mutual, if cold, respect. Their turning on us never made sense unless the Nimm somehow influenced them."

"They can do that?"

Gavin shrugged. "Never saw one before that night and haven't seen one since. Hope I never see one again. I only know what I've read about them. And as your retelling of that night in the woods illustrates, the truth doesn't always match the reality of the tale."

Chapter 57

Keegan crossed the room and knelt beside the nightstand. She shot a look to Gavin as she bent forward and began blindly fumbling beneath the base of the stand. There was a small space between the floor and the ornamental scrollwork of the wood at the base of the stand. Rather than reaching in from the front, Keegan leaned around the back. "There's a lot of strange stuff going on around here," she said. She bit her lip and started to look concerned. Finally, she found what she was looking for, grabbed it, and climbed back to her feet.

"What's that?" Gavin said as she passed him a fairly hefty leather-bound book. The covers and binding were well-worn. The volume was clearly ancient.

Rather than answer, Keegan watched his eyes. Gavin turned the book so the battered and faded cover caught the light. A shocked expression took the color from his face. Crios Talún was etched in an elaborate scrawl on the cover. He threw the book down on the bed and stepped back with raised hands. The motion made it look like the tome had scalded his flesh.

"Are you alright?" Keegan said and grabbed at his hands to check for just this kind of damage. There was none, but Gavin's gaze was fixed on the book where it had landed, cover up. The way the lettering caught the light, the title was unmistakable even at a distance.

Gavin took a deep breath, and she realized he'd been holding it since first seeing the title. "Do you know what that is?" he croaked in a cold, dry voice. His eyes finally met hers. "It's my family's grimoire."

She eyed him carefully. "I'm guessing it's authentic? You don't want to take a closer look? You didn't even crack the cover."

He slowly shook his head. "Authentic? There's no question. You can't feel it when you touch it?"

Her lips drew into a tight line. There was a power to the book; she'd sensed it even before first laying hands on it. She thought of the way she'd found it in the cavern—a cavern she still didn't understand and an experience she'd written off as a dream until last night. It was as if the book had called to her. No, maybe that wasn't right. But something had led her to the book, and something had masked the experience to keep it from her mind until only recently.

When she spoke, her words came in a whispered, conspiratorial tone. "I think we're being manipulated. This place…me being here. I wasn't supposed to stay more than a week. Then meeting you? It seems like it was supposed to happen. Then that book? The things that have been happening? There's a presence on this island. I'm starting to feel like a puppet—all these tiny tugs at my strings. At first they were nuanced. Now they're becoming more overt."

Gavin's gaze moved from her to the book and back again. Understanding registered. She sensed him beginning to make the same connections. "Where did you get the book?" he finally croaked. A sense of foreboding was visible in his expression. This was something she'd never seen in him before. He was ordinarily confident and in control.

"I found it. It's incredible. I have to show you," she offered her hand, then took his.

The only way to explain what she knew and demonstrate what she suspected was to show him where she'd found the book. The idea terrified her. Before seeing the horrified expression on his face, she would have wagered nothing could ever make her return to that creepy ass cavern. In a matter of minutes, that had changed. The book meant something more to him than even she suspected. How and why it had come to be here just became questions they needed answered.

Crossing the room to the full-length mirror, Keegan's confidence grew. When the idea first crossed her mind, she didn't know how or if she would be able to return to the cavern. In truth, she didn't know how she'd gotten there *the first time. But like her memory of the first visit, things were coming back slowly. The events of that night felt like a puzzle with most of its pieces missing. Still, those pieces were dropping into place in the form of tangled, disjointed, and fractured thoughts. They were less memories and more senses of the experience that night. And as she stepped within inches of the mirror, she realized she needed to return as much for her own understanding as Gavin's.*

His brow furrowing, Gavin looked at Keegan's hand in his and the way she stood squarely before the mirror. "Are you alright?" he whispered.

She looked at him over her shoulder and squeezed his hand tightly. Closing her eyes, she focused her senses on the mirror and whispered the Latin phrase that sprang unbidden to her mind, "reditum antro portam." The fingers of her free hand touched the surface of the mirror and a tingling jolt coursed through her body.

The room went wholly and utterly dark.

Chapter 58

Gavin's entire body tingled. Even his tongue felt numb. It was like he'd just been hit with a brief low-voltage current. "I don't know what you did," he whispered, "but I think you tripped the breaker."

Keegan gave a little laugh that sounded forced and nervous to Gavin's ears. "Hang on a second," she said.

A small blinding light pierced the darkness and brought a stabbing pain to the back of Gavin's eyes. He raised a hand to block the glare and laughed. "Easy with that thing." He felt Keegan tuck herself close to his side and wrap one arm around his waist. It was a defensive move, and his hackles instantly rose. His free hand went to the knife on the back of his belt. He slipped it free from the sheath in a silent, well-practiced motion. "What is it," he whispered.

Keegan panned the light of her cell phone across the floor before them. Thirty feet of uneven stone was all they could see. The beam of light ended at a perimeter of inky black.

"What the hell?" Gavin muttered. The sound of his voice was wrong in the space. It carried like they were standing in a vast empty cathedral. He instantly wondered how much space was out there beyond the perimeter of their meager light.

Keegan slowly panned her light across the stone floor surrounding them. Aside from a light layer of dirt and grit, there was nothing to see. A few seconds later, Gavin added the light of his mobile; it did nothing to help them understand their current location.

Long seconds of silence passed. Finally, Gavin looked at Keegan. "What did you do?"

She swallowed hard. "I'm showing you where I found the book," she said. Her voice dropped to a whisper before adding, "I think."

Gavin stepped forward and began playing his light more diligently across the floor. Keegan instantly seized his arm and pulled him to a stop.

"What are you doing?" she whispered as if they might be overheard.

"You were here before?" he asked.

She nodded, her eyes wide and bordering on panic. Clearly, she was rethinking the wisdom of this trip.

He pointed to the focal point of his light's beam. "I think you went that way," he said with a smirk. "I'd recognize your bare feet anywhere."

Turning a shoulder, Gavin guided Keegan's gaze to the small set of closely spaced footprints leading off into the darkness. Judging by the uneven gait and their ever-shifting direction, she'd been scared. He grinned wider as understanding struck. "You didn't have a light last time?"

Keegan gave a stiff shake of her head and clung tightly to his side. "I didn't know how I got here," she said. "I was cold, it was pitch black, and I think I was even too scared to scream." She went on to explain how she stumbled around until finally finding a wall. Sometime after the wall, she found a torch hanging in a wall sconce of some kind. She couldn't recall how she'd set it alight but felt like that part of the story was on the tip of her tongue.

They followed her small, unsteady prints in the dust until they reached a wall. Just as she'd said, the cavern was vast. Gavin guessed they had walked seventy or eighty yards. They followed the tracks to an empty wall sconce. Much to Keegan's consternation, she'd passed two similar wall-mounted torches before finding the one she'd eventually used. It seemed the perimeter of the cavern had been well-appointed with man-made light at some point since mounts for the torches had been placed approximately every hundred feet.

"Where was the grimoire?" Gavin asked, trying to coax Keegan along. He

could see frustration building as they retraced her path through the massive space.

Keegan pointed to the path her footprints took away from the wall. She had obviously struck out for the middle of the massive space to better understand her predicament. "That way. But it only gets weirder from here."

They made better time, moving quickly across the space with the benefit of their two handheld lights. Gavin moved quietly but could still hear their footsteps echoing into the distance. "How big is this place?"

Keegan shook her head. "Never figured that out," she admitted.

He shined his light toward the ceiling. The beam failed to penetrate the darkness above them, so he had no idea just how high the space might be. "Just where in the hell are we?"

Squeezing his hand, Keegan let out a rueful chuckle. "I was wondering when you'd get around to asking that." She took an audible breath and then sighed. "Haven't a clue. But it's gotta be somewhere on the island—" she froze suddenly in mid-step and met his gaze with a nearly panicked stare. "Doesn't it?"

Gavin laughed and pulled her close. "We stepped through a mirror to get here. If you ask me, we could be anywhere." He considered the Casting that opened a portal through time and space to deposit him centuries from the time of his birth and stopped short of voicing the primary concern on his mind. They could be anywhere or anywhen.

If there was an answer to the question, his mother's grimoire was their best chance of finding an answer. For perhaps the hundredth time, he was asking himself how the book could have come to be in a place like this. His list of unanswered questions was growing faster than he could tally them, and his patience was shot. A sense of frustration was just about to boil over when a shadowy form rose in the distance.

Gavin stepped between Keegan and the massive dark shape. "Get back," he warned Keegan. Raising his cell phone light in one hand and the blade of his bowie knife in the other, he readied for the oncoming attack.

She tapped him on the shoulder and moved carefully to his side. Her light came up and added distance to the beam of his. "It's ok," she said with a coy grin. "He won't hurt us."

Gavin stepped forward to examine the six-foot-tall statue depicting a World

War Two-era soldier resplendent in a tattered and torn Nazi uniform. The craftsmanship was incredible, if unconventional. Every detail of the uniform was captured, right down to the loose threads surrounding tears in the fabric. Even more strange was the unusual pose in which the figure had been sculpted. He appeared to be mid-stride, turning to look over his shoulder with an expression of fear. One arm seemed to be raised in defense, and the other was outstretched, perhaps for balance. His mouth was agape, his eyes wide, coarse patchy stubble coated his jaw and cheeks, and even his face was pebbled with sweat.

Turning to Keegan, Gavin said, "This is just..." his voice trailed off.

"Just like the cave at the top of the mountain," she said, completing his thought. Pointing into the darkness, she said, "there's more. A lot more."

She led him through a quick tour of the massive space. Along the way, they passed more than a dozen additional Nazi soldiers in all manner of unusual poses and positions. They passed a group of pirates who seemed to be gathered around a central object that was, for some reason missing from the scene, and then they came to a gathering of numerous robed monks gathered around the base of a massive, intricately detailed tree. Every figure they passed had been captured in the same exacting detail, and everyone was carved from the same unusual stone—even the tree, which Gavin failed to comprehend how something so massive and delicate was even possible.

"It was just over here," Keegan said finally, just after they passed the massive tree. She stopped suddenly, pausing mid-stride with a faraway look in her eye.

Gavin's senses were on high alert once more. His grip tightened on the blade in his right hand. He had yet to sheath their only defense since stepping foot in this strange place. "What is it?" he whispered.

"Brody?" Keegan said slowly as if tasting the word on her tongue.

"Brody?" Gavin repeated. He shone his light around slowly and examined the thirty or so feet within the bubble of visibility. "He's here?"

Keegan shook her head slowly as if trying to sort something out in her mind. "No," her voice sounded unsure. "But he was." Her tone was growing in certainty with each passing second. "He was here that night. Why am I only now remembering that?"

"Brody was here with you when you were lost?" Gavin was struggling to make sense of the new information.

She turned to look at him, confusion clouding her expression. "He wasn't...then he was. I think he found me. He led me to the book and then guided me out of here."

Gavin winced. "You realize you're not making sense, right?"

"Parts of this are foggy. It's like a dream, but I know it was real. I can't explain why I only just started to recall this," she waved her hands in the air as if to encompass the space around them. "I can't explain why parts of it seem out of reach even now. It's like someone did something to me."

"You think it's a Casting," Gavin said. It was a statement rather than a question.

Her eyes locked on his; this concept was clearly occurring to her for the first time. "That would explain a lot. I think you're right!"

Gavin felt his irritation grow. Until recently, he thought such concerns had died out long ago. Warring factions, covens, and sects fought themselves into extinction until they were little more than legends to the modern mind. He'd been shocked to find Keegan gifted with Casting ability. While he'd hoped such things were relegated to history, it seemed likely that the gifts of the past might filter down to the more in-tune of the modern generation. But if there was another Caster on the island, perhaps the covens of old were not as extinct as he had hoped.

"There's another Caster on the island?" Gavin said, his tone incredulous.

"I didn't tell you the weirdest part about the grimoire. There are two copies of the book on the island."

Gavin shook his head. "Not possible," he said flatly. "If the book is authentic, it can't be copied. Each coven had its grimoire, and each included a Casting to prevent duplication. It was a protection. Each book was unique to the coven who created it. Some were more powerful than others, so each group coveted them as the one-of-a-kind artifacts they were. Duplicating one would steal from its power."

"It's not a copy of the book," Keegan corrected. "It's literally two of the same book."

"That's just not possible."

She shrugged. "Be that as it may, I have seen them for myself. I'm certain of it."

Gavin felt his bile rise. Whoever had the second book was certainly behind everything strange taking place on the island. "Who has the book?"

"My father."

Chapter 59

"Maybe the book isn't authentic," Keegan decided. "I only flipped through it...parts were nonsensical. It might have been another language, but it looked like English—just English that didn't make any sense. Like it was written by a crazy person."

Gavin cocked his head but said nothing. His non-verbal response somehow managed to speak volumes to Keegan. "That means something to you?"

"Both copies were the same in that regard?"

"The nonsense?" she clarified.

He nodded.

Keegan shrugged. "Dad's copy stays in his safe, so I haven't had more than a few minutes at a time with it. But yeah, from what I could tell they seemed to be duplicates. Sections were entirely readable, even if I didn't understand what I was seeing. That would be followed by another section that was gibberish. All written in the same hand, maybe a code or something?"

Gavin looked suddenly pale, even in the lousy light of the cavern.

"What is it?" Keegan pressed.

"The books sound legit. It's not code. What you saw was a Binding. Those sections are called phases. Only members of the coven can read them. It's a protection meant to ensure the Castings recorded in the grimoire could only be used by members of the coven."

This was a logic Keegan found immediately satisfying. It was like locking the book with a key known only to members of the group to which the information belonged. "What about the English sections? It looked like there were Castings and wards documented there in cleartext. Is that just a wild goose chase?"

Already shaking his head, Gavin had taken on a sightless thousand-yard stare. "No," he said distractedly. "It's all useful to someone with talent. The really powerful or dangerous incantations were obfuscated. But any member of the coven would be able to read the book cover to cover."

That begged the question, just what use it might be to her father, Keegan reasoned. If the book was only useful to someone with innate natural Casting ability, what good would it do him? Then again, she had power. It was unpredictable and she was inexperienced, but that had to mean something. Where had it come from? Did such things happen randomly or was there some kind of biological link? And if the talent was hereditary, might her father have an ability she was unaware of? His sudden shift of good fortune in recent years suddenly seemed worthy of further examination.

Keegan knew more about Casting than most in the modern age. She'd had her first out-of-body experience while in veterinary school. Coming to grips with the experience had required the excessive application of her academic acumen. It was the first she'd ever heard of Casting beyond what was commonly available in fiction. Not to be confused with magic, the theatrical and illusionist art that was the mainstay of entertainers, charlatans, and con artists, she had come to learn that Crafting was, in fact, very real. Some had the ability, though most had absolutely no aptitude for it. According to her research, there was evidence that suggested Casting had once been more common—the ability more accessible to a greater portion of the population. Over the millennia, for whatever reason, it seemed the ability had faded from the populace just as understanding of it had disappeared from modern understanding. Those who knew of it now were versed in the most arcane history and reticent to share what they knew.

Looking at Gavin with fresh eyes, Keegan suddenly understood just what a link to the past he represented. So much arcane knowledge had been lost to the ages. But he had lived in that time. He'd come from a family of Casters. Even if he had no ability himself, he was a living link to information lost to the ages. If anyone could help her understand her abilities, it was him. Perhaps it was why they'd had such a connection from the start.

Keegan set these concerns aside and focused on the most immediate of problems. "Could someone have used a Casting from the book to duplicate it?"

Gavin snapped his attention back to the moment and offered a non-committal shrug. "Give me time with the book and I might be able to answer some questions. Not the least of which is how the hell I'm here." He met her eye. "I'll admit to ruminating on that one for more than a couple of sleepless nights. The power it took for my mother to send me here? It's unprecedented. She was powerful, but that was something an entire coven couldn't have done working in concert. I've never been able to make sense of it. Whatever she did, she tapped into a serious mystical channel."

"Mystical channel?" She'd never heard the term before.

"God level. But she never had the juice for that. If she did, I would have known."

Laughing, Keegan stepped forward. Sensing seriousness in his tone and expression, she quickly stopped. "You're not kidding? You're saying she asked God to send you forward in time?"

It was Gavin's turn to laugh. "God? No—well, not that God. A God. It's the only thing that makes sense."

"Wait, you're saying there's more than one God?"

Gavin waggled a hand in the air. "A handful, actually. Though none have much in the way of power these days. Even back then, their power was on the way out. As close as I can tell, the so-called witch trials in Salem were the end of an era for what remained of that power structure. All of the killing sort of put an end to things. People were too afraid."

Keegan didn't understand. The confusion must have been evident in her expression because Gavin continued as if prompted.

"We haven't talked about it, but you must be a part of a coven?"

Confused, Keegan shook her head. "There are no more covens. There's the silly Goths who dress up and play witches, but as close as I can tell, all of the legit covens were wiped out in the mid-1690s." Then, realizing what this would literally mean to him after his experience at that time, she stepped quickly forward and placed a sympathetic hand on his arm. "I didn't mean—"

He shook his head and smiled sadly. "It's alright. I shied away from doing a lot of research. I've meant to get around to it, but it's just nowhere near the top of my list. Call it the family business. I figured I would get around to looking it up sooner or later. It was easy to make assumptions and push the Google searches off till later."

Not knowing what to say, Keegan pushed on. "You were saying about Gods?"

"The Gods of Old," Gavin said without additional preamble. "A half dozen or so. Deities of varying degrees of clout. Think of them as the sponsors of the main covens. Any coven with significant power owed it to whatever deity they worshiped."

Keegan was dumbfounded. "You're saying the covens had their respective Gods to thank for their power? They offered some kind of fealty, and in return, they were granted power? How could I not know this?"

Gavin laughed. "They'd like to have everyone believe that. It was more the other way around. Well, maybe it was better described as a symbiotic relationship. The Gods of Old gained strength from the attention of those who worshiped them. The more followers, or the more devoted those followers were—ideally both—the more powerful the God became. In turn, the God rewarded that adulation by empowering the coven or covens which supported them."

Suddenly it made sense why Casting had fallen out of favor and legitimate Casters were so few and far between. These days it seemed modern man had little use for a higher power. Worship was out of vogue.

"Wait, so you're saying the decline of Crafting was the result of the Gods losing power…and the Gods lost power because those who worshiped them became disenfranchised?"

Gavin nodded. "Well put. Essentially, yes. But back to the point—my mother used her death curse to send me forward to this time and wipe out everyone present at her execution. Even if Karina and my father had somehow managed to contribute to the effort—impossible because they'd already been killed—Mom wouldn't have had the power for anything close to what she did. I can't even imagine where she would've found a Casting to do what she did. I've never heard of anything. And our coven didn't have the power for anything in that league. No Earth Caster could—" his voice broke off suddenly.

Keegan watched as a faraway look returned to Gavin's eyes. Long seconds passed. For some reason, she felt increasingly reluctant to break the silence. It *seemed his mind was in another time or place. Perhaps, as he'd just mentioned, he was starting to process memories and emotions that were long overdue.*

Eyeing the jumble of decaying fabric that marked where she'd found the grimoire, a dark form at the far edge of her cell phone's light caught her eye. Keegan walked forward and gasped as the upper half of a prone figure came into view.

"My God," Keegan whispered in the darkness. "Another one."

"What's that?" Gavin moved swiftly to her side.

"This is the creepiest one yet!"

Another stone figure lay face up on the cavern floor. Unlike all the carvings they'd found so far, this was the carving of a skeleton. It had been rendered from the ribcage upward. Only the body's upper torso was captured for whatever reason. Depicted in the same lifelike detail as the other works of art, this one demonstrated stunning familiarity with the human skeletal structure. The bones of the skull were detailed to the point that the occipital, temporal, and parietal bones were clearly distinguished. The jaw was complete with teeth that showed wear, two chipped, and several with cavities. Even the jaw looked like it might indeed be articulated.

The arms were socketed at the shoulder, Keegan observed. The way the elbow joint came together looked as perfect as any anatomy class skeleton she had ever seen, only this version was carved meticulously of stone. The ribs were carved in exceptional detail, showing what could only be described as a flare of artistic license as two of the ribs showed evidence of being broken earlier in life. Remodeling marks suggested the pair of ribs had been poorly set at some point and healed with thick scarring. That choice in the rendering interested Keegan. She leaned in closer with her light to take a look.

And then she screamed.

Her light clattered to the cavern floor, and she retreated in a flurry of gesticulating limbs.

Gavin swept her up in one arm, pointing his light quickly about with the hand braced on her shoulder while raising his knife defensively in his right hand. "What?" he shouted. "What did you see? Where is it?"

Keegan was on the verge of hyperventilating. Even as she fought for breath, she was chastising herself for a reaction that was uncharacteristic. What she'd just seen made her stomach flip flop.

"We need to get out of here right now," she said in a cold whisper.

"What? What did you see?"

"The body," she said in a quiet tremulous tone. "It's human."

Clearly confused, Gavin stepped closer to the body. She grabbed him by the arm but was stayed by his calming smile. "It's alright. Just wait here."

Gavin stepped forward and leaned over the supine body. Taking a deep breath to steel herself, Keegan paced forward, snatched her phone from the floor, and added her light to his.

The two lights shown down on the stone figure. Perhaps two-thirds of the rib cage had been captured in perfect stony detail. But the bottom right side of the figure's ribs was not stone. The stone strata ended abruptly giving way to what was unmistakably the pearl white of human bone. It was as if the body had fallen there and petrified over time, turning primarily to stone except for this one small remaining portion.

"What the hell?" Gavin muttered.

They both stepped back and stared at the half-skeleton on the cavern floor. The idea of a body petrifying over time seemed farfetched, but that was far preferable to the unavoidable truth. Turning as one, Keegan and Gavin spun to face the greater cavern and the dozens of intricately carved, impossibly lifelike figures.

Gavin nodded slowly and whispered. "You're right. Let's get the hell out of here."

Chapter 60

Gavin stumbled as Keegan's form materialized in a blurry fog around him. No, not Keegan's room, he noticed with a start. The contents of his stomach roiled as his bedroom snapped into focus. He turned in time to see Keegan take a deep, steadying breath. The disorienting step through the mirror clearly had less impact on her most recent meal.

"Sorry," she said. "Should have warned you. That first step's a doozy."

He grinned sheepishly, bent with his hands on his knees. Swallowing hard, he waved a hand in a lazy gesture. "How?" was all he could say.

Keegan shrugged and ran a hand around his back in a soothing motion. "Take deep breaths. The vertigo will pass in a few seconds." She looked back to the darkened room. A bolt of lightning filled the wall of windows to their left and reminded them both that the storm continued to batter the island.

"I can use most of the mirrors on the island," Keegan said after a brief silence. "I'm still working it out, so I have more questions than answers. I've had time for a little research. The prevailing theory is that the mirror has to be backed with real silver rather than the cheap silver knockoff crap most companies use these days. Meaning I can only use antique mirrors. There seems to be a size requirement as well. I can't use someone's handheld vanity mirror, for

example."

Gavin stood, still breathing deeply. "But how? A Crafting of some kind?"

Brushing a lock of hair from her eyes, Keegan met his gaze. "Great question. Not my Casting. I can tell you that for sure. It's like the out-of-body thing. I have no idea why it's happening. I'm only now starting to gain control of this...whatever it is."

Shaking his head, Gavin walked slowly across the room and then sat heavily at the foot of the bed. "It's hardly the strangest thing happening here," he muttered. His mind was already reviewing the catalog of intricate carvings they had just witnessed. He'd been thinking of the sigil marking the portal at the top of the mountain. At first the mark seemed vaguely familiar, though whatever memory associated with it eluded him. Seeing the partially ossified corpse in the cavern had triggered a connection, however. Now he wondered how a memory burned so indelibly upon his heart and mind had managed to resist him for so long.

"Hand me that?" Gavin said and pointed to the digital tablet on his nightstand. His limbs felt suddenly so heavy, the effort of retrieving the device seemed insurmountable.

Chapter 61

Keegan passed Gavin the tablet before slipping onto the bed beside him. She expected him to launch the web browser and reference some sort of occult website. To her surprise, he tapped the device to life and engaged a drawing app. "The symbol we saw at the top of the mountain," Gavin began. "It struck me as familiar the first time I saw it. When you and I went back…the sense was far more intense. I've had this nagging suspicion ever since. The sigil was clearly important. Why else would it mark the portal in such a way?"

As he spoke, he drew on the screen with the tip of his index finger. He made a crude circle, then added a thick wavy line directly beneath it at its six o'clock position. "This is the sigil my mother drew as part of the Casting that sent me to this time," he said at last. "It's a rune depicting the deity known as Nae'ja-dinn."

Keegan said the word slowly, as if tasting it and trying it out all at the same time. "Nae'ja-dinn…" the word was familiar. Speaking it brought a flood of memory that seemed to rush into focus from a mile away. She recalled a series of figures huddled around the base of a short stone wall. A well of some kind, she understood suddenly. The memory had the sense of a dream, yet she recognized it was an experience somehow repressed.

"Are you alright?" Gavin had placed a hand on her arm. Concern filled his *stare.*

Shaking her head slowly, Keegan processed the new information. "You know why the sigil is familiar, don't you?"

Gavin's blank expression was all the confirmation she needed. Keegan snatched the tablet from his hands. She tapped and swiped with skill and precision. It took only a matter of seconds for her to access her personal photo archive over the network. Another couple of seconds and she located the album with the photos in question. Tapping to enlarge the first shot, she handed the device back to Gavin. It showed a long stretch of tilled soil at the bottom of a long stone wall. A series of balled shrubs sat at the edge of the frame waiting to be placed in holes at the base of the wall.

"The new planting?" Gavin said, referring to the shrubs he and Willy spent three days transplanting several months earlier. "So?"

"Swipe," Keegan said simply.

Gavin flicked a finger across the screen. There was a shot of him muscling a shrub into a hole perhaps two feet deep. His face was covered in sweat, and his sleeveless arms were covered in mud and dozens of shallow scratches and welts. Certainly not the most flattering image, he supposed, and shot her a questioning look. She spun a finger in the air in a silent gesture for him to continue. He did.

The next photo depicted Gavin dragging another balled shrub across the clumpy, uneven soil. He must have been pulling it backward, the effort catching Willy off guard because the frame had been snapped just as Willy backpedaled to place a foot into the next planting hole. Willy's arms were windmilling, and a grimace of panic contorted his sweat-covered face. Keegan and Gavin laughed at the memory, Keegan's hand moving quickly to cover her mouth.

"I forgot about that one," she admitted. "Not the shot I was thinking of."

Gavin swiped once more and the photo of the last hole in the line came into frame. Like the rest, it was at the bottom of the stone wall, set away from its base by about eighteen inches. It was the last in the line because this was the corner of the wall and presumably the end of the line of new shrubs. Gavin's brows furrowed as he looked at the photo more closely. His fingers moved to zoom in on the image.

"The next photo should be a closeup," Keegan offered. She didn't know why she remembered this set of images so clearly. As with the memory of the ritual in the bowels of the citadel, this experience had suddenly come snapping back into focus.

Gavin flipped to the next photo and promptly dropped the tablet onto his lap. Carved into the face of the cornerstone of the wall was the same symbol they'd seen at the top of the mountain.

"Nae'ja-dinn," Gavin whispered.

Keegan nodded. "There are more marks like that all over the island. I don't know why I didn't notice them until now. It's like I was..." she struggled to find words lost just beyond her grasp.

Gavin met her eye. "Like you were made to look past them...or through them," he said. His words came as a statement rather than a question. She realized he had experienced the same phenomenon.

She suddenly wanted to explain what she'd witnessed the previous night in the subbasement of the citadel. But even now, her body seemed to repel her mind's ambition to voice the related thoughts. "Who, or what is Nae'ja-dinn?" she asked instead.

Setting the tablet aside, Gavin pushed himself further back on the bed. He took long seconds before responding. Keegan couldn't tell if he was searching his memory, collecting his thoughts, or perhaps he was fighting the same ingrained force that made it difficult for her to speak on this subject.

"She was one of the Gods of Old," Gavin finally offered in a low, toneless voice. "Some say the most powerful of the five."

Keegan grinned. "The Gods of Old?" She had a passing familiarity with the deities to which he was referring. Anyone who had attempted a deep dive into the arcane arts was bound to stumble across a reference to them sooner or later. But they were a legend that even the most fanciful of the lifelong Crafters didn't take seriously. Some said there were five Gods, some insisted there were seven. Some insisted the beings in question were simply powerful Casters whose legend had been exaggerated through countless tellings. But some were adamant that the Gods of Old were beings entirely unlike mortal men, and that they were, in fact, Gods here to rule us.

There were so many versions of the lore, most contradictory, and no one believed. At least not in Keegan's rational mind. Her laugh died on her lips, however, when she saw the pale expression on Gavin's face.

"Wait," she said suddenly. "You're saying they're real?"

Gavin shrugged. "Are real? Were real? I'm not sure of the proper tense. My coven worked tirelessly to eradicate the last traces of their power. Back in the seventeenth century, their power base was in shambles. They were nearly stamped out. The Nimm was the last of their ilk on our plane—demons with the ability to look human for short periods. I believe the last of the Nimm killed the last of my clan…but maybe I was wrong."

Keegan swallowed hard. "But those sigils? What does it mean if they're all over the island?"

Gavin seemed to be grinding his teeth. He glared at her. "This isn't right." His voice came out like a growl. "I was supposed to be the last. The last to know these things…the last to remember how things once were…the last with contact with the old ways. Once I was gone, everything about them was supposed to be lost to time."

He took a long breath. His eyes roved the room, though Keegan suspected he was really seeing the surrounding island and considering—perhaps reconsidering preconceptions. "The Gods of Old," he said after a long silence. "Forgotten for all time." His jaw clamped and gnashed once more. "Almost."

Placing a hand on his forearm, Keegan coaxed him along. "What does it have to do with this island?"

"It's said the Gods couldn't be vanquished, so they were locked away. Each imprisoned in a far-off land." He raised a free hand in the air and blew a breath out in a huff. "I guess you can't get any more far off than this place."

Though Keegan believed this was where his story was going, her blood felt suddenly cold. "You think that's why all of these sigils are here?"

"The sigils and the energy of this place? The fact that most of the world can't find this island even if they have a map? It's all connected. I just didn't put it together. It absolutely explains why every serious medical condition is cured after time here."

"The sigils of Nae'ja-dinn explain the medical miracles?" Keegan's tone was incredulous.

Gavin nodded. "People create gods with the power of their faith. Show the people something miraculous and you have their devotion. She's starting over, and she's using all of us to do it."

Keegan took long seconds to process this statement. She had always believed that a God or Gods cultivated faith in those who worshiped them, strengthening the worshipers through their understanding of their God. Was it possible she'd had it backward all this time? Had that been backward all this time?

"You're saying the Gods of Old draw their power from their worshipers?"

"All Gods have," Gavin clarified. "Been that way since the start of time." A smirk touched his lips. "Funny how they leave that out of the teachings, isn't it? Sort of puts the shoe on the other foot when you think about it. Undermining them, back in the day, was a matter of turning the people against them. When the people failed in their devotion, the Gods lost power. Those held under their thumbs gained the upper hand. They just needed to understand the rules to have a chance at setting things right."

Keegan felt lightheaded. Everything she'd believed about organized religion was being thrown asunder. "All the sigils spread across the island…does that mean Nae'ja-dinn is actually here somewhere?"

A long silence settled in the room. "I think so," Gavin said at last.

"Then there's one more rune we need to worry about," Keegan said. She turned Gavin's forearm over in her hands. His tattoo caught the firelight. The ink marking wasn't fresh, yet she was sure it hadn't been there two days ago. The inking was a complex etching of strangely geometric patterns with no apparent meaning. "Tell me about this."

Gavin's face scrunched in confusion. "What? You know the story."

She shook her head. There was no question he believed he'd had the tattoo for years. It stood to reason, by that same logic, he would think they had talked about it in the past as well. But they hadn't. The more she thought about it, the more she was sure their confusion was the result of a Casting. But was his memory being messed with, or was hers?

Looking increasingly uncomfortable, Gavin rubbed at the marking on his inner arm. "A misguided trip to Chicago a few years back with a couple of," his voice trailed off momentarily, "associates." There was no question that last word left a bad taste in his mouth and hinted there was much more to the story. "Too much to drink, a night blurrier than not, and now I'm stuck with this…thing."

Unable to stop herself from grinning at the distaste he clearly held for a mark that would forever scar his flesh, Keegan pressed on. "You don't recall the specifics, or you don't want to say?"

He glared at her. "Not something I'm proud of, but I don't have much in the way of memories from that night. I've had years to think about it, and I'm still coming up dry."

"Would you say your memories are artificially foggy like the night of the burning—the night your mother used the sigil and curse to send you through time?"

His expression souring, Gavin licked his lips. He began to speak but stopped short. The question seemed to require substantial consideration. Rather than address the point, he asked, "where are you going with this?"

Keegan pointed to the ink on his arm and began to trace a pattern set inside the more complex shape. Her finger traced a circle that an overlay of intricate geometric shapes had obscured. Then her finger found and traced a thick squiggly line that was offset from the circle in a now too-familiar way. She looked up to see Gavin's mouth hanging open.

"Nae'ja-dinn," he whispered. "How? Why?" He looked ready to become physically sick. "I've been marked."

Clearly, this was news to him. "It's more than that," she said and held tight to his arm. Her finger switched to the other side of the circle and traced another wavy line. This one also occluded by a tangle of unrelated shapes and patterns. The second line ran parallel to the first, though on the opposite side of the circle. "There's a balance here—something not present in the original sigil," she explained. "I need to do additional research, but this balance would seem to offset or negate the power of the Nae'ja-dinn."

"Offset?" Gavin's voice was more brittle than she'd ever heard it.

She nodded quickly. "More research is required, but if I'm right, this is a ward of protection. Are you sure you don't remember who gave you this?"

He shook his head, his voice coming in a tired and reluctant single word. "Why?"

"I think whoever did this was a witch."

Chapter 62

Gavin thumbed back the hammer on the .357 revolver and glared at Anakasta and his wife. The couple sat in a pair of high-backed chairs bracketing a cold dark hearth at the end of their bedroom suite. Though both looked uncomfortable, neither looked appropriately frightened, he observed. Tensions ratcheted up by several degrees when Keegan returned with the book from the wall safe and dropped it on the table at her father's knees.

As far as Gavin was concerned, the list of potential masterminds with mystical machinations had to be short. The Anakastas had spent a fortune to gain control over the island and they'd been searching every inch of it for months. This wasn't long division. The only real question was how hard he could squeeze them for the truth. And since Keegan was onboard with the interrogation, the knob on the proverbial juicer was entirely in his control.

"You broke into my—" Anakasta's words were cut off as his eyes settled on the grimoire before him. "What are you doing with that?" he practically spat the last word with vitriol.

Gavin tapped the revolver against the leg of his jeans and eyed Anakasta with a frosty stare. "I was going to ask you the same thing." His tone was calm to the point of being chilling. He'd used it many times in the past to great effect.

Anakasta was already shaking his head. He seemed more frightened of the book than the gun in Gavin's hand. "That book is dangerous. Put it away—just put it away."

Flipping open the shoulder bag slung across his body, Gavin pulled the copy Keegan had found in the massive cavern that was presumably located somewhere on the island. He handed the book to Keegan, who placed it on the table beside the copy from the safe. Two things were instantly apparent with the two books side by side on the table's surface. The first was that the covers were identical. Every blotch, crevice, and imperfection of the book's rough leather cover was duplicated with exacting detail. Conversely, the book from the safe was at least a quarter-inch thicker than the book from the cavern.

Obviously making the same observations, Asha leaned forward in her seat. She eyed the books with suspicion. Anakasta shifted uncomfortably in his chair but remained silent. Keegan flipped the cover of the thinner book and turned two or three sheets into the volume. She held the book open with one hand while repeating the same action on the thicker volume with her free hand. A moment later, she pushed the pair of books to the edge of the table bringing them closer to Gavin and catching the room's meager light.

Leaning forward, Gavin found identical pages in the books. Both had pages etched with a rich black ink scrawled by the hand he didn't know but could identify from many years of study. The writing was so ancient it had been penned using a quill, the words captured to a thick, coarse paper with fibers threadbare and as unique as a fingerprint. The pages were identical, both in content and physical composition.

Keegan directed his attention to the dark mark in the corner of the rightmost page. Gavin examined the smudge more closely. It was a fingerprint—a thumb mark, he was almost certain. And what he'd initially taken to be ink now looked more like blood long since dried, so dark and ancient it might as well have been ink.

"Look closer," Keegan said softly.

Gavin eyed Anakasta and Asha suspiciously. He tapped the revolver against his leg twice in a less than subtle warning, then knelt before the books. The thumbprints, too, were identical, right down to the L-shaped scar marring the pattern near the center of the print. It was unique and unmistakable. He switched the revolver to his left hand and tipped the pad of his right thumb to the lap light. The remains of the long-since healed L-shaped scar were visible.

The fingerprint was his, yet he had no memory of making it. More confusing, he had burned his thumb on the fuser of a laser printer more than ten years ago. He'd last seen the grimoire back in the seventeenth century. Everything was just as Keegan had described it, and that suggested only one conclusion. Someone had used the Casting in the book to travel with the volume through time. But there were problems with this conclusion.

The first of which was his own practical experience with the Casting. When his mother sent him here, nothing inorganic or non-living had made the crossing with him. At least that was his explanation for what had happened. He'd arrived in this time period bare-assed naked, after all. There was no logic to that part of the experience unless it was a byproduct of the crossing. It suggested that only living material could make the transition as part of the Casting. And if that were the case, if someone had used the book to reproduce his mother's death curse, they must have revised the rite to bring the grimoire along. It was the only reasonable explanation for the existence of more than one copy of the book. One had existed through time, arriving here and now through natural events, while the other had come here with whoever had manipulated time and space through the dark Casting.

The second problem was perhaps more troubling. Only members of the coven could read the most sensitive parts of the grimoire. A Casting protected the secrets recorded within the book, and the rite Dendra Kravenell used to send Gavin forward in time was a Blood Casting. It was a Dark Rite and outlawed by the remaining covens of his time. To read the book, one had to be a member of his coven...

Or of his blood.

Gavin rose, his grip on the .357 tightening as his gaze shifted from Anakasta to Asha. "Which one is it?" he said simply.

Keegan looked confused. She'd been lost with this new revelation.

Anakasta sighed. "That would be me," he said with an air of exasperation. "I'm your great, great, great-grandson." His gaze shifted to Keegan. "I hope you don't expect me to call you Grandmother? Even to me, that just feels... wrong."

Keegan had gone pale. She glanced from her father to Gavin. "What?"

Gavin stepped to Anakasta and glared. Through clamped teeth, he said, "explain."

A sour expression spread across Anakasta's face. It suggested the man was preparing to be less than forthcoming, at the very least he was about to shade the truth. Not a patient man to begin with, Gavin had no tolerance for additional foolishness. He shoved the table aside with a quick kick and placed the revolver's muzzle against Anakasta's leg, just above the knee. Twisting, he applied excessive pressure. "It's a bad time to think about bullshitting me."

Tears instantly wet the corners of Anakasta's eyes as he squirmed, this time from discomfort. "You wouldn't hurt family."

Gavin thumbed the hammer and practically growled, "maybe I should have kept a journal. Respect is earned, not inherited. You're nothing to me."

With each passing second, Gavin's concern continued to grow. Pieces were falling into place. They were on the lost island of Nae'ja-dinn. The sense of power surrounding this place was growing, and now that he knew it was related to her, they were all in serious danger.

Chapter 63

Great-grandson.

The words reverberated in Keegan's mind. What her father described should be preposterous…but somehow, it wasn't. Somehow, she'd known he wasn't the man she'd come to know off and on through her childhood. Raised mainly in boarding schools, the differences between the man she'd recognized then seemed so obvious. The man who made efforts to reach out to her in recent years was a far cry from the well-meaning, if emotionally distant father of her youth. But looking back, she struggled to understand when the transition had occurred. He certainly looked the same.

Her stare broke from her father's eyes—the man who had claimed to be her father—and for the first time, noticed the barrel of the gun Gavin had placed against that man's knee. "What's your name?" she said, the words interrupting whatever heated conversation the two men had been having.

Anakasta looked at her, question clear in his expression. Gavin was unfazed by the distraction, his attention fixed squarely on her father while he maintained what appeared to be extreme pressure as he drove the muzzle of the gun into Anakasta's leg. "Calling you father seems inappropriate," Keegan clarified. "It's time to come clean."

"Remove the weapon, and we can talk," Anakasta said. His effort to look smug was undermined by the unmistakable concern that clouded his eyes every time he looked at Gavin. There was a fear there that seemed to go beyond the moment. Almost like he worried over a volatility only he knew.

Gavin pulled the gun back but took a long look at Anakasta. Keegan was surprised when Gavin slid the revolver down the back of his jeans in one smooth, clearly familiar motion. He did not, however, withdraw from his perch over Anakasta. Without hesitation, Gavin seized the middle finger on Anakasta's left hand and twisted. A joint popped and her father—the stranger—howled in pain.

Gavin eased away and eyed Anakasta as the man bellowed. He cradled his hand as if bone had been shattered. Tears filled the older man's eyes. A stone-cold stare was Gavin's only reaction, that and the pair of white-knuckled fists that hung at his sides. He seemed like a snake, coiled and ready to strike a second time.

"You need to understand the rules," Gavin said calmly. "We ask the questions, and you answer. If a question is asked more than once, you will experience pain. If I think you're lying, I'll hurt you. If you try to call for help, you're going to be hurt real bad."

The look in Anakasta's eyes bordered on terror. Interestingly, he didn't seem surprised by the violent outburst. Keegan was. She had nearly pissed herself. Gavin's calm in the face of the high-stress situation was almost as shocking as the ease with which he'd transitioned to a state of controlled violence. Even now, she would bet his resting pulse was only fractionally above normal.

Asha leaned to the edge of her seat and raised a hand along with a querulous voice. "Chandler! His name is Chandler. Chandler Anakasta. He truly is your great-grandson, several times removed."

Turning on Asha, Gavin's eyes were blazing. "You know about this? You're part of it?"

A sudden numbness settled over Keegan. A weariness that came with understanding as missing pieces of the puzzle fell into place. "Of course she is," she said. Even her knees felt suddenly weak. "My fat—" she groaned. "If Chandler is who he claims, he has taken possession of my father's body. That could only result from a powerful Crafting...a delicate Binding that required the grimoire. If he used the death curse to possess my father, in his case traveling from some time in the future to steal his body, then he would need the help of a witch here. My father was a lot of things, but I can say one thing with absolute

278

certainty. He had no natural Crafting ability whatsoever."

She glared at Chandler. "That's it, isn't it. That's when you took over his body? When his financial fortune turned around? He chased one get-rich-quick scheme after another. Every single idea failed until one-day things changed. It was like his luck transformed overnight. But it wasn't his luck that changed...it was his soul."

Keegan snatched the gun from the back of Gavin's jeans and shoved it in Chandler's face. "What did you do? What happened to my father!" She pressed the barrel to the bony ridge beneath the man's eyes and then deftly thumbed back the hammer. "You killed him!"

Chapter 64

Gavin watched as the crotch of Chandler's pants grew instantly wet. The acrid scent of urine permeated the air. Asha whimpered but seemed rooted in her seat. Keegan had seized on a point that had yet to gel for Gavin. Whatever she'd surmised had driven her to a breaking point. Tears streamed down her cheeks, but he noted her gun hand remained absolutely steady.

If nothing else, she's good under pressure.

The thought almost made him smile. He'd never thought too far into their future, but if Chandler was to be believed, it sounded like he and Keegan made a go of it. Even had a kid somewhere down the line...

And that kid would one day use the family grimoire to craft a variation on his mother's death curse to hijack the body of Keegan's father.

That's messed up.

Gavin stepped slowly forward. He placed a reassuring hand on Keegan's outstretched arm. "Let's take a step back a second," he said in a calming tone. "I might be a little slow, but this doesn't make much sense. If you shoot him, I might never sort this crap out."

He took the gun from Keegan's hand, pointed the barrel at the floor and gently lowered the hammer to a safer position. The gun went to the back of his jeans once more. Keegan looked to be waffling between emotions running from staggering rage to near complete shutdown.

"Besides," Gavin said and flashed Keegan a mischievous grin. "If he doesn't give us answers damn quick, I'll just dislocate more of his fingers." He seized the ring finger on Chandler's left hand and made ready to twist.

"Wait!" Chandler bellowed. "Ask me anything. I'll talk!"

Satisfied, Gavin collected a chair from the far side of the room. He slid it to a position opposite Chandler and Asha and guided Keegan into it. Her complexion was ashen, but she seemed to be recovering from the shock of Chandler's reveal.

"Where did you get the grimoire?" Gavin asked. He needed to get the story going, and it seemed like as good a starting point as any. "How could you read it?"

Still cradling his injured hand, Chandler sagged in his seat. He looked defeated, both physically and mentally. "I need ice for my hand."

Gavin's hands closed into fists so tight that his knuckles popped audibly. Chandler's eyes went wide and he sat a bit straighter. Gavin observed that the man's gaze never managed to meet Keegan's eyes or his own. It was the mark of a man with a guilty conscience.

"It's a family legacy," Chandler said quickly. "It took me years to find the book—nearly two decades, actually. I thought I was chasing an old wives' tale, but I had the means and always wanted to understand the Poisoned Rock legend. My family was said to play a key role, after all," he said with a disappointed smile.

Gavin's brow furrowed. "What legend? I've never heard of Poisoned Rock."

The comment brought a chuckle from Chandler. "No, I don't suppose you would. Now that I think about it, I don't know when it took on that name. But you're standing on it. This is Poisoned Rock. A lot of what's to come is lost to history." He went silent for several seconds, seemingly lost in thought. "Though someone went on to detail portions of the tale in the grimoire. It's how I know more than most when it comes to this cursed island."

Gavin looked at the pair of duplicate books still on the table side by side. One was substantially thicker than the other. It added credence to what Chandler described. Among other things, the grimoire was a sort of living document in that it was added to over time. The clan chronicled the tale of their coven and the Bindings developed over time. It was part of the reason the book became more powerful with each passing year, stronger with each generation. Gavin had always assumed two things, both mistakenly, it now seemed. First, he thought the book had been lost to time or destroyed centuries ago. Second, he assumed he would be the last of his line. Rightfully so, he believed the goal of his coven had been to stamp out dark powers in every form—ultimately including their own.

Shooting a look at the silent form of Keegan, Gavin saw how her hands lay folded in her lap. Only the pads of her fingers moved, gently shifting against one another in tiny circular motions. His concerns over the book could wait. They needed to understand what had happened to her father. She and her father had never been close, but if nothing more could come of this, Keegan would need closure.

Gavin waved a hand at the pair of books. "I know the grimoire cover to cover. There's no Casting that would let you take over the body of another man, living or dead."

The pained expression on Chandler's face was telling. Whatever he had done, it now aggrieved him. He opened his mouth to speak but failed. His mouth closed and his head lowered. A shudder went through his body and Gavin suspected the man was fighting back tears.

"It was an act of desperation on his part," Asha offered. "He's not proud of it. He was just doing what was necessary to survive."

Irritation crept into Gavin's tone for the first time. "Necessary to survive? How does that justify stealing the body of his forbearer?" The idea was absurd, plus according to every sci-fi book he'd ever read, Gavin couldn't see that ending in anything other than disaster. He wasn't sure of the mechanics of such a thing because, well, it was simply too impossible. But then he'd been thrown forward in time himself, so who was he to say what was possible.

"In the original timeline," Asha explained, "Stanton Anakasta was murdered by his business partner for the insurance money. Gregory Ivankovich blamed Stanton for their mutual failed business ventures and considered the insurance policy his chance to recoup what he believed Stanton had cost his family."

Gavin and Keegan stared at Asha, neither understanding the significance of the point she was making.

"The Casting to which you refer was not a part of the grimoire when it was last in your possession," Asha went on. "Years from now, the book was found and added to by Keegan...at least in the original timeline," she clarified. "We're on the precipice of a pivotal time in history. What's about to take place will shape the world for centuries to come.

"Chandler had the ability, passed down through his bloodline. Passed down from his great, great—" blowing out a huff of air —"passed down from you," she said with a wave of her hand to Keegan. "You and Gavin were to find one another eventually. When Chandler took possession of Anakasta's body, he simply accelerated the timeline of your courtship by bringing the two of you together years before you would have otherwise met."

Gavin groaned. "Because if we didn't meet..."

Asha spun a bemused finger in the air, "Correct. He would never become."

"He was ensuring his own existence," Keegan grumbled, accusation clear in her tone.

Gavin rubbed the bridge of his nose. "Let's stay on point. How did Chandler become Stanton?"

Leveling her gaze on Gavin, Asha explained. "Keegan will one day document the death curse your mother used to send you here. She explained the invocation of Nae'ja-dinn, the sigil...she even managed to work out the rites used for the incantation. How? I have no idea. But she nailed it. According to what Chandler has told me of the family lore," her gaze shifted to Keegan, "you're extremely powerful in your own right. Legendary."

Chandler sat quietly. His wounded hand was now clamped beneath the pit of his right arm to keep pressure on the joint. Gavin could see the man was uncomfortable but suspected it had as much to do with the story now being told. That Chandler offered nothing to interrupt Asha's telling of the story suggested it at least remained accurate to the way he had explained it to her.

"So he used the death curse?" Gavin said. "How does that result in him taking the body of a past family member?"

"In his time, Chandler was very powerful," Asha explained. "It's the bloodline," she said with a smile and eyed Keegan. "He worked out a variation on the Rite. A crafting that leveraged not his death as the source of power, but the passing of a member of his bloodline. The key was knowing the exact time and location of the passing, all documented in the associated reports. Given it was such a high-profile spectacle, Stanton Anakasta's death in that elevator shaft was front-page news for weeks. On top of the police investigation, one was also conducted by the building's insurance carrier. A pair of bloggers added their own brand of investigative journalism to the mix. The event was thoroughly chronicled. It's all detailed right there," she said, eyeing the thicker grimoire.

Gavin considered this information. "So rather than using his own death in the Casting, Chandler used the power of Stanton's death in the Rite. The ritual allowing him to steal Stanton's body and prevent his murder. What happened to the partner? Yankovich, was it?"

"Ivankovich," Asha corrected. "Gregory Ivankovich." She shrugged. "Someone had to die in that elevator. It was important to keep the timelines as close to original as possible."

Keegan leaned forward in her seat and spoke for the first time in a while. "Keep the timelines close? That wasn't a priority when it came to placing Gavin and me in the same place ahead of schedule." She eyed Chandler with suspicion. "Oh, I get it. If you can maintain continuity with the timeline you know, you can game the system."

The growing pain behind Gavin's eyes was intensifying. Chandler really was a sonofabitch. All of his substantial financial success now made sense. It was challenging to make a bad investment when you knew how the markets would play out. Minimal impact on the timeline was the key to his scheme. He was using knowledge of the future to amass a fortune.

This was a lot to process, Gavin had to admit. At least a light was returning to Keegan's eyes. The shock of what they were hearing seemed to make a degree of sense to her. Perhaps it answered some of the concerns growing in her mind these recent months. Not understanding her power, and now the strange events of the last several days. He sensed they were on the precipice of understanding something much more significant that was starting to take form around them.

The Poisoned Rock legend, that's what Asha had called it.

"Tell me about—" the words died on Gavin's lips as the hair on his arms and neck danced to attention. It was as if static had suddenly filled the air. Keegan's eyes went wide, her head swiveling left and right in search of the threat he sensed.

"What is that?" Keegan whispered.

Gavin sensed something—danger, he just couldn't divine the source. His hand went instantly to the grip of the pistol, the thumb flicking back the *hammer even as his eyes probed the shadows of the surrounding room.*

A snapping sound came from their left, and the gun went up to target the sound in response. But rather than a threat, Gavin saw Chandler's mouth clamped shut. His eyes had rolled back to show only their whites, drool ran from the corner of his lips, and the slight shiver that had first seemed to shake his body quickly evolved into a full-blown seizure. Gavin and Keegan were both on their feet.

Chandler's eyes began to glow a ghostly white.

"That's not good," Keegan muttered as she backpedaled.

Gavin moved with her, the pair putting several feet between themselves and Chandler Anakasta. Turning to Asha, Gavin was about to shout a warning when he saw that she, too, was afflicted with glowing white eyes. Her body did not shake, and she did not drool, however. She rose smoothly from the chair to stand rigid and straight-backed. Hands raising, both palms extended toward Gavin and Keegan as if offering something unseen. Then a spiral of dust-like particulates materialized between her hands. The spiral danced and spun with exponentially increasing speed. Perhaps three seconds after the manifestation began, a piercing white light pulsed from the center of the small formation. It filled the room, causing all Gavin saw to go black instantly.

Chapter 65

Gavin's world had been reduced to a vacuum, a sightless, soundless void that, in all fairness, should have included a complete lack of consciousness. But he could reason, therefor some semblance of his mind remained intact. He knew enough to understand that his sense of time was misfiring with the rest of his sensory inputs. It called into question just how scrambled his mind had become. Logically this was beyond his control, so his mind moved on to matters worthy of the one faculty remaining.

He had time to think.

Stanton—er, Chandler Anakasta, and his wife Asha could be counted squarely in the pocket of the entity gathering power on the island. Though there was now little question that force was the Nae'ja-dinn, it would already be game over if she had found her way back into our world. And since the worldwide cataclysm had yet to unfold, events weren't that far along. She needed to rebuild a following before that could happen. This island would be the start. It was her gateway back into our realm. There was no question that Nova Derrota would be the front line in the war that was to come. There was one question that mattered more than any other.

Are we already too late?

Gavin didn't think so. Anakasta had the grimoire; with it, he could raise something powerful. Some lesser being, perhaps a demigod—something to convince the populous that Nae'ja-dinn was worthy of fear or respect. The emotion didn't matter so much as the fact that people believed. Their belief would give her the power she needed to reenter our plane. Ultimately, it would also be the force she used to subjugate humanity if the plan could progress that far. In the age of internet access and instantaneous worldwide news, spreading the message wouldn't be difficult. Creating believers wouldn't take long. People were sheep. They believed what they saw, and there was no question the force Anakasta and Asha planned to raise would put on a convincing show.

The power of the island had been incubating for years, centuries, judging by the stone figures stashed throughout the island. There was no doubt that something here was gaining power, but it was doing so slowly over time. Now, armed with the grimoire, the Anakastas were about to supercharge that force. And they were using the power of his family to bring about an Armageddon.

Gavin still wasn't convinced Anakasta was who he claimed. The Crafting he'd used to come to this time didn't make sense. Dendra's death curse was the first of its kind, as far as he knew. Nothing like it had ever been documented. For Chandler Anakasta to develop a variation on it would have required profound power. The kind of power that no longer existed. The covens were long since wiped out. Gavin was the last of his kind, and he had no power at all. The gift was known to skip a generation, and he was, without question, the last of his lineage.

Keegan had power, he reasoned. More power than any he'd met since arriving in this time. It stood to reason that a random soul might be afflicted with talent but lacking a coven to help them hone and develop their ability; what were the chances of a stray natural Practitioner developing any significant power in the modern age?

But Keegan had, he reminded himself. Afflicted by experiences she could not explain, she sought an understanding of what she was. Information in the modern age made the task easier than ever before. She'd come to understand what she was, even if it flew in the face of all that reason and logic told her to believe. But could there be more to it? Was her ability some wonder of chance— an arcane twist of natural selection? Or did she owe her talents to an ancient lineage lost to time? Gavin's coven was far from the only. They were simply among the last three left standing when the Nimm sought to murder his parents that fateful night.

According to Gavin's research, the other two clans had fallen within a week of the night his parents died in the fires. Thirty-three souls were burned at the stake in less than three weeks. History recorded no survivors. But what if there were? What if someone made it into hiding, keeping their family secret as it was passed down through the generations and their bloodline?

Could that explain Keegan's power?

It was a matter for another day, Gavin reasoned. First, he and Keegan needed to survive the night. Even adrift in a senseless void, Gavin knew that would be the challenge of a lifetime. But considering all he had experienced and learned since arriving in this time, maybe that was the point. Perhaps it had all been preparation for what was to come. His time with the Outfit was savage and violent. It had hardened both his body and his mind. Like a soldier subjected to a life-and-death boot camp, he'd undergone training ideally suited to prepare him for what was to come. As for his soul...well, that had been hardened by calluses long ago. Childhood had prepared him in that regard.

Chapter 66

The void split and coughed Keegan out with a blinding flash of light. She was all knees and elbows in the violent tumble across the cold stone floor. The world was still spinning when she rubbed at her eyes and fought a case of vertigo that had more in common with a lightning strike. The room had gone instantly dark—no, that wasn't right. It was dim. Pale light seemed to fight with shadows for control of the stone-covered walls. The buzzing in her ears quickly gave way to the low murmur of voices. It was a group in the middle of some sub-audible chant.

Bracing herself against the wall to steady her trembling legs, Keegan's eyes swept the room. Maybe a dozen figures, most dressed in ancient-looking cloaks of coarse material—was it wool? The group was gathered on one half of a medium-sized room with a roughhewn stone floor and matching walls. Lit torches hung from the wall secured in crude, ancient-looking sconces. Everyone in the room faced a stout circular well at the center of the space.

Keegan's stomach sank. She recognized this place. A memory, only freshly resurfaced, now ricocheted through her mind.

The basement of the citadel.

She'd been here before. How could she have forgotten? The ritual of only two nights prior seemed like a lifetime ago. But what was the purpose? She recalled the bloodletting. A Blood Casting. It was perhaps the most powerful, and certainly the most dangerous, because it was frequently unpredictable and challenging to control. Only the most reckless of practitioners would be crazy enough to attempt the rituals.

Movement on the far side of the room drew Keegan's attention. A large figure sat with his back to the base of the wall. His hands were tied in front of him, and he was brushing at something he held in his lap. Fearful of drawing the attention of those in the room, Keegan risked a step forward. Slowly dancing shadows resolved into the form of Zane Greeley. Tess Lindow lay sprawled on the floor at his side, her head laying in his lap. Like him, she was bound hand and foot. Her eyes were wide and staring at the congregation gathered opposite them at the base of the well. Greeley's lips moved in slow, silent whispers as he stroked Tess's hair. Keegan understood he was whispering words of gentle reassurance. They were, likely, the only thing keeping Tess from a complete panic attack.

Keegan looked around and realized no one in the room was paying her the slightest attention. The dozen or so present remained entirely focused on the short wall—the mouth of the well as she now saw it for what it was. This was where the bloodletting must be made. No one stood at the edge of the abyss. But that was certain to change, she knew.

Deciding to exploit her captors' lack of attention, Keegan turned abruptly. In her mind's eye, she knew where to find the room's entry. She froze mid-stride at the sight of two unconscious figures. They were bound hand and foot and lying between her and the door. Gavin lay on his side, hands bound behind his back with thin, coarse rope. Beside him, and bound in exactly the same manner, lay…herself.

The gasp escaping Keegan's lips went unnoticed by everyone in the room. So did the curse she uttered less silently. "Shit. Not now! Why now?"

Chapter 67

A piercing sound pulled Gavin's attention back from the void. The fog enveloping his consciousness seemed to coalesce into something with substance. Blinking rapidly, the haze inside his mind began to clear and the dull glow of lamplight swam slowly into focus. Another shriek, this time recognizable as that of a young woman brought him fully back to the moment. The cold stone and grit of the floor became suddenly apparent. Leaning on an elbow, he took in the block-walled chamber. It was lit entirely by torchlight. Numerous robed figures knelt with their backs to him, their attention focused on the curved wall of a short stone dais at the center of the room. No, that wasn't right. It was a well, he realized. This was the underground chamber Keegan had described. The stout stone wall surrounded the mouth of the well she'd seen in her out-of-body experience.

Gavin glanced to the left, his attention following the latest shrieking scream. A tall, lithe, very nude woman was dragging another woman, this one bruised and bloodied, from the open space behind the well. Shadows draped the woman like a living garment and hugged her naked form as if controlled by or possessed by some living, malevolent supernatural force. Long dark hair curtained the woman's face and cascaded over her shoulders. Each step had an economy of motion that teetered somewhere between the grace of a dancer and the predatorial menace of a stalking feline. She was smaller than the woman she *manhandled in the direction of the well mouth, yet she controlled the shackled woman with strength and agility that were out of proportion for her small size.*

Rocking first to a knee, Gavin attempted to launch himself upward in defense of the shackled woman. Though he didn't understand what was happening, he knew an occult ritual when he saw it. The sight of the supplicant forms and the slow murmur of their voices took him back to his childhood. These were Rites that had no place in the modern world. A ten-inch-long chain-linked Gavin's shackles to a steel eyelet sunk deep into the stone floor. He made it halfway to his feet before the chain played out. Still dazed and only partially aware of his surroundings, the chain had gone unnoticed. He crashed back to the floor where he landed hard on an elbow. Turning his head at the last second, Gavin avoided an even less graceful faceplant and smacked the side of his head against the cold stone in the tumble instead.

The girl screamed again. This time Gavin sprang to his knees. Taking up the chain's short slack, he flexed and leaned backward in an effort to pull the eyelet from the floor. Beads of sweat burst from his forehead before he finally gave up on the effort. It was no use. Dropping the chain and taking a deep breath, only then did he notice Keegan laying in a heap on the floor at his side.

Gavin shot a look to the well mouth. The dark-haired woman had the bound woman bent headfirst over the wall and tipping into the abyss. Since there was nothing he could do for her, Gavin focused instead on Keegan. Feeling quickly for a pulse along her neck, he sighed with relief. Eyeing her chest's steady rise and fall, a new appreciation for their dire circumstance threatened to consume him. She was breathing, though unconscious. Her hands were shackled the same as his, linked to the floor by a matching short length of shining silver chain and a thick steel loop anchored to the floor. He tipped her head to remove a kink from her neck. It would prevent obstruction to her airway in the short term. Beyond that, there was little he could do for her at the moment.

The girl at the well mouth...that was a different matter.

"Wait!" Gavin yelled. His voice boomed in the strange acoustics of the chamber's circular stone walls.

In his haste, Gavin first thought the strange nude figure was attempting to pitch the bound woman into the pit. Perhaps some sort of offering as part of the ritual? Seeing their paused pose, the truth became evident and far more chilling. The dark figure had a fist full of the other woman's hair and had maneuvered her halfway over the wall. Shockingly, she didn't intend to shove the woman into the depths of the pit. The prisoner's head was pulled back, and it caught the light for the first time. Gavin recognized Tess Lindow's dirty, tear-streaked face right before the dark figure pulled the double-edged blade of a dagger across defenseless flesh. Tess's scream became a gargle as impossibly thick, black-looking blood erupted from the wound. Her eyes rolled and her body sagged as her life's blood gushed into the depths of the well.

The tattoo burned suddenly on Gavin's forearm. It felt like a beacon warning of something he already knew. A dark Casting was in progress. They were at a tipping point. This Casting was the opening salvo in a much greater battle that would have dire consequences for the rest of humanity.

The Casting had to be stopped here and now.

All of this happened in scant seconds. Gavin's eyes registered the horror of the scene, his ears observed to crescendo of chat from the congregation keeping time with the sacrifice, and his mind struggled to find a way to stop the rapidly unfolding insanity. A scream of primal rage resonated through the chamber, and for a long second Gavin thought the sound had come from his own lips. Then the sound of rattling chains and scraping boots drew his attention to the far side of the chamber—somewhere to the dark figure's back. A bellowing sob followed, and Gavin knew he and Keegan were not the only prisoners in this hellscape.

The head of the nude dark figure rose, then cocked in response to the bellowed scream to her back. She did not, however, divert her attention from the effort at hand. She uttered a few unintelligible words, and the mewling voice from an unseen figure on the other side of the chamber went silent with a wheezing groan. The dark figure was undeterred. Torchlight flickered and shadows danced. With every motion, the gory tableau swam in and out of focus. With one hand still clutching a fist full of Tess Lindow's chestnut hair, the figure seemed intent on draining the sacrifice of every possible drop of blood. Though the flow had slowed considerably, Gavin was shocked to see blood still trickling freely from a wound that had cut Tess nearly to the spine.

The knife-wielding figure tipped back her head just as a massive gust of air shot from the depths of the well. It blew the hair and the inky black shadows back from the figure's face. Asha Anakasta stared unblinking, directly into Gavin's eyes. The cloying shadows that had until now hung across her naked form seemed to gain substance. They caught the wind and were flung across the chamber where they stuck to the rear wall as two separate, large amorphous oily blobs. As Gavin stared, the pair of shadows converged on each other. It was as if they were sliding across the surface of the stone. Upon touching, they grew thicker, darker, and more defined. All of this took place in the span of two dozen heartbeats. Then the single dark, featureless form grew and took on a distinctly *human shape, though one entirely unlike Asha. A mass seemingly two-dimensional in form appeared to rise behind her, at least three feet greater in height and more than three times wider than Asha at the shoulder.*

Gavin blinked, suddenly understanding he was witnessing the results of her Casting. Something was coming. It was gaining purchase on our plane—the invocation allowing something dangerous access to this world.

A throaty, resonant growl slipped from Gavin's lips. A sound so primal that even the chanting of the room went suddenly silent. None of the kneeling figures moved, and none of them turned to face Gavin where he knelt on one knee. The ropy muscles of his arms corded as they strained against the bindings at his wrists and the tether to the floor. Savage fury burned in his eyes as the animal growl continued to grow in ferocious intensity.

The dark figure of Asha finally turned her attention from the now lifeless form of Tess Lindow. Rising from where she stooped, half bent over the wall, she pushed the hair from her face with blood-soaked fingers. Asha Anakasta glared at Gavin, malicious satisfaction was obvious in her crazed smile.

A weak, tremulous voice came from beside Gavin. "Asha?"

Still grinding his teeth, Gavin clamped off the growl and turned quickly to see Keegan kneeling at his side. She swayed, looking as physically unsteady as she sounded. "It can't be," Keegan continued in a whisper. "What happened to her hair?"

The color of her hair was wrong, but that was the least wrong thing happening here.

Gavin took a deep breath and returned his attention to the predatory stare of the creature across the well. "That's Asha's body," he whispered to Keegan. "But she's not driving. Probably hasn't been for some time."

"Ah… Alright. Maybe that explains why she just killed our friend, but how does that explain the hair?"

Asha returned her attention momentarily to the limp body hanging in her hands. The blood flow had slowed to mere drops. She seemed to assess this. Apparently coming to a decision, she gave the body a couple of violent shakes, akin to a diner attempting to flick the last remaining drops from a catsup bottle. Then she turned and tossed the lifeless body aside. It splattered and thudded on impact with the floor.

Fresh concern instantly filled Keegan's voice. "She just threw Tess like she was made of balsa wood. What is she on?"

Gavin swallowed hard. His eyes swept the room. It was full of unmoving supplicants. Though he could only see the backs of their heads, he recognized most of them. They were their friends and coworkers here on the island. That no one was moving confirmed his suspicion.

"The strength and the hair," Gavin explained. "That's not Asha anymore. This is a ritual to raise…something. It's using Asha and some hardcore Blood Casting to bring it across the Vail."

Confusion clouded Keegan's already incredulous expression. "The Vail?"

"It's rising."

"What's rising?"

Gavin thought of all he'd seen on the island, the sense of building power, and the manipulation of time and space Anakasta had explained to bring them all to this place, here and now. Anakasta had alluded to something significant taking place—some event that changed the course of world events. It was the man's motivation for crossing the centuries; a desperate effort to get on the winning side of a world-changing crisis.

Asha slowly circled the well, all the while, her gaze moved slowly back and forth between Gavin and Keegan. Reaching the near side of the stone circle, she stopped and wiped blood-covered hands slowly across her naked stomach. She slowly wiped the last of the blood on her bare thighs, leaving black, oily-looking streaks on her alabaster flesh. Once more, shadows seemed to dance and roil of their own accord. It might have been a trick of the light, but Gavin knew better.

Pulling long black locks from before her eyes with newly clean hands, Asha gazed at the couple with a feline stare. "You are fortunate," she said in a husky feminine tone that sounded nothing like Asha. "You are here to bear witness. The rising of the oldest of the old, the first among the favored." A chilling smile crossed her suddenly black lips.

"Oh God," Keegan whimpered. "She means Nae'ja-dinn."

"No," Gavin said flatly, and with a sound of confidence that was out of place given their situation. His eyes never left Asha's form as he offered a slow shake of his head. "That's what she wants us to think. But there's a reason we're still alive. It's the same reason she's been using your fath—using Chandler to scour this island. They can't raise the God of Old until they find the Scalden Ara."

295

The look of satisfaction left Asha's face. Keegan looked confused. And terrified. But now, more confused than terrified. "Wait. What?"

"It's an artifact, and the source of Nae'ja-dinn's power on this plane. She can't return here without it...and they can't find it." Gavin tipped his head at the silent forms kneeling with their backs to them. "It's what this is all about. Using minions to search the island. They know the artifact is here somewhere. That's how she was entombed here in prehistory."

Asha looked at Gavin with a strange new expression. She knelt before him, her eyes level with his and her gaze becoming more penetrating. The moment she drew within two feet of him, Gavin surged against his bindings. He came up short of getting his hands on the woman when the chain linking him to the floor went taught. Not to be denied, he lashed out with his head and tried to smash the woman's nose. The shackles hindered the effort and he was pulled off course at the last second.

Asha laughed. "You are everything the prophecy foretold. That and so much more." Her brow furrowed. "I hoped you would be the second sacrifice. You have an untapped power that would serve my master well. Sadly, it seems you have a larger part to play. Your death today would be..." she seemed to search for the right words. "Counterproductive."

The woman's malevolent stare swung smoothly to Keegan and Gavin felt his rage flare anew. "Don't even think about it," he growled.

"Oh, no. She is most definitely off-limits," Asha said through a troublingly sincere smile. Her gaze shifted back to Gavin. "This one is perhaps even more vital than you."

Rising, Asha moved quickly around the perimeter of the well once more. Stooping from sight, she grappled with something on the floor. A deep baritone groaned, hinting at the next sacrifice. It was a pained, semi-conscious sort of murmur that spoke of immense physical agony and disorientation.

Chapter 68

Keegan watched Asha pull the semi-conscious form of Greeley from the space behind the well. The waif of a girl was all of one-hundred and fifteen pounds, but she lifted the man's two-hundred plus as if it were a feather pillow.

Definitely not Asha then, Keegan reasoned. Even after all she'd seen and experienced, the rational part of her mind had difficulty coming to grips with what was happening before her eyes. Her pinhead of a stepmother was possessed by…by what?

Greeley's eyes rolled and what little neck the man had lolled like it was made of jelly. He attempted to draw his feet for support, only to have Asha raise him higher and give him a violent shake. The brief, brutal wobble shot through him and seemed to rob him of equilibrium. Asha glared at Keegan. "If I can't sacrifice you," her gaze shifted to Gavin, "and I can't eviscerate you," a smile played at the corner of inky black lips, "I'll have to make do with the big one."

Locking one hand on the back of Greeley's neck, she held him aloft from a single outstretched arm. Her petite fingers seemed to elongate and somehow wrap nearly around the big man's throat. "Not the worst choice," she seemed to decide. "Plenty of blood in this one. Lots of life, too."

Keegan's attention was pulled from the spectacle by the sound of a low tone *from Gavin. He leaned close and reached the end of his restraints. He tipped his head subtly in his direction to draw her near. For the first time, Keegan realized she wasn't restrained the same as him. Her hands were bound at her front before being anchored to the floor. Adjusting her position on her knees, she edged closer to him.*

"You have to pop the lock on my cuffs," Gavin whispered.

Keegan's hands moved slowly as she tried not to draw Asha's attention from her inspection of Greeley. The woman—or whatever she was—seemed to be inspecting him the way a connoisseur did when selecting a fine bottle of wine, or perhaps more appropriately, a fine cut of meat. "I don't have anything you can use to pick the lock." The words were muttered in a barely audible reply.

Gavin's lips drew tight and his eyes bore into her. "No, I want you to pop the locks. Close your eyes and reach out with your mind. See the manacles and the inner workings of the mechanism." His eyes searched hers. "You have power you don't even understand."

Tears threatened at the corners of her eyes and Keegan's throat tightened. "I can't—I've never done anything like that."

After shooting another quick look in the direction of the well, Gavin met her gaze once more. "You haven't, but you can. You just don't know it. Think of it as a power-up. When I showed you how to read the grimoire, you bonded with the book. You bonded with the power of my coven."

Keegan flashed back to her brief examination of the grimoire. Sections of the book were legible, while others were complete nonsense. There were words, not exactly gibberish, but something that defied her mind's ability to interpret. Gavin had explained these portions of the book were legible only to members of his coven. They were the sections containing the book's most sensitive secrets. This Binding was ultimately the source of his family power. He'd pointed out a passage in the book that would give her the ability to read the volume in its entirety but warned that, by doing so, he would be inducting her into their coven. Since it had been his life's ambition to see the last known coven come to an end, she knew this was a difficult choice on his part. He'd made a choice based on their tenuous situation on the island as much as his confidence in her. The first factor continued to churn inside her gut while the second was the only reason she hadn't already succumbed to blind panic, given their current circumstance.

Though Gavin couldn't invoke the Casting himself, he could interpret the book. Though he had no ability himself, he was a member of the coven, and as such, could read the grimoire. He'd translated the Binding, a simple invocation with no immediate visible impact. This situation with the Asha-creature had interrupted before she'd been able to confirm the effectiveness of the Casting.

A tear rolled from the corner of Keegan's eye. "I don't even know where to begin," she whispered.

Eyeing the far side of the room, Gavin responded through clamped teeth. "There's no time. Reach out. See it. Release the latch the same way a key would. Do it with your mind and do it quick."

Keegan turned in time to see Asha stride to the edge of the well with Greeley raised from a single outstretched arm. She pinned his lower body against the base of the well with a twist of her nude hip and bent the big man face-first over the wall of the well. Greeley moaned, unable to speak and unable to raise his arms for any defense. Keegan wondered if his spine had been snapped to paralyze him, or maybe it was some kind of peripheral Casting employed by the creature inhabiting Asha's body.

There was so much she didn't understand.

The chain links binding Gavin rattled as he seized violently at the restraints. "Let him go, you bitch!" he bellowed.

The creature paused and looked at Gavin. "You realize this meat suit has nothing to do with my gender," Asha said with amusement. "I've been riding around in the trollop's head for over a year. I can take control whenever I choose. Even when I allow her control, she has no idea I'm here. But I've been watching you. I pulled the strings that brought this family to this place."

Keegan watched the creature and listened to the words, but inside, her mind was drifting. The experience was like her out-of-body episodes, but only in the sense that she felt her mind moving through a gauze-like haze as the transition took place. Until now, she'd never been consciously aware of the experience. Suddenly she understood it was a part of the process dating back to her first episode. Somehow she was now just slightly more aware of the nuances of the intermediate stages. In that, she sensed, would be her ability to control what came next.

Her mind slipped, and suddenly she saw massive gears and cogs. They surrounded her, some as tall as two-story buildings, others more the size of VW Bugs. Everything existed in a white spectral fog. Rather than blotting out the light, the fog seemed to bring weak, fuzzy illumination to the strange mechanical landscape.

The iron world around Keegan jolted suddenly. Her view bounced and swam in an effort to strike a balance. A part of her mind associated the experience with the sound of chain links rattling and binding somewhere in the distance. And with a jolt, Keegan understood what she was seeing. The massive mechanics surrounding her incorporeal form were the inner workings of the shackles locking Gavin to the floor of the chamber.

Chapter 69

"You faced my kind once before," Asha said. She rocked her hips against Greeley's bent form with obvious enjoyment and forced his head deeper into the mouth of the well. The hulking dark shadowy figure remained at the Asha-creature's back. It clung to the wall of the chamber and still lacked detail. It appeared two-dimensional as it only had height and width. It shifted from side to side, its motions independent of Asha giving the sense of a malicious intelligence waiting for an opportunity to attack everyone in the room. The next bloodletting would bring it fully onto this plane, give it form, and with that, the ability to act. This was the Asha-creature's goal, Gavin knew with unabashed certainty.

The Asha-thing was having too much fun. If it meant buying some time, Gavin was happy to engage. The longer he could keep the creature talking, the better he liked their chances. Getting the upper hand with Asha was their only opportunity to make it out of this mess. It was undoubtedly Greeley's only chance. But even if he could get free, Gavin wasn't entirely sure what he could do. The Asha-creature was clearly powerful. The only obvious chance of gaining the advantage would be critically damaging the host body. From the sound of the tale so far, Asha might still be in there somewhere. Reclaiming her would be a goal, but not at the cost of his life or Keegan's.

Understanding, or at least a hint of it, must have touched his expression because Gavin heard the creature chuckle.

"Sorting it out, perhaps?" Asha murmured, her tone a taunt. "They were right. You have no natural Casting ability at all, do you? You sense nothing in me?"

Gavin stared into the eyes of the Asha-beast and found something he'd seen only once before. "You're Nimm," he said. The newness of the understanding was evident in his inflection.

Asha's face split into a wide, sincere, if unnatural and malevolent smile. "No power at all, but perhaps a gift for observation."

"I saw you die," Gavin insisted.

"You killed one of us," the creature snapped. Her face turned into a mask of distaste. "We are many. You killed only one."

This understanding sent Gavin's hopes into overdrive. He'd just confirmed two crucial facts. First, this creature could be killed, even if he didn't yet know how to accomplish it. Second, this Nimm had little knowledge of the circumstance, which led to the death of the last Nimm he'd faced. If the events of that confrontation were known, it would have understood that Gavin hadn't killed the creature. His mother made the kill with her death curse. But since no one survived that night to tell the tale, this monster knew less than it wanted him to believe.

"You were one of many once, long ago," Gavin taunted. "But you're few now. You might even be the last."

Fury burned in Asha's eyes, a hint that his guess was close to, or perhaps even on the mark. She used her free hand to seize Greeley by the hair and tip his head back. The big man's short neck was suddenly as exposed as physically possible. Asha snatched the dagger from the top of the stone well; Gavin saw the ancient blade flash as it caught the flickering torchlight.

"Wait!" Gavin barked. It was a desperate and likely meaningless attempt to stay the big man's execution, but Gavin was out of options.

The swinging blade stopped suddenly. The Asha-creature's head tipped slowly as if in response to an unfamiliar sound. At first Gavin thought this was a response to his plea. Perhaps the creature wanted to toy with him some more? Then he saw the young woman's short nose twitch. She seemed to be sniffing the air. This lasted only a second. Then she looked up with wild eyes that bore into Gavin.

"You can't be," the creature growled. Its voice was suddenly very unlike it had been. A throaty rasp had seized those three words. At the same time, the dark pools around Asha's eyes seemed to expand to consume more of her face. "You have no power," the creature said in a tone that seemed pointed inward as it worked out whatever it sensed.

When Asha's gaze snapped instantly to Keegan, Gavin understood what the creature sensed. At the same moment, he felt the iron cuffs loosen from the bloody furrows they'd plowed into the flesh of his wrists. Without fully understanding it, he sensed that the far end of the chain linking the cuffs to the eyelets in the floor had also come undone. Twisting his grip and taking the cuff in his right hand, he lashed out and used the now loose chain like a bullwhip. The chain flicked through the air with lightning-like speed, the ring at the end impacting Asha's hand with a bone-cracking crunch. The knife spun through the air and rattled across the floor.

Gavin was already on his feet and closing the short distance between him and the close side of the well. Only the four-foot-wide gaping maw separated him from the creature.

The Asha-creature was still bellowing from the blow from the chain whip when the small woman somehow recovered. Fierce aggression replaced the surprise in her eyes and her lips began to move with unheard words. Gavin recognized them instantly for what they were. The creature was uttering the incantation that was part of the sacrifice.

Having lost the dagger, the Asha-creature lashed out with a talon-like claw. Gavin had one foot on the lip of the well and was vaulting its expanse as the claw slashed down to rake Greeley's throat. The chain in Gavin's hand was already in motion once more, but this time it missed the mark as the creature twisted to ensure the big man's lifeblood made its way into the well. While Gavin failed to score a direct hit to the creature's face, the end of the chain did impact Asha's shoulder. This seemed to distract from the effort put into Greeley's execution. The big man tumbled forward over the well mouth as the creature screamed and fell in the opposite direction.

Gavin's leap wasn't high, but it was long. He cleared the wall on the far side of the well and grabbed the back of Greeley's shirt before the big man went fully over the precipice. However, Greeley outweighed Gavin by a wide margin, and this factored in. Gavin tightened his grip on the fistful of Greeley's shirt even as they were both pulled over the lip of the well. Dropping low at the last second, Gavin's chest slammed into the outer face of the well wall. He slung his free hand over the wall to get a second fist full of the big man's shirt. Then heaving, he pulled Greeley back from the brink and dropped him to the floor with a wet splat.

Chapter 70

Gavin's head swam and he felt his feet leave the ground. The room spun in an instant, and he saw the still supine forms of the supplicant robed followers kneeling face down on the floor as he was launched bodily across the chamber. Tucking his head at the last second, his shoulders impacted the chamber's far wall. He covered his head in time to impact with the floor in a clumsy somersault. Wobbling to his feet as his mind struggled to make sense of the last two seconds, Gavin blinked and saw the massive two-dimensional shadow finish taking a three-dimensional shape. It was over seven feet tall—probably closer to eight—with shoulders at least twice as wide as Greeley's. The figure was shirtless with bulging, rock-hard muscles beneath a mottled flesh that was gray and pale blue. It was marked with scars too numerous to count. It wore only a troublingly small loincloth of unidentifiable animal skin and a pair of similarly fashioned boots. Oddly, the loincloth was secured with a semi-modern-looking belt, upon which a long-bladed flint knife was strapped.

The figure had no hair, but its massive head featured a pronounced brow line. A huge craggy nose suggested a history of numerous breaks and absolutely no medical treatment. Though all of this was concerning, the jaw made the creature identifiable. It jutted out like the bumper on a 1970s-era gas guzzler and sported a pair of thick vertical teeth so pronounced they could easily be mistaken for tusks.

Keegan's voice was tremulous. "What the fuck is that?"

The giant figure's flesh still rippled as it struggled to materialize on the earthly plane. Gavin looked at Greeley who still lay in a heap against the chamber's back wall. The big man had freed a rag of some kind and had managed to stem the blood flow from his neck wound by applying pressure. They needed to get him help soon or he might yet bleed out.

"It's called an Ory," Gavin said, his eyes fixed on the massive figure.

The Ory stepped forward. As one, Gavin and Keegan stepped backward and two paces to their left. Gavin watched as the gray-blue flesh of the creature still puckered, danced, and shimmered. A guttural glow came from the mouth of the creature, and a dark liquid oozed from the corner of its mouth.

"Is that normal?" Keegan asked.

Gavin shot a glance at Greeley and considered the question. Moving his gaze back to the Ory, his eyes passed over the mouth of the well. A smile touched Gavin's lips. When he spoke, the words were quiet and from the corner of his mouth. "You need to spend some quality time with that book. Everything I know is captured in there. No matter what happens here, everything you need to know is in the book." He felt her eyes on him for a fraction of a second but knew better than to share the moment. Breaking his stare with the creature again would be a mistake. The wavy appearance of its flesh was already beginning to calm.

"Asha didn't get enough blood in the well," Gavin went on. He eyed the Ory meaningfully and ground a foot against the stone to ensure his footing. "The big bastard is making a slow transition to our plane. Until that's complete, he's vulnerable."

The weakness in Keegan's voice was replaced by an air of knowing concern. "And when the transition is complete?"

The Ory stomped two paces forward. The couple retreated a commensurate two paces and moved further to their left again.

"The demonic version of the Terminator."

Keegan didn't miss a beat. "Then we take him out before he's fully manifest." It was a statement rather than a question, and Gavin was struck by how quickly she was growing to accept this altered form of her previous reality. "Any particularly weak points?"

"According to the literature, a heart twice the size of ours in approximately the same place. Also, I'm pretty sure I can use that shimmer along his gut to disembowel him. Either should do the trick."

"So we just need a knife?" Keegan said.

Gavin adjusted his grip on the handle of the thick curved Guker knife held behind his back.

"Where'd you get that?"

Gavin only chuckled. They didn't have enough time to explain, and even if they did, he wasn't sure he could. "I go on his next step," he said.

As if on cue, the Ory scowled and took another menacing pace in their direction. Gavin saw the shimmer of the mottled flesh on the creature's abdomen and judged it an invitation. Rather than retreat as he had previously, he charged the beast. The soles of his boots slapped stone as he closed the distance in three paces. Raising the Guker knife in a backswing that would give it the maximum amount of gut-eviscerating power, he caught sight of Keegan in the corner of his eye. She was matching him stride for stride.

Gavin's blade slashed the scarred flesh of the creature at the same second that Keegan's blade pierced its upper chest. It turned out Keegan had somehow lifted the sacrificial blade Asha had used at the well mouth. She plunged it deep into the heart of the Ory and was twisting the delicate, ornamental knife just as Gavin's slash was spilling the beast's intestines.

The Ory bellowed in anguish, its head thrown back and a gurgling snarl spewing thick viscous blood into the air. The shimmer of the creature's flesh escalated and spread in the span of less than a second. A blinding light emanated from the creature's core, and a thunderclap filled the chamber.

A scorching burn flashed up Gavin's arm, starting from the point where his hand touched the blade buried deep within the Ory. He saw Keegan's form illuminated in a gauzy silhouette as the searing light overcame him. Then the pressure wave struck, knocking the air from his lungs and causing the world to go black.

Chapter 71

The hammering pain behind his eyes was the first sensation to greet Gavin on his return to consciousness. A whooshing sound in his ears sounded strange, but at the same time, vaguely familiar. An attempt to open his eyes brought an instant sense of gut-churning vertigo, causing him to roll to his side just in time to vomit. Reluctant to attempt opening his eyes again, he rolled onto his back. Rainfall splattered his face.

His eyes still clamped tight, Gavin slapped a palm against the ground and attempted to rise to a sitting position. His hand splashed in a puddle and a fine grit met his hand where a smooth stone floor should have been. "Kay?" His voice was a hoarse whisper against vocal cords still stinging from his rising gorge. He needed to check on Keegan. "You alright?"

A horn blared in the distance and was answered instantly by another. A honk from yet another sounded in response. His pulse quickened and his hands instantly closed into fists. Gavin spun to one knee before vaulting to his feet. The world swam around him as he blinked through driving rainfall. He stumbled a step, and then another, his gaze flashing left and then right in search of attackers. But there were none.

Gavin stood in the nighttime shadows of an alley between a pair of tall urban buildings. The sounds of traffic were now plainly identifiable nearby, as was the impact of driving rain on pavement. The foulness of his regurgitation was nothing compared to the wreak coming from the handful of massive steel dumpsters lining the walls of the surrounding alley.

It was night and Gavin was alone. In a city.

How?

His mind swam as he once more searched the shadows for assailants. He truly was alone. His foot brushed against something and it skittered across the pavement a few inches. The dark object was unidentifiable. Stooping, he retrieved it. The long-curved blade of the Guker knife caught the small sliver of streetlight emanating from the mouth of the alley. Though most of the blade had been washed clean by the downpour, a thick strand of black organic matter still hung tangled around the hilt. The intestine or abdominal lining from the Ory, he understood instantly. He shook it free from the blade with a sharp flick of his wrist and heard the gore strike the pavement with a splat.

Still kneeling in the puddle, Gavin realized something else. The bare flesh of his knee was grinding into the grime and grit of the alley floor. His gaze traveled along his own body. Through nothing more than an inky black cloak of shadow in the confines of an alley, it was suddenly impossible to miss that he was entirely naked.

The pounding in his head somehow seemed to double as concern for his predicament skyrocketed. His grip on the handle of the curved-bladed knife went white-knuckled as he climbed to his feet. He stumbled for the mouth of the alley, concern for his naked form already forgotten in favor of his new predicament. Vertigo still plagued him, though it seemed to be less of a problem with every passing minute. He probed his hairline and skull for a cut, gash, or swelling; anything to explain his loss of time. By the time he reached the street, he was reasonably sure the disorientation wasn't the result of a head wound.

The glare of the streetlight some thirty yards distant sent a fresh stab of pain through Gavin's head, and he reasoned that, whatever happened, his brain was scrambled in addition to his mind. He had no idea where he was or how he'd gotten here. He was about to call for Keegan once more when a hiss sounded to his left. His muscles tensed, and he raised the knife defensively as a massive city bus rolled into view. Its brakes hissed again as it eased through the narrow side street and turned through a tight intersection. The driver seemed not to notice him, likely obscured by the driving rain and the blurring stroke of the overmatched windscreen wipers.

Blowing out a breath, Gavin shook his head and moved for the same street *corner. Only then did he notice the buzz of traffic passing the stop sign at the end of the block. Cars were zipping by at perhaps 30 miles per hour and throwing up thick curtains of pungent water as they went. The night was oppressive, the darkness and sheets of rain curtained the city. He shivered, realizing for the first time just how cold the downpour was.*

Stepping onto the sidewalk of a far busier city street, Gavin tucked himself close to the nearest brick building to avoid the torrents of water thrown by passing cars. The sidewalk was devoid of pedestrians, and he could see why. Drivers paid foot traffic no attention, and anyone walking the streets was likely to be hit with enough water to be knocked from their feet. Either the rainfall was too torrential for the sewers to keep up, or the nearest drains had been plugged with debris. With a glance to the forbidding darkness overhead, he reasoned it was likely a little of both.

A sight weakly illuminated in the distance caught Gavin's eye. It was a building a dozen or more stories tall lit by dozens of sodium vapor work lights. An intricate scaffolding framework crisscrossed the entire front of the stone building, and even in these foul conditions, dozens of workers scurried about with backpacks and equipment. He watched as a massive crane, one blocking two lanes of the four-lane road, lowered an enormous sheet of stone from the side of the building. Another similar sheet of stone sat on a double-wide semi-trailer. It was either recently removed from the building or about to be raised to replace the section which was just removed.

"The Kronenburg building," Gavin whispered. "This work was completed months ago."

Chapter 72

The booming sound of voices jolted Keegan to consciousness with a start. Blinking against the glare, she slapped a hand against the floor and forced herself into a sitting position. Her stomach instantly revolted, gorge rising to the back of her throat. She fought her body's need to purge the contents of her last meal even as her mind struggled to make sense of the blur of light and the shrieking hammer of strange sounds assaulting her ears. Something in the back of her mind suggested danger—mortal danger—and Keegan struggled to find her feet. The effort was a waste and she landed in a pile on the floor once more.

Struggling to slow her breathing, Keegan blinked back the harsh light. As she did, the hammering in her ears began to dissipate. It was the sound of her heartbeat, she quickly realized. A strange texture became apparent beneath the tips of her fingers—a coarse grain—sticky? A hardwood floor. A sticky hardwood floor. She shifted and noticed two things. First, the churning deep in her stomach was less violent, and second, the unmistakable tacky, sticky sensation beneath her palm and fingers was equally present against her hip and back.

Keegan gasped and slapped her hands against her naked form. Her head turned back and forth, the glare of unfamiliar light was beginning to materialize into potentially recognizable shapes. The booming thunder of numerous simultaneous voices sounded in the near distance and Keegan's heart went into her throat. She jumped to her feet, or at least attempted to. Still off-balance, her feet crossed at the ankles and she went tumbling. There was an instant impact with at least one semi-stationary object which seemed to, in turn, collide with several other things. This produced a skittering crash, and a half-second later, something unyielding fell upon her.

The impact would have caused Keegan to scream, if the startling strike hadn't left her briefly without air in her lungs. By the time she gasped enough breath to bellow, she understood the object on her was inanimate and not altogether heavy. Taking another breath to steady her nerves, she blinked away the last remaining blurry streaks obscuring her vision to find herself tangled amongst a set of toppled wooden chairs. Her gaze quickly took in the room. Coarse wood planks on the floor, plaster walls adorned with few decorations beyond the occasional dimly lit, modern-looking lighting sconce, a dozen or so three-by-three foot square tables—three of whose chairs now entangled her, and dozens of additional chairs, all of which had been flipped upside down to rest upon the square tables. A pair of rather expensive prints of the Chicago skyline hung on each wall. They were printed on stainless steel rather than canvas. A set of wide wooden French doors filled half of the far wall. Beyond them, she could hear the sound of numerous raucous raised voices and the low murmur of a radio or television set.

Keegan took a slow breath, realizing she had the room to herself. It was the backroom of some restaurant or bar, she guessed by the layout and decor. She looked down across her own naked body and tried to push back the fog still clouding her mind. The last thing she remembered…

The shadow-figure in the basement of the citadel slammed to the forefront of her mind and she shot to a sitting position. Fallen chairs tumbled away in a clatter. "Gavin," she called before she could reconsider giving away her position. She cringed at the thunderous sound of her voice in the silent space.

Her eyes traversed the room once more. She was clearly alone. And on her own.

Crap.

The double doors at the end of the room crashed open as a woman plowed through. Her gaze swept the space as she entered, trepidation already creasing her brow. "The room's off limits you—" she was already bellowing. She stopped short when her focus fell on Keegan in a heap on the floor, tangled between the table and chairs. The fury in the woman's expression disappeared and her face went blank. Long seconds seemed to pass. Finally, worry or confusion softened her features.

The woman stepped slowly into the room, her eyes fixed on Keegan. Keegan didn't move. She didn't know what to do. The woman was in her early twenties, if Keegan had to guess. She was tall, had long blonde hair, and wore short form-fitting shorts and a matching short-sleeved top. An apron was tied around her trim waist.

Anger suddenly flooded the woman's expression. She turned quickly and closed the double doors. Keegan heard the sound of a bolt being thrown—some kind of heavy lock had been set. "Honey," the woman said as she turned back. Concern blanketed her face once more as she advanced. "Did those bastards do this to you?"

Keegan was confused. Then she eyed herself once more before recalling the room and the voices beyond. The woman's outfit, the noise…This was some kind of bar or tavern. Easing her arm from between the legs of a chair and then pushing a table away, Keegan shook her head. A headache the likes of which she had never experienced stabbed behind her eyes, but it wasn't the most pressing concern. "No," she said in a quiet voice. "It's not what you're thinking."

"Are you hurt?" the woman asked. She offered a hand and pulled Keegan to her feet.

The question caused Keegan to take a mental inventory for the first time. Yes, she thought. Just about every inch of her body hurt. An incredible ache seemed to permeate her frame. She felt like she'd been hit by a car, only to have it park on her for good measure.

Keegan took a second to look herself over quickly to confirm the pain was internal. She saw no bruising or bleeding. Her head throbbed hard enough that she wondered if the stranger could hear it pounding from a couple of feet away, but aside from that—and being naked—she was in good working order.

"Honey," the woman said. "Where in the devil are your clothes?"

Keegan looked at herself once more. The confusion of the circumstance must have been clear on her face because the woman just gazed at her disapprovingly. After a long second, the woman turned suddenly and headed for the door. The lock was thrown, one of the double doors was cracked, then the stranger slid from the room. The door was closed silently behind her.

Not understanding the silent rebuke, Keegan was more concerned with Gavin's disappearance. The room had no other doors, so it was obvious he wasn't there. This was unquestionably, the most concerning part of this experience.

The door cracked open again as the waitress slipped back into the room. She had a long overcoat draped over one arm. She advanced cautiously, her eyes fixed on Keegan. After a moment, she offered the coat.

"Are you sure no one...are you sure no one hurt you?" the woman said slowly.

Keegan nodded confidently. "It's the only thing I know at the moment." She slipped the coat over her shoulders and pulled the single-breasted lapels tight. It was a man's coat, dwarfing her small frame. She tied the oversized belt tight around her hips and suddenly realized how cold she'd been.

"The coat belongs to our assistant manager," the waitress said. "He won't be in until tonight. In any case, he won't miss it." She eyed Keegan with obvious concern. "You sure you're alright? I mean, what the hell happened? Sorry for saying it, but you don't look strung out or drunk. How'd you end up like this?"

Keegan's mind swam. She had no idea where she was. Keeping a low profile while she sorted it out seemed like a good idea, but that meant finding the right thing to say. The wrong words now would only draw more attention. Her gaze fell on the logo stretched taught across the front of the waitress's ample cleavage. It was a circle with blocky numbers in the center. The thick white lines of the art were cracked and worn from many washings, but the numbers were still clear: 10-31. Above the numbers was a single word, nearly worn away. Code.

The waitress saw Keegan looking at her shirt. "Sorry," she said. "I checked my locker. I don't have any spare stuff. The coat was the best I could do. Can I call someone for you?"

"Code 10-31," Keegan said. "That was a bar in Chicago, wasn't it?"

The waitress's already concerned expression darkened. "Maybe you should sit down, honey."

Confusion must have been apparent in Keegan's eyes.

"Honey, are you saying you don't know where you are?"

Keegan eyed the intricate, highly detailed image of the Chicago skyline imprinted on stainless steel hanging on the wall just to the right of the waitress. She felt her stomach drop with the suddenness of the realization. "I'm in Chicago," she said in a flat, far-away voice.

The waitress chuckled. "Girl, if you don't know you're in Chicago, you really need to get your act together. I was going to say you're standing in the 10-31 right now. Are you saying you don't even know what city you're in?"

Keegan's eyes went wide. "Code 10-31? This is Chicago—a bar called Code 10-31?" Her mind was already racing. She met the waitress's concerned gaze. "I was told the bar burned years ago. When did they rebuild?"

The waitress laughed. "Girl, you're a trip. I don't know what you're talking about. There's never been a fire. And I promise you, this is the one and only Code 10-31."

Keegan felt the room begin to spin.

A Note from Xander Weaver:

Thank you for reading Black Rock: The Rising. I hope you've had as much fun reading it as I've had writing it. If you did and feel like showing your support, please post a review with your online retailer of choice. Each review makes a big difference to new readers and is instrumental in spreading the word about my work. Just a brief statement explaining what you enjoyed is all it takes.

Your time and effort are sincerely appreciated.

Thank you!

—Xander Weaver

Acknowledgments:

Some believe that writing is a solitary endeavor; the result of a single author slaving over a keyboard until the story that needs telling has been expressed in its entirety. This has never been the case for me. I do my best work when receiving input and feedback from trusted friends and colleagues.

The cover design is thanks to Paramita Bhattacharjee from https://www.creativeparamita.com. After countless hours working on a manuscript, it's crucial to have a cover that properly represents the story being told. The quality of the work speaks for itself.

As in the past, I'm also fortunate to have a support team of fact-checkers, proofreaders, and cheerleaders who help me improve the quality of my work. For their time and effort, I want to give special thanks to: Wayne and Terri Manke, Tom Nielsen, Wenzel Roessler, and Jamie Dresser. Jamie Dresser, in particular, championed this book from its roughest draft to its final proof—truly a level of support that goes above and beyond. He read this manuscript more times than anyone, tenacious in his will to see it in print.

With friends and colleagues like these, the writing process is anything but solitary. I am incredibly fortunate to know the true meaning of "friendship."

Newsletter:

Want to hear about the latest book release, contests, and giveaways?

Join the newsletter:

XanderWeaver.com/newsletter

About the Author

Thank you for reading *Black Rock: The Rising*. This is the first book in the "Black Rock" series and a departure in theme and tone from my previous books. It explores darker characters, dipping one foot firmly into paranormal waters. But as always, the focus of the story concentrates on the characters at all times. The more realistic they are, the more believable the plot.

Like most authors, I am first a reader at heart. I write the genre of stories I *want* to read—that I *love* to read. I desire action, mystery, and suspense—I want to be thrilled! Books need to make me think, even while taking me on a wild ride that sticks in my head long after the tale is finished. Learning things along the way is a great deal of fun, but at the core of it all, I thrive on characters. Whether I love them or hate them, the greatest characters ever written are those that spark an emotional response that makes reading and writing, fun.

If you would like to be notified of future book releases in advance, I welcome you to join my newsletter at: www.XanderWeaver.com. Rest assured, your personal information will never be sold or traded.

While I'm working on the next thrill ride, I frequently post updates to Facebook (Weaver.Books) and Twitter (@XanderWeaver). Please follow the progress and join in the fun!

Cyrus Cooper Series:

Book One: Dangerous Minds

Book Two: Rogue Faction Part 1

Book Three: Rogue Faction Part 2

Book Four: Halon Seven

Book Five: Surviving Origin Part 1

Book Six: Surviving Origin Part 2

Other Books:

Sleepwalker: The Journal of Grady Ledger

For more information, please visit:

XanderWeaver.com